Also by Chelsea Pitcher

The Last Changeling
~ the beginning of Taylor and Elora's story ~

D1557229

THE LAST
FAERIE QUEEN

CHELSEA PITCHER

THE LAST
FAERIE QUEEN

flux
Woodbury, Minnesota

First Edition
First Printing, 2015

Cover design by Kevin R. Brown
Cover photo: Marwane Pallas
Additional image: iStockphoto.com/6524824/©ANGELGILD

Flux, an imprint of Llewellyn Worldwide Ltd.

Library of Congress Cataloging-in-Publication Data
Pitcher, Chelsea.
  The last faerie queen / Chelsea Pitcher.—First edition.
    pages cm
  Sequel to: The last changeling.
  Summary: When the faerie princess Elora attempts to unite the divided Faerie realm by overthrowing her mother, the Dark Queen, she is betrayed by her people, who kidnap two of her human friends.
  ISBN 978-0-7387-4349-3
[1. Fantasy. 2. Fairies—Fiction. 3. Friendship—Fiction.] I. Title.
PZ7.P6428Lc 2015
[Fic]—dc23

                                                                    2015023109

Flux
Llewellyn Worldwide Ltd.
2143 Wooddale Drive
Woodbury, MN 55125-2989
www.fluxnow.com

Printed in the United States of America

To Stephanie, Ryan, and Heather
Thank you for the mortal magic

1

TAYLOR

I was seventeen when I met a faerie princess. Before that, I'd only dreamed of someone magical walking into my life. But late one night, the Princess of the Dark Faeries snuck into the human world in search of a mortal offering. She crept out of the shadows and reached for my hand.

I didn't know who she was then. I had no idea who I was leading out of the darkness.

I took her home.

After that, things got really messed up. While the princess searched for an offering, I fell desperately in love with her. I helped her enroll in my high school. I pointed out the cruelest guy in my class: Brad Dickson, King of the Dirtbags.

I didn't know she was going to steal him.

It happened on prom night. Right after Elora kissed me, and confessed to having *all kinds of feelings*, she disappeared into the darkness with Brad. I mean, what the hell? Of course, I still thought she was a mortal then, thanks to a very impressive glamour (a.k.a. magical illusion). I was convinced she was a teen runaway who'd escaped an abusive family. And I was right. That night, her abusive family came looking for her.

They just happened to have horns and wings.

So here's how it went: I went sneaking after Elora, and three of my friends went sneaking after us. We ended up at the local graveyard, and that's when all hell broke loose.

I mean, literally. Hell on earth. The faeries of the Dark Court came down from the sky, and crawled out of the dirt like corpses. They wanted to punish their princess for fraternizing with humans. (They had no idea she was stealing a human, or why.) They captured us in a matter of minutes, because they had magic, and all we had was a buzz from the whiskey we'd drunk at the prom.

Oh God, I sound like a cautionary tale about teen drinking.

It's just one drink!

Yeah, but you almost got murdered by faeries!

Harmless?

But guess what? We got the upper hand. See, the dark faeries decided a long time ago that humans were drooling, destructive idiots, so they never imagined a scenario where we could outsmart them. And while they tortured Elora, we managed to slip out of their grasp, and save her.

Well, most of her.

My gaze traveled down, to the place where Elora slept. Here in the Bright Court, the glittering forest illuminated the paleness of her face. Her fiery hair was plastered to her forehead. She looked peaceful. She looked safe. But if I trailed my gaze farther down, to the space between her shoulder blades ...

"No, no, no," I whispered, closing my eyes. I told myself that when I opened them, her wings would be there. I'd only seen them once. Back in the graveyard, they'd unfurled like waves rising out of the darkest sea. Higher and higher they'd risen, beating back the wind.

Then they'd fallen.

No, a blade had fallen on them. An iron blade, which caused Elora's skin to bubble and hiss. And her brother, the Prince of the Dark Faeries, had towered over her, grinning maniacally. Sawing maniacally, until those wings fell away.

Now, two jagged stumps rose out of her back like shards of obsidian.

"It's okay, we brought your wings with us," I promised, unsure of how much she remembered from the previous night. "We're safe in the Bright Court now. Your allies snuck us in." That part had been a surprise. Massive winged horses had rescued us from the graveyard and carried us into the sky. Carried us across the worlds. "The Seelie Queen welcomed us and used her magic to heal you. I only had to give up—"

A scream tore through the forest. I want to say I got chills, but honestly, I was too exhausted to feel that kind of thing. Instead, I just froze, listening like an animal that's about to be ripped to pieces by a bullet.

The scream came again. This time, it felt never-ending, and I recognized the voice.

"Kylie." My friend. The second-most-amazing person I'd ever met, after Elora. Definitely the sweetest. Kylie was in danger. Or *pain*.

I slid my body out from under Elora's, laying her head gently on the ground. There was grass, at least enough of it to cradle her head like a pillow. "It's okay," I told her. "I'll go." I couldn't help but touch her face. That red hair had a habit of falling over it. "You stay here, where you're safe."

Safe?

The word tasted funny in my mouth. Was she ever safe? Were any of us? So far, the bright faeries had been nothing but nice to us, but that niceness had come at a cost.

I had to find my friends.

"Kylie?" I called, pulling on my clothes as I went. I leapt over logs, the hems of my pants already muddy, trying to button my shirt without losing momentum. Hours earlier, I'd stood in front of the mirror in my bedroom, checking that shirt for wrinkles and pretending my life was about to change. Pretending Elora was going to kiss me at the prom and I'd finally get to tell her how I felt.

Be careful what you wish for, right?

Now I was stumbling through a faerie forest, wishing for invisibility. The sun was beating down on me, but it wasn't the only source of light in this place. The trunks of the trees glowed, the leaves glittered like emeralds, and white flowers peeked out between branches, bright as lightbulbs. As I pushed through some brambles into a clearing, I tried to prepare myself for anything.

But I wasn't prepared for this.

The second I entered the clearing, where fat, golden fruits hung from every gnarled branch, I was pretty much accosted by my friends. They burst out of the forest, one by one, like they'd already been inducted into some Seelie Secret Society.

Kylie was the first.

"Taylor!" she called, her dark hair in tangles and her brown eyes bright. She was gliding toward me in the most elaborate wheelchair I'd ever seen. The base appeared to be crystal, and the back rose up into two winged swans, heads dipping toward each other to form a heart. The wheels seemed to have no trouble moving over the grass. It was magical and extravagant—the kind of thing Kylie would love but never ask for.

Oh, and she had wings. Glamoured, of course, but they looked so real, with shiny black feathers like she was a raven queen. Like she might transform into a bird and disappear into the trees.

"They made me a throne," she gushed, and opened her arms to hug me. She wore a dress that looked like the midnight sky—black fabric with a thousand tiny lights. Same old boots. "I'm practically a princess."

"And every princess needs a queen!" Keegan announced, jumping out of the bushes. It was a funny thing for him to say. Kylie's twin brother never dressed up in drag or anything; even now, with faerie couture at his disposal, he'd gone the simple satyr route, with hooves and horns and a brown velvet suit that helped him blend in with the forest. But maybe that was the joke, the point he was making.

Or maybe he was just having fun.

"What happened?" I asked as Kylie squeezed the breath out of me. Her olive skin looked especially sun-kissed in the light. "I heard screaming—"

"We're fine."

"Everything's fine," Keegan agreed. They were acting weird, smiling so big but not meeting my eyes.

A shiver went up my spine. "Where's Alexia?"

"Here," said a liquid voice from above. "There. Everywhere. If you know where to look."

The words startled me. She sounded so much like Elora.

She'd been in the faerie lands for less than a day, but already she was assimilating. Just like Elora had, back home.

The thought didn't soothe me.

"Come out, my little Cheshire Cat," Kylie called to the creature hiding in the trees. I followed her gaze. When Alexia dropped down from the branches, she did so with the grace of a cat.

Her transformation was the boldest.

She hadn't done much to change her face, not that any of us would blame her. With ancestors in Africa, South America, and Japan, Alexia was what guys at school called "*painfully* beautiful*.*" But now her brown eyes were entirely black, and her lips were stained like she'd been eating blackberries.

Or drinking from someone's neck.

In fact, she looked a bit like a vampire—or a vampire and a faerie mixed. Her long, slinky dress was burgundy, and her wings were red and black, in the pattern of a Monarch's. I had the most disturbing vision of her pinned.

"It's nice to see you've made yourself comfortable," I said, not bothering to mask my sarcasm.

She didn't seem to pick up on it, though. Her tone was actually warm when she said, "Isn't it? It's strange. I spent my life avoiding nature." She shook out her hair, and it fell in dark waves around her. "You have no idea what rain does to my hair. But here, it doesn't seem so important. It's almost as if I've finally come home." She inhaled, planting her light brown feet in the dirt. In all my years at Unity High, I'd never seen her without break-your-leg heels.

"You're not home," I told her.

"How can you be so sure?" She kept staring at the trees like they were filled with pixies. All of my friends did.

I squinted my eyes but I didn't see anything. Or any*one*.

"I never really felt at home before this," Alexia said. "None of us did. Why shouldn't we enjoy the show?"

"What show?" I asked. What was wrong with all of them? It was becoming alarmingly clear what Elora had meant when she said humans were easily lured into Faerie. Now, without even meaning to, I'd brought the people who'd be the most vulnerable to that trick. The ones who'd never felt accepted in the human world.

"The *show*!" Alexia spun in a circle and leaves fell around her head. *How does she do that?* "The revelation. Don't you want to be welcomed here properly?"

"Yeah, Taylor," Kylie said, and that worried me more than anything. Alexia and Keegan were always messing with me. But not Kylie; she had sincerity in her bones. "Don't be so negative. We all know we *were* in danger, but we're safe now. These are the good faeries."

"There are no good faeries," I snapped. Branches shook above my head. The sound could've been attributed to the wind, but I knew better. Someone was listening.

The entire forest was probably listening.

I chose my words carefully. "It's not as simple as that. All faeries come from the same place. Some of them associate with light, and some with darkness, but they're all immortal, and much more concerned with the planet as a whole than individual human lives." I knelt in front of Kylie to evade the ears of spies. "We're like animals to them. Puppies to play with. Do you understand?"

Kylie giggled. She was *giggling* while I was trying to save her life.

"Kylie, please," I said. "The Bright Queen sent Elora to the human world to find a mortal offering. A *person* she could keep as a pet." I looked around, a nervous feeling in my chest. "Wait. Where's Brad?"

It wasn't that I *wanted* to see the puffy-chested, slur-slinging asshole of Unity High. But Elora had stolen him from the human world, and as bad as he was, I wouldn't abandon him here.

Kylie waved a hand. "The Queen said she was sending him home."

"She didn't want him," Keegan agreed.

"Who would?" Alexia asked, erupting in laughter. They all followed suit.

I dropped my head into my hands. "You don't understand. The Seelie Queen isn't going to just *give up* an offering for no reason. If Brad gets to go home, that means she's keeping someone else. Someone like—"

Me.

But I couldn't say it. I couldn't admit what had happened last night. Elora had been *dying*. Like, bleeding to death in my arms. And the Bright Queen had been happy to help, *if* I told her my full name...

"Taylor, relax," Kylie cooed. It was patronizing, and I'd never heard her be patronizing before. What had happened to all of them? What had the faeries done? "If we entertain ourselves a while, they'll come through and give you a new look."

"A makeover," Alexia deadpanned.

"Isn't that what you've always wanted?" Keegan teased,

fluffing up his chestnut hair. Unlike his sister, whose dyed-black hair framed her face at an angle, Keegan was sporting his natural color.

Kylie frowned at them. "You're making it sound stupid. It's not stupid. It's to make us look like we belong, in case of spies."

"They can even give you wings," Alexia added.

"Oh, well maybe they can do the same for Elora," I snarled. "Give her a set of imaginary wings to make up for the ones that were *cut off of her*."

They didn't say anything. They just looked at me with those wide, newborn baby eyes. It scared the shit out of me.

"Wait a minute." I looked around, like the forest would suddenly reveal what it was hiding. "Where are her wings? What did you do with them?"

"Taylor, calm down." Kylie reached for me. "Some ladies picked them up right before you got here. The ones with branches for hair and dragonfly wings. They handed them over to the Queen."

"They did? You don't think … " I ran my hands through my hair, afraid to hope. "Do you think they can reattach them?"

"Sure they can," said Kylie. "They're faeries; they have magic. They're probably sewing them on right now."

"Not sewing," I mumbled, shaking my head. "Not if there's iron in the needles."

God, what was I saying? Of course faeries could make needles without iron. They could probably make anything. And the thought of Elora flying again should've set me at ease.

But it didn't. I felt panicky, and angry enough to take

someone's head off. "I need to sit down," I said, slumping onto the grass. I clutched my hair in my hands.

"Taylor?" Kylie's voice filtered in from far away, even though she was right next to me. When she touched me, I jumped.

"He's coming out of shock," said Alexia, standing at Kylie's side. I looked up at them through my hair. "He needs a little something to calm him down." They all laughed that tinkling laugh, like a wind chime that starts out pleasant and becomes annoying fast.

"Luckily, I have just the thing." Alexia reached up, plucking a piece of pale, glowing fruit from a tree. When she tore off the stem, golden liquid oozed out of the top.

"I'm not eating that," I said.

"It's okay," Kylie said. "I know what you're thinking: *Don't eat their food*. But that's just in the stories. Humans get the rules twisted."

"What the hell do you know about the rules?" I demanded. "You didn't even know faeries existed until last night!" Again, I felt disproportionately angry. If I really thought about it, it made perfect sense that Kylie would know certain things about Faerie. She'd always ironed faerie patches onto her clothes. She carried that Tinker Bell lunchbox. Girls like that collected old poems and hung faerie calendars on their walls. She was probably a great source of information.

So why did I feel so angry?

Shock, shock, shock, my brain said, repeating Alexia's diagnosis. Then, *relax*.

Alexia held out the peach-that-wasn't-a-peach. Peaches don't usually glow. They *definitely* don't bleed. But now that gold, gooey liquid was dripping down her fingers, thick as blood, and she went to lick it.

Keegan stopped her with his hand. "Don't be greedy."

Alexia glared. But the anger didn't last, and soon that freaky Cheshire grin returned to her face. "He's right," she said to me. "One drop for each of us. That's what they said."

"You think I'm going to eat this?" I knocked the fruit from her hand. "You're not eating it either."

This time they exploded in laughter. I realized Alexia's eyes weren't the only ones that were liquid black. They all stared at me with those dilated eyes. Seeing things I couldn't see.

"Holy shit. You guys are tripping."

The laughter reached a fever pitch.

"You've got to be kidding me."

"It's not a drug, Taylor." Kylie plucked a piece of fruit from a low-hanging branch. "It's just to help you come out of shock. We all needed it." Her voice dropped to a hushed whisper. "I kind of freaked out."

"She started screaming," Alexia said. "Her, of all people."

"They weren't supposed to be monsters." Kylie frowned for about two seconds, and then she was mesmerized by the fruit again. "I just needed to calm down, and they helped with that."

"They *drugged* you," I said.

"No." She giggled at her hand. "They made me feel happy. And you can feel happy too."

"Oh my God. Seriously?"

Keegan knelt beside me, plucking the fruit from his sister's hand. "The doctor's in, Taylor."

Kylie laughed so hard I thought she was going to fall out

of her chair. But Alexia had other plans. She came up behind me and yanked my arm behind my back, piercing my finger with her nail. "It's quicker if it goes directly into the blood-stream."

"Fuck!" I wrestled free of her grip. "That hurt, you psy-chopathic—"

"It won't in a minute."

I crawled backward, away from her. I wasn't about to let her put that poison in my veins. But I made a mistake. I guess I wasn't thinking. I stuck my injured finger into my mouth.

Crap.

A few feet away, the group was laughing again. The whole thing had been a ploy to get me to suck on my finger. The fin-ger she'd smeared with nectar.

"I hate you," I mumbled as a wave of nausea hit me. If only I could stick my finger down my throat, I could get rid of most of the nectar. If only I wasn't falling down a hole that had no bottom.

From the depths of the darkness, Alexia's voice floated down. "You'll love me soon enough. You'll love all of us. And you'll be able to see everything they've kept hidden."

2

ELORA

I awoke to dizzying pain, though the reason did not occur to me right away. For one brief instant, I was blissfully ignorant of the source of my agony. I even entertained the fleeting fantasy that insects were feasting on my wings.

Perhaps some jokester had dripped honey over them.

That would explain the warm, wet sensation creeping down my back. Funny, the things the mind conjures to escape reality. Rising to my knees, I rustled my wings to shake the insects away.

Oh, Darkness.

Pain, searing and hot, shot through the length of my body. My limbs gave way under the weight of it. My heart constricted as if stabbed.

Please, let it have been a dream.

I opened my eyes. The Seelie Forest sprawled out before me, a reminder of where I was and where I had been. But Taylor was gone, and he'd taken my happiness, my sense of peace, and left only the memory of the trauma I'd endured. The battle in the graveyard. The blade . . .

No.

I reached behind my back.

Please, no.

I searched with my hands, my fingers clawing at the air.

They cannot be gone.

Sobs rose up from the deepest parts of me, unfurling in my gut and barreling up my throat. I tried to swallow them down, but who can swallow oceans? They swelled inside of me, pouring out my eyes, my lips, everything.

"Looking for these?"

I jerked my head up. In that moment, I felt more vulnerable than I ever had before. Unable to fly. Barely able to move. What would my people think of me when they saw what Naeve had done? What would Taylor think?

He'll be disgusted. He'll never want to look at me again.

But my mind changed as I lifted my gaze. My world changed. In the back of the clearing sat Lyndiria, the Queen of the Bright Faeries, and at her feet were wings.

My wings. "How … "

"I presume the boy is responsible," said Lyndiria, light pouring off of her in gales. It was difficult to see her clearly.

I closed my eyes, wary of being blinded. "Taylor brought them? He's so—"

"Perfect?" she suggested.

A chill crept through me, like spiders hatching beneath my skin. But I had no time to think on it. Every cell in my body propelled me forward as I crawled on hands and knees to those black, tattered wings, those things that looked so much like home to me. And felt like home. And smelled of blood and earth.

What are faeries, if not blood and earth?

I cradled the wings in my arms. They were cold, encrusted

in ice. Just above my head, snow fell softly on the wings, but only there. The Queen must have cast a spell to keep them cold.

"I am sorry for your loss," she said as I studied her handiwork, my heart a frantic butterfly in my chest. There was only one reason I could think of to keep my wings in the snow. When blood freezes, it cannot escape.

I looked up at her. "Lady," I murmured, "you don't suppose..."

"Certainly," she said, and my heart rose like a wave. She rose, too, and that light bled away from her like rivulets into the sea. Now unburdened by her luminescence, I could see her more clearly: those curves, bound tightly in a gown of diaphanous green; that skin, warm and brown as the earth kissed by sunlight. She was larger than life, this great forest queen. And she had power I could not comprehend.

"Would you help me?" I asked. "I did everything you asked of me. I went to the mortal world, I found a boy who was a young leader of men. I brought him here—"

"I asked for *the bane of the darkness*," Lyndiria scolded, the emerald strands of her hair darkening to red. "I asked for a boy who was *perfect for light*. We spoke of this last night—"

"I hardly remember last night," I said, images of horror flashing through my mind. Here, Naeve tossed his sword into the air, letting it shatter on the ground. Here, he slid the iron shards into my back, one by one. "But I remember your riddle," I added, reciting the Bright Queen's riddle from memory:

"Bane of the darkness, perfect for light,
Steal him away in the dead of the night.
Bind him with blood, this young leader of men,
And bring him to Court before Light's hallowed reign."

The Queen had tucked that riddle into my palm and sent me off to the mortal world in search of an offering. If I could provide a proper offering, she would help me take down the Unseelie Court. She would bind the Dark Queen, I would rally the servants, and together we'd overthrow the nobles.

The Dark Court would fall.

Then, after the dust had settled, the Bright Queen would disband *her* court as well, so that all could be free. She'd promised she would, the last time I saw her. But now . . .

"I brought you a proper offering," I insisted, scanning the bower for the boy I'd stolen on prom night. I saw no one except for the Queen. "Brad Dickson ruled his school with an iron fist, making him a *young leader of men*. He was cruel, which made him the *bane of the darkness*. And because he had a habit of harming his classmates, the human world would be better off without him, making him *perfect for light*."

"You twisted the riddle to mean what you wanted. You brought me something sour instead of something sweet. I've already sent the boy—"

"I brought you *exactly* what you asked for," I said, feeling desperate with my wings so close to me. If I didn't convince the Bright Queen to help me soon, I would lose everything. My ability to fly. My revolution. All of my efforts would be for nothing. "If you wanted something sweet, you should've *asked* for something sweet."

"I suppose that is the danger of riddles. And you have made quite the sacrifice," the Bright Queen said, her gaze flickering to my wings. "But if I were to help you—"

"I will give you everything I promised. The Dark Court will fall. My mother will be ruined. You can finally be free."

"Free?" she repeated, as if the word tasted funny in her mouth. "What makes you think I want to be free?"

"Because I know how it feels to be shackled by nobility." I glanced down at my wrists, at the shadows that clung to me like jewelry. Like *chains*. "We are wild things who built up cages and called them castles. We have lashed ourselves to our thrones. But once upon a time ... "

" ... there were no queens, and no courts. I roamed the earth as I pleased." The Bright Queen smiled, but it fell away quickly. "Then *she* came along and ruined everything."

"The Dark Lady has a talent for that."

"She wanted to destroy humanity, so I had to stand against her. I had to build my court to stop *her* court—"

"Yes, but not anymore. There will be *no need* for a Bright Court if we destroy the Dark Court." I looked up, studying the flowers in her crown. Opalescent blossoms sat beside fat green leaves. But if you looked closely, you could see the places where thorns curved into her skin, keeping the garland in place. "Nobility comes at a cost. But you can be free."

The Bright Queen peered down at me, her eyes sparkling as if ablaze. She looked *hungry*. "I will do as I promised," she said. "I will bind the Dark Lady."

"And?"

"If the Dark Court falls, I will relinquish my throne." Her gaze dropped to my wings. "Now, give those to me."

"Thank you, Lady. Thank you." The tears had only just dried on my face, but already they were falling again. Those oceans were pouring out of me, drowning my sadness, giving life to hope. "Have you ever heard of such a thing? Of sewing a part of one's body—"

17

"Never," she said, "outside of the human world. But then, I've never heard of a faerie cutting away another's wings. Certainly, I've never heard of one faerie using iron against another."

I laughed a little, heavy under the weight of hope. "At least Naeve will have the remembrance he's always wanted. And the adoration of his queen."

Lyndiria was silent a long moment. I inched toward her, anxious to begin the ritual that might return my wings to me. Finally, when I reached the place where she sat, she took the wings from my hands and said, "I do not believe he will risk telling her the whole truth."

"What do you mean?" I knelt at her feet, facing away from her. My body cringed at the thought of being touched now that I was so wounded. How would she heal me? Would she use needles or wind or webs? Would she use all of them?

"He tried to end your life." The Bright Queen swept my hair over my shoulders, and her touch was soft. Motherly. Unlike anything I'd ever felt. "He broke the laws of Faerie, using iron against you. And on top of it all, you got away from him. Would *you* confess such shortcomings to the Queen of the Dark Faeries?"

"I would, but I don't mind angering my mommy."

She laughed. We both did. After all, we were conspiring to take away everything my mother cared about. Her court. Her crown. Her wretched, villainous smile.

"Now then." Lyndiria leaned in, lips close to my ear. "I'll just be needing the name of the faerie who will take your place." The pads of her fingers trickled over my back, making my body scream.

"Take my place?" I managed between short breaths.

"In the battle against the Dark Court. Surely you didn't think you'd be going yourself? You'll be on the mend."

"I'm on the mend now," I said, growing angry. I was so close to regaining my wings, and still she was taunting me with the power she held over me. Teasing.

Wasn't she?

"You do not understand," said the Queen. "As things are now, the worst is behind you. My magic flushed out the iron in your veins. Together with the mortal's love, it healed the worst of your wounds. But if you are to bond with something that has been torn away, your body will be in a constant state of healing. The process could take months. You will not be able to go about your usual activities. You will not be able to fight. You'll have to rest."

"No."

"You'll be incapacitated. The best you could do is sit in the trees surrounding the battle and act as defense, and even then, why risk it?"

"No, there has to be another way." I could not lose this opportunity. Even now, I could feel the edges of my wings brushing against my back. I yearned to make them a part of me again.

"What if we wait until the battle is ended?" I asked. "I could return to you, and—"

"We could attempt it. But the places where they were cut away will have healed by then, and we'd have to open you up all over again."

My body shuddered at the thought.

"The pain would be great," she said, echoing my fears. "The first cut alone might—"

"I could suffer it."

"I suppose you could," she said, and her tone was kind. But there was something beneath it, satisfaction or hunger. I couldn't quite place it. "Of course, the wings would not fit so nicely after all that. If we do it today, we might be able to slide them right back into place. Sew them together with wind and webs. Fill you up with light again, to lessen the pain. I cannot promise your body will respond to the ritual, but there is a much greater chance now than there will be then."

"And there is no chance I would be able to fight? You are certain of that?"

"Naeve nearly bested you the last time. What do you think will happen when so much of your strength is dedicated to healing these wings?"

My wings. The greatest part of me. My freedom, my identity. How could I say goodbye when I didn't have to? But how could I ask my people to fight if I were not brave enough to stand alongside them?

"Please ... I need some time."

"Do make your decision quickly," the Queen said. "I've places to be, and people to govern."

"Yes, Lady."

She rose. My back remained to her, but I could hear her movements. Before she left the clearing, she set the wings in my lap. Then, transforming into her favorite form, a great black-eyed doe, she scampered toward the trees.

I clutched the wings to my chest and sobbed.

3

TAYLOR

I'd never taken drugs before. It wasn't that I was a kiss-ass or anything, though I knew to stay away from the hard stuff. Anything you snort or inject could stay the hell away from me. But the natural stuff, the stuff that grows in the forest, well . . . I'd thought about it.

The sad truth was, I'd never had anyone to experiment with. I wasn't about to try drugs alone. How sad would that have been, tripping in my bedroom above my parents' garage, the place where I'd been serving the self-imposed sentence for my brother's death? One look out the window and I would've seen the tree I'd stupidly let him climb, knowing full well it was dangerous for a little kid to be up so high. What if my drug-addled mind got stuck on that thought and I saw him falling all over again? I would've lost it completely, torn my room apart.

I would've gone insane.

But this was different. I was with my friends, and though they'd essentially dosed me, there was nothing I could do about it now. And since I was suddenly incapable of feeling anger, or shame, I settled in with the three of them and watched the world unfold before me. Not the world I'd known, the human world.

The real world.

The first thing to change was the air. Had the air always been so *alive*? Had there always been little beings there, beings of color and light dancing just outside the corners of my eyes? Even the shadows moved, where I could find them: in little patches underneath the leaves, and under my body. Creatures were everywhere, saturating the air, changing shape as I reached out to touch them.

That, too, was amazing. Rainbows of light followed my hand, the way a trail of light follows a shooting star. I could hear my friends laughing around me, looking at my movements too, but nothing could hold our attention for long. Soon we were moving around, shifting the dirt with our fingers, approaching the trees.

We wanted to touch everything.

There were *things* living in the dirt, but it wasn't that simple. The entire ground was breathing, in and out; I could feel it. I pressed my hand against the dirt—something I'd done at my brother's grave a hundred times—and the ground pushed back, greeting me. To my left, on the edge of the clearing, Kylie was reaching up and checking which leaf was a leaf and which was a faerie. Half the leaves touched by her fingers curled back to reveal some green-winged thing, and others scurried away like animals. Everything was something other than what it seemed, and everything was alive. Rocks rose on little legs and hobbled past us. The wind sang in our ears, beckoning us the way sirens beckoned men into the ocean.

I wanted to feel the ocean then, to feel waves pouring over

me, showing me all the creatures that lived underneath. But the light felt a lot like water, like something warm and fluid moving over me. Or maybe there were faeries there made out of light, touching me. It was impossible to know what was real. Was all of it? Was none of it? And, more importantly, did it matter?

All the worries I'd carried for most of my life—my father's disappointment in me, the loss of my brother, my never-ending quest to gain love from Elora, from anyone—just slipped off of me, and I felt clean. Unburdened. I leaned against the trunk of a tree and felt arms reaching out for me, lifting me into the branches. The bark scraped my back but I didn't care; it felt like scratching an impossible itch. It was only when those hands started getting too friendly that I detached myself from them and really looked around.

The sight should've been ordinary—a host of branches dangling green leaves. But it was anything but ordinary. A world existed between those branches. Each tree was home to a civilization. I poked my head into a hole and saw a dwelling way bigger than the space implied. Little creatures scurried around inside, with backs like pinecones and faces like men. The creatures were not lounging, they were re-arranging. A bed of moss flew into the air, barely missing my face, and landed on the other side of the room. Tables and chairs moved of their own accord. A particularly small creature raced this way and that, screeching, "Different! Different!" and another one, sitting surprisingly close to my face, hissed like a talking snake. "Which kind of flowers?" it asked.

I couldn't imagine the right answer, so I said, "Roses," thinking I could give them to Elora. I missed her, even now.

In fact, I may have missed her more, because I wanted her to be able to share this experience. But my eyes started to wander, and my brain followed as roses sprang up out of every wall, climbing over the bark and twisting around branches like a living tapestry, a painting you could smell.

And they smelled amazing. The entire world smelled like roses. I reached out to take one and immediately regretted it. A thorn pierced my thumb so hard, I thought it was deliberate.

"The beauties bite back," said the hissing faerie.

"No shit." I stuck my finger in my mouth, sucking away the blood before the flowers could get to it. *Evil roses. The vampires of the garden.* Well, they wouldn't get my blood! The Bright Queen already had my name, and that was plenty, thank you very much. Sure, I was having a grand old time, but I had to keep a sense of myself, or I'd be lost.

I remembered that much. I remembered...

The hands were back, caressing my legs in a way that made me feel special and very uncomfortable at the same time. Pulling my knees into my chest, I lifted my head out of the tree to find so many nymphs, I thought I must have been hallucinating.

Well, duh! I am hallucinating.

Except some of the nymphs were probably real. I was just seeing three or four for each one of them, or maybe I wasn't. It was hard to tell, and it was hard not to stare. They weren't exactly wearing much, except in the weirdest places, like a leaf covering a shoulder, or a vine wrapped around the thigh. Clothing as costume rather than covering. Something Keegan would dig. He liked to use outfits to screw with people, like Alexia used words to screw with people. But Kylie—she never screwed with people. She was just honest. God, they were awesome. I missed them.

I fell out of the tree.

"Ow," I said, more because I thought I should than out of actual pain. I mean, when you fall ten feet onto your ass, it's supposed to hurt, right? But it didn't. I thought, with a kind of detached fascination, that someone could pull my arm out of its socket and I wouldn't feel a thing.

God forbid the doctors get ahold of this shit. With faerie drugs at hand, the medical industry would have a field day. I started busting up then, because *we* were having a field day. We were actually *in a field*, or a reasonable facsimile of one. *Field* day. *Oh my God, I'm hilarious.* I was laughing, and then my friends were laughing, and then the trees started laughing, which made us laugh even more.

Then everyone was dancing with everyone, and I feared the nymphs might start to kiss me, but instead they twirled in circles, waving their hands. At first I thought it was some kind of ritual—a Welcome to Faerie dance—but then I realized they were manipulating the light around me. Ever since I'd spoken my name to the Seelie Queen, that light had clung to me the way it clung to her faeries, but now it *solidified* behind my back. Turning this way and that, I saw the tips of golden wings, veined in green. It was only glamour, but it looked amazing.

The dancing continued, and I started to spin around, trying to get a better look at my wings. Then Kylie and Alexia were kissing in this totally frenzied way, like they might never see each other again, which gave me this creepy-crawly sense of premonition, and Keegan was sneaking into the forest with a satyr. I thought I should go after him, maybe warn him against getting too caught up in the happy faerieland illusion, but he didn't get far because suddenly trumpets were blaring. And pipes, and, and ... what was that sound? A sort of tinkling, crinkling sound, the way glitter would sound if it *had* a sound. I mean, the way laughter would sound if you were underwater. I mean ...

I had to sit down. My legs had gone all gelatinous, and it was kind of serendipitous because someone was sliding a chair *right under me.* One of those recently crafted chairs where you could still see the shape of the branches, with a pillow made of moss. As I sat down, the others gathered around, and this huge, elaborate dinner table was constructed right in front of us, out of branches and vines and a tablecloth that *I swear to God* had to have been spun from sunlight because it was so light and soft.

When the food arrived, I realized how hungry I'd become. I could've eaten a horse, except I wouldn't be doing that here because horses were probably centaurs in disguise, and besides, faeries didn't eat meat due to their aversion to iron. And I was okay with that. I was more than okay with that. If everything was alive, I didn't need some animal to die for me. I didn't need anyone to die for me. Especially not Elora.

Elora.

And there she was. Dressed in glowing teal, the same exact color as her eyes. The Seelie Queen had probably put her foot down at Elora's usual black. But this was nice too; it was better than nice. God, she was so beautiful. I wanted to pull her into me and kiss her and tell her I'd give anything to make up for

what she'd given me. I would have, too, right in front of everyone, if my legs hadn't turned to jelly.

The shaking I felt was worse now, with her standing so
close. Across the long table. To the left of the Queen. How
angry the bright faeries must've been to see the daughter of the
Dark Lady taking her seat next to their queen. But if they only
got to know her, they'd fall in love with her.

What was not to love?

She was amazing.

Now that she had joined us, I couldn't care less about anything else. Faeries were closing in around me, filling my goblet,
dropping treats onto my plate, but I couldn't focus on them. I
started drawing an image of Elora with my food: her fire-lit eyes,
bright as blue and green flames dancing. Her pale, luminous
skin. Her wings.

Wait.

"Oh my God."

"What?" Kylie asked, following my gaze. She nudged me,
like I'd simply been taken in by Elora's beauty.

Hello, that was two minutes ago. Catch up.

"Her wings," I breathed, barely able to produce simple
sentences.

"I told you," Kylie said, juice dripping from her mouth.
Alexia's hand was in her lap like they couldn't stand to stop
touching each other.

"That was so … fast. The healing … "

"It's magic." Kylie grinned like she was some amazing
faerie expert. I wondered how she was going to feel in the
morning.

"It must be. I have to go talk to her." I pushed back from

the table, determined to make it over to Elora, no matter how wobbly my legs were. But something else stopped me from moving this time. A hand on my shoulder, holding me down.

"Not so fast, little mortal," a voice whispered in my ear.

I looked up to see a faerie with hair made of light. Her pale skin was glowing, like she was lit up from the inside, and her green dress clung to her so tightly, I thought it might fall away at any moment.

"Why can't I go over there?" I asked.

"You can," the faerie said, crouching next to me. From this angle, I could see the wings poking out of her back. Unlike Elora's wings, which were black and tattered, even before the dark faeries got to them, these were green and glistening like a dragonfly's. "But *should* you?" she pressed.

"I ... yes."

"Are you certain?"

"Oh my *God*. Just say what you're thinking. Don't hint. *Say* it."

The faerie laughed. And she placed her hand on my knee, making me all kinds of squirmy. "I know about your deal with the Queen."

A hitch caught in my throat. "What do you know?" I asked, pretending to drink from my goblet. I wanted to hide the movement of my lips, in case anyone was watching.

"I know you offered your name to save the princess."

"Can you tell me what that means?"

She hesitated. On the other side of the table, the Queen was leaning into Elora, whispering about something, but she could glance our way at any second. "It means she can control your every move, if she is so inclined."

"But will she?" I asked, and my body twitched. It was like I wanted to feel fear, but I couldn't quite *get* there.

"She is not a dark faerie. She will not harm you—"

"There are lots of ways to harm a person," I said, glancing at my knee. At *her hand* on my knee. "And they don't always require a sword."

The faerie took back her hand. "Forgive me," she said, blushing. "It has been so long since mortals have graced this land."

I know, I thought smugly. Elora had told me all about the sanctions between the courts. The dark faeries had agreed not to attack humanity if the bright faeries agreed not to befriend them. It was a tentative agreement, but it had put centuries of fighting on hold. Now it was all unraveling because of me.

"I will respect your boundaries," the faerie said. "*I* will, but…"

"The Queen won't?"

Again, she paused. Across the table, the Queen of the Bright Faeries sat like an embodiment of Mother Earth, waiting to cradle us in her arms. But I had seen another side of her, a side that would kill as easily as give life. She would've let Elora bleed out if I hadn't offered up my name.

She was beautiful and powerful, like nature itself. But what did *nature* want with a human boy?

"Will she … force me to do things?" A tremor ran through my back. For a second, the fear was real. "Is that why you're keeping me in my seat? Will the Queen be jealous if I sit by Elora?"

The faerie lowered her head, speaking softly into my ear. "I would never say anything bad about my queen. The bright faeries love humanity. We will not intentionally hurt you—"

"But?"

She lifted her gaze. "The idea that you could be kept, like a captive … "

"Wait. Are you saying … " I studied her face, not believing what I was hearing. "You think humans should be free?"

The faerie nodded. "I cannot say it. Anyone could be listening in." She glanced up, at the trees. "But there are those you can trust in this place." She pointed across the table, to a nymph with great, curling horns. Pale brown skin peeked out of a dress so low, I could practically see a belly button. "The royal seamstress. And over there … "

I looked to the left. Next to Keegan, there was a lady with branches for limbs. Her rich brown skin was dark as the earth, and leaves shot out of her head. When she smiled, I saw she had twigs for teeth. Sharpened, of course.

"The royal storyteller," the faerie said.

"And you?"

"Me?" She blushed, like she'd been nominated for an Oscar. Like she was just happy to be considered. "I am Maya de Lyre, the royal songstress. The three of us, together, are the Queen's favored ladies. We are the closest to her, and yet she has not trusted us with her reasons for keeping you. This concerns me."

It concerns me too, I thought. But I didn't say it. Instead, I decided to take a chance. "So you'll help me break free?"

The faerie sucked in a breath. *Maya de Lyre*, I reminded myself, trying not to forget her name. Trying not to forget any of this.

"The punishment would be dire," she said. "But I can investigate. If there is a possibility that you could be freed … "

"Do you think there's a possibility?"

"I think this is a riddle, and I've yet to hear a riddle I couldn't solve." She flashed white teeth. Her smile was fierce, like everything in this forest. The light. The drugs.

"I solved the Queen's last riddle," I boasted. "I figured out she wanted a nice human instead of a nasty one."

Maya de Lyre frowned, her hair flickering like I'd struck a nerve. Slowly, that light trickled back into her.

"Ah, so you've met him?" I asked. "Brad, I mean. The asshole of Unity High."

"The Queen told me to take him home."

"And you already did?" Vertigo washed over me. Something about her wording felt familiar, like it had been rehearsed. "How long was I asleep? Or is he, like, tied up somewhere, waiting to be transported?"

She laughed. "Don't worry so much, darling. The path to the mortal world can be treacherous, or it can be swift. If you travel to the sea of the Undulari, there are merfolk who will carry a mortal through the waterways without harming him in the slightest."

"So he really is gone." I should've felt relieved, but cold dread was settling over me. Pressing into me. If Brad was gone, I was *definitely* the offering the Seelie Queen had wanted. She wasn't changing her mind, calling Brad back, and releasing me. She wanted me for some nefarious purpose, and even her closest confidants didn't know why.

"So you'll help me?" I asked, just as the Queen glanced over. The leaves in her hair brightened to gold at the sight of me. *Shit. Shit. Shit.* I took a gulp from my goblet, trying to look busy. Naturally, liquid sloshed down my shirt.

Still, the stain provided us with an opportunity. Maya de Lyre knelt in front of me, turning *away* from the Queen, to blot at my shirt. "I will give you what you want," she said softly, "but you must do something for me. You must not tell the princess that you are the Queen's offering."

"Why not? Elora could help me."

"She could," Maya de Lyre agreed. "That is the problem. Wouldn't she do *anything* to set you free? Even unravel *her* bargain with the Queen?"

"I … oh, crap. I didn't think about that." Elora's revolution depended on the Seelie Queen's help. No one else was strong enough to bind Elora's mother, the Unseelie Queen. I couldn't mess that up.

"You're right," I said, lifting my goblet again. It was a cheap trick, but it would work for the moment. "We'll figure this out on our own."

Maya de Lyre grinned, and I thought she was going to throw her arms around me. But she didn't. She simply squeezed my shoulder, respecting my boundaries.

I thought that was significant.

"We'll meet again in private," she said, rising to fill her own plate.

My heart started to race. For the first time since I'd arrived here, I felt *grounded*. Like I was actually gaining control, even though faerie drugs were still swimming in my veins. I decided two things in that moment: I would regain my freedom from the Seelie Queen. And I would fight in Elora's revolution.

4

ELORA

As the mortals ate, the Queen made conversation, and I tried to appear interested. But I wasn't. Much more interesting was the scene playing out in the periphery of my vision, the faerie hovering around Taylor, finding excuses to touch him. Here, she placed her hand on his cheek, pretending his untamable hair was bothering her. Here, she pressed her bosom against his arm to reach for a berry.

How subtle, I thought, anger pulsing through me. He seemed so at home with her, all green eyes and golden hair. They'd even given him wings, to make him look like he belonged in the Seelie Court. In fact, all the mortals had been glamoured to look like faeries for their own protection, but on Taylor it looked *natural*.

A shudder ran through my back and I closed my eyes.

The Queen was prattling on about some banquet she was planning for the mortals. A banquet! Wasn't that what was happening now? But the Bright Queen's claim to fame, more than her ability to heal, was her ability to throw a fabulous party. It was how she kept her people controlled. She lavished gifts upon them, kept them drunk and happy. Then, when she needed them to go into one itsy-bitsy battle, who were they to argue?

Who would say no to that?

When she turned to me and said, "It is my expert opinion that oak-aged whiskey tastes better after the first three centuries," I nodded politely, forcing myself to pay attention. The timing was good, because if I'd only pretended to listen to the Queen's next statement, it would've been great folly.

"Tonight, we will allow the mortals to rest and rejuvenate themselves after the terrible things they have seen," she said. "Tomorrow, we begin our journey to the heart of the Seelie Court, where they can seek refuge."

"No." My voice was louder than I expected it to be. The faeries of the Seelie Court took notice. "We cannot take them farther into your lands. We have to send them home. You have no claim to them."

"No claim to them?" She raised her eyebrows.

A trickle of fear crept down my spine. Was *this* why she had agreed to help me? Was she plotting to keep four humans instead of Brad?

"Oh, I have something better than a claim to them," the Queen continued. "I have affection for them. And you would throw them to the wolves?"

"Keeping them here would be selfish."

"Would it?" she shrieked. Her body flashed with light, and her green hair began dropping leaves. Then, lowering her voice, she turned to the humans. "And why did you come to this place, my dears? Did you do it for your own delight? Or were you seeking sanctuary?"

"Sanctuary," Keegan said after a moment. He was hanging on her every word, even if he only understood half of them. "We wanted to go home after those faeries attacked us in the graveyard. But they knew what we looked like, and we thought they might follow us to our houses. Hurt our families." His body twitched, as if it realized the seriousness of his words before his brain did. Honestly, the humans were acting far more casual than the situation required. Had they drunk too much wine?

The Bright Queen smiled. "Hurt your families? Oh you kind, precious babies. Did you hear that, Elora?"

Princess, I wanted to correct, because ignoring a person's title was a sign of disrespect. Then again, I was planning to render all titles meaningless, so I might as well get used to the sound of my name on other people's lips.

"I suppose I hadn't thought of that," I admitted. "Still, once the dark faeries have me, they won't bother with the humans. They'd only use them as collateral to get me back."

"Are they getting you back?" Taylor asked.

"You know they are," I said, my eyes glued to the Queen. I was afraid to look at him, and be *seen*. "But only until I can destroy them."

The bright faeries gasped at that. Surely the Queen had told them *something* of my reasons for being here, but she clearly hadn't told them everything.

"And you're doing that alone?" Taylor pressed. Oh, how I longed for the days when these conversations took place in his bedroom, away from prying Seelie eyes. Of course, back in his room, he hadn't known that my stories of the dark and bright faeries were *real*. It had been a lot easier to talk about things when he thought I was telling him a "fairy" tale.

Funny, the difference a few letters can make.

"I will not be *alone*," I said, trying to strike a balance between saying too much in front of the faeries, and saying too little to satisfy the humans. One human in particular. "Many of the dark servants will come to my aid."

Another gasp from the bright faeries. This time, I couldn't help but roll my eyes. Such drama. Didn't it get tiring?

"So what if they will?" Taylor asked. "Is there such a thing as *too much* support?" He was staring at me, his eyes burning into me, and I hated the feeling of disappointing him. But regardless of the cost, I would protect him from the wickedness of the faeries, both bright and dark. Even if he hated me for it.

"This isn't your fight," I said, finally meeting his gaze. "I will not lead you into battle, risking your life—"

"You don't get to decide that. It's *my* decision—"

"It is *my* world and *my* revolution and I *do* get to decide."

"What revolution?" Kylie asked, looking over at me. A couple of deer had crept out of the forest, and she was feeding them sweets.

"It is … complicated," I began, swirling jam around my plate. "I am not sure how to explain it simply."

"I can do it," Taylor offered, and I looked up, surprised. But why was I surprised? From the moment I'd met him, he had always been kind, and understanding, and clever.

"Tell us," I said, staring into his leaf-green eyes. "Tell us about my plans for the Unseelie Court." My unspoken message was clear: do not mention my plans for *this* court, or my dealings with their queen. Do not mention that, if my revolution is a success and the Dark Court falls, the Bright Queen will disband *her* court in response.

Taylor nodded solemnly, in understanding. I wanted to pull him into my arms and kiss his lips. Instead, I sat quietly and listened.

"Let me see if I remember this correctly," he said, holding my gaze. "Back in the Middle Ages, two courts of faeries were created, one who loved humanity, and one who wanted to destroy them."

"*Why?*" Keegan asked playfully. "Who would want to hurt *us?*"

"Um, people who don't like murderers," Alexia said. "Or pedophiles. Or hipster doofuses."

Kylie almost laughed. But she caught herself, hand slapping over her mouth. She never did like talking about the worst kinds of humans. Here in Faerie, she could almost pretend they didn't exist.

Almost.

"Well, you're half right," Taylor said, tilting his head. "The faeries of the Dark Court did hate humans because of our destructiveness, but they especially hated us because we used iron."

"Oh! Because iron keeps faeries away," Kylie said, clasping her hands. "I read that in this crazy-old book. People put iron on their horses and their doors and around their necks. That really works?"

Taylor nodded. "It got so bad, the faeries stopped being able to have babies. Because iron was so poisonous, and it weakened them."

"That's terrible," Kylie said, and my chest surged with

warmth. The bright faeries were leaning in. "So they're dying off?"

"We are immortal," the Bright Queen announced.

"Then you can't be killed?" Keegan asked.

"We *can* be killed," I explained, "with weapons or magic, but our bodies don't decay."

"So you don't die of natural causes, but you can be hurt, and iron hurts you the worst," Kylie said.

Taylor nodded. "*And* their land is constantly being taken over by humans, because, you know, we don't adapt to the natural world. We make it adapt to us."

"De-evolution," Keegan said.

"Exactly," Alexia agreed, and her eyes went wide. I think it was the first time she and Keegan had ever agreed on anything.

After a moment of heavy silence, Kylie began putting the pieces together in that careful way of hers. "So after humanity started poisoning the faeries, and took over their lands, the dark faeries decided to fight back. Okay. Where do the bright faeries come in?"

"How did you put it?" Taylor mused, looking at me. His gaze flickered to my back, where dark wings unfurled like shadows. I turned away. "All faeries believe the earth is to be protected, because the earth is like their body," he said. "But while the dark faeries are willing to protect the earth by any means necessary, the bright faeries believe humans are *part* of the earth, and fall under their protection."

A slow smile took over my face, born of adoration. Affection. Maybe even…

"That's pretty messed up," Alexia said, brushing her dark, wavy hair behind her back. "I mean, say your body got sick, like you had a disease or something. And it was killing you, but you were all, 'Oh, no, I have to protect it, because it's a part of me.'"

"Okay, you're sympathizing with the *dark faeries*," Taylor said, his tone growing harsher. "You do know these are the people who almost killed your girlfriend? The people who almost killed ... " His gaze shifted, and all eyes turned to me.

That was all right. It was my turn to speak. "Over the centuries, the faeries of the Dark Court grew worse and worse. They didn't simply fight with the Seelie Court, or with humanity. They fought with each other. They abused the servants that waited on them hand and foot."

"They attacked their own princess," Kylie said, shaking her head. "In the graveyard. That was them, right? The faeries of the Dark Court?"

"Ah, yes," I said, nodding. "The courtiers, and Naeve."

"Is that ... was he ... " But Kylie couldn't say it. Naeve had taken a special interest in her, realizing she was the sweetest of the humans. He'd commanded his favored courtier, the Lady Claremondes, to attack. And that slithery creature, half-woman and half-snake, had slid her venomous tongue along Kylie's neck, making her shake and scream.

"Yes, Naeve is the worst of them," I said. "Of course, being the Prince of the Dark Court comes with a certain sense of entitlement."

"Wait, the prince? Like your *brother*?" Keegan gaped at me.

"Adopted brother. Adopted, in fact, long before I was born." I lowered my gaze. I did not want to get into the specifics of my relationship with Naeve. Did not want to admit how he had treated me since I was a child.

But Taylor took the reins for me, before I even had to ask. "Remember how I said the faeries were losing the ability to have babies? Well, for a long time, they thought Naeve was the last faerie ever to be born."

"So he was born in the Middle Ages?" Kylie asked, wide-eyed. "He's *centuries* old?"

"Yep, he was born toward the end," Taylor said. "And the Dark Lady swooped in and adopted him, thinking she could use him as a symbol of her court. A symbol of everything the faeries had to lose if they didn't take down humanity."

"So Naeve grew up as a prince," Keegan said, "even though he wasn't related to the Queen."

"That's kind of an important point." Taylor glanced at me. "Because years later, when Naeve was an adult, he and the Queen kind of … hooked up."

"Wait, *what*?" Keegan asked. Kylie dropped her roll. Only Alexia looked unsurprised.

Taylor jumped in. "Look, none of us has a perfect family. If we did, we probably wouldn't be here." When nobody responded, he went on. "Sure, the Dark Lady's relationship with Naeve was messed up, but that's the point. He was obsessed with her, and he saw her as a mother and a lover. She was *everything* to him."

"Until I came along," I murmured, my face flushing with heat. But Taylor had begun the story of Naeve, and he would finish it for me. Nodding, he said, "Centuries after Naeve was born, the Dark Lady realized she was pregnant. Turns out, *Elora* was the last faerie ever to be born. So Naeve lost all of his fame, and the attention of the Queen, in one fell swoop. And even though it wasn't Elora's fault, considering she was a baby and all, he took out all his anger on her."

"He essentially tormented me throughout my life," I admitted softly.

"So brother fought sister," Keegan said. "The courtiers abused the servants. And the Queen abused them all."

I lifted my head. "Yes. That is it exactly. You see, then, why I plotted a revolution. My goal is to take them down from the inside."

"Like we did back at school." Kylie gasped. "I mean, the way we all came together to take down Brad and his goons."

"Yes. But more life-and-death," I pointed out.

Kylie nodded, but she wouldn't look at me. I felt the cold weight of guilt pressing into my chest. After all, Brad had made Kylie's life a living hell. I hadn't meant to belittle her experience.

Then she said the last thing I expected. "So what can we do to help?"

"What?" I blinked at her, utterly lost in that moment.

"You defended us back in the human world. You helped us throw our own revolution."

"Yeah." Keegan nodded. "We should return the favor."

"You could die," Taylor said, surprising me. I hadn't expected him to interfere with their offering.

"We could die every minute back home. We could be crossing the street, and *bam*!" Kylie slapped her hands together. "Car crash."

"Dying here is much more likely," Taylor said.

"So you don't want us to help her?" Alexia asked.

"I don't want you to get hurt," he explained. "But I'm going to help her." He turned, catching my eye. "She's insane if she thinks I won't."

"Taylor—"

"Right, like we're just going to sit on our asses in faerie-land while she faces the guy who cut off her wings? Fuck no," Alexia said.

"It isn't our fight," Taylor said. "She's right about that."

"It wasn't her fight back home. She still stood with us. She *led* us," Kylie said, taking Alexia's hand. "And what do I even have to go back to? Parents who stopped loving me the minute I had feelings for a girl? The minute I realized I *might*, at some point?"

"They didn't stop loving you," Keegan said, and it was the first time I'd heard him speak kindly about his parents. Then again, they had kicked him out at age eleven for being gay. Kylie, who'd jokingly called herself "half a heathen" for being bisexual, had been quick to follow him.

But perhaps Keegan wasn't really defending his parents. Perhaps he just wanted Kylie to feel loved.

She smiled, barely. "I want to do something meaningful with my life. And sure, I want that life to be long—"

"I always thought I would burn fast and bright," Alexia murmured.

"But that's why we have to prepare," Kylie said. "I bet there are wands and arrows and all sorts of things here. We could—"

"Darlings, darlings!" The Queen stood abruptly, towering over us like an ancient oak. "I believe I speak for all the bright faeries when I say I am enchanted by your offering. Here, more than ever, we have proof of the value of humanity. Let us make a toast in your honor!"

The bright faeries exploded with cheers and applause, and the humans beamed, not understanding what was happening. Not understanding that they were being dismissed. Distracted.

Still, after a moment, Taylor surprised me one more time. He turned to the Queen and said, "So you think we should fight?"

The Queen's smile slipped, but oh, she was so practiced at wearing the mask of nobility, she caught it quickly. "Far be it from me to stop you from doing as you please. That is the dark faeries' game ... "

Subtle, I thought, biting my tongue to keep from biting her. I mean, to keep from lashing out at her. Verbally.

Oh, who was I kidding? I wanted to bite her at this point.

"But first, let us show you all the Bright Court has to offer." She waved a hand dramatically. "There are crystalline pools so deep, you can dive hundreds of miles into the sparkling depths, and mountains so high, you can see countries splayed out below you. There are cities built into the trees!"

Taylor perked up at that. I remembered, suddenly, my first night in his bedroom, when he'd told me he used to daydream about a city in the trees. He and his brother had even drawn up the plans. I'd almost forgotten he was an artist. Or at least, he used to be, before his brother died.

I waited for him to take the bait.

To bite.

To sink into the Bright Lady's hook.

But even the lure of seeing his visions come to life was not enough to distract him. "After the battle, I'd love to see those things," he said calmly. "And more. But until then, I'm going to be very busy, learning how to fight."

"Young man—"

"And if you respect me, you won't try to stand in my way."

"I respect you a great deal. But I also respect the princess, and if she does not want you to fight . . . "

Oh, clever, shifting the blame to me. That way, she could be the hero, rooting for the humans. And I could be the villain.

I chose my words carefully. "You've been through a great deal," I said to Taylor. "You risked your life for me. Your family. Your home. The last thing I want is for you to get killed in my name—"

"Indeed," the Queen agreed, cutting me off. Then, more softly, she added, "The poor babies wouldn't stand a chance."

"They aren't babies," I snapped.

"They are *humans*," the Bright Queen said. Her tone was not laced with disgust, as my mother's might've been, but still, it was heavy with condescension.

"*Human* is not synonymous with *helpless*," I said. "Even in battle, they would not be *helpless*. I simply think—"

"Of course they wouldn't," she agreed. "Many mortals are experienced in warfare. But when it comes to magic, and the wickedness of the dark faeries—"

"*The dark faeries* were thwarted in the graveyard. *The dark faeries* underestimated the humans. That's why they lost," I said, a thrill racing through me. A thrill of possibility. Of hope.

"Young princess, you cannot possibly believe—"

"Wait."

"Excuse me?" The Queen frowned, clearly startled by my command. But I was speaking as much to myself as to her.

"Wait, I have an idea. What if the mortals could aid my revolution without risking their lives in battle? What if they used their magic to—"

"*What magic?*" the Queen interrupted. "Mortals are many things, but they are not magical."

I shook my head. "That's where you're wrong. Kylie's more talented at craftsmanship than anyone I've ever met. Alexia's a natural chameleon. Keegan can see into you, into the depths of your soul—"

"And the leader?"

I froze, narrowing my eyes. "What?"

"The boy who's led this conversation," the Queen said, gesturing to Taylor. The light was clinging to him the way it clung to her faeries. Her devotees. I needed to get him out of here. I needed to crawl across the table, pushing the plates aside until I reached him—

My gaze dropped to his plate. There, in the center, was a haphazard drawing of me. And just like that, an idea blossomed in my mind, something so powerful, it could bring the dark courtiers to their knees. The missing element in my revolution.

And all of it hinged on Taylor's ability to paint.

My gaze shifted up, to the artist who'd saved my life. "Tonight, after the Queen has drawn all the forest's light into her body so the mortals can sleep, I will meet with you under the stars, and together we will discuss your part in my revolution."

5

TAYLOR

She came for me in the darkest part of the night. First I saw nothing, just darkness clinging to the sleeping forms of my friends. Then she appeared, stepping through an opening in the trees that hadn't been there a second ago. Her hair was tangled like she'd been caught in the rain, and her eyes, miraculously, were bright.

Why were her eyes always so bright?

The Princess of the Dark Court beckoned to me, her body surrounded by mist in shades of purple and black, like the petals of a flower that only blooms at night. And in the center of the flower, a face so pale, it looked like the moon the Seelie Court was missing. Red hair spilled over her shoulders in waves, curling at the ends. I wanted to slide my hands into that hair and lower my face to hers. Her head would tilt, the tiniest bit, and then we'd be kissing, really kissing.

Elora would step closer, wrapping her arms around my neck. My arms would go around her waist. I'd tug her a little, fingers digging into her hipbones, and she'd just fit, body curving into me. Slowly, we'd fall to the forest floor. We'd fall like leaves, but we wouldn't be dying.

We'd be coming to life.

In the real world, Elora was hesitant. This, at least, was a side of her I'd come to know intimately. (I know, the irony.) She lingered in the shadows like they would somehow protect her, though from me, or from some unseen danger, I didn't know.

I wanted to tell her to come closer, but I didn't. As usual, the Taylor that took the wheel in my fantasies was much braver than the one who sputtered along in reality. Then again, fantastical Taylor didn't have to worry about the very crushing weight of rejection. The ever-present sting of defeat. So, instead of doing what I wanted, I did what I always did.

I gave her an out. "You're leaving, aren't you?" I asked, meeting her at the edge of the clearing. In the middle of the space, our friends slept soundly, resting on beds of leaves and moss. The beds were surprisingly comfortable, except for Kylie, who'd called herself "the inspiration for *The Princess and the Pea*." Still, after several minutes of careful rearranging, she'd curled up against Alexia and fallen asleep.

"I'm leaving," Elora confirmed, stepping closer. Just like that, I took her hands. I don't even know what compelled me. Maybe fantastical Taylor was sliding into the drivers seat. Maybe he was just taking the wheel for a second. Either way, she felt amazing, and she wasn't pulling away, so I didn't question it much.

"Where are you going?" I asked, playing with her hands.

"You know where," she said.

"And I can't come with you?"

"You know that too."

I laughed, pushing my boundaries and hers. "You said that before, but here I am."

That was a mistake. She stepped back, almost untangling her hands from mine. "You aren't supposed to be here. You're supposed to be home, with your family. I can't keep you here."

"You aren't." *The Seelie Queen is.* "And besides, my parents pretty much disowned me before I left."

Who am I kidding? My dad never wanted me in the first place. And my mom didn't have the guts to stand up to him.

"You could still reconcile..." She looked up at me, her eyes dark and beautiful in the night. This is how I remembered her best, surrounded by branches and shadows. A creature that was equal parts forest and darkness. "You should never have been brought into this place. It is not safe—"

"What if, for once, we looked at things the opposite way?" I reached out and tucked a hair behind her ear. Even I couldn't believe it. Who was this person taking over my body? How could I get him to stay? "Instead of looking at the downside, let's look at the positives here."

"I'm a faerie of the Dark Court. I was trained to look at the dark side of things."

"Trained?"

"Raised? Created? I don't know anymore." She shook her head. "And what are the positives, exactly?"

It hurt that she even had to ask, considering I was standing right in front of her. But I knew she didn't mean it that way. She was just worried for me, worried for both of us.

"Well, you're going to fight in your revolution," I said. "That's still happening, right?"

"Yes."

"And I'm going to help you—"

"Without putting yourself in danger."

"Without putting myself in danger." Possibly. I hadn't decided yet. "And, best of all, you got to smuggle your secret boyfriend into the Seelie Court, where the dark faeries can't get to us."

She laughed, lowering her lips to my ear. I was startlingly aware that she hadn't dismissed the "boyfriend" comment. I was startlingly aware of, well, *everything*, because her touch was so electric. It lit me up from the inside. It did the exact opposite of what you'd expect from a Princess of the Dark Court. But in the vast darkness that was the Unseelie Court, Elora was the moon, fully belonging in the night sky, yes, but also lighting it up.

"You *are* here, aren't you?" She smiled, her body inching closer to mine. This was my favorite part, the way we would start out close and get … *closer*. I'd never known how close I could get to someone, before her.

This time, *I* lowered my lips to *her* ear. "I kind of thought that was obvious," I said.

This time, she shivered.

And this time, just this once, I told the truth. "And I kind of think that's what you wanted all along."

"It is." Her gaze drifted up, holding me in place. "From the moment I met you, I could see you here, standing under the leaves. Vines wrapping around you, not choking, just holding you gently. But that is the danger of the Seelie Court: it is beautifully inviting, but it does not do what you expect. And so … " She stepped back. "I knew I couldn't bring you, not if I wanted to protect you."

"How about this?" I followed her, taking her hands again. "You worry about what you need, and I'll take care of myself. I don't need you to protect me."

"You don't know what you need—"

"See, that's the problem here. You wanting to protect me? That's sweet, okay, because I want to protect you. But you thinking I'm helpless? That's condescending."

Her smile fell away. "I didn't ... that isn't what I meant."

"I know what you meant. But you talking like that makes me feel *bad*. Like some pathetic little boy who can't possibly stand up to your greatness."

"It isn't a *male* thing. It's a *mortal* thing." She kissed my cheek. "I have nothing but respect for you. But you are in a forest of magic, and as magical as you are, my darling, you are not prepared for the illusions here."

My darling. Those words drifted through my head, whispering, pulling on me. Always, she was pulling on me. Even when she was walking away. "So you're going to the Unseelie Court," I said.

"Just to the border between the courts. I need to reconnect with my followers, to let them know that I survived Naeve's wrath."

"Are you going to lie about what happened? I mean, are you going to tell them ... " *That you risked your life for a human. Me.*

"Haven't I told you?" she asked, brow furrowing. It was the cutest thing I'd ever seen. "Faeries cannot lie."

"For real?" The breath whooshed out of me. "So, when you tell me how you feel ... "

"It is *really* how I feel."

I thought of everything she'd said to me in the mortal world. She'd called me her sweetest salvation. A force of nature. "Okay, that's wicked."

I expected her to smile, to flash that *wicked* grin that whispered all kinds of things. But she didn't. She looked worried.

"What aren't you telling me? Are you afraid of what your followers will think?"

"It isn't that." The shadows hovered around her, circling her arms like they were tasting her skin. I didn't like it. "I realized something in the graveyard," she said. "When Naeve captured you, there was a look in his eyes—"

"Pure, unadulterated hatred?"

"Fear. He's afraid of you."

"Me?" I resisted the urge to look behind me, to make sure she wasn't talking to someone else. "Why?"

"Because you are a human," she said simply. "Humans have always been a great and terrible mystery to the faeries. Nature created you, and yet you seek to destroy her at every turn."

"Aw, shucks. You flatter me." I didn't exactly love it when she talked about humans like that. Even if it was true.

"Taylor. I did not mean—"

"I know." I tightened my grip on her hands, keeping her close. "You don't blame me for nuclear war. I don't blame you for the fact that your mother's a psycho. That's why we're so good together."

She smiled. "We are, aren't we?"

"The best," I said softly. "So tell me more about The Great and Terrible Taylor, capable of striking fear into the hearts of dark faeries everywhere."

"You have a power they do not understand. And your

world … " Her eyes glittered, and for a second I believed everything she'd said. Believed I was great and terrible. "Nothing quite terrifies them like the human world."

"It's too bad we can't transport them to the middle of a city, and *then* attack. God, can you imagine the look on Naeve's—" I froze, staring at Elora. She had the wildest grin on her face.

"Have I told you how brilliant you are today?"

"Well no, but if you stay a while … "

She laughed. "We cannot transport the dark faeries to the mortal world, true. But perhaps we can bring the mortal world to them."

"How?"

"All it would take is a few quick sketches. Simple renderings of the mortal world. Nothing fancy. Then I could use glamour to make them *think* they'd been transported … "

"Renderings?" I stepped back, pulling my hands from her grip.

"Just a few quick sketches. We want the illusion to be realistic, and you know the mortal world better than I—"

"You want me to draw?" My pulse was pounding and my heart was racing, like I'd woken up in the Seelie Court all over again. Woken up and remembered what I had done, and what it had cost.

"I know it's a lot to ask. But Taylor—"

"A lot to … " I huffed, shaking my head. "I haven't painted since my brother's death. You know that. You know it was my fault! How could you ask me to … "

"Taylor, please. It wasn't your fault."

"You weren't *there*. He climbed that tree because of *me*. To get my father to stop ... "

Abusing me.

But I'd never said those words. I'd never even framed it that way in my head. Abused kids got thrown into walls and locked into rooms and touched in ways they didn't want. My dad was a hardass, sure, but he hadn't *abused* me.

He'd only broken me down every time I felt good about myself. Ridiculed me in front of my brother. In front of my friends. He'd taken every good thing I could do and found something wrong with it.

I could paint, but only when something was right in front of me. Never from memory. Never from my own mind. So what?

"He *taunted* me," I said, leaning into a tree. "People were calling me a prodigy, and my dad made me feel so stupid. Like nothing was good enough. Aaron was just trying to help. He was the best kid brother you could ever hope for. He was my best friend, honestly."

I closed my eyes, resting my head against the bark. When I opened them, Elora was standing in front of me. "I've relived that moment so many times," I said. "Aaron racing out of the door, and me running after him. He was convinced I could paint from memory if I just saw the right thing. He climbed that tree for me, so I would have the perfect image to remember, so my dad would stop taunting me." I ran my hands through my hair, swallowing and swallowing. "He was just a kid, you know? Growing up in that house, with all that yelling ... He thought he could fix everything."

Elora crept closer, like she was approaching a wounded animal. "Forgive me," she said softly.

"There's nothing to forgive." I turned away from her, looking up into the trees. Looking anywhere but *there*, into those eyes. "It isn't your fault I'm *useless*."

"You aren't useless, Taylor. You're brilliant and sweet and—"

"Brilliant? Please. You're the one coming up with all these big ideas, and I'm the one dragging you down."

"No." She took my face in her hands. "You're the one keeping my feet on the ground. My ideas are big, yes, some might say out of this world, but I need them to work in this world. Do you understand? I need a plan we can execute, not something so grand and dramatic that we'll never pull it off."

"You can pull off anything."

"That's what I thought when I entered the human world. I thought I could sneak into a high school, steal a mortal offering, and be off before my enemies caught me. *Why* did I think that?"

"Because you've got that killer self-confidence that's so common in people our age?"

She laughed. "I thought I could prepare for every eventuality. I *always* think that. That's why Naeve was able to capture me in the graveyard. He found the one thing I wasn't prepared for, and used it against me. He found ... "

"Me."

"Yes, you. And tonight, when you offered yourself up to fight in my revolution, I realized something."

"What?"

"People are going to *die* because of me. I know it sounds

ridiculous that I should only realize this now, when mortals have offered to fight, but ... " She swallowed, looking away. "I think, deep down, I truly believed I could keep my people alive if I prepared for everything. That's why I spent *years* gathering up the servants of the Unseelie Court. There are thousands of us, and only hundreds of courtiers. Surely, with those odds ... "

"Your plan is going to work," I told her. "The Bright Queen will bind your mother, keeping her out of the battle. Your army will overpower the courtiers. You're going to *win*, Elora."

"And people are going to die. Good people, who only wanted to be free. The ground will be littered with broken bones and blood as bright as poppies. And I will know who is to blame."

"The courtiers who abused them. The queen who enslaved them."

"And me. That's why I wanted you to paint, my sweetest salvation. It isn't because I am cruel. It's because I am *desperate*. I thought, if I could truly shock the courtiers at the beginning of the battle, they would have no chance to ... " She looked up, eyes glistening. "I thought I could protect everyone, and I ended up hurting you. It was terrible of me."

"No, I'm the one who's being terrible. I'm the one who's being selfish." I pushed off from the tree. "You're trying to use my ability to save your entire world, and I'm just trapped in this cycle of beating myself up, when I don't *have* to be. After Aaron fell, I locked up my paints, even though painting made me happier than anything. It made me feel like I fit in the world, you know? Like I could contribute something." I reached for her hands. She took mine instantly. "And instead of trying, instead of letting myself be a part of the world, I'm going to keep them locked up, while you do this life-changing thing? This world-changing thing? No, I'm going to help you. I'm going to *try*."

She closed her eyes, head dipping toward me. For one brief second, the shadows broke away from her, and she was *mine*. "We can save the world," she said. "Together, we can save the world. I can even create a double illusion, glamour upon glamour, so when Naeve rips the first glamour away, he will think the city around him is real!"

"Slow down there, turbo," I said. "You're getting ahead of yourself." Or at least, she was getting ahead of *me*.

"Trust me, it's going to work. Everything will be an illusion." She started to break away from me. "When I come back—"

"Whoa, whoa, whoa. You're not leaving yet." Again, I was bolder than I'd ever been. But I didn't care. I couldn't leave it like this.

Elora paused, her lips curling, like maybe she knew. "And why is that?"

This time, I wasn't taking any chances. As gently as I could, I pulled her into me. Still, even with all my gentleness, it felt like a collision of some sort.

A force of nature.

Isn't that what she'd called me? Here, now, she was a storm, twisting me in circles. Torrential rain covering me. I wanted to go swimming in her, to come away soaked and invigorated.

I lowered my lips to hers.

"Taylor," she whispered, but it wasn't a protest. It was more like a surrender. Because I wasn't the force of nature, and neither was she. It was *us*, together. *We* were the force of nature. And you can't fight nature.

We both surrendered.

My leg slid between hers, and then I was backing her up against a tree, but I stopped myself before we reached the bark. I didn't know how much her wounds had healed, and I wasn't going to risk hurting her the tiniest bit, not for passion. Not for anything.

The true wildness could wait. Because this girl, when she was at full force, could handle anything I had to throw at her. I was probably the one who needed to worry. But I would rise to meet her, every time. I would make myself good enough, make myself strong enough, because this? This was better than anything.

Her lips parted to let me in. Her breath was hot, and so was mine. I could feel heat rising between us. Here, between our lips, and lower. Electricity shot through our entire bodies, reaching out to meet in the middle. Tangling in the air.

But no, there shouldn't be any space between us. I wove my fingers into her hair, grasping, pulling her closer to me. She didn't pull away. She kissed me harder. I could hear her breathing. She was making these sweet little sounds that were halfway between a sigh and a moan, and my legs got shaky.

"Just stay a little longer," I begged, lowering my lips to her neck. "Just one night. A couple of hours." Her back arched when my lips touched her skin, and I thought I was going to lose it. I thought I was going to die. How could anything feel this wonderful, and make me ache so badly at the same time?

"I can't," she whispered, but her hands were cradling my face, and then they were gliding past my neck, down to my chest. She couldn't stay still any more than I could. "I have to go."

"You always have to go," I said, and I turned us around, so that I was up against the tree, and she could do anything she wanted with me.

"I always come back, don't I?" Her hands slipped under the bottom of my dress shirt. I couldn't believe that, only a day earlier, we'd been at the prom. I couldn't believe something so mundane had been so important to me.

But it had never been about the prom, not really. It had always been, would always be, about her.

"Maybe someday, you'll actually stay," I said, and I knew it sounded harsh. But I couldn't help it. "Because even when I have you … " I looked up, into her eyes. Her skin was so pale, and her lips were so red, but all I wanted to see were those eyes. "I don't really have you. You keep pieces of yourself—"

"I know." She looked down. Why did she always look down when I needed her to look at me? To actually *see* me?

"And I get it, okay? You're trying to keep yourself safe."

"I am." She spoke to the ground.

"But nothing here is safe."

She looked up. I met her gaze, *showing* her that I didn't need to be protected. Showing her I could face the truth head on.

"And none of us is safe, regardless of how we *feel*," I said. "So maybe, just this once, you could go all-in, you know? And I'll go all-in too."

For a minute she just looked at me. Really looked at me, and let me look back. Finally, she said, "You'll go all-in too?"

"Yes. God, yes."

"No matter what I … do, or what happens to me?"

"Of course."

She looked so relieved then, I thought she was going to cry. But she didn't. She said, "All right, then. Yes."

"Yes?" My heart jumped so high, it couldn't be contained within my chest. It cleared the trees and shot for the stars.

"Yes, it's what I want." She held my gaze. "You are what I want."

"Oh my God. Seriously?"

She laughed, and then she kissed me. "From the moment I met you. Before it even made sense."

"I know what you mean." I kissed her back. And just like that, our hands were back, and our lips were exploring, and I was holding onto her so tightly …

"Taylor." She pulled away, eyes shimmering. But she didn't look sad, exactly. She looked *hurt*.

The breath rushed out of me. "What did I do? Did I hurt you?"

She started to shake her head, but didn't. God, I *had* hurt her. "I am … still healing," she said, and my heart sank to my knees. Up one minute, and down the next. This roller-coaster of agony and bliss. "But I will be all right. Perhaps when we meet again."

"How long are you going to be gone?" I moved aside a little bit. Giving her space to breathe. To *heal*, without me.

"A few days, if all goes well. The battle itself will not take place until the Solstice, when the dark faeries are at their weakest."

"The Solstice? So we'll have more than a month to—"

"Reconnect, yes. The Queen has agreed to set up camp at the borderlands, to keep you happy. She'll provide whatever is necessary to help you with your tasks."

"Tasks?" I asked, wrinkling my brow.

"Painting, for you," she said. "And as for the others, well, she'll find a way to draw out their *mortal magic*."

I grinned, but it fell away quickly. "Be careful. *Please*."

"I have always been careful. Except…" She let the unspoken words drift between us.

Except with you.

"Of all the things that could hurt me…" She stepped up, planting the softest kiss on my lips. She lingered, and I loved it.

"I won't," I promised. "I'll do anything I can to protect you. I'll cut out my heart and hand it over to the Unseelie Queen."

She closed her eyes, and a chill ran through me. Then she kissed me again, long and deep. As she disappeared into the darkness, her voice drifted back to me. "Let us hope it does not come to that."

6

ELORA

There were few neutral spaces left in Faerie. No wide expanses called "No Fey's Land" by faerie children. No faerie children, but that's another story.

The faerie courts had snuffed neutrality out.

In order to survive, you had to pick a side, or else go into exile—and who would choose that? Who would wander into the human lands, to be forgotten, when they could be kissed by a queen's loving lips? When they could, at the very least, be graced by her smile?

They all chose sides, long ago, before I was born into this travesty of a world. They all chose light or dark, and bent themselves accordingly. Just like that, the neutral wild was reclaimed, and renamed. Bright Court *here*, Dark Court *there*. No in-between.

No place where we could hide.

Still, if you were resourceful, and very clever, which I believe I am, you could sniff out the places the royals refused to go. The places the courtiers wouldn't deign to visit, because the land might sully their precious robes. I started seeking out these places as a little girl, perhaps already understanding my difference. Perhaps knowing from the beginning that I would be the reason the courts would fall. I hated the niceties, hated the etiquette that came with courtly life. We were faeries, shouldn't we be dancing in the dirt? Shouldn't we be shedding our stately robes and letting the rain clothe our skin?

Shouldn't we be free?

But no. Not according to my mother, and not according to the Bright Queen, who was supposed to be her opposite, and yet...

They are so alike.

Two sides of the same coin. Light and Dark, playing off of each other. Creating the same divided courts, where the queens control everything, and the rest are just pawns. Laying waste to their people in different, yet ultimately similar ways. After all, does it matter how you stifle and kill your brethren? You are betraying them all the same.

And so it went, for the young Princess of the Dark Court, the little faerie with strangely tattered wings: I'd wait for my mother to tire, and I'd go slipping away into the ubiquitous darkness. I'd travel through caverns and tunnels and mountains and burrows. I'd find places where I could simply be myself: The underwater caves beneath the Sea of Kalayna, where great, multi-colored crystals jutted out, casting prismatic rainbows all across the walls, and if you twirled just so, your wings would catch the light and send everything spinning. The Lost Ruins of the Lord and Lady, where, centuries ago, the faeries had come to worship the earliest forest beings to walk the earth. There, I'd climbed over the broken stones reclaimed by moss and ivy. I'd danced in the circle where the Lord and Lady were rumored to have been born.

Now, centuries later, the two Queens of Faerie shunned the Lost Ruins, refusing to admit there was a time when *other* beings were revered. And the courtiers, ever eager to please their jealous mistresses, perpetuated the illusion. That's the thing about faeries: we may not be able to speak a lie, but we built empires by avoiding certain truths.

When I was seven, the Dark Lady learned of my affinity for the ruins and stopped me from visiting. No matter, there were other places to see. And if she'd never forbidden me, I never would've discovered the Courtyard of Everlasting Love, which existed right on the borderlands, half in the Dark Court, and half in the Bright.

In the circular Courtyard of Everlasting Love, couples danced for all eternity, staring into each other's eyes. Not because they wanted to, necessarily, but because they'd made a promise there, centuries ago, to never be apart, and Faerie takes such promises very seriously. As a young girl, I'd woven in and out of the couples, sometimes spinning, sometimes studying the look in their eyes to see if the spark of love had survived.

Sometimes, they looked on each other adoringly, more deeply in love than when they'd met. Sometimes, they looked detached, or even appalled, because a hundred years is a long time to love someone, especially if you didn't know them very well to begin with. Five hundred years can be agony if you realize you've made a mistake. And a thousand years? Well, would you still cling to your lover, as desperate and devoted as the first time? Or would you long for death, the only thing that could offer you release?

Still, they danced. Each of them, dressed in the decadence

of their time: in velvet robes and corsetry and armor, horns curling out of their heads, or wings from their backs. Wearing garlands of flowers, or vines in their hair. Dancing to whatever song most reminded them of their lover. A concerto, perhaps. Or flute music. The pipes, or a grand, joyous band.

And me? I heard music too, as I stepped into the outdoor courtyard, between the dancers. I heard the song that had played, not when Taylor and I had danced together at the prom, so awkwardly, but the one that had screeched to life after we'd escaped the ballroom and went running across the grounds to the darkness beyond. The singer was a woman, someone fervently singing of love and devotion against a backdrop of heavy beats and frenzied piano. Violin, at the climax of the song.

The crescendo.

The music had faded as we'd run into the night, but still, parts of it stayed with me. I remembered it so vividly. Remembered Taylor's fingers tripping over my skin, sliding under the folds of my skirt, lips tasting, kissing, loving—

Stop.

I leaned into a tree, pain pulsing through me. At any other moment, I might've chuckled at the irony of a seventeen-year-old depending on an elderly tree to hold herself up. But there was no humor in this.

I'm still healing, I insisted, taking slow, metered breaths. *That's why it hurts. It has nothing to do with him.*

"I'll be all right," I told myself, straightening up in a way the tree never would. And yet, to my utmost surprise, the tree laughed.

I spun around, my heart thundering in my chest. It was

funny how one could grow up in Faerie and still be surprised at how quickly stillness could transform into agility, how trees, and rocks, and even the ground herself could shift, so quickly, to reveal someone living there. Waves unfurled to reveal horses. The sky peeled back the layers of a gown, offering you just a hint of what lay beneath. Trees became wise women, or old chuckling men, or boys with horns. Scampering off into the forest to tease you. Coming forward to seduce you.

Still, no boy scampered forward to take my hand. No face appeared in the bark. I had to shake myself, wondering if I was going mad, until a figure emerged from the darkness. I almost shrieked and pulled her to my chest. But I needed to be cautious, so I whispered the riddle we'd created to weed out imposters: "What happens when the light touches darkness?"

"The fractured fragments of Faerie become whole."

My chest surged with warmth. "Illya, my little survivor!"

"Littler now than I used to be," she said, scampering to the edge of the closest branch. She was a marsh sprite, a creature that mortals would never understand: born with the legs of a frog, the upper body of a human, and dragonfly wings. But to me, she made more sense than anything. To me, she was sea and land and sky, all wrapped up in one perfect package.

She was also my favored servant; though, if I had my way, the very idea of "servant" would be tossed aside. We would be equals. And now, with her dragonfly wings burned up like paper, courtesy of Naeve, we were equals in another way. Equally wounded.

"How do you fare?" I asked, wondering why she wasn't

coming closer. Was she afraid to be seen, like I was? Or was it something else?

"Better, now that I know you're alive." She smiled, but it was grim. Her eyes trailed to my back, to the glamours and shadows there.

I was all smoke and mirrors, these days.

"Lady," Illya said, eyes growing wide. "Did you somehow … were you able to—"

I lowered my gaze. I wasn't ready to speak of what I had chosen in the Bright Queen's bower, or what it had cost. "I … I can't—"

"I understand. Does it hurt much?" she asked after a minute.

"It is mostly a dull ache. I'm able to push it aside, except—" *When he touches me.* "When it catches me off guard."

She nodded, watching me intently.

"Where are the others?" I asked, my gaze flickering to the edge of the clearing. The trees grew darker there, gnarled and grasping at the wind with clawed hands.

"Farther down."

"How much did you tell them?" I took a single step. Three more, and I'd be crossing over into the Dark Court.

She hesitated.

"Illya?"

"I told them you went to the wasteland, yes, but only in search of something to help our cause. I didn't say what, or *why*."

"Clever Illya. What else did you say?" I took another step.

The dancing couples were spinning around me, making it difficult to maneuver with ease.

Illya took in a breath. "I told them Naeve caught up to you there, and took your wings, but you managed to get away."

"What did you say of the mortals?"

"That we wanted to bring you home, but they insisted on taking you to the Seelie Court. That we were outnumbered—"

"Illya."

"We were! And everything I told them is true. We didn't want to carry you into the Seelie Court. We didn't want to leave you—"

"I'm sorry. I didn't plan to … " I paused, lowering my head. "You cannot blame me for what Naeve did."

"No." She was silent a moment, kneading her hands into her hair like she did when she was nervous. "But you stopped him from hurting that human. You sacrificed yourself—"

"It was necessary," I said, because that was much simpler than explaining the whole truth. Naeve was going to hurt Taylor, so I placed myself between them. "I needed an offering for the Seelie Queen."

"*One* offering. You could've let the boy die and taken the others. Any of the others!"

"No. I couldn't have. The Queen would never have helped me if I'd caused a mortal's death. These things have consequences."

"All things have consequences," Illya said.

We had reached the line that separated the Bright Court from the Dark. Here, the checkerboard pattern of the courtyard floor turned from red and white to red and black.

Blood and death, rather than blood and life.

Now the dancers spun away, to let me pass. It should have been a relief to breathe fresh air, but it didn't feel cool in their absence. It felt *populated*, as if a hundred figures lingered in the trees beyond the courtyard, breathing heavily, in anticipation of ... something.

"Illya ... "

In anticipation of me?

"Illya, where are my followers?"

She didn't reply. Instead, she skittered away, into the shadows. But that was all right; I needn't have felt alone in this place. For the moment Illya disappeared, the very trees came to life, branches curling like fingernails.

They formed a line in front of me, forbidding me to pass.

7

TAYLOR

In the morning, I woke to the sound of whispering in my ear. I rolled over, hoping to see Elora's beautiful face. But my disappointment was twofold—it wasn't Elora, and the effects of that damned drug hadn't worn off.

Faeries were still everywhere.

They crawled through the trees, across the ground, *in the air*. My head felt dizzy just looking around. But this time, they weren't interested in surrounding me and making me feel uncomfortable. They passed me by, or flew over me, ignoring me completely. Like I wasn't even there.

I turned around, looking to commiserate with the twins, only to find that they weren't actually there. Alexia was gone too. It was just me, and the faeries, and this giant oak in the center of the clearing, which now had something in front of it.

I stepped up to the tree. The oak's body spilled across the ground, separating into four fat legs. A flat, bench-like space, covered in leaves and mosses, sat between the two front legs, and a large easel, complete with brushes and paints, rested in front of it.

"Oh, boy. This is going to suck."

"Better to suck than to blow," said a voice, and I whipped my head around.

"What the—who said that?"

Something giggled into my ear.

I looked up. The creature was twice the size of my thumb, with a humanoid body and a heart-shaped mouth. Dragonfly wings. But the weirdest thing was the way her head shot up into a red point, like a horn. Or maybe a blood-tipped thorn.

I hope that's not what it is.

When the faerie tugged at my earlobe, I resisted the urge to swat her away. I didn't want to accidentally break her arm. Besides, there's something really awkward about swatting a naked thing. Especially if that thing is kind of a person.

Kind of?

No wonder the dark faeries hated humanity.

I decided to be polite. "Hi there," I said, running my hand over the canvas. It felt familiar, like shaking hands with an old friend. "Where'd everyone go?"

"Different places, with different faeries."

"Who? Where?" I asked, nervous that we'd all been separated so quickly.

"Who?" the faerie mimicked. "Where? You know, for someone who speaks Human as his first language, your verbal skills are incredibly stilted."

"I can speak with perfect eloquence if I feel so inclined," I said, drawing out the words dramatically. "Forgive me. I'm adjusting."

"I forgive you," she said, ignoring my sarcasm.

"I'm ever so grateful," I muttered as she landed on my outstretched hand. Her skin had a violet sheen, like she'd been rolling in glitter. "Will you tell me where they are?"

"No."

I yanked my hand away.

She fell several inches before catching herself. "But I might tell you with whom. If you're nice."

"I'm nice. I'll be nice."

"And do *everything* I say."

"I'm not an idiot."

She giggled. "Smarty," she said, tugging at my pants. "Smarty pants. Isn't that something they say?"

She looked up, and I thought she was talking to the oak. But when I followed her gaze, I saw dozens of tiny, horn-tipped faces staring back at me. They shrieked, disappearing into the holes in the tree.

"Can we focus?" I sat on the bench and gestured for the faerie to join me. She settled in on my knee. "Tell me about my friends."

"The little one's off with the brownies," she said, "making a secret weapon for the princess. Brownies know all about tools and trinkets and general forms of blacksmithery."

"Blacksmithery?"

"Yeah, uh ... " She looked to the tree. "Isn't that what humans say? Blacksmithery and jackassery and general buffoonery?"

"They say lots of dopey stuff," replied a voice.

"Tough talk coming from someone who won't even show her face," I said.

A face appeared in one of the holes of the tree, all teeth

and tongue. I stuck out my tongue at her. I couldn't help it. These faeries brought out the kid in me.

"What about Alexia?" I asked when the face disappeared.

"The one who could've been a nymph?" asked the faerie. "She's in session with the Bright Queen."

"Session? Like school?"

"Uh huh. Acting school," she said vaguely. *Typical faerie.*

"What part is she playing?" I asked.

"The part of the princess."

"What? Why?"

"Because the princess cannot tell a lie. But if her followers ask about you ... "

"She can't tell the truth."

"Exactly. So if things go badly at the border, the mortal girl can travel there, pretending to be the princess, and put on a show."

"Do you think things are going to go badly?" I asked, blood rushing through my ears. I tried to listen for sounds of distant distress, but Elora was too far away to be heard.

"I think the princess is very clever," the faerie said. "But it is better to be safe than sorry. At least, that's what the mortal girl said."

"Sounds like Alexia," I agreed. "What about Keegan?"

The faerie was coy. "Oh, *him*? He refuses to tell the Bright Lady how he can help. He'll only tell the princess." She giggled into her hand. "He's off with the satyrs, studying *other* things."

"Lucky him."

"Aw, is the mortal lonely? Does he need me to make him feel better?"

"I don't even know how that would work," I said.

She shrugged. "We always find a way."

"I bet. But I'm not interested. As you've probably heard, I'm in bed with the enemy. Or, at least..."

"You'd like to be?" She flashed a grin.

I studied her for a minute. "It doesn't bother you, does it? You don't dislike her like the others do."

"I live in the borderlands."

"Meaning?"

"Meaning..." She rose, fluttering directly beside my ear. "The servants on the borderlands sometimes become friendly."

"Seriously? Elora didn't tell me anything about that."

She laughed, and it reverberated through my ear canal. "She doesn't know! You think we'd tip off the royals? They'd have our heads."

"Our *heads*!" came a chorus from the tree.

"Well, your secret's safe with me," I promised, wondering if Elora knew more than this faerie suspected. Wondering if Naeve did.

"Hey, when we were in the graveyard," I whispered, so only this faerie could hear, "the Prince of the Dark Court said something about Elora. He said she'd always been her *father's* daughter. Do you know what that means?"

The faerie shook her head. But she didn't say no, and I thought that was significant. Like, maybe she *couldn't* say it.

"He said it was a secret," I pressed. "And since *secret* couplings are something you know about, I wondered..."

"I cannot speak of it!" the faerie hissed. Darting away from me, she disappeared into the tree.

Ah, so I've struck a nerve, I thought. But it wasn't that surprising. Elora had pretty much told me the entire history of

Faerie, but she'd never mentioned her father. I didn't think she even knew who he was. I didn't think her mother wanted her to know.

"Okay, well, I'll just be here," I said, picking up my paintbrush. "All alone in the forest."

The faerie poked her head out of a hole. At least, I thought it was the faerie I'd been talking to, but I couldn't tell for certain. They all had pale skin and scarlet horns. Still, it was probably annoying when people couldn't tell them apart. If I could just study her more closely...

"Hey, I have an idea," I called, dipping the paintbrush into some red paint. "It's been a long time since I've done this. If I could paint an actual subject, it'd really help get the creative juices flowing."

The faerie flitted out of the opening but didn't come any closer. "Oh yeah?"

"Yeah," I said. Brushing the canvas in an upward stroke, I drew a little red horn. "The color is just perfect."

She inched closer, those wings buzzing furiously. "Is that going to be *me*?" she asked. Her entire body was blushing.

"That's the idea," I said casually. "You could even keep it after, if you want."

"I do. I *want*." Her gaze shifted from me to the canvas, and she was smiling so big. It kind of made my heart hurt to see how obsessed the faeries were with humanity. The bright faeries *needed* to be close to us. The dark faeries *needed* to destroy us. What had life been like for them before humans came along? Were they happier then?

The dark faeries were, I thought, and a shiver ran through me. The dark faeries would do anything to revert to a world without humanity. But if I could discover the Dark Lady's secret, maybe Elora could use it to gain leverage over her. Or over Naeve.

"I just need one little piece of information," I said, pulling the brush away from the canvas.

The faerie zipped close to my ear. "I don't know the secret," she said.

"Who *does*?" I swirled my brush in a little bowl of water. Next, I mixed white paint with red and blue, to match the faerie's skin tone. Her eyes followed me hungrily.

"Naeve knows," she confirmed. "And the *other* Lady. The one whose name I'm forbidden to speak."

"Who's forbidden you?" I asked, trying to remember the Dark Lady's name. Virayla?

"Who do you think?" She fluttered closer, breath tickling my ear. "The same faerie who has the information you seek. The Bright Queen."

———

That night, after I met up with my friends, the Queen's "favored ladies" gave us humans a tour of the grounds. They showed us a waterfall where we could bathe, and strange petals we could rub against our bodies to get clean. They even had leaves that tasted like mint and left our teeth feeling like they'd just been brushed. The only thing left to hope for was a toilet, and while I wasn't expecting running water and porcelain, the faeries' version of a bathroom was actually pretty impressive.

First of all, it was private, situated beneath a gigantic tree that split open at the base to let us in. Even Kylie could wheel in and out with relative ease. There were vines hanging over the entrance, to block passersby from looking inside, and the toilet itself looked fairly comfortable, formed out of mud and covered in vines. To the left sat a stack of moss-colored leaves.

When Maya de Lyre came up behind me, whispering, "It's mostly a hole glamoured to look like a toilet," I actually laughed. There's something unsettling about being given *everything* you want, without even having to ask.

So I leaned back and said, "As long as there's not poison ivy glamoured to look like TP, I'll be okay."

She smiled, taking my hand. "I have a surprise for you."

My heart leapt. Had she already figured out a way to free me from the Seelie Queen? And how? A dozen scenarios danced through my head as she led me down a path filled with brambles and vines. Had she sacrificed a virgin? No. That's something the dark faeries might do, but not the bright. Had she performed an amazing, non-stop dance for twenty-four hours? Had she given up *her* freedom? I was about to ask. But suddenly we burst into a clearing, and the words died on my lips.

In their place, new ones were born. "Holy wicked arsenal, Batman."

Maya de Lyre smiled, turning to me. "You like it?"

I stepped up to the green, woven blanket spread out across the grass. And on the blanket was, well, everything my mind could conjure. Knives, all laid out in a line, arranged from smoothest blade to most jagged edge. Beside them was an ax, big enough to take down a giant, and next to that—

"Good God, is that a *flail*?"

Maya de Lyre giggled like I'd asked her on a date. "It is indeed."

"Whose weapons are these? Are these yours?" I asked, heart pounding and hands tightening to fists. It was hard to keep my distance, hard not to pick up one of those blades and start swinging.

"No. They're yours," she said.

I spun to face her. "Um . . . what?"

"I gathered them for you. I thought you would like them."

The hairs stood up on the back of my neck. "I do, but . . . " I tried to stay rational, tried to remind myself of the rules of Faerie.

Faeries rarely do anything for free. Isn't that what Elora had told me, back in the mortal world? *They like trades.*

"What will it cost me?" I asked.

"Nothing, dear mortal. *Taylor,*" she added, as if we were fast friends. And maybe we were. Maybe we could be.

Maybe this was exactly what it seemed. I stepped forward, not touching any of the weapons yet, just looking at them. They were so shiny. God, they were so sharp. They were perfect.

"So I can take them and not give anything back?" I asked.

"Yes."

"What made you think I'd want them?"

She tilted her head like the question was strange. Like all of this—the water to bathe in, the weapons, my *every desire* being granted—was perfectly normal, and I was the weird one.

"Isn't it common for mortal boys to dream of weapons?" she asked. "Admittedly, we do not have guns or . . . explosives. We faeries have other ways of dealing with adversity."

"Like magic."

"Like magic. We can bring the storms. Bring floods. Bid the forest to wake. Shooting a single bullet seems … unnecessary."

I started to shiver a little with all this talk of death. I mean, yes, I wanted to defend myself, and defend Elora, but I wouldn't kill for fun. There was nothing fun about it. I remembered that from the graveyard. I'd only slammed the branch into Naeve's head to save Elora.

Well, that, and you wanted to see his blood run over your hands. Wanted to see him slumped on the ground. Until it actually happened.

I took a step back, because now I could see another version of myself. Not Taylor the hero. Taylor the bloodthirsty warlord. I mean, honestly, how many people entered into battle thinking they were the former, only to wind up the latter? How could you ever really tell if hacking someone up was justified? Because that guy, on the other side, wanting to hack you up? He thinks he's the good guy too.

I mean, he must.

"You didn't do this because I'm a mortal boy," I said, the gravity of my thoughts centering me in reality. "You did it because I said I wanted to fight. Last night, at dinner."

"Do you still want to?" she asked, green eyes glistening. They were lighter than mine, a bright, golden-green, and that soothed me somehow. When my eyes were too much like a faerie's, it freaked me out.

"What about the Queen?" I asked. "I'm pretty sure she doesn't want me to."

"The Queen is distracted. Each night, she holes herself up

in her bower, blocking out every possible sound, to practice the spell that will bind the Dark Lady." Maya de Lyre smiled. "Besides, if my investigation goes well . . ."

"It won't matter if she wants me to fight." Finally, I smiled back. "But I'm doing something different now. Something Elora wants me to do."

"Ah yes, the little pictures."

"It's what Elora wants."

"Well, aren't you obedient?" She sashayed over to the swords. Her dress went swish, swish, swish around her legs. "And here I thought the *bright* faeries had a reputation for making humans into pets."

"I'm not her pet," I snapped. "I'm her . . ."

"Lover?"

"That's none of your business."

"Fair enough. Boyfriend, then?"

"We haven't discussed . . . I mean, she hasn't explicitly said—"

"Much of anything, has she?"

"I know how she feels."

"Tell me." And she waited, expectantly, while I tried to pull something out of thin air.

"I know that she cares about me," I said.

"We all care about you. We all want you to be happy."

"It's more than that."

"What is it, then? I'd truly love to know."

"It's . . ."

Love? Elora had never said that word, never admitted to loving anyone. Now she was gone, and I didn't even know when she was coming back.

Days, if all goes well...

"What if I want to practice fighting?" I said, taking a single step. "I mean, no promises. No deals. No caveats. No tricks."

The faerie nodded, but she didn't speak.

I knew there was a significance in that, but I'd already started. "I'll still paint during the day. But at night, after everyone goes to sleep, we can sneak away here and practice. All of us can. Just in case we decide to fight in the revolution."

"If you're allowed to fight," Maya de Lyre said solemnly.

I felt a flash of anger, and picked up a sword. It felt heavy in my hand. It felt *right*. "I'll be the judge of that."

8

ELORA

The forest grew darker before my eyes. Trees reached out long, gnarled branches and clasped hands. Trunks grew wider until there were no spaces between them. Surely, a faerie with wings could crest those branches easily, but I could climb for days and never reach the top. I could climb until my limbs gave out and I fell, uselessly, to the ground.

So here I stood, watching the Unseelie Forest block me out. Once the trees had finished their dirty work, they slid their roots back into the ground, and were silent.

"What is the meaning of this?" I called. "Why are you keeping me out?"

"Not us," said a voice, and Illya peered out of the darkness. She sat on a branch just above my head. "Your mother."

"My mother?" Her words knocked the breath from me. "Surely, she doesn't know…"

"What you've been up to? Well, yes and no." Illya skittered down the branch, finally climbing onto my shoulder, so we could talk privately. "Naeve spun his yarn. Painted you as the human-loving harlot. Made quite a show, actually—"

"Illya, please. I need you to focus. Does she know of the revolution?"

"No, nor of your deal with the Seelie Queen. She doesn't even know where you are. Not for certain."

"What, then?"

"She knows you were spotted with humans. She knows they put their hands on you—"

"To carry me to safety. To save my life!"

"Not as Naeve tells it. He believes you have chosen *them* over *us*."

"So I'm banished, then?" I asked, trying to still the fluttering in my chest. Trying to still the fear and the chill and the panic.

"No, not banished. The Dark Lady believes we can bring you back. Believes we can ... *cleanse* you of the human filth on your skin."

Good luck, I thought and snorted. But to Illya, I said, "What do I have to do?"

She paused, kneading my hair with her hands. "Something you will not do."

"Meaning?"

"Provide your mother with a proper offering. Bring the mortals to her, to show your allegiance. If you hand over the people who helped you, the people *you* helped in the graveyard, she'll know you don't care for them, and she'll welcome you back into the fold."

"Oh, is that all?" I said with a laugh.

Illya was not amused.

"Oh, come now," I said, softening my voice. "This doesn't change everything. It doesn't have to change anything. Come the Solstice, she'll be weakened, and you can smuggle me in through the tunnels running under the court. We'll use glam-our to make me look like a servant. The revolution will go as planned, and you can—"

"I'm sorry, Lady. That isn't going to happen."

"I know you're scared," I said, reaching up to touch her hand. She didn't reach back. "But I will protect you. I will fight for you, if we're caught. I will go down swinging—"

"I cannot let you enter!" she shrieked. This close to me, the sound reverberated in my ear.

I fell silent.

"Have you rejoined her, then?" I said after a moment. The thought was worse than anything I'd imagined. But the Dark Lady could be very convincing, and if Illya believed I'd fallen prey to the wasteland...

The human world, I reminded myself.

"It isn't that," Illya broke in. "We would love nothing more than to follow you into battle and overthrow your moth-er's court."

"But?"

"*We* are beginning to doubt your loyalties. And your moth-er's edict is clever..." Illya looked away, into the darkness. "What better way to prove you don't care for humans than to hand—"

"Four of them over to you? To torture for sport? Illya, you cannot be serious."

"Don't be silly, princess. We do not want four humans."

The breath rushed back into me. "You don't? Oh, thank Darkness. I thought—"

"We only want one."

"*What?*"

"The boy whose life you saved."

"The boy who—why *him?*"

"Because your actions indicate that he means something to you."

He means everything to me.

But I couldn't say it. I would lose everything if I said it.

"Illya, what do they believe?" I asked, studying the forest. Searching for the faces of my followers. My friends. "Do they think I went traipsing off to the wasteland for a vacation?"

"They believe what I told them. You went in search of something that would help strengthen our cause."

"Then what am I missing?"

She turned, speaking softly. "They believe something happened *while* you were there, something that changed you."

It did.

"But if you hand over the mortal, it will prove that you are still the same," Illya finished. "That he hasn't corrupted you."

"Illya," I whispered. "He hasn't corrupted me."

He has saved my life.

"Please, you have to believe me," I begged.

"I'm sorry, princess. We cannot let you pass. Not without proof."

"And if I bring him to you, you will … sacrifice him? Spill his blood on my mother's court?"

"Perhaps if we had time, a ritual could be performed," she said casually. "Something to strengthen our revolution."

"But?" I asked, feeling sicker than I'd ever felt. These were my *people.* My family. They were supposed to be.

"But, as it is, we have much to accomplish, and very little time to do it," she said. "So—"

"You'd let him roam, then? Wander the forests unharmed?"

"We are busy, princess. We are not fools."

"So you'd lash him to a tree somewhere and forget about him? Forever?"

She paused, and I turned to look at her, resting on the edge of my shoulder. Her eyes were alight with fire, as if hungry. "Have you truly forgotten the ways of the world? The natural order of things—"

"Just say it, Illya. Say what you're going to say, and be gone from here. I have to think."

"Humans don't live forever. A blink of an eye, and they're gone."

Thankfully, we used to say. But I did not say that anymore. "How much time do I have to decide? The Summer Solstice is over a month away—"

"We are not waiting until the Solstice to strike," Illya said. "We attack on the seventeenth of this month, the morning after the full moon. You'd need to be here by the fifteenth, to give yourself time to reach the castle."

"*The fifteenth?* No, no, no. That's less than—"

"Two weeks away. I know."

"It isn't enough time! By the time I return to the mortal—"

"It's plenty of time," Illya said. "You infiltrated the wasteland, befriended a host of mortals, and lured them into the Seelie Court in a matter of weeks."

"I didn't *lure* them. They saved my life—"

"Lady, please." She stepped closer, speaking into my ear. "We will not last until the Solstice. The Dark Queen is going through us one by one, trying to get to you. She is torturing us. We have to attack soon."

"But the full moon..."

"It's the brightest night of the month," Illya said. "The courtiers will sleep poorly, and your mother is already growing weak, with summer fast approaching."

"Faster and faster it comes, each year," I murmured, looking back toward the Seelie Court. Looking toward *him*. "What if I fail the test? What if I cannot bring you a human sacrifice?"

"We will carry out your plans without you."

I laughed, but there was no joy in it. "You cannot take on the Dark Lady yourselves. She will obliterate a third of your army."

"It's a risk we are willing to take."

"Do you really hate me so?" I reached up, as if to draw her into my hand. She scuttled away, climbing onto an overhanging branch. "Would you really forget everything we have been through?"

"I never forget," she said fiercely. "I can never forget. That is why it breaks my heart to think you've fallen."

"I … " I began, but I couldn't finish the thought. The truth of it was, I'd fallen many times. Fallen from the sky's loving embrace. Fallen to the dirt. Fallen for a human. Now, with so much at stake, would I fall back into my old beliefs, or fall away from my mother's court forever? My home?

"This is a riddle I cannot solve," I said softly. The darkness responded to me. Reaching out its tendrils, it brushed the hair from my face and kissed my cheeks.

It wants you back, a voice whispered, and I leaned in, letting it soothe me. *All it needs is one little offering.*

Offering? I thought. *They asked for a sacrifice.* But those words weren't so different, were they? It all depended on how the offer was made.

"Illya," I said, a fluttery feeling in my chest. My guts were clenching, but what choice did I have? "Suppose I could bring you the mortal. Wouldn't he be better suited to fight alongside us in battle? We could use the bodies."

Oh, Darkness. I hadn't meant it that way. Hadn't meant to speak of him as a body. A corpse. But Illya heard the offering the way she wanted to, and it piqued her interest.

"What human would offer that?" she asked.

"A human who wants to be a hero." I glanced at the Seelie Forest. "A human who is already painting pictures for me." Lowering my voice, I told her of my plans to glamour the battlefield to look like a human city. "If we all work together, we can create a fantastical illusion and turn reality on its head."

For a moment, Illya looked impressed. Then, as always, she began to pick at the details, making sure my plan was foolproof. "Relying on glamour is risky," she said. "What if Naeve suspects your illusion and tries to pull it away?"

"Ah, but I've thought of that. You see, after we apply the first glamour, a second glamour will be used, which he *can* pull away, and—"

"Dual glamours. Crafty," she said with a grin. "But what of the other senses?"

"The other senses?"

"Well, yes. This glamour will only cover sight," she reminded me. "Scent is easy enough, if you're bringing the mortal. But what of sound?"

"Sound?"

"Yes, sound. If the courtiers wake to birds chirping and leaves rustling, they will suspect they are still in Faerie. But if we could distract them with some strange and horrible noise ... Lady!"

Her voice was so loud, I jumped at the sound of it. "What is it?" I asked, heart racing.

"Remember the device you sent me from the mortal world? The communication device with the horrible shriek?"

"Cell phone," I said with a laugh. "Yes, the *mortal* gave it to me, so I could stay in contact with *you* while I was away from home."

"I imagine he thought you were contacting a human. But think of it, Lady. Think of Naeve waking up to that shriek. Then, when he looks around, and sees the world changed—"

"Oh, it's brilliant! You're brilliant." I clapped my hands. "Sweet Illya. I knew you would understand."

"I don't," she said, surprising me. "No human will offer himself up. No human will *sacrifice* himself. None of this is going to happen."

"And if you're wrong?"

Illya turned, facing the darkness. I could've sworn I heard someone whispering. Finally, she turned back to me, her face solemn. "You'll have to bring him across the border yourself," she said. "The Dark Lady has enchanted these woods to snatch up any mortal who enters unattended."

"I understand."

"It is decided then." Illya skittered backward, into the trees. "You bring us the mortal, and we will welcome you back into the darkness," she called.

Then she was gone. I was alone, grappling with the realization that I had solved her riddle after all. Taylor would have his moment in the sun. The dark faeries would have their offering. Everyone would get exactly what they wanted.

Except me.

9

TAYLOR

I woke up with sore arms to find Kylie and Alexia returning from the forest. Their hair was messed up, and they looked like they hadn't slept all night. Well, that was okay. They could have their fun, and I could have mine. For the first time since I'd arrived here, I felt invigorated.

For the first time since I met Elora, I felt like I had a purpose of my own.

And so I painted, with arms that could barely manage to draw a smiley face, let alone an entire city, until evening came again. I smiled and talked through dinner, while pixies and sprites performed acrobatic tricks in the sky. But after the faeries had retreated into their quarters and we'd settled into our beds of leaves and moss, I turned to my friends with a grin.

"I have something to show you," I said.

Together, we snuck through the forest to my secret space in an already secret land, all of us trying to creep but still managing to snap a bunch of twigs. We weren't exactly used to being stealthy, and we didn't have the practice—let alone the wings—to keep from making noise. Still, we made it to the clearing without being caught.

I picked up a sword the minute I entered the space.

"Holy mother of God," Keegan said, coming up beside me and reaching for the sword. But he reached for the blade, and I pulled it back before he could touch it.

"Careful. It's sharper than you think."

"I understand what a sword is."

I shook my head. "Look." Reaching into the overhanging branches, I pulled down a leaf.

"Most swords will cut a leaf," Keegan said, as Kylie and Alexia neared the blanket holding all the weapons. But while Alexia immediately began grabbing things, getting a feel for them in her hands, Kylie scanned the entire arsenal, choosing slowly.

"Watch," I said to Keegan, dropping the leaf in the air. As it fluttered toward the sword, I turned the blade so that the sharp side was pointing up. The second the leaf touched the blade, it was cut clean in half.

"Okay," Keegan said, clearly unimpressed. "The weapons have been sharpened. And?"

I smiled, giving him the same show that Maya de Lyre had given me last night. She'd even cast an enchantment over the space to muffle the sound of the weapons. "Hand me that branch," I said, pointing to a thick, gnarled thing a few feet off.

Keegan did.

This time, I performed the exact same movements, and when the branch hit the sword, it didn't bounce off, or come away with a tiny nick. Again, the blade sliced it clean in half.

"Impressive," Keegan said, crossing his arms over his chest. But he was smirking a little, like I was putting on a puppet show for kids. Like I was a dime-store magician, and he wanted to play with the big kids.

That's okay, I thought. *I can play with the big kids. Hell, I can run with the wolves.*

"Now hand me a rock."

Keegan's head snapped up, and I knew I had his full attention. Even the girls were watching now. It was Alexia who brought me a rock, as big as my fist and heavy enough to make a sufficient clang.

"Give me some space," I said.

Keegan and Kylie did as I asked, moving toward the edge of the trees. Only Alexia took her time, taking one exaggerated step, then two.

"Good enough," I said. Then I threw the rock into the air.

This was the tricky part, the part where I had to get the timing just right. Sure, I'd played baseball as a kid, but the hilt of the sword was thicker than a bat, and the rock was heavier than a ball.

Besides, I wasn't trying to hit a ball across a field. I was trying to destroy something. To transform it.

I hit the rock just as it finished its upward trajectory, the blade catching it square in the center. And, just like the branch and the leaf before it, the rocked sliced easily into two equal parts.

"Whoa," Keegan said, bending down to pick up half of the rock. In the place where the blade had touched it, the rock was smooth like it'd been cauterized.

"I've never seen a sword do that," Alexia said.

Kylie just laughed, grinning like she'd known this would

happen. Like she'd finally found a place where the rules (or lack of rules) made sense.

"That's what I learned last night," I said.

It had, in fact, taken me all night to perfect that move, but they didn't need to know that. For once, I was the teacher, instead of the one being taught a lesson. For once, I was the leader, and it felt comfortable, like I'd been born to do this.

"These are the rules," I said, and I wasn't imitating Maya de Lyre anymore. These were *my* rules, and my friends would stick to them or they'd have to leave.

It was for their own good.

"We aren't here to play." I tilted the sword so they could see how it caught the light. "These aren't toys. If you stay, you stay to practice for battle, not because you're fulfilling some childhood fantasy." That part was as much for me as for them.

"So if we pick up a weapon, that automatically means we're fighting in the revolution?" Alexia asked, and I could tell she was inching toward the blanket. Just to pick something up without my permission.

Just to prove that she could.

"No," I said, my gaze flicking to Kylie, who was looking into the trees for some reason. When I followed her gaze, I saw nothing. "You don't have to agree to anything. I just need you to take this seriously, because these weapons are incredibly dangerous, and you need to respect them."

"Master Blade." Alexia tipped her head at the sword.

"I'm serious."

She smirked. "I know. It's just funny to see you like this."

"Like what? Caring about something?"

"Oh, we've seen you care about something," Keegan said with a wink.

"This is more like … you taking initiative." Alexia smiled, eying me coolly. "The Taylor that takes charge. I like it."

"Imagine that." Keegan knelt beside the blanket, running his hand over a hilt. "You letting someone else take charge."

"Oh my God. Shut *up*!" Kylie exclaimed, and we all turned to her. "Oh, please, like that wasn't a sex joke."

"Alexia's the sex joke," Keegan quipped, but he picked up a sword. Bowing at Alexia, he said, "This shall be our final battle."

Alexia growled, lifting a sword with a shiny purple blade from the ground. Of course.

"Um. Guys?" I watched, one hand over my face, waiting for the first limb to fall.

"No, this is good," Kylie said. "This could work. Channel the anger," she joked, and I didn't know which one she was talking to. But it didn't matter, because Keegan and Alexia had found their sparring partners.

And I'd found mine.

"So what do you think," I asked, my arms already screaming for rest. "Duel with swords, or practice shooting arrows?"

Kylie shook her head, staring down at the line of knives. They looked medieval, all jagged with animals carved into the hilts.

"I think I'd like to throw something," she said.

———

For three days, we ran ourselves ragged, working on our tasks during the day and practicing our battle skills at night. Keegan stuck with an ax or a sword (pretty much anything you could swing) while Kylie worked with anything she could throw. Meanwhile, in typical knight fashion, I practiced with my sword, while Alexia tried *all* the weapons, finally deciding on the bow and arrows as her staple.

On our third night, the Queen's favored ladies came by to watch our progress, and I learned the other two's names. The faerie with horns was Maya de Lume, the royal seamstress (Keegan dubbed her "Horny"), and the one with twigs for teeth was Maya de Livre, the royal storyteller (Keegan dubbed her "Scary Spice.")

Meanwhile, Alexia was putting her SAT prep to good use. "Music, clothing, and books," she said, studying them with interest.

"Wait. What?" Kylie said, pausing in mid-throw. I winced, afraid the knife would go shooting from her hand, but it didn't. She was better at stopping momentum than I was.

"Lyre, Lume, and Livre," Alexia said. "You're named after what you can do."

Maya de Lyre shook her golden head. The hair filtered around her, blending with the forest's light. "We are named for our greatest passions," she corrected. "And that which can best serve our Queen."

"Well, I think it's fitting," Alexia said. "More so than a Princess of the Dark Court named after the light."

"What?" I asked, swinging my sword left and right. Whenever I held it, I couldn't help but swing it.

"You didn't know?" She looked at me. "Elora means *light*. In Greek."

I narrowed my eyes. "That doesn't make any sense."

"Does it have to? They're faeries," Kylie said nervously. She must've noticed the way the ladies were scowling, thoroughly unnerved by the mention of the princess.

My princess.

"Dark faeries have little need for sense," the faerie called Horny agreed. I mean, Maya de Lume. God, Keegan was getting into my head.

"Let's just finish up here," I said, trying to shift focus. "Keegan and I have been practicing. We can duel for you, and you can tell us—" I paused, hearing a sound in the nearby forest. The sound of a foot breaking a twig. But when I listened again, I heard nothing.

"Hold on," Kylie said. "I've been thinking about something."

"Yeah?" I turned to look at her. We all did.

"Well, we're going up against faeries who have magic *and* weapons, right? But we only have weapons?"

"Way to put a damper on things," Keegan joked.

"But I'm right. You know I'm right. And I was thinking..." Kylie looked up, into the trees. "Maybe you guys should practice climbing. To give yourselves an advantage."

"What about you?" her brother asked.

"I've always wanted to ride a horse," she said quickly, like she was afraid of being shut down. "And I think I could do it. I mean, I've watched videos about it and stuff. If I had a saddle with a back—"

"We could make you a saddle." Maya de Lyre jumped in,

eager to help. Eager to provide us with *anything*, to tend to our mortal needs.

"Really?" Kylie's eyes lit up.

"I think it's a decent idea," Alexia said, which was pretty much her version of giving someone a gold star.

Kylie beamed. "That way, you know, I could ride into battle, and you guys could drop down from above. We'll have more options when we're fighting."

"Dueling on horseback," I said. "Hell yeah. Maybe tomorrow, we can—"

"Purposefully defy me?" a voice said.

The sword clattered from my hand. A creature emerged from the forest, her red hair in tangles and her eyes glittering in rage.

"Elora."

"Well, well, well. Isn't this cozy?" she asked. She looked like she'd been through hell.

Maybe she has.

"Listen," I said, stumbling over to her. I wasn't suave anymore. I was clumsy, Taylor the kid. "We were just—"

"Doing the one thing I forbade you to do?" She stepped forward, and there were leaves in her hair. That teal dress was torn. Dirt splattered her ankles.

"That's the thing," I said, not wanting to argue in front of everybody. "You can't *forbid* me to do things."

"He isn't your property," Maya de Lyre said, her golden hair sparkling like fire.

"He isn't a pet." Maya de Lume lowered her horns in warning.

"He is a man, and he's perfectly capable of making his

own decisions," Maya de Livre agreed, flashing that dangerous smile.

With the three of them flanking me like soldiers, I felt strong. Capable of speaking my voice and defending myself. I knew I should've felt that way without their help, but damn. Elora was intimidating. Especially when she was pissed.

Plus, in spite of the anger, it was taking every bit of restraint to keep from wrapping her in my arms. Kissing her. Saying *screw it* and just doing what she wanted.

I needed her to love me, but I needed her to respect me more. Needed her to respect me first.

I stepped away from the faeries. "Look, you don't have to like it," I said. "Frankly, I don't like the idea of you going up against Naeve again. But I respect you, and I have faith in you, so I'm not trying to stop you."

"Taylor—"

"Just listen," I said, reaching for her hands. To my surprise, she let me take them. "I know I went against your orders, or instructions, or whatever, but you have to understand it was wrong to tell me that. You should've at least talked to me about it before you *decided* I couldn't fight."

"I was only trying to protect you," she said, and her eyes didn't flash with fury anymore. Now the look bordered on despair. I had to remind myself that she'd only just returned from the Unseelie Court, and anything could've happened there.

This wasn't just about me.

"I know," I said, stepping closer. Now it was just me and her in our own little world. It was how it should be, even if it wouldn't last. "I know, because it kills me not to be able to protect you every second. But we have to be able to trust each other, if this thing between us is ever going to be more than an escape for you."

"Is that what you think?" Her gaze flicked to the faeries behind us, like she thought maybe they'd been putting ideas into my head. But they hadn't. I could come up with these insecurities on my own, thank you very much.

"I didn't, until you made plans without me," I said, hating the sound of it. Hating the truth of it. "You keep making plans without me."

To my surprise, Elora came up close and kissed me. Right in front of everyone, she kissed me. "Not anymore," she said, squeezing my hands. "Let's take a walk."

10

ELORA

Taylor and I bid our friends adieu and traveled to the top of a hill overlooking the forest. From here, we could see where the borderlands split the terrain into green and black. In the Unseelie Court, everything grew darker: trees, insects, plants.

Faeries.

I could only appreciate the difference now that I had left.

"Come and sit beside me," I said, settling onto the ground.

When Taylor sat down, his hand immediately twined with mine. He must've known what I knew, that these moments had to be stolen when they could. But what happened next could determine whether we'd be able to keep stealing these moments or lose them entirely.

I took a deep breath. "Taylor, I don't want you to fight in this battle."

"That's not your decision. I—"

"I know."

He looked up at me. His hair was wild and his eyes were bright. Gold and green, like the forest below.

I studied those eyes as I said, "I don't like it, but I know it. All this time, I have been trying to protect you, believing it was my place. But—"

"But?"

I sighed. "Every time I hear the faeries, bright or dark, speak of mortals, it makes my skin crawl. I cannot think like them, if I am to be with you. You were right about that."

"I was *right*?" His face broke into a grin. "Can I get that in writing?"

"Taylor, please do not joke. Something terrible has happened." I tried to steady my voice. "Something terrible, which will allow you to enter the Unseelie Court unchallenged."

"What? Did hell freeze over?"

No, it has always been cold there, I thought. Then, quickly and quietly, I recounted what had happened at the borderlands.

For a moment, Taylor was silent. Finally, he said, "You'll sneak me in through an underground tunnel?"

"Yes," I said, squeezing his hand. "Together, we will travel up the mountain, and when we arrive at the palace, the battle will begin. My mother will never have to know—"

"And you'll let me fight?" Taylor broke in. "You won't try to stop me?"

I swallowed, trying not to see blood spattered across his chest. Trying not to see the light going out of those eyes. "I will not make that decision for you. But I think it would be best if you acted as a guard—"

"Ah, so I can go to the battle. To watch."

"I'll station you in the surrounding trees. You'll be able to use bows and arrows, should you choose to."

"But—"

"But nothing, sweet." I reached up to touch his face. He turned, kissing each of my fingers slowly. "This arrangement is no slight to you. However strong you are, physical strength is no match for magic. You will need to rely on your cunning, and keep your wits about you always. If someone should come for you, your mind will be the thing to save you. Do you understand me?"

"Yes," he said. He must've understood how hard this was for me, to not do everything in my power to protect him.

But I would not keep him in a cage. "There is something else, and this is important."

"What?"

"I saw the way you looked when you believed you'd killed Naeve with that branch. I know how much of your strength is born of morality. Of compassion. If you enter into this battle, you are agreeing to defend yourself—at least yourself—at all costs. You will see death, Taylor, and you may be the cause of it. I need you to deeply consider the consequences of this, not only to others, but to yourself. The taking of a life affects the taker in an indescribable way. It is profound and everlasting. It will always be a part of you."

Silence. I was struck with the quietness, not only of the land below, but in the trees above. For once, it seemed we were alone.

"I understand." Taylor's voice felt loud in this quiet space. I heard it reverberate off the edges of the world.

"You will not understand until the blood stains your hands."

"I know, but I understand what you're saying, and it's worth it to me."

"We have until the fifteenth. That's ten days from now."

"That's it?" He whistled, looking out across the land. "Just ten?"

I nodded. "I would use that time to think on it."

"All right."

More silence, deeper this time. When he said, "So ... " I jumped a little. Another time, my wings might've rustled at my surprise.

But not now.

"So, what?" I asked. My face must've fallen, because he reached out to touch my arm. I inhaled at the feel of him, and a dull pain unfurled in my back. I told myself it was simply a result of my blood rushing faster.

"So, how did you pull it off?" he asked.

"Pull it off?" I looked to the border, confused.

"I mean, your wings. How did you get them back?"

I lowered my head. Shame pulsed through me, hot and fast. I knew it wasn't my fault that Naeve had taken my wings, knew I had made the right choice in the Bright Queen's bower. Still, there was a part of me that felt so embarrassed by the loss, the mutilation, that I couldn't imagine ever lifting the glamour from my back.

"Elora? I ... oh God."

I glanced up to see Taylor's face had fallen. I was peering into a mirror of grief and despair.

"I didn't ... " I began, swallowing. "I couldn't ... "

"Oh *God.*" He reached for my hands, but I pulled away from him. I couldn't bear to be touched in this moment. "Why didn't you *tell me?*" he asked.

"I didn't want you to know. I thought if I shielded you from it…"

You wouldn't be sickened by me.

Disappointed.

Sickened.

"I'm such an idiot," he said, shaking his head. "I let myself believe you got them back. I just assumed—"

"I understand. But magic is limited, and if I were to attempt such a thing, I would spend the time healing that I need to spend fighting."

He touched my face, surprising me. "I would take your place in battle."

I almost lost control then. Almost cried. Almost kissed him. So many desires flooded through me, and slipped away. "I know," I said softly. "But none of you will. I alone must stand against Naeve."

"Are you in pain?" he asked after a minute. That gaze was intense, and it made me want to curl into myself. Made me want to hide.

"They hurt from time to time," I said, avoiding the entire truth. How could I admit when my wings hurt the most? I could barely admit it to myself.

"Can I look at them?" he asked, his words feeding my fears. But my heart responded, as it often did with him, and I let it take the lead for the moment.

"Yes." I held my breath. Even as he crawled behind me, and I ripped the glamour away, I hardly breathed. I hated his curiosity. No, I hated myself. The tattered remains of me. It must've been horrible to look at me.

"Taylor?" I said after an eternal moment.

He didn't speak. Instead, he ran his fingers along the small of my back, far below where my wings had been. It hurt. With each brush of his fingertips, the pain pulsed. But I didn't stop him.

"What do you see?" I asked, suddenly aware of the darkness. It must've been so different for him. Humans weren't exactly nocturnal creatures. I unleashed a soft glow around me, mortified and vulnerable under his gaze. Still, I couldn't stop myself from letting him see me.

He inhaled sharply.

I dimmed the light, humiliated.

"No, don't," he said. "I think I saw something."

"What?"

"It's hard to explain. You know how new growth grows out of trees that have been cut down?"

"Yes?" I couldn't think about what his words meant. Couldn't allow myself to think.

His hands trailed around my waist. I had to grab them, to stop him.

"Taylor, it hurts."

"It does? I'm sorry. I didn't think that would hurt—"

My breath came out in short gasps. I was terrified to tell him. But I had no choice, now. "It's not the wings. It is, but it isn't. It's you." I twisted to look at him. "It hurts when you touch me."

"Only?"

"No. But it hurts the worst."

His eyes closed. My words must have crushed him. But when his eyes opened, he did not look pained. He was almost smiling. "Wait," he said.

"What?"

"Maybe it's not what you think."

"What do you mean?"

"I mean, it's pretty dark here, but I could swear, when I touch you, it's like … it's almost like I can see them growing."

I waited a beat. Two. Three.

"How certain are you?" I asked. Could it be true? Was it even *possible*? My heart rose like a wave, flooding my chest with warmth.

"Not very," he admitted. "Like I said, it's dark. My eyes could be playing tricks on me. But—"

"Then why would you say it?" I asked, suddenly angry. My heart crashed on the rocks.

"I—"

"Why would you give me hope when you know how hard this is for me? You have no right to do this." I jerked away from him.

"I'm sorry," he said, following me. It was as if he couldn't help it, as if gravity drew him to me. I knew the feeling, usually. "I'm so sorry. I thought you'd want to know," he said. "I know how important flight is to you."

"*Was*," I said bitterly.

"What?"

"It's over now, Taylor. You have to let it go."

"Why should I let it go? If there's even a possibility— Hey," he said as I crawled farther away from him. "Where are you going?"

I couldn't stay there any longer. I couldn't be close to him, couldn't have him looking at me. "Why are you doing this?" I demanded. "Why are you focusing on the one thing I cannot do, instead of all the things I can?"

"Hey—hey, listen." He reached for me, stopping just short

of my waist. "I would *never* do that. I mean, if I thought for a second that flying again was impossible for you. If I even thought *you* thought that…" He looked at me, and his gaze pierced into the deepest parts of me. Past my anger, my hurt. Down into my hope. "But you don't think that, do you? You still believe there's a chance, I can see it. I can *feel* it. Tell me I'm wrong."

He waited. But I couldn't answer.

"Listen to me." He put his hand on my leg, so lightly. I thought, for an instant, that he was being careful with me because I'd been hurt. But then I remembered that he'd always been careful with me, never pushed too hard. It was just the kind of person he was. "If it hurts you to hear me talk this way, I'll stop. I'll never bring it up again."

I lowered my head, ashamed that he had seen my vulnerability. "Thank you," I began, but he broke in again, gently.

"But let me say one thing, one time. Please? And trust that I say it because I believe in the magic of this place and I think it *might* help you. And if that possibility exists, I want to give it to you. I want, at least, to try."

I lifted my head. I felt heavy, weighted down with fear, with apprehension. But I was finally learning to trust him. I couldn't go back on that so quickly. "Speak," I entreated.

"What if it doesn't hurt to be near me because I'm bad for you? What if it hurts because my love for you is speeding up the healing? Or even … helping them grow."

I inhaled slowly. The possibility was too much for me. But even more than that … "You love me?"

The look in his eyes was so sincere, I almost cried. "Are you kidding? I think I've loved you from the beginning. I know that sounds crazy, but...I knew you. Even before you told me who you were, I knew you. And I love you more than anything in the world."

Tears stung in my eyes and I didn't blink them away. I'd never wanted to cry in front of anyone. But that wasn't the strangest thing. At the sound of his confession—the mention of his love—a stinging pain shot through my back.

Could he be right? Is there any way...?

But maybe it wasn't so impossible. Love had always been the greatest healer. And here in Faerie, magic took physical form.

"And you would do this for me? You would let me...use you?" I asked.

"Oh my God, use me. Yes." He was laughing. I wanted to laugh too, but I couldn't. Our situation was too dangerous. The ease with which I could hurt him...the ease with which he could hurt me...did I dare risk it?

"Taylor."

He grinned, taking my hands. "You wouldn't be using me."

"Yes, I would."

He shook his head. "You'd be using this as an excuse to do what you've wanted to do all along."

It was a preposterous thing to say. The power of flight, a mere excuse? I looked into his eyes, wanting to protest. I looked down at his hands, ready to pull myself from his grip. But eyes and hands, lips and skin, drew me in without even trying. I realized something right then.

"You're right," I said, and brought my lips to his. He tasted of mint and berries. I wanted more. "Come with me into the forest."

11

TAYLOR

She led me, or rather, I led her, through the trees. I tripped over more branches than I could count. I couldn't wait to touch her, kiss her, taste her. I wanted to memorize every inch of her skin.

We came to a stop in a clearing filled with silvery light. I was unlacing her dress before we'd even touched the ground. "Come here," I said, pulling her close to me. And I kissed her, slowly, sweetly, as her body curved into me.

"I missed you," I said, pulling back to look into her eyes.

"And I, you," she murmured, brushing the hair from my face. The intensity in her gaze surprised me. Every time she looked at me like that, I couldn't believe it. Then I was kissing her cheeks, her neck, her throat; everything I could reach before I managed to take off her dress. And when it fell away, and I saw her without anything between us, I was struck with a funny thought.

When Elora had come to the human world, she must've thought it was strange that people wore so many layers of clothes. I don't mean the way we dress in the winter—I mean the way we keep our private areas bound up even on the most sweltering days. I still remember that shame I felt, as a kid, when I realized the other guys would see me in the locker room showers. I knew how dangerous it was to let them see me.

But here in Faerie, they must not have worried about those types of things. Underneath her dress, Elora was naked.

"Oh my God."

"You say that a lot," she said, staring at me unashamed. "Do you believe in God?"

"I do right now."

She laughed. And she pulled my head back to her neck, so that I could kiss some more. It was all the reassurance I needed. I'd been afraid, leading her clumsily through the forest, that she'd take one look at me up close and change her mind. She'd pulled away from me so many times before. But something was different now. She was different now. I didn't have to wonder every second if she wanted me.

I knew she did. I could feel it.

When she lifted my chin and kissed me, I started to lose control of my limbs. My legs shook as we sank to our knees. There were so many places I wanted to touch, my hands were completely overwhelmed. I started at her shoulders—they seemed a safe-enough place—and trailed my hands down her arms. I couldn't imagine ever getting tired of touching even the least erotic places. I wanted to feel everything, no matter how innocent. I wanted to make her shake just by breathing on her neck.

And I did.

It happened when I slid my hand into her hair, just at the nape of her neck. I leaned in and took her earlobe between my teeth, kissing her softly. "I love you," I said, whispering the words I'd been practicing in my head. "I've never loved any-body as much as I love you. And honestly, I want to make love to you so badly, but ... "

"But?"

"I think we should go slow," I said. I mean, sure, I wanted to do *everything*, but we'd hardly done *anything* before this, and we needed to be careful. I could hurt her with the brush of my hand. I could humiliate myself with my lack of experience. Better to take things slowly, and figure it out as we went.

"I can kiss every inch of your body," I whispered, "until you feel better than you've ever felt. Will you let me do that for you?"

Her whole body was shaking when she said, "Only if you let me do the same for you."

"Come here, baby." I guided her onto my lap, so that she was straddling me. I wanted to keep her safe as much as I wanted to make her feel good. I couldn't stand the thought of anything hurting her, even though I knew my touch could hurt her. But she was here, in my lap, in my hands, kissing me like she would die if we broke apart. And I really believed what I'd said, about helping her wings grow. I'd seen something when I'd looked at them. I knew, in the deepest parts of me, that I was right about this. But could I hurt her to prove it?

"Is this okay?" I asked, gliding my hands down to her waist.

"Yes," she breathed as I reached her hips. It was incredibly difficult to keep my hands from traveling to her most private places. But I'd waited this long for her, and I wouldn't mess things up by moving too fast. I waited for her to guide me, each second, to show me what she wanted, when she wasn't saying it.

The word "yes" on her lips was the sexiest thing I'd ever heard.

I wanted to hear it again. I slid my hands back up her waist, over her stomach, rising, rising. "Can I touch you?" I asked, my lips still close to her ear.

"Yes."

Oh, God, I was in heaven. I hadn't been kidding about believing in God. Or *gods*. Everything, maybe. Ever since we'd met, I'd thought anything and everything was possible. And as my fingertips grazed the skin over her heart, and spread outward, I felt like I was worshipping her.

She inhaled sharply. For a brief second, I felt exceedingly pleased with myself. She liked me. I was making her feel good. But when she bit her bottom lip, I pulled back.

"Am I hurting you?"

She didn't answer.

"Elora. Please tell me."

She turned, looking into the darkness. "Yes."

Funny how a minute can change the power of a word. This time, her "yes" was a knife in my chest. But I'd known this could happen. I'd encouraged her to do this, knowing full well it might hurt her. Was I so selfish that I'd compromise her well-being for my own pleasure?

"I'm sorry," I said, pulling back. "I'm so sorry. We should stop this."

"What? No." She took my hands and put them back on her thighs. I knew I should pull away but I couldn't. There was power in her touch that I couldn't fight.

Didn't want to.

Couldn't.

"I don't want to hurt you," I said.

"It's not so bad." Her lips found mine, and lingered.

My resolve weakened. Pretty soon it would dissipate into the air. "Even a little is too much," I managed.

She shook her head. "It's all right, if you're careful. Because ..."

"What?"

"I think you're right."

I inhaled slowly, trying to steady my spinning head, but it backfired. Her scent filled my head, woodsy and sharp like the forest after the rain. Flowers and fruit and something spicy, like cinnamon. I ran my tongue from her throat to her neck.

She giggled a little, like maybe it tickled.

"Is this okay?" I asked.

"Better than."

"Good." I trailed little kisses around her throat. "This?"

"Yes. Mmm." Her body shuddered, and I realized my hands had been slipping toward the center of her. She was warm there, and I wanted to move closer, to touch her at her core. I'd never felt like this before, never felt this urgency. Even when I'd wanted to get closer to someone, it had been a purely physical desire. But as her lips touched mine, pressing into me, the whole of her pressing into me, I felt every part of me drawn to her. I felt my body rise and reach out for her. I felt my heart straining against my chest. And my spirit too—I felt clearly what I'd only just suspected before. Maybe it was this place. Maybe it was Elora. Or maybe it was because I was completely and totally in love with her.

My hands slid farther up her thighs and she wrapped her arms around me, pulling me close with an urgency I recognized in myself. I was kissing her mouth now—couldn't tear myself away from her lips—and I couldn't see or smell or taste anything but her. When she murmured the words, I wasn't sure I'd heard her right.

"Hmmm?" I said, thinking that if I hadn't heard her right I could pass it off as a moan rather than a question. But she looked up at me, right into my eyes, and said, "I'm in love with you."

Every part of me froze.

"I'm so in love with you," she whispered, like the words held power. Or danger. I guess for her, they did. They erased everything she'd ever believed about humans. But they built something new in its place. Something terrifying, yes, but beautiful too.

I wrapped my arms around her waist, down low where it wouldn't hurt her. The skin was burning up there. All of her was burning up; a sudden heat went searing through her. I loosened my grip, letting cool air rush in between us, but she pulled me back, almost violently. She held onto me, nails digging into my shirt and I held her there, trying to protect her from whatever was hurting her. When she pulled away, to look at me, I expected to see a pained expression on her face. But the look she wore was awe.

"Kiss me," she said.

I did.

Her breathing quickened and she ran her fingers through my hair. The look of awe hadn't lessened. But a slow smile cut into it. "Taylor."

"What is it?"

She grinned, kissing me once, twice, three times. "It doesn't hurt so badly anymore."

"What—really?"

She nodded.

"That's amazing. Your own love helped the magic to work."

"Not mine." She shook her head. "Ours," she said, pressing into me until I was lying on my back. Now she crawled over me and she was the animal, the wild thing, the goddess. She led my hand up her thigh, her face so close to mine, holding onto my gaze with ferocity. Maybe memorizing me the way I always tried to memorize her. But this, I would never forget.

The image was burned into my memory.

When she said, "Heal me," I did as she asked.

12

ELORA

In the morning, I awoke to a gasp, but it didn't sound like Taylor's. I reached for my dress, which was covering me like a blanket. As my eyes tried to adjust to the hideous light, I caught flashes of the person peering down at me: her dark hair was tangled, and her brown eyes were narrowed into slits. That crystalline chair sparkled in the light.

"Kylie," I said, scanning the space for Taylor. He was nowhere to be seen. "Where did—"

"He needed to take care of something," she said. "And I offered to watch over you, because..." She paused, studying my back. Studying whatever growth Taylor had seen the previous night. Or maybe there was more, considering...

"He told you?" I pushed myself to a sitting position. My limbs ached, but it was less of an all-consuming pain and more the feeling you get after a long night of flying. A welcome soreness in the muscles.

"He didn't have to. The whole forest is talking about it." Kylie scoffed, a short, scalding sound. "I thought you'd already got them back, you know? Thought the Queen had sewed them on. But this... this is much more magical, isn't it?"

I was having trouble lacing up the low back of my corset, and suddenly I didn't want to use magic in front of Kylie. So I just held onto it, looking up at her as she blinked in the early morning light. Her hair was tufting up in the back, like perhaps she and Alexia had slipped away last night when Taylor and I did, but any joy it might've brought was gone now.

"You're angry with me," I said.

"Oh, no." She shook her head and just kept shaking it. "I'm not angry with you. I'm just angry."

"What can I do?"

"What *can't* you do?" she responded, not really answering me. "What can't the Dark Princess do? You get love. You get your wings. You get everything you want. And I get nothing."

"You have Alexia," I said before I could stop myself. "You have us."

"Oh, good. I guess I'm set then." She made a move to leave, but I stopped her with my hand.

I took it back when she glared at me. "But that doesn't change things, does it?" I asked. "Nothing you *have* changes what you *don't have*. Just like Taylor's love didn't make up for the loss of my wings."

"But it *does*, that's the point." She ran her hands through her hair. "You're going to get back your wings. You're going to get back everything they stupidly told me I could get back, if I just *prayed* for it. Or made up for what I'd done to anger God. Someone actually said that to me, do you believe that?" She looked up at the trees. "And I knew they were wrong, but they wouldn't let it go. If God didn't fix me, science would. There are so many new advances to science! They kept me locked in a fairy tale. Locked in a tower."

"Kylie. I'm sorry. I—"

"I don't want you to be sorry. I want to be able to be myself without having my differences *thrown* in my *face*." Her eyes shimmered with tears. "I mean, honestly, is that asking so much? I feel normal. I *am* normal. The only time I feel different is around *other* people, you know?"

I do, I thought, studying her eyes. When I was a child, I realized there was something very different about my wings. Unlike my mother's, which were grand and full, mine appeared to have been sliced along their curves. They looked *tattered*, and the courtiers called me the Tattered Princess behind my mother's back.

Still, through it all, I had been able to fly. As for Kylie…

"I am truly sorry," I said, reaching for her hand. "Honestly, if we could trade places—"

"Don't do that." She pushed away my hand. "I don't want your pity. That's what I've been trying to tell you. I'm happy for you. I *am*. I just…"

"What is it?" I said softly, worried the worst of it was yet to come. Worried she'd never forgive me, or she'd do something rash.

"I'm just sick to death of waiting for the slightest bit of decency from the world, and being disappointed," she said, wiping away the tears. "I'm sick of being forced to live in a universe where the logic doesn't make *sense* to me, and when I finally get to a place where magic exists, the same stupid logic applies."

"But—"

"Not for everybody. Just for me."

"It isn't just you."

"Okay, well, anybody who isn't a *faerie*. God, maybe I'll sew your old wings into my back, so that I have faerie blood running through my veins, and then I can be magical too."

"*Kylie*—"

"But that wouldn't work, would it? The world changes, and you change with it. Only I stay the same. And I'm just *done …*"

I knelt before her. I didn't even realize I was crying until my tears fell onto her knees. And when I reached up to touch her face, she didn't pull away. She just looked at me.

"I'm not making threats," she said. "I just can't carry everyone anymore. It's too much weight."

My thumb trailed across her cheek, catching a tear as it fell. "That is the secret, isn't it? Everyone sees you as the sweetest among us, and that is true. But beyond that lies something different. You are the strongest. Not because of what you've endured, but because you insist that we will win, even when none of us dares to believe it. You make it true, with that insistence."

"Kylie the insufferable optimist." She snorted. "Good riddance."

"We all wear masks, and Faerie will strip them from our faces. That is the danger of bringing you here."

"The danger and the power," she said softly. "And what about those who've always been here? What about *you?*"

I laughed. "I had to go to the human world to shed my mask."

"Which was … ?"

Elora the singular entity, never depending on anyone but herself. Denying the possibility of love to survive.

"The untouchable princess," I said.

To my surprise, she laughed. Her eyes trailed to the place where my top threatened to fall away. "Not so untouchable anymore, huh?"

I blushed, looking down. "I've been ... working on it," I said. "Sometimes it's hard for me. To trust him. I keep thinking the moment I do, he will disappear. Or betray me."

"Why?"

I shrugged, as if we were discussing algebra equations or the process for making jam. "It's what I know."

She was quiet a minute, studying my eyes with an intensity that made me nervous. Finally, she said, "Your parents?"

"Well, I only know my mother, but that's enough." I huffed, a sharp sound. "It's more than enough."

"That bad, huh?"

"She's the Queen of the Dark Faeries," I said, as if that explained it. And I suppose it did, if you knew the slightest bit about her.

"And you never met your dad?"

"Plenty of faeries grow up only knowing one of their parents, or none. We're all related, all connected by the same earth, which is our original body, and so we raise each other. The specifics of our parentage aren't fussed over like in the mortal world."

"So not knowing your dad is normal."

"It would've been normal if we hadn't been forbidden to speak about him. *That* made his absence clearer than anything else. *That* made me wonder why he'd left. If I'd simply had a bit of information, I could've let it go."

Instead I'd obsessed over it. Obsessed over the coldness of

my mother. Obsessed over the idea that my father would save me from her. From being alone.

"It makes you hate yourself, doesn't it?" Kylie asked softly. "Or, at the very least, you question your worth. If you can even *be* loved."

"Yes."

"My parents are jerks too. I mean, maybe not jerks-with-magic, but still. They made me hate myself for a long time." Her gaze shifted down. At first, I thought she was looking at the grass, but then I realized she was looking at herself. "You're never going to ask me, are you?"

"Ask you what?"

"If I was born this way, or … "

"You can tell me if you like."

"Well, we were talking about our parents," she said, tugging at a thread on her dress.

My eyes widened, and my heart nearly stopped. "*They* did this? Your parents—"

"No. Not exactly. It's just … " She shook her head, and I feared she was going to stay silent. But after a moment, she said, "My dad used to hunt."

"Like … animals?"

"Yeah, like deer," she said. "He'd go on these weekend trips with his friends. And when Keegan was old enough, he'd take him along, because you know, boys hunt! Girls … gather, I don't know. Like we were all cave men." She laughed, and I laughed with her.

Then, nothing. "And this bothered you?" I pressed. "This inability to hunt?"

"Not that. Just feeling inferior. I mean, I was *eight,* and I already knew he loved me less."

A shiver, slow-starting, skittered up my spine. "You offered to go with them," I said.

"I thought I could win him over."

"By hunting?"

"I wasn't going to *hunt,*" she said, as if it were obvious. "I was going to swim and eat s'mores and they could go hunting down the road … "

"But they didn't?"

She fell silent again, looking off into the trees. "That was probably the plan. But the second morning we were there, this deer came into our camp. A girl. Fully grown, you know, but without any horns. I thought, *Aw, maybe it's a mama deer searching for food.* I thought I could follow her back home, real quiet, and catch a glimpse of her fawns."

This time, I waited a beat before saying, "Did you?"

Kylie blinked her eyes, but no tears fell from her lashes. "Everybody was drunk. I mean, not me and Keegan, but the guys would bring, like, four eighteen-packs and stay hammered the whole time. One of my dad's friends picked up his shotgun and fired without even batting an eye. He caught her in the leg."

"What did you do?" I asked. I could see it all so clearly. The panic. The blood. And eight-year-old Kylie trying to make sense of it.

"I just *lost it,*" she said. "I started screaming and running over there, waving my hands. And my dad was yelling at me to come back over, but I didn't. The second I moved, the deer was dead, you know?"

I nodded, closing my eyes. "And he…shot you?" I asked.

"It was his friend. He wasn't trying to shoot me. He was just drunk, and he thought he could hit the deer behind my back. When the shot fired, the deer took off, and he hit me here." Kylie twisted, pointing to her side, down low. "You'd be surprised at how many people suffer spinal injuries that way. Except mostly it's guys shooting their girlfriends. Or wives."

I winced, fingers tearing at the grass. I'd come so far, gained so much faith in humanity. But faith could bleed into fury in an instant.

"Did he go to prison?" I asked softly. Perhaps if humans had taken vengeance on the man, I wouldn't feel so angry. I wouldn't ache to see his blood running over my hands.

Kylie shook her head. "When the whole thing happened, everyone was screaming, and my dad was yelling at the guy. Saying he was going to kill him."

Perhaps he should have, I thought. I kept that to myself.

"When I woke up in the hospital, things had shifted. I could hear my dad talking to the nurse, saying, 'Why did she step in front of the deer? Why did she insist on coming?'"

"Oh, Darkness," I breathed. But it was a foolish thing to say. Darkness hadn't done this. People had.

"I think it was easier for him, you know? If he blamed me, he didn't have to blame himself." She sniffed, tilting her head to look up at the sky. "I just needed him to say that he loved me no matter what had happened before. No matter what happened after."

"But he never did?"

"He didn't say much after, in general." She lowered her head. "And then Keegan came out, and our parents kicked him out, and ... I was just done waiting for them to come around, you know?" Her eyes shimmered again. "To *see* us as we were, not who they wanted us to be."

"I see you," I said. "I know it isn't the same thing. I *know* it isn't. But we're making a family, the five of us."

She nodded. "We are making a family," she agreed. "And families stick together in times of turmoil. In times of battle ... "

"Kylie." I froze, my chest tightening. "We've been over this. Each one of you is helping me—"

"We are," she said, flashing a mischievous smile. "I'm making you a secret weapon that'll knock Naeve on his ass. But I'm also making armor, made out of iron—"

"Iron is forbidden."

"Not to humans. It'll keep us protected."

"Kylie, please! You cannot go to battle. It is too dangerous."

"Alexia's going. Keegan's going. I don't even know what Keegan's plan is, but I know it's a big one. Can you stop all of us?" She paused, staring into my eyes. She wasn't crying anymore, but those eyes were bright. Filled with possibility. "I know you're letting Taylor go."

"Yes, because I need ... " *An offering.* But was that really why? Or had I simply realized that I couldn't make the decision for him?

I lowered my head. "Please ... " I whispered. "Please reconsider."

"Go talk to the others," Kylie said. "Everyone has a good reason for wanting to fight. I think you'll be surprised."

"What's your reason?" I asked.

She looked out at the Seelie Forest, glittering with light. "Faerie isn't what I expected. I expected a world of elemental beings. A world of chaos, maybe, but a world where everyone was free. A world you're working toward. I want to work toward that too."

"It will not be easy."

"No, it won't. But if I wait here, *hoping* things go well in the battle, do I even deserve the world you're fighting for?" She looked up, and her gaze was fierce. She looked like a warrior. "I'm ready to fight for what I believe in."

I nodded, taking her hands. "Thank you," I said. "I wish you would stay behind. I wish you all would. But I understand why you want to fight. I'll speak with the others."

———

After an afternoon of tracking down Alexia, then Keegan, I finally went to see Taylor. He sat in the center of a clearing, making careful strokes on a makeshift easel. When I entered the space, a dozen horn-tipped pixidellies darted away from him, taking shelter in the surrounding trees.

Little gossips, I thought. *What stories are they spinning for him?* And then I forgot them, mesmerized by the sight of the boy who'd healed me all night.

"Taylor?"

He looked up, red blossoming in his cheeks. At first, I thought he was bashful about the previous night's adventures. Then it hit me.

"You did it?" I said, unable to stop myself.

He cocked his head to the side, his attention split between me and the canvas. His smile was sheepish and suggestive at the same time. "Sort of," he said, turning the easel in my direction.

I approached slowly. Teal eyes stared back at me. Waves of scarlet cascaded around them, falling over snow-white skin. And just a hint of wings.

It was me. He'd painted me.

My breath hovered on the borderland between lungs and lips. "I look dangerous," I said after a moment.

"You are dangerous." He stood, wrapping me in his arms. "You appeared that way last night."

"And you remembered? You drew from memory?"

"Your image is burned into my mind." He kissed my throat. "It was all I could think of when I woke up this morning." His lips traveled up to my ear. "You were all I could see."

His kisses were melting my resolve. But I had to remain strong today. "Then let me be your inspiration to draw other things. Didn't many of your painters claim to have such inspiration—muses, I believe?"

"You aren't some spirit flitting around my ears," he replied. "You are my muse in flesh and blood. Everything about you inspires me. Your touch." He clasped my hands in his, pressing them to his chest. "Your lips—"

"Taylor."

"I'm just being honest," he said with a grin. "I thought you'd appreciate that."

"Then you might appreciate this." Unlacing my fingers from his, I stepped back, crouching on my hands and feet. I gave him a threatening growl.

"Miss Elora. You're trying to seduce me."

"I'm posing for you," I explained.

"With clothes on?"

"If you do what I ask, I'll take them off."

He dropped his gaze, bashful. "I have to say, I've never heard that one before. What do you want me to do?"

"Draw me," I said, catching his eye. "Like a gargoyle. On a building."

"In a human city," he finished, already shaking his head. "I've been trying. But everything ends up looking like a Surrealist nightmare."

"I can work with that," I said. "Just promise you'll keep trying."

"Okay. But don't you have work to do? Some meeting with the Queen, or, I don't know, strategy to plot?"

"Always," I said, tossing my hair over my shoulder. "But this is important. You are important. I've tried too long to keep myself away from you. But last night, I came to you unafraid, unhindered by fear of consequence, and offered you my heart and my soul, and I found what I needed in you. Through you."

Taylor sat down at the oak, his gaze lingering on my face. "What could I possibly give to you that you couldn't give to yourself?"

"Love."

Three hours later, he'd painted a single glittering skyscraper. By the end of the night, a city was forming.

13

TAYLOR

Now that Elora was back, Maya de Lyre stopped coming around. I guess it was too risky to conspire in front of the princess. Still, I knew Maya de Lyre was busy investigating how to free me from the Bright Queen, because she started leaving me little notes. Two days after Elora's arrival, I awoke with a leaf in my hand (which promptly dissolved into dust) that said, "I'm getting close." Three nights after that, the vines on the bathroom wall spelled out, "Just a few more days."

She was actually going to pull it off.

It was a good thing, too, because *my* investigation (about the identity of Elora's father) had hit a dead end. With Elora back in the Bright Court, I just couldn't get the Seelie Queen alone. In fact, I could hardly get Elora alone, because I was so busy painting or practicing for battle. By the time I finished my work for the night, my arms were exhausted, and if you've ever tried to *heal* anyone, well … you need your arms.

So we mostly just slept.

We did manage to sneak away a few times, in the days leading up to the fifteenth, but it wasn't enough to satisfy me. My desire for Elora spilled over into my dreams. I could hear her voice, hushed and whispering, with an urgency that made my blood shift. I could feel her breath on my ear. I started to laugh a little, murmuring all the things I wanted to say to her when I was awake. As first, she was responsive, murmuring back in pleasant tones, but when her tone grew harsher it pulled me right out of the dream.

That's when I realized the voice I was hearing wasn't in my subconscious. And the ear it was whispering in? Not mine.

I sat up and looked around. Elora was gone. Kylie and Alexia were sleeping a few feet away, wrapped up in each other's arms, but Keegan was missing. Or maybe he was just misplaced. I could hear his voice in the distance, bobbing around the forest like a ghost without a body. I crawled across the ground in its direction.

As I got closer, Elora's voice rose to a shrill pitch, stopping me in my tracks. "*No*," she said. "I've told you all week. I will not allow it under my leadership."

"Why not?" Keegan asked, his pitch rising too. "You know it's a good idea. If it wasn't, you would've said so already."

"We think ourselves so clever, don't we?"

Pulling myself onto a moss-covered rock, I peered through two trees into the space where they were standing. It wasn't really a clearing, but eerie light filtered through the forest, and I could make out their silhouettes.

Keegan's hands waved in the darkness. "I want a life of meaning," he said.

"Then fight along the fringes with Taylor."

"Do you know how tired I am of living on the fringes? Just once, I want to be the hero."

"You'll be the martyr. The fool."

"Better me than you. Last time, he made an example out of you. But that, with all its consequences, was just a game to him. This time will be different—"

"No, Keegan."

"What happens if he kills you? You think your followers can survive without you, but what if they can't? What if they take your death as a sign that they've lost the battle?"

"How nice of you to speak of me as if I'm already gone."

"Come on, Elora, he's going to do everything he can to kill you. It's pretty much his life goal, from what I can tell."

"I can best him. I've done it before."

"But isn't there a chance that you can't?"

She said nothing. Their conversation disturbed me in a way I couldn't even articulate. But I had no time to work through my confusion. I needed to take in every word.

"Please." Keegan took her hands. I felt a surge of jealousy—not because I thought he would take her from me, but because I needed that closeness. I needed her near me in those final days.

"Let me do this," Keegan said. "I'll go in head-to-toe armor. I'll take the most magical sword in the world."

Elora huffed a little at that. I couldn't believe what I was hearing. Did Keegan really think he could go up against Naeve? It was ridiculous. Preposterous. A suicide mission. Besides…

Why him and not me?

"Come on," Keegan said. Even in the dim light, I could see he was searching her eyes. "You know I'm right. And if you won't help me do this, I'll find someone else. I bet the Seelie Queen would—"

"Peace, Keegan." Then she said something I couldn't understand. I inched forward, just a little, and lost my balance, tumbling into a fat pile of leaves.

Crap.

The two of them turned in my direction. I could *hear* it. With the exception of my impromptu collapse, the forest had been dead quiet. I knew it was only a matter of time before they came over to investigate—or ran away like frightened deer—so I did my best impression of the Lady Claremondes and slithered backwards in the underbrush.

And yeah. It hurt.

Slithering through the forest is probably different for snakes. For me, my legs and elbows and shins met with every tiny rock and twig. But what are a couple of scrapes to a guy who's about to go into battle? I mean hey, if Keegan got to face off with the Prince of the Dark Court, there was *no way* Elora was keeping me on the fringes. I would fight alongside the servants of the Dark Court.

I would fight to defend their princess.

She was coming for me. I could hear her, even though her steps were much more calculated than a human's. It never really occurred to me, back home, that she was quieter than the rest of us. But then again, I was too busy being infatuated with her to notice her strangeness.

Fearing I was about to be caught, I rose to my hands and knees and crawled backward through the forest. That was probably my dumbest mistake. I ran smack-dab into a tree and my tailbone started to throb immediately. At least I thought it was a tree, until I heard the voice.

"Going somewhere?"

I shot to my feet, turning around as quickly as I could without falling. And there she was, struggling to hold in the light that spilled easily from her fingertips, her mouth, her hair. I could see it, just under the surface of her brown skin, threatening to break free.

I bowed out of habit. "Your Highness."

The Bright Lady grinned. "I thought you'd be sleeping, young mortal. After all, you've been *quite* busy."

"Painting is hard work."

"But that is not all you've been doing."

Heat rushed to my cheeks. Did she know I'd been fighting? Did she know I'd been doing *other* things? Out of the corner of my eye, I caught sight of a faerie hovering between two branches. She looked familiar, her tiny horn tipped in red.

"You're right," I said. "I've been investigating."

"Investigating?" the Queen said with a smile. "Trying to find a way out of our bargain?"

"I still don't know what our bargain is," I said casually. "I mean, I don't know what it *entails*." She held up a hand, but I went on before she could stop me. "Besides, I've had other things on my mind."

"Oh?"

"Elora's brother said something in the graveyard. I mean, her adopted brother." The difference seemed significant, considering his relationship with the Dark Lady.

"What did he say?" the Queen asked, leaning in. Farther off, I could hear the sound of feet crunching against leaves, and I knew Keegan and Elora were returning to our camp. Once she realized I wasn't there, would she come looking for me?

I spoke quickly. "He called her 'her father's daughter.'

He said he *knew* she'd go to the human world. How could he know that?"

"He couldn't. Not for certain." Now the footsteps were coming closer, and I could hear Elora whispering my name. Soon, she'd start yelling. I knew, because it's what I would've done. And she wanted to protect me like I wanted to protect her.

"There's something else," I whispered. "Alexia said Elora's name means *light* in Greek."

This time, the Queen stepped back. "It means *Crown of God* in Hebrew," she said after a second.

"Do faeries believe in God?"

"Not in the way that humans do."

"But they do believe in light. In fact, light and darkness might be the closest things you have to gods."

"You flatter me, young mortal. But this time, it will take more—"

"Taylor?" Elora's voice called out into the darkness. Soon, she'd catch a glimpse of the Bright Queen's light. Soon, she'd be here.

"You'd better be off," the Queen said.

"No."

"Excuse me?"

"No. You owe me this. I gave you my freedom."

"In exchange for Elora's life."

"Just tell me one thing." I could see shadows moving, could see Elora's beautiful form getting closer. I had maybe ten seconds. "Why would a Princess of the Dark Court be named for the light?"

The Seelie Queen laughed. She was *laughing* at me, taking pleasure in my distress. "Isn't it obvious?" she asked.

"*No,*" I said. "That's why I'm asking."

But maybe it should've been obvious. Maybe I should've figured it out by then. But I hadn't, or I refused to see it.

One piece of the puzzle was still missing.

"You know the rules," the Queen said. "You give me an offering, and I'll respond in kind."

"What do you want?" I asked, following her into the darkness. But the shadows seemed to be repelled by her, and wherever we went, eerie light trickled in.

"There is a ritual," she began, "which will make you stronger. It will bond you to this place, perhaps help Elora's people accept you."

That sounds awesome.

"What's the catch?" I asked.

She glanced behind my back. "The princess will not be happy about it."

"Will it hurt her?"

"It will not harm a single hair on her head."

"What about the rest of her body?"

Her lips twitched, amused by my thoroughness. "It may cause her to worry, nothing more."

"What about *my* body?"

She paused. "The ritual itself will cause some pain. But you will come away stronger, and that pain will fall away."

"Will I still be … myself?"

"You will have your body. Your heart. Your mind. Your spirit—"

"Again, what's the catch? What are you keeping from me?"

"The ritual is strange. When it comes time to perform, I will need you to trust me. And forgive me for the strangeness."

"But it won't mutilate me? I won't wake up a monster?"

She shook her head. "The ritual will not cause that level of transformation."

"Why are you even giving me a choice?" I asked, as Elora called out from behind me. Branches shook in the distance. "You have my name…"

"I am not like the dark faeries," the Queen said, her eyes going wide. "What will it take to convince you of that? I *want* you to have free will. But there are certain eventualities that I must prevent—"

"Like?"

"There isn't time to discuss it. Do you agree or not?"

"If I don't, will you perform the ritual anyway?"

She was quiet, and the most terrible feeling settled over me. *The answer is yes. She pretends to be different from the dark faeries, but in the end, she'll get what she wants. You don't really have a choice.*

Well then, I might as well get something out of the bargain.

"I will agree to the ritual," I said softly, "as long as you've told me the truth and Elora won't be harmed. And I'll still be myself."

"You will be better," the Queen said, eyes flashing in the darkness. Then she disappeared into the shadows, leaving me alone in a forest of illusions.

When Elora burst out of the trees, she told me she'd been looking for me, and I told her I'd been looking for her. We kept our secrets, and a wall formed between us. But soon, the Queen would tell me what I wanted to know, and that wall would shatter.

Then nothing would keep us apart.

14

ELORA

The night before our departure, the Queen offered to tell us a story. From the way her entourage reacted, it was obvious this was a rare treat. For a few chaotic moments, I heard more whispering at the dinner table than I'd heard in the hallways of Unity High. Then a nymph called out, "Tell us a Naiad and Dryad!"

"Oh, Darkness." I chuckled into my goblet. Naiad and Dryad were characters in old folk tales, the kind used by mothers to warn their children away from humans: Dryad Discovers the Iron Railway; Naiad Gets Caught in a Fishing Net. I must've heard dozens of them. They always had a lesson.

"What do you say, Lady?" I asked, my tongue properly loosened from the wine I'd been sipping. "Surely, the mortals would enjoy a good folktale."

The Bright Lady grinned, her eyes settling on Taylor. "I believe I have just the story. Maya de Livre?"

The Queen's royal storyteller, in all her gnarled glory, climbed *onto* the table and began waving her hands through the air.

"Telling stories is complicated for the fey," I explained to the humans as images took shape: a green and brown creature raced through the forest, while a lady with shimmering blue skin swam in a lake. "Surely, we can tell stories of things that have come to pass. But 'fairy tales,' as you call them, or stories that we have made up to entertain children, cannot simply be spoken, for speaking them would be a lie. Therefore, we must use glamour to *illustrate* what we are saying, and in this way, we are no longer lying. We are merely describing that which dances before our eyes."

"Wow," Kylie breathed, as the creature called Naiad circled in the air as if swimming. That long blue hair trailed out around her, and tinted waves unfurled at her back. Meanwhile, Dryad danced on the land, spinning and spinning while leaves fell from her hair.

"Once upon a time," the Seelie Queen said, "Naiad and Dryad were sisters, in the way that all creatures of the universe are sisters. Both reveled in the beauty of the earth, and each adored the other. They were kindred, Naiad sticking to the shallows, and Dryad running alongside the shore, so that they could be together."

As the Queen spoke, the creatures in the air shifted, illustrating her words: the lady of the forest ran along a green, mossy bank, while the lady of the river splashed along beside her.

"For many years, it was this way," the Queen said. "But times change. The earth was ever shifting, ever lifting up her petals to unveil new layers, and while Dryad delighted in each revelation, Naiad grew afraid. She did not like the changes that were happening on the land. She clung to the old ways—the fluid, but constant, waters. She clung to the dark, where she could believe that things would always stay the same. And she began to distrust Dryad, and moved away from her, into the depths."

Together we watched as Naiad disappeared into a cool, dark body of water, until only her glowing blue eyes could be seen. Meanwhile, Dryad traveled the shores, searching for her friend.

"Naiad retreated to the deep, moving farther and farther away from the world of the land. Eventually, she forgot how it felt to feel the sun on her skin. Even worse, she forgot her love for Dryad." The Queen looked up, her green eyes glistening. "Enlisting the help of the creatures of the sea, Naiad came up with a plot to overthrow the creatures of the land. To usher in a new age of darkness." More eyes appeared in the water, glowing gold and silver and green. "And though they could wipe out most of civilization in their quest for safety, many of them believed in Naiad's plan. To them it seemed safer than the alternative. It seemed safer than change.

"So it began. The war between two sisters. The battle that should never have been. Blood stained the rivers and soaked into the roots of the trees. Midsummer came, and the leaves were already red. Dryad began to fear for the lives of all of them. She had to find a way to get Naiad back."

Here the Queen smiled, a small, sinister thing. "And so Dryad came up with her own plan. You see, Dryad had known Naiad for thousands of years. She knew the way her sister thought, and what she feared." She paused a moment before she said, "What she desired. So Dryad scoured the land for a creature that could warm Naiad from the inside."

"Why a creature of the land?" Keegan asked, as Maya de Livre waved her hands, pulling Dryad back into the forest.

"You're so impatient," Kylie said, elbowing her brother. "Don't you think she's going to answer that?"

"It doesn't hurt to ask."

"It does if it wastes time—"

The Queen cleared her throat and the leaves in the clearing took flight. They settled in around us, adorning our clothes, falling in our hair.

"Sorry," said the twins. They seemed unusually cheerful, considering we were about to go to war. Then again, the faeries had given Kylie a high-backed saddle earlier this week, which she could use to ride into battle. And Keegan was sneaking into the forest more and more often, returning with a lazy smile and joking that "a gentleman doesn't kiss and tell."

I suppose we were all taking pleasure where we could find it.

"I forgive you." The Queen smiled down at the twins. But she didn't answer Keegan's question, not then. She was too busy studying the figure that Maya de Livre was creating out of thin air. The boy with tanned skin and fiery hair. "Dryad found a boy she deemed to be an appropriate lover for her friend. And using old magic, she transformed him until he looked like a creature of the sea." Slowly, the boy's features darkened, until his hair was blue-black and his skin was cerulean. "She even granted him the power to breathe underwater for a short time. But an ancient creature like Dryad was still limited in certain things, and she warned the boy never to swim too deep." The Queen paused, touching her lips. "It seemed a simple enough instruction."

"But it wasn't?" This time it was Kylie who asked the question, and I expected Keegan to retaliate with all manner of protests. But he didn't. It was clear he wanted to hear the rest of the story, and even the prospect of arguing with his sister could not distract him.

"Alas, Dryad was foolish," the Queen said. "The creature she chose to seduce her friend was a young thing."

"How young?" Taylor asked, tightening his grip on my hand. I closed my eyes at the feel of him.

But they opened again when the Queen started speaking directly to him. "Not much older than you, sweet," she gushed. "And just as beautiful, with your sun-kissed skin and untamable hair. Naiad didn't stand a chance against his sweetness and beauty. His bravery."

"So she fell for him?" Taylor asked, squirming under her scrutiny.

"She fell for him quite wholeheartedly," the Bright Queen said, as Naiad led the boy into the shallows. "More so, even, than Dryad had anticipated. But just when Dryad was set to remove the glamour and prove to Naiad that dwellers of the land were worthy of loving, tragedy struck."

"Oh God." Taylor turned to me, his eyes widened in shock. "He drowned."

"No way," Kylie said, narrowing her eyes at him. "Why would you say that? He didn't drown—"

"He did indeed," said the Queen.

"*What?*" Keegan and Alexia shouted together.

The Seelie Queen nodded. "The boy was foolish. They all were, in a way. But Dryad was the biggest fool of all, for not seeing it coming. You see, being a creature of the water, and a lover of this particular boy, Naiad wanted to make love to him in her favorite place—a secret, underwater cave. He made it so far as the opening before his lungs began to cry out. He tried to swim back to the surface, but Naiad was confused. She thought she'd done something to upset him. She swam after him."

"Oh, no," Taylor said, as Naiad chased after the drowning boy. Grabbing him around the waist, she dragged him back down into the depths.

"She restrained him," the Queen said, "begging him to tell her what was wrong. Believing wholeheartedly that he was a creature of the deep, she did not understand his struggling. And as she pressed her lips to his, he took his final breath." The boy went limp in Naiad's arms. "She let go then, and watched him float to the surface. In that moment, she realized what had happened."

"She figured it out?" Kylie asked.

"She saw it," I said, and they all turned to me. "Glamour applied in life dissolves in death. Living cells respond to it, but glamouring a dead thing is simply covering it up. That's why I ran into trouble in the mortal world. I witnessed a mortal's death, and glamoured her body to look like a log, hoping to *borrow* her identity. But I lingered too long, and the glamour faded. Her body was discovered."

"The real Laura Belfry," Taylor murmured, and I nodded.

"The glamour left this boy when he died, revealing his true form to Naiad," the Queen said. "And in that moment, she understood everything." Now Naiad's lake grew darker, while Dryad's forest grew thicker, each blocking the other out. "Thus, in her attempt to bring her friend back to the light, Dryad had pushed her over the edge, into an abyss from which she would never return."

"They never made up?" Kylie asked, trying to see Naiad in the darkness.

The Queen shook her head. The change was subtle, but I was nearly certain I could see strands of red bleeding through her hair. "Naiad blamed Dryad for the death of her lover. Where there had once been discord, hatred bloomed between them."

"And the war raged on?" Taylor asked. He was studying the story the way he'd studied mine back in the mortal world. But this was only a fable. A story used to enrapture mortals.

"The war worsened," the Queen replied. "And Dryad grew even more desperate."

"Did she come up with another plan?" Taylor pressed.

The Queen looked at him a long moment. "That is a story for another time."

"So that's the end?" Keegan asked.

"*The end?*" Kylie crossed her arms over her chest. "That's a horrible ending."

She cowered a little when the Queen narrowed her eyes. "Tragic, I mean."

"What are we supposed to take away from that?" Alexia asked.

"Always be nice to your friends," Keegan said, clasping his hands together in mock giddiness.

Only Taylor remained silent, looking up at the Queen and studying her face. "It's about difference," he said after a minute. "Or perceived difference." He waited for the Queen to nod before continuing.

She did.

"It's about the way people destroy each other over imagined difference. And they all end up lonely, or dead." After a moment, he added, "Am I right?"

"You need to trust your instincts," I murmured.

To my surprise, he turned to look at me. "If I trusted my instincts, I'd say it's about something else entirely."

15

TAYLOR

That night, I couldn't sleep. I felt *charged*. Not only was I getting better with the bows and arrows (and the sword, in spite of Elora's insistence that I fight on the fringes), but I was finally gaining headway in my investigation. Tomorrow, I'd figure out how to tell Elora what the Bright Queen's story had revealed.

Her father was a bright faerie.

But not tonight. Because we'd taken the day off from fighting, to rest up for our travels, there was only one thing left to do. Turning on my side, I buried my face in Elora's hair. She laughed. The sound was so soft, almost a sigh, and when she turned to me, she smiled.

Her eyes were so bright, I just … couldn't help myself. I knew my friends were sleeping nearby, but there was maybe twenty feet between us, and besides, there wasn't time to sneak off into the forest.

This had to happen now.

I started at her neck. I was still figuring out when to use my lips and when to use my tongue—I mean, what was the best, and where, but she didn't seem to mind either way. She was sighing, hands curling into my hair, pulling me closer. But I wasn't going to stay close, not tonight. Not like this.

Pushing onto my hands and knees, I started trailing my kisses down. First over her shoulder, then down her arm. It was awkward, not nearly as smooth as it was in the movies; but then, I bet actors got a hundred takes to get it right. Me, I just had to dive in and hope things worked out.

So I did.

I inched past her waist, which I didn't kiss because she was wearing clothes. After that came the skirt, and it was billowy and long. I thought maybe she'd stop me long before I got to my destination, but she didn't. Instead she lay there, turned onto her side, facing me, because it hurt to lay on her back. Maybe it always would. But I could improvise.

I was good at that.

I reached the end of her skirt, finally, after twenty years of searching. Or so it seemed, but still, she didn't stop me. She was following me with her eyes, this soft smile on her lips. And when my hand slipped under the hem of her skirt, she grinned.

Then I was gone, into the darkness. I could hear Elora murmuring softly as I slid my fingers past her ankle. Then a soft sigh when my lips trailed up her calf. I licked her playfully, just above the knee, and she gasped.

I had to stop for a minute to catch my breath. It wasn't because of what I was doing. It was *her*. She intoxicated me. My limbs felt shaky and my entire being strained to reach her. I thought I would die if she didn't touch me. I thought I would die if I didn't taste her.

One thing at a time.

My heart started to race as I neared the center of her. My

hands were heavy. My body was electric. I was running my tongue up the length of her thigh when the voice pulled me out of the darkness.

"Okay, seriously, I'm happy for you guys," Keegan said. "But for fuck's sake. There's forest all around."

I mumbled, "Sorry," crawling back out of Elora's skirt, and Keegan turned on his back, away from us. On the other side of the clearing, Kylie giggled, and Alexia shushed her. So I guess we weren't the only ones awake after all. Or maybe I just wasn't as stealthy as I thought.

I looked at Elora, and she reached out her hand.

I lifted her from the ground and we hurried into the surrounding forest, and suddenly we couldn't keep our laughter in anymore. That's the thing about getting some, or being about to get some, or giving some. It puts the world in perspective.

Nothing could ruin our mood right now.

We found a place relatively quickly. Or maybe we didn't try that hard. Her hands were on my waist, following me through the forest, and when I turned, she started kissing me, and that was that.

We weren't going any farther.

Her lips were sweet. How had I ever survived without her? I wove my hands into her hair as she pushed me against a tree. Her leg slid between mine, her knee bent, and I could feel her pressing against me. My hands dropped to her hips, pulling her closer. I wanted her to touch me, but I also wanted to finish what I'd started. Maybe both, if we were incredibly lucky.

We hadn't always been, but it seemed like things were changing. Or maybe we were changing things.

I lowered my lips to her ear, gripping her skirt in my hands. "Do you want me to . . . I mean, before we got . . . "

"Interrupted."

"Yeah. Do you want me to keep doing that?"

"I wouldn't say no to it."

"That isn't what I asked."

"Yes," she said after a minute, kissing my cheek. Her lips were soft, but her hands were holding me fiercely. Then they were sliding into the front of my pants, just barely.

"We should lay down," I said. Again, in the movies, people would just *do* this without having to say it. But here in the real world, we weren't mind readers, and I needed to be sure. However awkward it might make me feel.

Elora didn't seem to mind. She didn't even seem to notice my nervousness, but maybe she was just focused on the task at hand. Or maybe she was nervous, and that was making my fumbling seem normal.

Yeah, let's go with that.

I lowered myself to the ground and pulled her on top of me. She was laughing, her hair falling over me. I tucked it behind her ear. Still, it broke loose again, and I didn't care. I was breaking loose too. I started to lift her skirt.

"I could take it off," she said.

My first thought was: *Yes, please take everything off. Just stay naked all the time.*

My second thought was: *Anyone could walk in on us like this.*

And that would be . . . unfortunate. I mean, I was already attempting something I'd never done before, and feeling awkward about, well, *all* of my movements. Did I need to be caught in the act?

"It's okay," I said, slipping one hand under her skirt. She inhaled sharply, biting her lip.

God, she was gorgeous.

"Are you sure?" she asked, eyes fluttering closed as my other hand joined the first.

"Yeah, it's fine. This way, I'll be undercover."

She laughed, leaning into me. My hands inched up without even trying.

"Well," she said, "I can do *this*." For a minute, she sat still, and in spite of my intense desire to be touching her always, I stopped the movement. All around us, the world was growing dark. It wasn't like smoke, exactly. It was darker than that, like ink drifting through the air. It curled around the trunks of the trees, blocking us out from the rest of the world.

"Wow," I said, my thumb sliding over her skin. Such a small movement, but she cooed softly, bending down to kiss my lips.

"You're so amazing," I said.

She shook her head, pulling away. For the first time since the attack in the graveyard, I noticed the symbols pulsing on her arms. Black and curving, it looked like an ancient language had been carved into her soul and was trying to break free through her skin. Something about the Seelie Court's light had caused those symbols to fade, but now they were back.

"I am what I was born to be," Elora whispered.

"Like I said: amazing." I smiled and returned to the task at hand. Well, the task at tongue. Yeah, that task.

Lifting her skirt over my head, I said, "I still think it'd be better if I went undercover."

Elora laughed. I loved the sound of it. I hoped I could

always make her laugh like that. "Are you sure you don't want me to lie down?" she asked as I kissed up her thigh.

I shook my head, and she giggled. "I figured this would be more comfortable for you," I explained.

"That's ... probably ... true," she said, sighing in between words. Murmuring, "Mmm."

I thought I was going to die.

"Are you all right?" she asked as I shifted.

"Yeah, I'm fine," I said, guiding her closer to me. "There's just something under my back. I think it's a rock."

"I can move."

"No, you're fine." I reached behind my back. Pulling out the rock, I threw it into the forest. "You're perfect." Then I lifted myself to meet her.

16

ELORA

The universe exploded in a world of colors. I felt the way it must feel to exist inside the Aurora Borealis, with all those colors pouring down. The light, the beauty. The wonder.

It rushed over me and I crashed into it, a girl made of storms. Of waves. He was bringing me to life with his kisses, with that soft touch. His hands curved into the backs of my thighs, holding me close. We were two beings, and we were more.

We were the entire universe.

I wanted to touch his face then, to tuck his hair behind his ear, but it was difficult. That skirt had a mind of its own. Every time I tried to maneuver around it, I encountered another fold. I told myself to relax, to simply revel in the sweetness of what was happening. And it was sweet, like moonlight on the skin. Sweet like nectar dripping down your fingers.

I gasped, and a thrill went through me. All around us, the air was moving, inky black from the darkness I'd created, but also permeated by cool, glittering light. Light coming off of *him*, I realized, and shivered in the air. Now the colors were mingling, black bleeding into purple, and gold fading into white. There were violets and blues, dancing the way that we were dancing. My body. His lips.

Entangled, but not close enough. Those colors were blending, but they weren't becoming one, and for the first time, I wanted them to. Wanted to stop being Elora the singular entity, and become a part of the world. I'd still be myself when it was all over, still be able to stand on my own. But there was strength in collective power. Strength in trusting another.

Suddenly, I could feel the distance between us. Could feel the distance between our lips. The hands that weren't grasping each other. And I needed that right now. I needed him.

"Baby," I whispered, and I felt foolish saying it. Like I, myself, were a child, needing to be cared for. But I couldn't care anymore what I sounded like. What I looked like. All that mattered was how I felt. How we felt, together.

"I need you," I said.

Taylor retreated from the folds of my skirt. When he appeared in the dim light, his cheeks were pink and his hair was all mussed up.

I started to laugh. I loved him so much.

"I'm here," he said, sliding his thumb across his bottom lip.

"Yes, but I need you *here*." Adjusting a little, I scooted down until I was in his arms.

"Do you want to stop?" he asked. He looked a bit ... disappointed.

"No. I just wanted to be close to you."

He nodded, but I could tell he wasn't entirely convinced. Moments ago, we'd been *very* close. "Was I ... did it—"

"You were wonderful," I said, and he relaxed. After all, faeries can't lie. "I just missed you."

He nodded, looking into my eyes. "I'm right here."

"I think we should undress," I said, fingers stumbling over the button of his pants. Dresses were so much easier. You could simply pull them up or down.

He laughed, because I must've sounded very solemn. And he unbuttoned his pants for me. "Here. I have more practice."

"Oh, I imagine you do," I joked, and he blushed a deep red. It was beautiful.

Then he turned away from me, and it physically hurt. That distance, that inability to look at him—it felt like a chasm inside of me.

"Come back." When I kissed him at his collarbone, he moaned and turned to me. "And tell me about this practice," I added.

Now he was laughing, as I guided the pants over his hips. "Not a chance," he said, but I didn't care. Now we were both laughing, and then we were kissing.

Soon, we'd shed all our clothes.

"Can I touch you?" he asked, hand resting on my side. We were both on our sides now, facing each other.

"Do you really have to ask?"

"At this point, I feel like I should." He kissed my cheek, then trailed to my ear. "I mean, better safe than sorry."

"Then I should ask you?"

"Oh, never." He shook his head, and I giggled. "I mean, you can literally touch me anytime."

"Really?" I pressed my hand against his heart, slowly moving down.

"Oh yeah." He was nodding, his face a mask of serious-ness, but I could tell he was fighting a grin. "Just *whenever* you feel like it."

"All right then." I trailed my hand past his navel. "I'll remember that next time we're at dinner."

He laughed. "Let's cross that bridge when we come to it," he said. And then he didn't speak anymore, because I was doing what he asked. I slid my hand down. He slid his hand down, too. We were hands and lips and hearts, weaving together like vines. We were love and light and darkness. We became that which we'd always wanted, and always *were*, but never felt until now.

Whole within ourselves.

Unstoppable together.

———

In the morning, I awoke feeling stronger than ever. I could hover ten feet above the ground! Unfortunately, my efforts ended the same way they always did: with me slumped on the forest floor, gasping for breath, as pain radiated through my back.

I would not be able to fly during the battle, and it ter-rified me.

Still, the day had its gaiety. Taylor revealed his paint-ings and Kylie revealed the armor she'd been making: crude plates of iron hammered into intricate patterns and designs. Together, we fawned over it.

"I've never seen such detail," I gushed, my eyes trailing over the places my hands could not go. If I went my entire life without touching iron again it would be too soon. But Taylor touched the armor for me, as did Alexia.

Only Keegan kept his distance.

"I made emblems for everyone," Kylie explained, holding up each chestplate so that it caught in the light. "A lion for Taylor, a raven for Alexia. A sneaky fox for you," she said to her brother, trying to get him to join in the fun. "And a unicorn for me."

"Hey." Alexia grabbed Kylie's chestplate, examining the horned horse in the center. "Why do you get a unicorn? All I get is a raven."

"Ravens are very powerful beings," I interjected. "Back home, I had a train of them following me around. Telling me secrets."

"Actually, I think ravens are pretty cool," Alexia admitted. "But they're not *supernatural*."

"Why did you pick a unicorn for yourself?" Taylor asked.

"Because . . ." Kylie avoided our gaze.

"Because why?"

"Because I made them! So I got to pick." She was blushing.

"I think it suits you," I said. "Unicorns are pure of heart. Protective of those around them. I think it's perfect."

The blush worsened.

"In fact, I think they all suit you," I went on, to shift the focus from her. "Alexia's wisdom, Keegan's craftiness. Taylor's courage. His wildness." I stepped closer to him, touching his chin with my fingers.

"I have something for you, too," Kylie said, beaming up at me.

"What is it?" For a moment, I shuddered, thinking she'd

give me something made of iron. Even though it was an irrational thought, my body was unable to forget the way it had felt to have those iron shards slide into my skin in the graveyard.

But perhaps Kylie hadn't forgotten either. "Here," she said, procuring a crown from behind a patch of bushes. The obsidian frame was adorned with jewels that glittered like gold in the light. Perfect for…

"It reminds me of Naeve," Keegan said, and I expected Kylie to frown. But she didn't.

She smiled. "It is for Naeve," she said. "And it's for Elora. Let me explain."

I nodded, watching her turn the crown upside down. All along the bottom, thin slats appeared, but I did not know what they were.

Until Kylie flipped a little switch on the side, and spikes shot out of the bottom.

"Oh, Darkness. Is that…"

"Iron," she said, flipping the switch again. The spikes slid back into the crown, perfectly hidden. "Here."

I took it, worried the bottom of the base would burn my fingers. But it didn't. The spikes were perfectly concealed, until…

I flipped the switch, holding the crown by its tallest point. When the spikes shot out, I grinned. "This is brilliant."

Kylie grinned back. "I thought you would like it. And when you wear it into the battle, Naeve's going to be distracted by it."

"God, he'll be mesmerized," Taylor said. "I mean really, it

represents everything you have that he wants. Your mother's blood. Your mother's crown. Her love."

I laughed, because love was something I had never felt before him. Even with Illya, I had kept my distance, afraid she would turn on me. And she had.

"So I simply pretend to surrender," I said, as Taylor reached for the crown. "Then, as I hand it over to him, feigning submission, I flip the switch, and he presses those iron spikes into his head. He uses iron against *himself*. Oh, it's poetic."

"It's perfect," Taylor said, studying the crown. Turning it over in his hands, he touched one of the spikes, so softly. "Ow." A single drop of blood appeared.

I stepped up, willing to kiss his wound even though the iron in his blood would hurt me. But Taylor slipped the finger into his mouth, eager to protect me. He stared at me. I stared at him. Then my hands went into his hair.

"Oh God," Alexia drawled. "Surely you can refrain from jumping each other's bones for five more minutes. I want to showcase my talent."

"Ah yes, all the world's a stage," Keegan muttered from behind our backs. "And Alexia's the star—"

"What's the matter with you?" Kylie rounded on him. "Why are you being so mean?"

"I'm not." His tone was cold, almost emotionless. A volcano waiting to erupt.

"Don't you think we've done a good job?" she asked.

"I think you're all very talented."

"Then why are you acting like this? What is your problem?"

"*I'm* not acting like anything! All of you are acting like

we're having a fucking tea party. We're about to go to war. A war that doesn't have *anything* to do with us. And even that's fine, because I know it's important. But you shouldn't be acting like you won a prize."

Kylie stared up at him, eyes wide. It didn't take a genius to understand that he'd never spoken to her this way before.

"You could die," he said after a minute, his strong voice cracking. "And you don't even care."

"Of course I care. What do you think the armor is for? Why do you think I've been practicing riding horses? I've been working day and night to protect us and you haven't even—" She broke off, shaking her head.

"Say it."

"Nothing."

"Say it!"

"I didn't mean anything."

He shrugged. "You're all thinking it, you might as well say it. I'm useless and you have no need for me." He looked at me then, looked right through me. "But at least I'm not fooling myself. You're a bunch of humans going to war with monsters and you think you're going to survive this." He turned back to his sister. "You're a fool."

"Oh, right, I'm an idiot," she said. "I'm stupid and I'm helpless and I'm going to get myself killed. Thanks for saying what I always knew you thought. Thanks for spelling it out."

Taylor went to step between them, but hesitated. None of us knew what to do. They'd always been playful and sweet. Best friends. But war makes enemies of all of us.

"I don't think you're helpless," Keegan said. "But don't act like you can go up against some great evil and survive. Don't act like you're invincible."

"I don't think that."

"But you act like it. You act like nothing can hurt you because you don't *want* it to. That's not how the world works, is it?"

"You have the nerve to tell me that?" She wheeled forward, forcing him back. "You think I don't know that?"

"I think you need to be reminded."

"Well, here's a newsflash for you, Keegan. You know why nobody's found a job for you? Because they don't know who you are. Nobody does. Not me. Not our family. Not anyone."

He stared at her, dumbstruck.

"You don't let anyone in because you think they'll only see the bad in you. But they can't see the good in you, and that's why—"

"I don't have to listen to this."

"Yes you do," she shouted, because he was moving away, into the trees. "You have to hear it. If you keep shutting people out you'll always feel useless, because no one will know all the wonderful things about you."

But it was too late to placate him with compliments. Keegan was gone.

Now the wind had gone out of Kylie. Now she was crying. "Damn it," she said to her hands, covering her face so we couldn't see. "Why did he have to do this? Why did he have to take this away from me?"

I knelt beside her. Alexia did the same. Taylor stepped up behind us, and we all tried to console her, but we didn't know how to make things right. I think we were all coming to the same conclusion, realizing what Keegan had kept hidden: he didn't protect his sister so fiercely because she needed him. He did it because he needed her.

Now everyone knew it. I knew it, and she knew it, and he must've known she knew. There was no undoing this revelation, no putting back what had been pulled away. I could only hope that, in his desperation, Keegan wouldn't seek an audience with the Seelie Queen. She might allow what I had forbidden.

Then Keegan would find his purpose and seal his fate.

17

TAYLOR

Elora went off in search of the Queen, and I didn't try to stop her. I didn't want her to know that I'd overheard her talking with Keegan in the woods. Besides, at this point, finding him was the most important thing. So splitting up made sense.

Still, I didn't exactly love being away from her this close to the battle, and I found myself making up ridiculous scenarios as Kylie, Alexia, and I pushed through the underbrush. I envisioned the Queen covering Elora in vines until she looked like a part of the forest. I envisioned Elora sneaking into the Dark Court without me. The longer we looked, screaming Keegan's name, the more I was convinced things were about to get ugly.

And I was right. I just had the reasons completely wrong.

We came across Keegan on the outside of a thicket: something so covered with vines that it was impossible to see inside. We were on a bit of a hill, so I could see the location of our camp from up here. I could also see how close we'd come to the border between the Bright and Dark Courts.

I shuddered, wanting to get Keegan away from here as soon as possible.

I crouched down in front of him. "Hey. Let's get you out

of here," I said. I wasn't even sure why I was treating him like a frightened deer. Then I saw the look in his eyes, and I understood why my instinct was taking over. Keegan was sitting on the ground, his back up against a tree, and his eyes were completely *blank*.

"What's wrong with you?" Kylie asked, coming to a stop before him. She reached out for his hand, but he didn't take it. Probably for the first time in their lives, he didn't take it.

He didn't even acknowledge her.

He was rocking a little, and I started to get really freaked out. We had no idea what kind of creatures lurked in this forest. Sure, the Queen and her ladies seemed protective of us, but they were four faeries out of what? Thousands? Millions?

Probably thousands, at this point, I thought as Alexia started poking around the space. *Because of human expansion. Because of human destructiveness.*

Which meant they had a right to be upset with us, which meant we never should have trusted them in the first place. Yeah, the longer Keegan went without saying a word, the worse I felt about this entire place. We'd turned our backs for one second, and something had gotten ahold of him.

But what?

Kylie reached down to brush the slick sheen from Keegan's forehead, and he jerked away. When he moaned, I actually jumped, because his mouth hadn't even shifted. Then I realized why: *he* wasn't moaning. The moaning was coming from inside the circle of trees.

Kylie and I looked at each other. Alexia was already circling around the back and couldn't be seen.

"I'm going in," we said at the same time.

"No, you stay here, and I'll check it out," I said.

Kylie shook her head. When it came down to it, she was as stubborn as me.

"Fine," I said, helping her out of her chair. Then I knelt down and crawled under a patch of vines. I could feel them scraping against my back, drawing blood with the slightest bit of effort. When all was said and done, my clothes would be torn to shreds.

Thanks a lot, Seelie Court.

Still, I'd had it pretty good since I'd arrived. I mean, things could've been worse. For example, I could've been tied to a tree by my wrists, half-starved and half-clothed, moaning like I hadn't moved in weeks.

I could've been like him.

"Brad?"

I stepped up to him slowly. I thought maybe if I moved slowly enough, he'd disappear before my eyes like a mirage. Like a simple creation of smoke and mirrors, here one minute and gone the next. A glamour.

Not a person, made up of flesh and blood.

A lot of blood, I thought, my eyes trailing to his wrists. Thin red lines crept down his arms. The blood was dried, which meant he hadn't been struggling in a while. God, had he been here the *entire* time?

"Who did this to you?" I asked, while Kylie called to me from the outside. I actually considered ignoring her. Sure, she'd be mad, but she'd be spared the sight of … this. I wished I'd been spared. I already wanted to gouge out my eyes.

"Taylor? Can you pull me through? This branch is sticking in my back."

I could see Kylie's hand poking through the branches. For a second I was frozen. Trapped between staring at Brad, still in the black jeans he'd worn to the prom, and Kylie's hand, poking through the branches into hell.

"Can you hear me?" I whispered to him.

He wouldn't look at me. Wouldn't talk to me. But he was talking to himself, mumbling like the air was filled with faeries. And it wasn't, this time.

"*Taylor?*" Kylie called.

"Fuck." I knelt down and took hold of her hands. Pulling her through to the other side, I didn't even say anything as I set her beside a tree, three feet from Brad. I just waited for her to see.

"What took you so long?" she asked. "And where did Alexia—"

She froze, trailing off in mid-sentence. Her eyes fell over the mess that was Brad. The body that remained of him. I mean, sure, he was alive, but how much now?

"What have they done to him?" Kylie breathed.

I shook my head, then realized she couldn't read my thoughts. Still, speaking was taking an incredible amount of effort. My tongue felt heavy. All of me did. "I don't know."

"Who—"

"I don't know."

Kylie pushed a hand through her hair, but it fell right back in her face. It was probably better that way. Better to see the world through dirty lenses, through clouds, through smoke.

Better not to see it at all.

"I didn't think Faerie would be like this," she said, so softly, as she stared at Brad. Her greatest tormentor, back home. The boy who'd taunted her and drugged her and tried to photograph her naked.

At least photograph her.

When Kylie reached up to set Brad free, the word just slipped out of my mouth: "Wait."

She turned, hand on the vines. "What?" she asked. "God, I should've brought one of my knives."

"I have to ask you something," I said. From the other side of the thicket, Alexia was calling, "How did you guys get in?" but we could barely hear her, and it didn't matter anymore. The only people in this space were the people who were supposed to be in this space. Just me, Kylie, and the boy who'd made her life a living hell. The boy who'd made my life hell too, before Elora came along and convinced us to take him down.

I lowered my voice. "That night you went over to Brad's ... "

Kylie huffed, struggling to slice the vines with her fingernails. "Taylor, I really don't want to talk about this right now."

"I need to talk about it right now," I said as Brad squirmed. I thought maybe he could tell we were talking about him but couldn't find the words to respond.

I closed my eyes, blocking out the sight of him.

"Okay, well, I guess I'll just stay with Keegan," Alexia called from another dimension. That's how it felt, like she was in a made-up world and we were in the real one, where terrible things happened for no reason. Unless ...

"You told us Brad wanted to take your picture," I said, keeping the rest to myself. How Brad had told everyone at school that Kylie had "boy and girl parts," because she was bi. How the photo was going to "prove" it.

The first vine broke free, and Kylie turned to look at me. "So?"

"So, is that really true?" I asked, and she narrowed her eyes. I'd never seen her look so mad before. "I mean, is that *all* he did? I'm not questioning that he would do that to you. I know he would. But I always thought..." Again, I had to look away from him in order to say these things. I had to separate the guy in front of me from the guy he'd been. "I just wondered if maybe he'd tried to do something more."

Kylie stared at me a long minute, her hand frozen in the air. She'd managed to slice the second vine, and now she'd only have to pull on it to set him free.

But should he be free?

I hated myself for thinking it, but I couldn't get away from this thought that if Brad had tried to do more than take her picture, if he'd tried to touch her, or...

"What are you doing, Taylor?" Kylie was staring into my eyes, and hers were so bright. Like she could see into the depths of me. See the darkness there.

"I just need to know," I said softly.

"Because why? Because then you'll feel justified in leaving him here? Are you really using me as an excuse for that?"

"No! I wasn't—"

"Yes you are." She shook her head in disgust. "You did the same thing back home. You used what Brad did to me, or tried to do, as an excuse to hurt him, but you want to know the truth of it? *You wanted to hurt him all along.* Long before I came into your life, you hated him, like so many people did, but you wouldn't retaliate."

"Maybe that's true. But—"

"Maybe you didn't think you were worth the effort. Maybe you even thought he was right to torment you."

"Kylie…" I'd never heard her talk like this. It scared me. But here we were, three feet from a boy being kept as a slave, and I was trying to justify it. Maybe it was the only way to keep myself from going completely insane. I needed to believe there was some reason for all of this, that the universe was exacting its vengeance, unleashing karma on the boy who'd hurt so many people. Because if it wasn't, if life was just one bad thing happening after another, one more person hurting someone for *no reason*, who could live in a world like that?

Who could *fight* for a world like that without contributing to the problem? Without perpetuating it?

"You know I'm right," Kylie said, still staring into my eyes. "Until I came along, you mostly just put up with his abuse. You told yourself it was better to not fight back, because it would only get worse. Trust me, I know the mentality." She reached out to touch my arm. "But do not convince yourself that hurting someone for me makes it okay. Because if he did something to me… if he hurt me, then it already happened. You didn't stop it, and he didn't stop it. It's over. That moment is *gone*. Do you understand?"

I slid my hands over my face, trying to hold myself together that way. "No. I don't. Are you saying something *did* happen?"

She shook her head. "I'm saying that if it *had*, you didn't protect me, or save me, or whatever you think I needed at the time. So if you go after him after the fact, you aren't doing it for me. You're doing it to appease your own guilt, and using me as an excuse. And I'm not going to be used for that, or anything."

She moved back from the vines, and from Brad. One of his wrists was still tied in place. "So do what you're going to do, Taylor. But don't use me as an excuse."

She watched me, and Brad watched me too, his eyes struggling to stay on my face. Barely coherent, but not entirely gone.

We could still save him, I thought, and relief rushed over me. I couldn't even explain it to myself. I'd hated Brad for so long. But I guess the truth of it was, I didn't want to hurt him the way he'd hurt us. I'd just wanted him *gone*.

No, I'd wanted him to not be cruel in the first place. To choose to do the right thing, instead of putting more evil into the world.

In one swift movement, I unsnapped the vine that held him.

"I loosened it for you," Kylie said with a smile.

I smiled back, but it was shaky. Brad was just slumped there, staring at his wrists. I crouched in front of him. "Who did this to you?"

He narrowed his eyes, like he could hear me but I wasn't speaking the right language. "*Taylor*," he said finally.

I jerked back, affronted. "No. I'm Taylor."

Brad started to laugh. "No, no, no," he said, shaking his head.

"What's going on?" Kylie asked.

"I don't know." I peered at Brad. "Who tied you up? Was it the Queen? Tall, curvy, kind of … tree-like?"

"Like a mother oak," Kylie supplied. "But also a person."

"Taylor," Brad said.

"What about the faerie with twigs for teeth? She looks like she sprouted up from the ground? Kinda scary looking?" I asked.

"I know the name," Brad murmured. "Taylor. Taylor. Taylor."

"We need to get him out of here," Kylie said. "He needs help."

"That's the thing," I said, as Brad poked at his wrists. "We don't know who can help him, because we don't know who did this to him. I don't even think he can walk."

At that, Brad started shifting his legs, just a little. Bending his knees, as if testing them.

"What about horns? Did she have horns?" Kylie said, but I could tell she was just humoring me. She probably thought I was a fool for thinking Brad would tell us anything.

Brad shook his head.

"Was it even a *she*?" I asked.

Brad huffed at that.

"Most of the faeries here are girls," Kylie said. "I mean, Keegan found some satyrs. But I haven't seen many."

"Maybe the Queen prefers girls in her court."

"Maybe the Queen prefers girls."

She let the statement hang, and I couldn't help but think of the Bright Queen's story. After all, Naiad and Dryad had been "close" for many years. Maybe the Bright Queen hated the Dark Lady because Elora's mother had rejected her. Possibly for Elora's father.

Then again, if the Bright Queen had set Elora's parents up, that didn't make sense. Unless she and the Dark Lady had been estranged for so long…

I shook my head, telling myself it wasn't important. But behind all the pondering, a single thought floated into my head: if the Bright Queen did prefer girls, she wasn't keeping me to be her lover.

Me *or* Brad. Which meant someone else must've done this to him.

"Taylor, we have to go," Kylie said as Alexia's hand appeared under the brambles. "We'll get Elora, and not tell anyone else until he's taken care of."

The thought of Elora tending to Brad made me feel sick. But the thought of abandoning him here made me feel sicker. Just as we were about to slip back under the branches, I noticed a streak in his hair that didn't match the rest. It looked *blond*.

I turned, my heart pounding. "There's one more faerie we should ask him about," I said. The faerie who'd been the nicest to me. The one who'd promised to free me from the Bright Queen's grasp. But how could she, unless she had someone to take my place?

"Her wings are like a dragonfly's, but bigger," I said.

Brad's head snapped up.

"She wears this tight green dress that looks like it's *clinging* to her."

He started to shake. I thought he might pass out. We needed to get him some food.

Still, I had one last description. "Her hair is made of light. I mean, it looks like it's made of light. I don't know for certain ... Brad?"

"*Taylor.*" He stumbled to his feet. I hadn't even expected him to sit up. But now he was standing, taking one shaky step. His eyes were so wide, I thought they would fall out of his head. "I *know* the *name.*"

"Is it Maya de Lyre?" I asked. "Is that the name?"

Brad took one look at me and bolted. He moved so fast, I wouldn't have believed it if I hadn't seen it. But I guess when you're scared for your life, and your freedom, you'll do anything to get away. You'll push your body to its limit. Crawl under thorny vines.

I heard Alexia say, "Ow! Holy shit." Then, "Where did *you* come from?"

And then she didn't say anything, because Brad must've run past her, into the forest. I could hear him heading west.

I hoped I was wrong about that.

"We have to go," I said to Kylie. She nodded, eyes wide. And together, we crawled out of the thicket, me first, and her on my heels. I helped her back into her chair.

"What the hell just happened?" Alexia said as Keegan pushed himself to his knees. "Did I just imagine that?"

Keegan said, "No. No, that happened." He still looked dazed, but he sounded coherent.

"I think he's heading to the border," I said, dread washing over me like darkness.

"Let's go." Alexia nodded at me. "You can fill me in on the details after we've saved his ass."

We bolted through the trees. Keegan and Kylie followed

more slowly, her chair weaving around the rocks, and his legs stumbling as he tried to get them to work.

And yet, Brad manages to race. I couldn't understand it. Then again, I hadn't been held captive for weeks, bound and starved and God knew what else. I found myself hoping that Maya de Lyre had *only* kept him like a pet. It was a ridiculous thought to have, but things could've been worse.

They were about to get worse, still. Brad wasn't just nearing the border. He'd reached it. Now dark hands were beckoning to him, calling him into the darkness. Calling him into the place where the light couldn't hurt him.

"Don't do it," I yelled, and Brad's head snapped back to me. He smiled, like I was so stupid. Like I didn't know anything. As he crossed over the border, those hands surrounded his body. They clawed and reached and scratched. In one second, he'd been swallowed by the darkness.

"Shit, shit, shit," Alexia cursed as she ran. "What is he thinking?"

He's thinking the bright faeries won't follow him there, I thought, struggling for breath as we neared the border. Behind us, I could hear Kylie and Keegan crashing through the trees. None of us was trying to be quiet.

"Stop," I called as we neared the darkness. Alexia screeched to a halt, already in front of me. A short distance away.

So why was my heart in my throat?

"He's gone," I said, hunching over and taking big, heaving breaths. "We need Elora. She'll know how to get him back."

"No," Alexia said, her hand reaching. Not toward *me*, but toward the darkness that hovered along the border like a living entity.

"No? Alexia—"

She turned to me, eyes alight with fire. She looked ravenous, the way I'd felt when I'd first met Elora. The way I *still* felt every time I looked at Elora. "If they keep him, it will be my fault."

"Why would it be your fault?" I asked, in barely a whisper. I wanted to grab Alexia, but I thought it might make her bolt. I felt like the first responder on a bridge where there's a jumper.

And in a way, I was.

"Because I knew what Lora was doing," she said, using the name Elora had given us back home. "I knew she was taking him and I didn't stop her."

"It's okay."

Alexia shook her head, and she couldn't stop shaking. "I *wanted* her to take him. I wanted him out of our lives."

"We all hated Brad," I said, taking a single step. "We all wanted..." But I couldn't say it, not now. "You *can't* go in there."

"I can't stay," Alexia said, swaying a little. She lurched forward, and Kylie screamed.

I shot toward the border. But Alexia was too close to it; two more steps, and she'd crossed over to the other side. We all waited with bated breath for the hands.

This time, they brought their bodies with them. It was like a wave of darkness rising up from the ocean. First, a shadow danced and twisted. Then another joined it, and then a third. Soon Alexia was surrounded, and we could see the hands first—why, always, with the hands first?—and then the wave crested.

Then it crashed.

Alexia screamed, a deep, guttural sound, like crows were feasting on her entrails. Then, as if intuiting my fears, the wave contorted, separating into a swarm. A swarm of crows, a swarm of bees. Then Alexia was screaming, and the bees were stinging and the crows were diving, and God, I almost wished she'd stop screaming, because then it would be over.

Back on our side of the world—that is, back in the Seelie Court, where things like that didn't happen, or couldn't happen, or hadn't happened yet—a cloud of self-loathing descended over us all. Even Kylie, who was scrabbling against her brother's grip, had taken to attacking him with nails rather than fists. All of us wanted to help Alexia, and none of us did.

Even when the faces came, grinning with impossibly long, impossibly sharp teeth, we didn't move. Frozen by fear, or self-preservation, we reached for each other's hands, Keegan and I, with Kylie wedged awkwardly between us. And we watched an entire person disappear into the darkness.

Once, in the human world, I'd watched Elora disappear into the darkness, but she'd only been using glamour to make herself blend in with the night. This was real. Alexia had been surrounded. Tortured. Now the darkness lifted her up and carried her away.

"*No!*" Kylie howled, a final cry, but her strength was gone. She glared up at Keegan with so much hatred, I wondered if he'd ever get over it.

I wondered if either of them would. And then I couldn't wonder anymore, because Elora was charging out of the forest behind us. "What happened?" she asked, eyes wild.

"They took her," Kylie screamed. "They took Alexia.

Please. We have to go after her." She was struggling against Keegan so much, she almost broke free. But he grabbed her around the waist and wouldn't let her go. I thought for a minute she might fling herself from his grip and crawl into the Dark Court if she had to. I could imagine her climbing the mountain that way, doing whatever it took to get Alexia back.

"Why was she in there?" Elora asked, kneeling in front of Kylie.

"She went after Brad." I ran a hand through my hair. I felt like my brain was going to fall out. But then the dark faeries would just steal that too.

Elora's head whipped up. "*Brad?*"

"They were keeping him as a slave," Kylie said, staring out into the darkness. It called to her now, just as it had called to Alexia.

But I wouldn't let it hurt her.

"When we let him go, he bolted, and Alexia—" Kylie choked on the words, doubling over. "She tried to save him. The darkness *swallowed* her."

"It's a spell." Elora shook softly as she touched Kylie's hand. "She'll be taken up to the palace. But we can get her back."

"We *will* get her back," I promised. "We'll get them both back. We just need a plan."

"I don't think so," a cool, calculating voice said. A low voice. The voice of a queen.

I turned to face her. "You can't stop us. Not after we've seen who the bright faeries really are. How you really treat humans."

"And what, exactly, are you going to do?" The Bright Queen asked. Her gown was trailing on the ground behind her, pulling vines and leaves as it went. Or maybe they were growing out of it. For a second, I was afraid she would use the entire forest to contain us. I could see it rising up around us the way the darkness had risen up around Brad. Around Alexia.

I took a step back. "Whatever it takes to save the person you were keeping as a slave."

The Queen's eyes widened, and her cheeks flushed like she'd been slapped. But it was all an act. All of this was an illusion.

This whole stupid Court.

It is beautifully inviting, but it does not do what you expect.

Why hadn't I listened to Elora? All this time, I'd been warning my friends that there were no "good faeries." Still, I'd wanted to believe it. Wanted to believe in goodness *somewhere*.

I turned to Elora and saw it. I turned to Keegan and Kylie and remembered myself, and my purpose.

"We're going to the Dark Court," I said. "We're going to clean up your mess."

"Is that so?" the Bright Queen asked. I hadn't noticed before, but her brown skin was flecked with gold. Her green dress shimmered like crushed-up leaves had fallen over it. She wasn't simply the queen of this forest, she was a part of it. The *heart* of it. "And you thought I would let you leave? Undo all that I have done? All the tireless work, for years—"

"What?" Now she was babbling. And honestly, I didn't have the patience. "Look, you're off your rocker. I get it. But we're not, and we have a job to do, so if you don't mind … "

I'd taken three steps when her voice hit my back. But unlike a wave, it didn't knock me down. It held me in place.

"By the power of your name, I command you to stay."

18

ELORA

I waited for Taylor to take another step. To laugh. To call the Queen an idiot. Sure, she might've lashed out, but that would have been better than this. Anything would have been better than this.

"No." I turned to look at him. I turned, and felt I was looking at a corpse. A body preserved in a casket. "You didn't."

"I had to," Taylor said, so casually, as if there were no thought required. As if offering up his name to the Seelie Queen had been a natural thing to do. As if giving one's freedom away did not go against the very laws of nature. And now, knowing what she'd done to Brad, I felt so sick I couldn't even speak. I couldn't move.

Together we stood, immobilized. Together, with a world between us.

"Why?" I managed, finally closing the gap. Taking his hands, looking into his eyes. Doing anything to convince myself he was still mine.

No, I thought, shaking myself. *Still his own,* to offer his time to me. His lips. His love.

"I needed to save your life," he said, and again, it sounded so simple. Perhaps to him it was. Perhaps he'd simply do anything to protect me, the way I'd done everything to protect him. Convinced myself the Queen wanted a wicked mortal, instead of a sweet one. Lured Brad into these wretched lands. Allowed the Queen to ... to ...

Again, I felt sick and clamped a hand over my mouth. And Taylor put his arms around me, as only his legs were unable to move. I had a crazy thought, then, of throwing him over my shoulder. Sure, the Queen could stop him, but she couldn't stop me.

Then I looked up at the leaves growing out of her hair and remembered who I was dealing with. Remembered why I'd agreed to solve the riddle she'd given me in the first place. I was not strong enough to stand against my mother, a great Queen of Faerie, and win. Now, this great Queen of Faerie loomed over me, taunting my limitations. Taking away the one person who'd ever loved me unconditionally.

"Just tell me why," I entreated. "Why did you ask for a young leader of men if you wanted a toy? Why did you only pretend to send Brad home? This makes no sense!"

"Because you do not understand the riddle yet."

"The riddle is completed! You have what you wanted, and then some. I was simply the body you used to get it. And isn't that what it's always been about for you? A body to do your bidding in the mortal world? Another to do your bidding here? And even that wasn't enough." I turned toward the Dark Court. "You needed yet *another* to fulfill your sick, twisted—"

The Queen struck me across the face. It happened so fast, like a bolt of lightning striking a branch. I fell to my knees.

But I would not bow to her, or any Queen of Faerie. I was

done playing their games. "Release him," I said, rising to my feet.

"Fine. You may walk again, sweetness," the Queen said to Taylor. "As long as you do not cross over any border."

Any border to the Dark Court. Any border to the human world.

Clever little wretch.

"He does not belong to you," I insisted. "Let him go completely."

The Bright Queen shook her head. "Why?" she asked. "So you can bring him into your mother's court? Lead him proudly to death, or dismemberment? Let your mother make an *example* out of the boy who loves you?"

"Oh, Darkness forbid she should make an example," I spat. "Darkness forbid she should tie him up and torture him. Only you're allowed to do that?"

The Queen scowled, and her three ladies slid out of the forest. Together, they flanked her, as if they were going into battle at her back. And perhaps they were. Perhaps this was war, one more battle I hadn't anticipated. Would life always be this way? Beginning to trust, only to find myself tricked and betrayed? Again?

I opened my mouth to attack them, but Kylie beat me to it. "You!" she shrieked, wheeling toward Maya de Lyre. "You sick, psycho—"

"Whoa, there," Keegan said, struggling to hold her back. But I could tell he was exhausted, and Kylie was just getting started.

"This is your fault!" she screamed as Maya de Lyre reared back. "You're the reason she's gone."

The faerie's eyes went wide, and her body flashed as if she might set the place on fire. Still, she wasn't the one we needed to worry about here.

The Bright Queen turned, vines curling out of her hands. "What did you do?" she whispered, soft as a dragon's breath. Quiet as smoke.

"I . . ." Maya de Lyre stammered, trying to step back into the forest. The trees slid together to keep her from passing.

"I told you to take him home," the Queen said.

"But you didn't say *his* home, Lady. So I took him to mine." Maya de Lyre smiled, the tiniest bit. That wicked, glittering wretch nearly grinned as she thought about what she'd done to Brad.

I really was going to be sick. "You expect us to believe you didn't know about this?" I asked the Queen, swallowing back bile. Swallowing back anger and fear and disgust.

"Actually, I believe it," Taylor said.

I turned to face him. "Why?"

"Because Maya de Lyre's been helping me all along," he said, eyeing the royal songstress. "When no one was watching. When we were alone."

"Has she now?" This time, when the Queen exhaled, a small trickle of fire slipped out of her lips. No, not fire. Light. Illuminating, scalding light. The kind that could burn away the forest and leave only the skeletons of trees behind.

"She gave me weapons," Taylor said. "She wanted me to fight."

"Did she?" I asked, narrowing my eyes. "Or did she lead you to believe that without actually *saying* it?"

"I . . . I don't remember," he said softly. "It feels like forever ago. But why would she pretend to help me? Why would she give me weapons, if..."

Maya de Lyre said nothing, but her gaze trickled across the clearing. It settled on *me*. This time, she didn't smile.

"*No*," Taylor breathed, and he looked deflated. Like all the air had gone out of him. "You were trying to break us up! That way, Elora would storm off to the Dark Court, and you could have me for yourself."

I thought of that moment when, returning from the border, I'd seen the humans playing soldier with the bright faeries. I'd been furious until I realized they were fighting for me. They weren't reckless, and they weren't helpless.

They were brave.

"I wanted to keep you safe," Maya de Lyre said, frowning at Taylor. Her hands were curling in on themselves, like she wanted to grab him and run.

"No, you wanted to keep me captive, like you were keeping Brad." He looked up, at the Queen. "She was going to secretly trade me for him. She was *glamouring* him to look like me. I didn't know until I saw—"

"Is this true?" the Queen demanded, looming over the royal songstress. "You kept a mortal captive for these purposes?"

Maya de Lyre cowered under her gaze. "I never touched him," she said. "Not in the way you think. I only fed him, and slept by his side." Her eyes trailed to the forest. To the place where Brad had been kept. "It was just one human! You were going to keep *four*. It wasn't fair—"

"*Enough*," the Bright Queen shouted, and it shook the trees. "Did you intend to take this mortal for yourself?" She pointed to Taylor.

Maya de Lyre was still staring into the forest. "I never touched him," she said again. "Not in the way you think. I knew it was important to you—you said never to touch them like that, unless they asked." She tilted her head, a bird searching for prey. "Then I met the offering, and he was just so *sweet*, like a succulent peach. I could've sunk my teeth into him—"

"You're insane," Taylor spat.

Maya de Lyre grinned. "We're *all* insane, pretty mortal. All faeries. All humans. All of us killing each other, and making love in between, to convince ourselves it's worth it. This destruction of the natural world. This destruction of the body. The soul." She turned to the Queen. "I'm ready to be done. You've given me nothing but empty promises and empty beds."

"I never promised you my bed," said the Queen.

"No, why would you? Why would you promise your bed to anyone? No one can measure up to your precious Vi—"

"*Stop.*"

"I will not stop. You cannot make me do anything. I renounce my queen."

"Maya de Lyre—"

"That is *not* my *name*," the faerie said, and she was crying. "I am not my voice. I am not my body. Do it now, *please*."

"As you wish," the Queen said softly. "You have bound a mortal against his will. May the punishment fit the crime."

She reached out her fingers, releasing a single, slithering vine. It wrapped itself around her longtime servant, sprouting limb after limb like ivy suffocating a tree. For one quiet moment, I thought it would end like this. Softly. Peacefully. Then those vines constricted, and Maya de Lyre began to scream. Faster and faster they wrapped around her, until they had covered her completely.

Then, just as quickly, it was over, and she was silent. Only a wild, twisting bramble remained.

"It is done," the Seelie Queen said. "She will remain bound until the boy she stole takes his final breath. You are safe—"

"Safe?" Taylor said, trembling. His face had gone white. "We'll never be safe here."

"We'll never be safe again," Keegan said. "Not as long as you keep trying to control us and manipulate everything."

"And what would you have me do?" the Queen asked, rounding on him. "Hurl you into danger? Somehow convince myself you will survive?"

"We've been practicing for weeks," Kylie broke in. "We can ride into battle. Hide in the trees."

"*They've* been practicing for *centuries*," the Queen said in reply. Her gaze shifted to the darkness.

"I don't care. I'm getting my girlfriend back," Kylie said.

For a moment, I thought the Queen was actually considering her words. Her face softened as she looked at Kylie. There was something missing here, some piece of the puzzle I hadn't found yet. The Queen seemed to genuinely want the humans to be happy, and yet she tried to contain them.

What game was she playing?

"You disappoint me, princess," she said finally. "I thought you, of all people, would forbid them from entering this battle. After the graveyard, after seeing what your people can do … "

"I know what my people can do. I am one of them," I said, and it shocked her to hear me speak of myself this way. It shocked the humans, too, but what could I do? Pretend I was different? I was not a mortal. And I'd never be a bright faerie.

I didn't want to be.

"I believed you would do whatever it took to protect them," the Queen scolded.

"I would. But this isn't my decision. I love them, but I do not own them. Can you say the same?"

Again, the Queen hesitated. I thought, for an instant, that we might win. But as the smile spread over her face, a cold, sick feeling unfurled in my stomach.

"Perhaps you are right," she said. "Perhaps I have been unfair to the humans, trying to keep them safe by keeping them contained. But if I am to allow my mortal offering to enter the battle, you must do something for me."

"What is it?" I asked, my heart fluttering in my chest. First fluttering, then thundering, then silent as the Queen spoke her request:

"Admit to me the risk you're putting him in. Admit that bringing him into the Dark Court could mean handing him over to the Unseelie Queen. Admit that you are leading him into your mother's lands, and possibly your mother's hands, and you are free to go."

My heart sank to my knees. For I couldn't admit it. I couldn't lie, but I couldn't admit that it was the truth. Because if it was the truth, I couldn't bring Taylor into the Dark Court. Couldn't seal his fate like that.

And the Bright Queen knew it. Oh, she was crafty.

But so were the humans. For a moment, they were whispering together, and then Taylor leaned in and told me a secret about shackles and offerings. The solution to this riddle.

"All right," I said, my heart springing to life once again. "If I bring Taylor into the Dark Court, I might as well hand him over to my mother."

And that's exactly what I'm going to do.

19

TAYLOR

That night, Elora bound my wrists and led me through the forest. But these weren't breakable vines, like Maya de Lyre had used on Brad. These were metal shackles, with thick chain links between them. The kind of thing dark faeries just kept on hand, apparently.

Or maybe the Bright Queen had them. I didn't ask, because I didn't really want to know. I just held out my arms and let them close around my wrists. And my friends did the same, like good little humans. We were going to make such wonderful gifts for the Unseelie Queen!

Don't worry, I hadn't lost my mind. I was just playing the part that was required of me. Because the Bright Queen was right: we couldn't just sneak into the Unseelie Court and take back what had been stolen.

We'd have to be stolen too.

So here's how it went: Elora bound us with shackles and led us, like animals, to the border between the courts. Keegan and I went on foot, and Kylie rode a pretty golden mare that she'd bonded with over the past few days. When we reached the border, we were stopped by a host of wicked-looking things. There was a faerie in rusting armor with long, silvery hair and a lady scarecrow that could give a guy nightmares for centuries. There was a giantess with an eerie rabbit's head, and a faerie with a body like a frog sitting on her shoulder. A lady in a moth-eaten dress sneered down at us, her skin scarred and pockmarked beneath the red velvet. But more horrifying than anything was the woman whose head was *birthing* ravens. Her entire body was black, her dress was black, her gloves were black. Even her umbrella was black. Or maybe it was a parasol—you know, that thing Victorian ladies used to keep the sun off their pasty skin. The air around her was inky black, like her body was bleeding into the night, and birds peeled away from her face, disappearing into the sky. Birds that were half feather and half smoke. Their eyes were a glowing red, and even after they were gone I could still see them.

When I closed my eyes, I could still see them.

Fantastic, I thought as Elora tugged us toward them, her dress swirling around her feet in a deep shade of red. She'd glamoured it before we'd left the Seelie Forest.

"I believe an offering was requested?" she said to the dark faeries, dipping her head. She wasn't wearing Kylie's crown yet, but she'd tied it to her waist, along with my sword. The armor was floating behind us in an enchanted bag.

"And you're giving them to us?" the faerie in armor said. Her face was beautiful, the kind of face men killed for in fairy tales, but those eyes, man . . . they looked haunted. Like she'd lived a thousand years and seen a thousand evils.

Human evils, I thought, and took a step back.

Meanwhile, Elora's face betrayed nothing. How did she do

that? For a second, I wished I had the ability to hide what I was feeling.

Then I remembered there was value in letting people see you.

"I am not giving *you* anything," Elora said. "I am leading them through my mother's lands, up to her palace..."

I'm not sure why she said it like that. Not *our* lands. Not even *the Unseelie Court.* But maybe she was reminding them that they weren't free yet, and they needed her to make this land *theirs.*

"In chains," the faerie said, smiling hungrily as she eyed my wrists. *Oh, goody,* I thought, *another psychopath who likes to see us tied up.* "Have you come to your senses then? Seen humans for the filth that they are?"

Elora grinned. It was eerie and otherworldly and entirely *fey.* It reminded me of the differences between us, which weren't really obvious until her people were around. "Either that," she said, teeth glinting in the moonlight, "or they have offered themselves up willingly so that I might return home."

The silver-haired faerie scoffed, looking at us with undisguised hatred. "Mortals, offering themselves up to the darkness? Allowing themselves to be chained?"

Elora shrugged, all teenager again. "I daresay stranger things have happened. But either way, you're getting what you wanted. These mortals are entering the Dark Court. And once I give them to my mother, she will have no choice but to trust me again."

The faerie eyed her warily, but there was respect in her gaze. "What game are you playing?"

"A good one." Elora laughed, those eyes twinkling with mischief. "Would you like to play with me?"

Who wouldn't?

The faerie stared at her for a minute, like she was trying to see into Elora's soul. Finally, she stepped aside. "The princess has returned," she announced, and the servants cheered. Wings opened. Talons curled. I thought someone might slit their wrists right there so they could all dance in the blood. But there would be no veins opened here, not so close to the Seelie Court. If someone was going to bleed, it was going to happen at the Unseelie Castle.

And it was probably going to be me.

I shuddered, and Elora turned back like she'd felt it. For a second, we were the only ones in the forest. I remembered our first day at school together, the way it had felt like we were standing in a single pool of light. Now darkness surrounded us, but it had the same effect. We were the only people in the world, and we were having a conversation without words. She studied my face. I nodded, just enough for her to see it. I thought, *there's no going back now. Not if I'm going to become the man I've always wanted to be. The one who can defend the people he loves. The one who can defend himself.*

Elora watched me carefully. Then she smiled. "Let us venture, then."

Together, we walked from the light into the darkness. A host of winged faeries followed at our backs. Still, as long as they kept a respectable distance, I could stay close to their princess without getting attacked.

So I did. I walked at her side as we entered the darkness. The Unseelie Forest didn't reveal itself the way the Seelie Forest had. But then, that's the nature of darkness. It doesn't show you its monsters; instead, you have to check around every corner, constantly looking over your shoulder. And hey, there might be no monster at all.

Or they might be everywhere.

And so we walked, like kids afraid of their closets, through brambles that whipped away their vines to let us pass. All the trees were black, but they came in two forms: some were fat, with gnarled branches that looked like hands, and others were so tall, their tips impaled the sky. So, on top of any creatures that lurked in the forest, we had to be wary of trees that might stab us, or snatch us up.

Well played, Unseelie Forest.

I tried to joke with myself to keep from freaking out. Keegan was doing the same thing. He kept looking at all the dark places, all the sharp edges, and whistling, saying, "*Subtle.*" Eventually, we all started doing it, and laughing, even though our skin was crawling. At one point, Keegan took my hand, and I took Kylie's, and we walked together, the three of us, not shackled by fear or hate but bound by love.

Soon the forest was dotted with red as tiny berries peeked out of the branches. Blossoming before our eyes, they grew into red flowers that dropped petals onto the ground. It looked like the forest was bleeding.

"Subtle," Keegan and I said together. He turned to me and grinned.

Now those flowers were changing, giving way to fat, glowing fruits, almost identical to the ones we'd been drugged with in the Seelie Court, except these ones were red.

Of course, I thought, shaking my head. I hardly even noticed when my hand reached up and plucked one from a tree. It was like something was acting for me, or maybe some deep, instinctual part of me was responding without my knowledge. I'd almost lifted the fruit to my lips when Elora smacked it out of my hand.

"Careful there," she said, wiping the red, oozing liquid from my skin. "You don't want to do that."

"Why not?" I asked, though I had no doubt the fruit was dangerous. I just wanted to understand what I was dealing with. "And why did I do that?"

"Decades ago, my mother enchanted these woods to torment humans who entered our lands."

"Meaning?"

"Meaning this isn't poison, is it?" Keegan already had a piece of fruit in his hand. This time, Kylie slapped it away.

"Bad," she scolded.

He smirked, his lips twisting. But his eyes had followed the fruit to the ground.

"It is not poison," Elora confirmed, leading us past the tree. "If anything, it will make you wish for poison."

"Could you be a little less ... cryptic?" I asked, passing more trees with more bulbous fruits. My mouth started to water.

This is bad, I thought, as Keegan laughed, shaking his head. "Yeah, we don't take kindly to subtlety here, princess," he said.

Swooping down, I picked up a stick from the ground and started knocking fruit from the trees.

"What?" I asked when Elora turned around. "If you can't beat 'em, join 'em, right? But if you can't join 'em ... "

"Beat 'em off?" Keegan suggested.

Kylie laughed, clapping her hand over her mouth. Of the

three of us, she was the only one who hadn't reached for the fruit yet.

"So what does it do, exactly?" I asked, showing another piece of fruit who was boss. Maybe it was reckless, but it made me feel like I had *some* control in an uncontrollable situation.

"It shows you what humans are capable of," Elora said. "One bite, and you will see the darkest moments in human history. You will see your darkest moments too, the ones you keep hidden even from yourself."

I closed my eyes and saw my brother falling to his death. I saw Elora falling, too, into Naeve's clutches in the graveyard. Saw myself with the branch I'd slammed into Naeve's head.

"I don't need a spell to show me that," I said.

"Perhaps you will see other things, then," Elora suggested. "Things that have not yet come to pass. Things you are capable of in your worst moments. Would you mutilate another, out of vengeance and fury? Would you kill? Tear a person limb from limb, and smile as they screamed?"

"So it's like the Tree of Knowledge," Kylie said. "From the Bible story."

I tried to remember the story, but my parents were atheists. Still, I knew there was an apple, and a girl that got blamed for eating it. Something about a snake, too.

"Except here, every tree is the Tree of Knowledge, and it isn't the kind you want," Keegan said.

Elora nodded. "The knowledge of murder and assault and mutilation, of people who own continents while others starve in the streets."

"Child armies and child brides," Kylie said.

"Nuclear weapons. Napalm. War after war after war."

Keegan shook his head. We were all getting a little sick with ourselves. With our people.

"The knowledge of what men can do to each other under the right circumstances," Elora said. "Of what *you* could do, if you chose to—"

"It's not that simple," I said, and I wasn't talking to her. Not only. "It can't be. How can evil be a choice? How could you choose that? How could I choose that?"

"You're going to war *right now*," Kylie said. "You're going to kill people. People you haven't even met."

"People who tortured Elora. People who tortured their servants for centuries."

"And that's how you justify it."

"Why are you arguing with us?" I asked, looking up at Kylie. "You're going to war too."

I expected her to laugh, to shake her head. To say she would rescue Alexia and then bail.

But she didn't. "I'm just showing you how easy it is," she said, patting her horse on the back.

"It is easy to justify killing when you know who the villain is," Elora explained.

"Except we all have different ideas about that," I said.

"Yes," Elora said, as Kylie said, "Exactly."

I stopped in my tracks. "Then the dark faeries are right." If humans were gone, we'd take all that murder, assault and mutilation with us. Then what would be left? Faeries and animals. Plants. Flowers. Trees. The beautiful earth filled with beautiful creatures, instead of man.

Nature's big mistake.

"The spell is working," Elora said, touching my cheek

with her hand. The space around us felt darker, like she was using her magic to conceal the movement. "The magic preys on your desire to be a hero, Taylor. Your desire to be right."

"But there is no right, no absolute," I said. "Not if being *right* means killing whoever's *wrong*."

"That's right. That's it," she said, and just like that, my muscles began to relax. I could feel the spell dripping off of me like an oil slick.

"The danger is in simplifying," she said. "The danger is in forgetting your mercy. Forgetting the cost of taking a life, and the burden you will carry for the rest of your days."

"But what if there's no other choice?" I asked, looking up into the trees. Damn, that magic was strong. I *knew* the Unseelie Queen was speaking through me, getting into my head, but I couldn't stop it, because it felt like my own thoughts.

It mirrored them.

"What if I'm standing in the battle," I continued, "and someone's going to hurt me, or someone here, and I know I can stop it?"

"Then stop it." Elora took her hand from my face. I felt heavy the minute her fingers fell away.

I felt burdened.

"But there are many ways to defend oneself," Elora said. "And sometimes a soul is worth more than the body that carries it."

"What does that mean?" I asked.

"It means that dying is better," Kylie said, simplifying in a way Elora couldn't. Or wouldn't. "If the choice is dying or killing your soul—"

"By killing somebody?" I said, because I wasn't sure souls

could be killed. Stained maybe. Weakened or damaged for a time. But killed? No. I didn't believe that. I couldn't believe it, now that I knew I had a soul. Now that I'd felt it, through her. Through love.

Maybe that's the answer, I thought, but like a butterfly or a raven made of smoke, it flew away before I could catch it.

Before I really understood what it meant.

"If a guy was bearing down on me, and I knew I had to kill him or die, I might die," Kylie said. "I might do that, because my soul is more important than my body."

Might, Kylie had said. Not *would*. *Might*. Something had shifted. Faerie had changed her, made her harder, just like the rest of us.

"It doesn't call to you, does it?" I said, looking up at the fruit.

Kylie shook her head. "I already know what I'm capable of. I've known it since they took her, and it isn't pretty, Taylor. I may not kill to save my own life, but hers ... "

"You would?" I asked after a minute. I didn't really want to hear the answer, but I felt like I needed it.

"I would do things you can't imagine. Things I didn't imagine, before I watched the darkness swallow her whole." She reached up, plucking a piece of fruit from a nearby tree. She brought it right to her lips and I feared the worst. Then she tossed it, so carelessly, behind her back. "That's why I'm not drawn in by the power of the spell. I don't need some psycho to show me the dark side of my heart. I know what I'm capable of."

"And?" Keegan asked, shaking softly as he stared at her. She must've sounded like a stranger to him. Still, her words were familiar. We'd all thought them at some point.

"And I would do anything to protect the people I love," she said.

"Do not forget mercy," Elora reminded her. "There is room for both mercy and justice."

Kylie huffed, and her horse trotted ahead of us. "Mercy is earned." She tossed the words behind her like rotting fruit.

———

After that, we fell into a kind of dazed silence, and soon we were so exhausted, even the Dark Lady's whisperings couldn't get in. Elora walked beside us, using glamour to hide the fact that she was holding my hand. I wished I could lean into her and whisper helpful things like, "Remember the night I healed you with my tongue?" I wished we were alone.

I wished and wished, but under the cover of the Unseelie Forest, there were no stars, and no wishes came true. I felt alone, even though I was surrounded by friends. Then, just as I decided I'd never see any light again, I saw too much. I saw more light than my eyes could handle. Curling into myself, I peered out under my arm.

"What is that?" I asked as colors sped past my eyes. Blue and green and purple, gold and red. Silver and white. Everything shimmering against the deep blue backdrop of the sky, like heaven falling down. Or, maybe, the place where heaven and earth met.

"That," Elora said with a grin, "is the Aurora."

"The what?"

"Aurora Borealis," Kylie said. "Of course!"

"The Northern Lights," Keegan simplified.

Slowly, cautiously, I lifted my head. And then I could see it pouring down, like a waterfall cascading through the sky. Every color in the universe, coming together over our heads.

"We're going past this?" I asked.

Elora shook her head. "Not past. Through."

"Whoa," Kylie breathed, as I looked around. The Unseelie Forest was at our backs, as ominous as ever, but it felt like the air had shifted. Like autumn was bleeding into winter.

"How long have we been walking?" I asked.

"It isn't an issue of distance," Elora said cryptically. *Again with the faerie vagueness.*

"Translation to Human?" I requested.

She laughed, glancing behind her back. The dark faeries were still following us, but they weren't close enough to hear our conversation. "Remember when I said Faerie is the place where the physical and spiritual worlds meet? That night in your bedroom?"

"Yeah."

"Well, the spiritual realm makes for easy travel. It takes us where we wish to go. Call it concentrated will, or magic, or—"

"Flibbertigibbet," Keegan said.

"Or that." She smiled. "In the spiritual realm, one can pass easily from place to place, if one knows the way."

"Enchanted wardrobes?" Kylie suggested. "Train platforms?"

"Black holes and vortexes," Keegan added.

"However you're able to understand it," Elora said. "But magic is not science. It cannot be explained in simple terms of space and time."

"Time ... wait, did you Rip van Winkle us?" Kylie asked, looking around for signs that a century had passed in the blink of an eye. "If we went back home, would everyone we cared about be dead?"

Elora narrowed her eyes.

"Would years have gone by?" I said. "I mean, for every night we've spent in Faerie—"

"No, no, no." Elora shook her head. "Nothing like that. Although time here *is* fluid and cannot be charted with clocks. In fact, clocks move backward here, or they don't move at all."

"Okay, that's wicked," Keegan said, which was funny because, you know, we were in the land of wicked faeries. Still, I knew what he meant. I kind of wanted to look for a clock.

"Of course, if I wanted to, I *could* Rip van Winkle you," Elora said with a grin. "But those places are few and far between here."

Kylie nodded, and I could tell she was relieved. I was relieved. I mean, yeah, I had no intention of running back to my folks, but I wanted to think I *could,* if something changed. If I stopped being afraid of them.

Afraid of their rejection.

Maybe get your insecurities under wraps, I thought, *before we meet up with the Unseelie Queen.*

After all, any weakness I had, any fear, she would use against me. I tightened my grip on Elora's hand just as she moved away from me.

"We'll need a little help from here." She opened her hand to reveal a tiny black dot. The dot grew, taking over the rest of her palm. Turning to smoke, it fluttered away on wings.

"A butterfly!" Kylie gasped, temporarily forgetting her fury. Her anguish. That was the thing about magic: it could be horrifying or mesmerizing, depending on the minute. And now more butterflies peeled away from Elora's hand. I noticed the symbols on her arms were getting darker, and I thought, *Good, she's becoming her old self again.*

Then I thought, *Shit, she's becoming her old self again.*

Then I watched the butterflies disappear into the sky. Soon, two horses emerged from the darkness. Two *faeries*, wearing the shape of horses. Either way, I recognized them. They'd helped us carry Elora into the Seelie Court when she'd been on the brink of death.

"Lhiannon and Lamia," Elora said, nodding to the left, then the right. "Well met, old friends."

"A pleasure to see you alive, princess," Lamia said. And she dipped her black, massive head, rustling her wings.

Meanwhile, Lhiannon snorted, and smoke drifted from her nostrils. "Let me guess," she snarled. "You wish for us to carry the humans up to the palace."

"The humans, and your princess," Elora said.

Their eyes trailed to her back. Before we'd left the Seelie Court, she'd reapplied the glamour that made it look like she had her original wings. She just wasn't ready to reveal the newly budding wings to the world. Besides, in spite of our healing sessions, she could barely hover above the ground, let alone fly.

I didn't know if she'd ever be able to.

Finally, the horses knelt, and we climbed onto their backs. It took a minute to remove Kylie's saddle from her mare. Ten seconds later, we realized there was *no way* it was going to fit on these massive horses, and we ended up slinging it to Keegan's back with vines. Then, impressed with the effectiveness of the vines, Elora summoned more to strap us to the horses.

Then we were off.

Kylie's mare bolted back toward the Seelie Court as the ground dropped out beneath us. Soon it was a golden dot on the landscape. Then the landscape itself disappeared as the Aurora Borealis poured over me. No, *became* me. I looked down to see that my body was changing too. First it turned blue, then green, then violet. Then everything, all at once, flashing and rushing over my skin, transforming me into something else entirely.

I closed my eyes and became one with the stars. The universe.

Sitting at my back, Elora pressed into me, holding me close now that no one could see us. But I couldn't even feel bitter about that, couldn't feel bitter about anything. I just felt … good. Like everything was as it should be, and everything was going to be all right.

I twisted around, as best I could without losing my grip, and I found her mouth. Her lips parted and she crashed into me. Her hair spilled over me. The stars poured down on me.

On us.

"I love you," I whispered into her lips, and she whispered it back. And then she went back to holding me, leaning into my back, arms around my waist. We separated, but we didn't.

We never would entirely.

Then, just as I realized this, we came into the darkness again. The Unseelie Mountains rose up before us, jutting into the clouds. And there it was, that familiar black forest. But this time, red rivers cut through the darkness.

"Is that … are those … ?" I leaned back, into Elora.

She rested her head on my shoulder, just long enough to say, "It's not what you think. Look closer."

I did, peering at the rivers of red that crawled across the

landscape like veins. I mean, *exactly* like veins. The pattern was so similar, it made me feel queasy. Or maybe that was because the rivers looked like rivers of blood.

Well, they did and they didn't. A closer inspection revealed water that sparkled like rubies, rather than the thick, sticky substance that ran in my veins. Still, the Dark Lady must've been going for a blood-in-veins motif, and I couldn't help but think mortal blood *did* stain those riverbanks, even if the main substance was something else.

Elora spread her hands over my stomach as if to soothe me. She leaned in, speaking in my ear, "She told us to think of this land as her body, and warned us never to sully her form with human filth."

Subtle, I thought, and looked to Keegan, but he was too far away to laugh along with me.

We laughed to shake off the terror. The sickness.

We loved to scare off the hate.

I tilted my head back farther, thinking Elora might bury her face in my hair, when the stars caught my eye. Even though we'd passed through the Aurora some time ago, the stars still seemed to be falling. When I squinted my eyes, I realized that smoky black hands were reaching up and *pulling* them out of the sky.

Probably just a glamour, I told myself. I mean, you couldn't pull stars out of the sky without it affecting the universe. Still, the metaphor was effective. I heard Keegan whispering *subtle* in my mind. The Dark Lady not only hated the sun, and the bright Seelie Queen that represented it; she hated *all* suns (that is, all stars warming all galaxies) and was desperate to banish them from the sky. But she wasn't content simply glamouring the sky to look black—she wanted to show herself actively snuffing them out, wanted to show that her reach extended beyond the known world and into the sky. There was nothing she couldn't reach, touch, and destroy. She was omnipotent.

Yeah, in your dreams, lady, I thought, because the glamour was impressive, but it wasn't real.

I started to wonder if most of her power came from her ability to create terrifying illusions. When the dark faeries had captured us in the graveyard, they'd been quick to pull out the spiders and the snakes, since humans feared such things. But spiders and snakes didn't scare me.

Only one thing scared me, at this point. And the Dark Lady wouldn't have to be a genius to figure out what it was.

Now Elora leaned closer, brushing her lips across my cheek. She did it so fast, it would've been next to impossible for the faeries following us to see. Then she whispered, "Not long now," and as soon as she did, I felt us speeding toward the clouds. But rather than stopping at the mountain's highest point, which seemed like the best course of action, we stopped several hundred feet below it, in front of a great, twisting path that got thinner and thinner as it went.

Elora dismounted from our horse, holding out a hand. "Are you ready?"

My gaze trailed to the structure up ahead, forged out of the darkness and hardened into obsidian. Twisting spires slid into a scarlet sky, like a sword into the belly of a beast. I thought of blood dripping down. Of muscles tearing and bones breaking.

Unsubtly, I shook my head.

Elora laughed. "Welcome to the last seventeen years of my life," she said, helping me down, because really, I couldn't stay there forever. "Now, come on. Let's go meet my mommy."

20

ELORA

When the road narrowed to a razor-thin ledge, the mortals began to fret. First Taylor faltered, then Keegan, and Kylie, the only human permitted to ride up the path, kept peering over Lamia's back at the darkness below.

"Trust," I said softly, all-too-wary of spies listening in. The servants of the Dark Court still followed us in a swarm. And between the spindly branches of the nearby trees, snowy tree owls peeked out with impossibly black eyes. This close to the mountain's summit, everything was black on white. Tufts of mist drifted across a landscape of jagged stones, while the snow-capped mountain rose up into the twisting black spires of the Unseelie Castle. Of course, the great obsidian structure up ahead was merely the tip of the Unseelie stronghold, its inner workings weaving all the way down into the mountain.

We dark things needed a place to hide in the summer months, when the veil that covered our land could not keep out the light. And in the winter months, when the world was cloaked in glorious blackness, we climbed out of the earth like dead things, and we danced. We would dance tonight.

"Come along," I said, walking ahead of the group, showing them how it was done. Even without my wings, I had little fear of falling. I'd walked this path since I was a child, hurrying down the winding ledge until I reached the forest below, the snow-tipped trees that rose black and leafless no matter the season. To the mortals it must've looked like a lifeless wasteland, but they did not understand the things we did. Without death, there would be no new life. No growth without the decay. If nothing ever died, the earth would've been overpopulated centuries ago.

None of us would've been born.

And so the snow falls over the world, quietly lulling its creatures to sleep, so that all may be reborn in the spring. So the rocks sit, the blind and silent judges of the world, cold as the faeries here and almost as endless. And so my feet curved over the stone, like a seashell curving over a pearl.

"Faith," I said softly, and my voice carried on the wind to the mortals behind me.

"Trust." I wobbled playfully, and then caught myself when the mortals gasped.

"And connection." I took a tiny leap and landed on one foot, perhaps showing off a bit. I just wanted them to get comfortable, to believe in the earth's protection. Ironically, the only way for a human to travel this path successfully was to believe the earth would protect them on their passage. Most humans had long since lost their connection to the planet. Lost their faith in her goodness. Stopped trusting themselves.

Those humans would fall.

I slid my foot across the path, fast enough for the ledge to slice me, and as my blood slipped over the rocks, disappearing into the crevasse below, I turned to the humans and smiled. "And, if all else fails, a little gift is always appreciated."

Taylor let out a sound of disapproval—not, I think, because he was angry with me, but because he hated to see me hurt. Chances were, he'd be making that sound many times in the coming days.

A shiver went up my spine as a dark thought blossomed in my mind.

Five mortals enter the Unseelie Court. How many come out?
And, if I tip the scales, what will the cost be?

I glanced back at the faces of my friends. Kylie, who would do anything to protect the people she loved. Keegan, who had no vested interest in the High Faerie Courts or their subsequent downfall, and was only here out of loyalty to his sister. Perhaps, also, to me. And last, but never least, Taylor. My love. My heart.

How many lives would I sacrifice for him? Here, as the leader of the revolution, in a position of near-absolute power, I had control over who lived and who died. Who stood at the front lines, and who lingered in the back. Certainly, I would stand among the first wave, as any leader should, but Taylor? The boy who'd saved me so many times, in so many ways? What would I do to make sure he survived? Or, in uglier terms...

Who would I place in front of him?

As we entered the Unseelie Palace, the servants pressing in around us, I saw the answer to my question right in front of me. She sat in the entryway, in one of the many thrones situated throughout the castle. Red velvet curtains hung on either side of her to illustrate her importance.

"Don't look into her eyes," I warned quickly. "She can intuit your darkest fears and use them to break you."

"Wait, that's a person?" Keegan muttered. "She looks like a statue."

It was a fair point—*until* she stood. The Queen of the Dark Faeries towered over us in layer upon layer of black. Ribbons laced up her bodice and her arms. The tops of her snowy breasts billowed out of her corset, bluish-gray veins crawling like lines through marble, and her ebony hair was lined with scarlet. Oh, she was beautiful.

As beautiful as death after lifelong starvation.

I took a step forward, my gaze trailing from her face to the humans resting at her feet. Alexia knelt in her burgundy dress, a crown of crimson flowers in her hair, and farther down, in a kneeling-dog position, was Brad.

I opened my mouth to speak. But before I could give my mother a false offering, Alexia looked up at me, her eyes narrowing into slits. "*You!*" she shrieked.

I gasped, Alexia lunged, and together we slammed into the wall. One of the curtains came crashing down, wrapping around us like a blanket, and as we rolled across the floor, pulling hair and gnashing teeth, it covered us completely. That's when she covered my mouth with her hand and whispered dirty secrets in my ear.

"Follow my lead," she said.

21

TAYLOR

"What the hell?" I muttered as Alexia stumbled out of the curtain, disheveled and eager to reach our side. Elora, on the other hand, took her time. She stood up slowly, smoothing a single flyaway hair. I didn't know what was going on, but I wasn't about to risk drawing the attention of the Dark Lady. So I kept my mouth shut, staring at Alexia like she was a stranger and wondering if maybe she was.

Maybe the dark faeries were controlling her like a puppet, and she was going to kill us the second we were alone. Maybe she actually *was* a dark faerie, and that's why she'd sympathized with them so much.

Wait. That was insane. This place was making me insane, and I'd only just gotten here.

I closed my eyes and tried to breathe in slowly. But the place smelled like must and flowers and slowly drying blood, and I almost choked on the air. Over by the throne, Elora was talking.

She had the strangest smile on her face. "Now that we're all here, I can tell you my story," she said to her mother. The Dark Lady looked down, a look of great pity on her face. Or maybe it was disdain. Either way, Elora didn't blink as she said, "Little over three moons ago, I heard tell of a Seelie plot to infiltrate the human lands and steal a group of humans. Word on the wind was, the Seelie Queen had grown tired of the sanctions between the courts and was hoping to procure a whole host of playthings without the Dark Court ever knowing." Elora smiled, slowly, and I felt a surge of admiration at her ability to trick her own mother. I'd always been a terrible liar, and my mother was the hardest person to keep a secret from. It was a miracle I'd kept Elora hidden in my room for more than a day.

Now she circled around us as if we'd never met. "Still, I was cautious. What if this was only a rumor, a trick to get the Unseelie Court to break the sanctions first? I had to be certain, and so I lingered on the crossroads, where the border between the courts meets the border between Faerie and the wasteland. I did not have to wait long."

Wait a minute. A cold trickle of doubt made its way up my spine, and all the hairs on my arms stood on end.

"On a warm night in April, the sentries of the Bright Court set their sights on a mortal high school and made plans to steal a group of students."

This isn't right. Faeries can't lie.

"Sick, isn't it?" Elora asked, pausing to look at us with pure and utter disgust. "Cavorting with humans is terrible enough, but children? What game was the Seelie Queen playing?"

"Methinks the Lady hath lost her mind," the Unseelie Queen said, and she started to chortle. Soon she was guffawing, and Elora joined in, both of them cackling like witches, like evil things. My entire body had gone rigid with fear.

Elora grinned. "Lucky for us, I swept in and befriended the mortals before the Bright Queen had the chance to have her way with them." She turned to us, her face so mocking, it was unrecognizable. "Really, beasties, you should be thanking me."

The Dark Lady snorted, and I caught a flash of her true nature. Beneath the mask of marble white skin and ruby lips, I saw the face of a monster. Teeth so long and sharp they jutted all the way down her chin, and up *through* her cheeks. Eye sockets that were empty of eyes, but filled with the dark abyss of space. Of eternity. Blood dripped down her chin, but it couldn't have been mortal blood because of the iron.

God, had she been eating her own kind?

I envisioned her courtiers bringing in platter after platter of little faeries, each sprawled across a bed of greens, cowering and terrified. I imagined that first bite, the crunch. Did they wriggle as they slid down her throat? Did their wings beat against her chest cavity, fervent and frantic at first, then slower, like a heartbeat, until her stomach acid ate away at their wings and they fell into silence?

She caught me staring and licked her lips. A whisper trickled into my head: *Elora's lying,* it said. *She told you she couldn't lie, but she can. You can't trust anything she's said.*

I shook myself, trying to focus on Elora. But it didn't help. She was glaring at me like she wanted to see me cooked alive. "She can't lie," I whispered to myself.

That's even worse, the voice said. *If she cannot lie, she's telling the truth now. She stole you to give to her mother. Either way, you're . . .*

"Fucked," I muttered, and Elora laughed so hard. Together with her mother, who really did look a lot like her, if you looked in the right light, she laughed until she couldn't laugh anymore. And she leaned in to speak to me in a condescending voice. "Oh, human, we'll do a lot of things to you here. But that won't be one of them."

"Perhaps we should've left them with the Seelie Queen," her mother said, and they shared a smirk.

"Really, it's as if they can only think of one thing," Elora agreed, dipping down to stroke Brad's hair. He looked up, his eyes glassy, and licked at her hand like a dog. She stared disdainfully at her own palm before wiping it on her crimson dress. "This one seems a bit broken," she said with a laugh.

"He came to me that way." Her mother looked down with delight at the mess that was Brad. "Quite nice of the Seelie Queen, really, to break him in for me. She must know I like them that way."

Anger surged through me, and I fought against my bonds. More laughter ensued. More hilarity. God, I was so fucking funny! Wasn't I nice to entertain them? But man, when the chips are down, you kind of go for broke because you've got nothing to lose. And Brad may have been a terrible person, but he *was* a person, and we would decide what to do with him.

Not them.

Us.

Still, all of my struggling was for nothing, and in an effort to not tire myself out, I settled down and studied the layout of the place. The many twisting hallways leading into nowhere like an Escher painting. The doors hovering near the ceiling with no way to get to them at all. How the hell were we going to get out of here?

Through it all, Elora kept talking. Telling her version of

what happened. "I actually befriended the idiots in a matter of days, and was all set to bring them to my mummy."

"But you lost them," her mother said, peering at us with a curious frown. "You never brought them to my court until now."

"We were ... intercepted," Elora said with a snarl. "On the night we were set to return and teach those Seelie faeries a lesson once and for all, I found myself surrounded."

"By whom?" her mother asked, hanging on her every word.

But before Elora could tell the ending of her story, an ending we humans knew too well, the hall was flooded with faeries. These were not the ragged servants of the Unseelie Court, oh no. These were the spoiled, pampered courtiers with their heads up their respective asses. Well, not literally, though it wouldn't have surprised me here. They stormed into the room, dressed in their fancy-pants finery with their chins tilted up, as if they couldn't stand to breathe the same air as the *lowly humans*. I could've laughed, it was so damn ridiculous. But I didn't. I was far too close to death to tempt the fates.

Because here, among the beloved courtiers of the Dark Court, I recognized three key players: the Lady Claremondes, slithering across the ground like a serpent, the jagged remains of her tongue dripping poison onto the marble floor; Olorian, the beefcake idiot who could send me crashing through the wall with a flick of his jet-black wrist; and Naeve, the leader of them all, the last faerie ever to be born before Elora came along and stole his birthright.

His black hair was writhing like snakes. His golden eyes were glinting.

"Brother, darling," Elora cooed, bowing her head just a

little to mock his lack of royal blood. "Your timing, for once in your sorry life, is impeccable."

The Dark Prince bristled and crossed the courtyard to greet his queen, but the princess stopped him. "Not so fast," she said, turning to scowl at her mother. "You want to know who ruined everything? Who stopped me in the graveyard, just short of bringing the mortals into your court? Whose stupidity and pride allowed the mortals to escape to the *Seelie Court* with me in tow, laying waste to my plans?"

She turned, her gown swirling around her like water, like a whirlpool of blood that would swallow us all. And she bowed, dramatic and low, to her almost-brother. "I present to you the fool of the Unseelie Court: Naeve."

After that, it was only a matter of seconds before the servants surrounded him, covering his body like insects.

First, he was bound.

Next, he was pushed to his knees, his nose digging into the ground.

Then the Queen of the Dark Faeries rose to mete out judgment.

22

ELORA

There are few moments in life when one feels completely vindicated. Here, watching my greatest tormentor make friends with the dirt, I wanted to laugh openly and kick him in the gut.

I wanted to make him bleed the way he'd made me bleed.

An eye for an eye, my wings for his.

"Oh, *suffer*," I whispered as the Queen delivered the first of her blows. "Oh, *bleed*."

Naeve tried to scream, but the Dark Lady wouldn't stand for it. He tried to defend himself, but it was too late. Already, thin threads were crawling out of his lips, sewing his mouth shut. Darkness wrapped around his wrists, binding him tight. When blood dripped from his temple, spattering his ebony cape, I envisioned my nails digging into that wound, making it bigger.

A laugh jumped from my lips.

As if noticing me for the first time, one of the servants turned my way and gave me a look. I shut my mouth after that.

Not that it mattered much. Once first blood had been

drawn, Alexia looked my way and gave me a wink. In a voice that sounded much like mine, she said, "Take them to the dungeon. I'll deal with them once Naeve has learned his lesson."

Then, as if intuiting my desires, she leaned over Naeve and kicked him in the gut.

After that, the servants led me away.

23

TAYLOR

The second the cell door clanked shut, I slunk to the floor. What was the point of standing anymore? What was the point of breathing? I'd loved and lost, oh lucky me.

I wanted to scream.

In the background, from somewhere much, much farther away, I heard Keegan telling Brad to sit down, while Kylie and Alexia *reunited.* There was lots of whispering and hugging, and I wondered if they'd jump each other's bones right there, since there was no forest to slip away into. My hands slid over my face, trying to block them out.

It wasn't that I wasn't happy for them. I was very happy for them. I wanted them to have love. But I was also so jealous it made me sick, and I didn't like that about myself. Which meant that between me, Elora, and the make-out queens, I hardly liked anyone right now, and it was all so *unfair.*

I'd done what I was supposed to do. I'd risked my life for all of them. Put their happiness above my own. And now . . .

"Taylor?" Alexia's voice startled me from the depth of my despair. A part of me worried she'd mock me for having a pity party, and I'd actually cry. How strong and powerful was I, breaking down in a cell where everyone else was holding it together?

Then I looked into her eyes and the breath rushed out of me. "Oh my God."

"Shhhh." She lifted a finger to her lips, staring back at me with Alexia's mouth, Alexia's nose, Alexia's dimples.

Elora's eyes.

"How … "

"It's glamour, silly." She said it so casually, I almost did cry, out of relief this time. And I pulled her into my arms.

"Oh my God, oh my God, oh my God," I murmured. "Don't *ever* do that to me again."

"I'm sorry," she said, pulling away. Her eyes looked like Alexia's again. But I knew better; the twins and I did. We gathered in around her, including Kylie, who didn't even look that mad. She must've realized that Alexia—the *real* Alexia—was safer outside the cell, playing the part of the princess.

"Damn," I said, shaking my head. "She really nailed you."

Elora's lips curled, like I'd said something dirty. "She had plenty of practice."

"You mean … you *planned* this?" It seemed impossible that Alexia's Oscar-worthy performance had been anything but impromptu. They'd had no time to plan it. Alexia and Brad had disappeared across the border, and before that we'd all been working on …

"Oh. Oh! This was her task."

Elora nodded. "Of course, when she pitched her idea to the Seelie Queen, she claimed she would only perform for my followers at the border. Wearing the guise of glamour, she'd put on a show, and convince them I didn't care for you humans. But all along, she was planning on crossing over the border and coming to battle."

"And you agreed to let her?"

"Only after I agreed to let *you*." Elora smirked, looking at each of us. "You all got what you wanted, whether I wanted it or not. Of course, this worked out better than anything I could've plotted—"

"How is this *better*?" Kylie said, finally speaking after minutes of stunned silence. She kept squinting at Elora, like maybe she could see her true form underneath. But if this disguise was meant to fool faeries, I doubted there was any human in the world who could see through it.

"Thanks to her capture, Alexia was able to perform directly in front of my mother," Elora said. "Now, the Dark Lady has no choice but to believe her story. To believe *me*. She'll never see it coming when I betray her."

Kylie frowned, not ready to admit that any part of Alexia's capture had made things "better." I didn't blame her, though I knew what Elora was saying. She didn't think Alexia's capture had been a positive thing; she was just making the best of an awful situation. That strength was inspiring.

Keegan was, for the moment, strangely silent. He'd returned to the task of guarding Brad. But whether he was protecting Brad from the faeries, or protecting us from Brad, I didn't know.

"So how do we get out of here?" I asked, studying the curiously unguarded door. The cell was old-timey—dirt floor and metal bars, the latter placed too closely together for even the smallest human to slip through. You'd have to be some sort of sprite to get through them. Unless …

"Are the bars made of iron?"

Elora shook her head. "Why suffer the stench of iron when any old metal will do? Humans aren't so good at slipping through bars, or bending them with magic." A slow smile took over her face, and even though she looked like Alexia, I could see Elora beneath it. Her joy. Her mischievousness. "That power lies with faeries alone."

"So you're going to bend the bars?" Kylie asked.

"Making an escape through the castle proper is not a good idea. We'd be caught as soon as we set foot outside the dungeon." Elora paused, trailing her hand across the dirt of the back wall. "Taylor may not have told you, but sanctions have been in place for many years, forbidding faeries from interacting with humans. Dark faeries are not supposed to harm them, and bright faeries are not supposed to keep them as pets." Her gaze drifted to Brad. "But what Taylor does not know is that these dungeons were built *before* the sanctions, and thus built exclusively for humans. Faeries tend not to lock up their own kind." Her lips twitched, and I didn't know if it was from fear or satisfaction. "We find other ways to punish those who break our rules. Often publicly."

"Old school," Keegan muttered from his place in the corner. Ever vigilant, he watched as Brad made pies with the mud—or maybe Brad was making weapons: rocks surrounded by mud, to look more innocent, right up until they busted your nose.

I never could tell, with Brad.

"But humans," Elora continued, "we could lock away without ever fearing they'd escape. Even if they managed to garner a spoon … " She looked at the freshly packed dirt of the walls. "They'd spend days tunneling through the mountain, struggling with starvation and dehydration, only to find themselves right back here again."

"Ya'll are fucked up, you know that?" Keegan said.

Elora shrugged. "All of this took place before I was born."

"And yet, you say *we*," I muttered. Elora's eyes flickered to mine, and I shrugged too, mimicking her.

"I suppose old habits aren't murdered easily." She turned back to the wall. "You see, what mortals do not know is, the tunnels behind these walls are *magicked* to bring captives back to this place. But if one knows how to pull the spell away..." She held her hand against a patch of dirt until it reddened, as if warmed. There was a soft rumbling behind the wall, like an avalanche of small rocks. Elora smiled and yanked her hand away. "You will find escaping is quite an easy thing to do."

Keegan crept up to the wall, touching the place Elora had warmed. His hand went *through* the dirt as if there was nothing there. "But why?" he asked. "Why create passages leaving the cells if you didn't want humans to use them? Just to keep them spinning in circles?"

Elora shook her head. "Back in the old days, the dark faeries found much delight in terrifying mortals. So rather than entering the cell through the barred door, faeries would wait until the mortals had almost fallen asleep, and then they would crawl out of the walls. The mortals were often so exhausted at this point, they didn't know if they were awake or dreaming. It was like living in a never-ending nightmare. Some of them were actually scared to dea—"

"*Enough*," I said, and everyone turned to me. I felt my face redden, but I couldn't stand to hear another word. Elora seemed all too casual talking about the torture of humans. "Can we focus on the plan?"

She looked at me, her eyes pleading silently. I knew she wished we had a quiet moment alone. But I'd wanted that since the day we met, and we so rarely get what we want. More than anything, I wanted to get out of this place.

"I'm sorry," I said, when Elora didn't speak. "Your mother ... *did something* to my head. I'll feel a lot better about this whole messed-up place if I know how we're going to get out of it."

Elora nodded, stepping away from the wall. "When our sixth member returns, we'll make a final switch, and the five of you will travel down the mountain. I'll send some of my allies to meet you at the first fork in the path, and from there, they will take you where you wish to go."

"Meaning?" Keegan asked.

"Meaning the Seelie Court, if you wish to return. Or the human world—"

"We could go home?" Kylie looked at her, wide-eyed, like she'd spoken of magic and eternal life.

But she hadn't. She'd spoken of the opposite of that.

"Now that I've returned to court," Elora explained, "my enemies have no reason to follow you home. They only would've done that to get me back."

"And what if *this* is our home?" I asked. "I mean, what if we're not going back?"

Elora trapped me in her gaze. "Then my people will lead you into battle. But you must act as a guard, as you've promised—"

I nodded, but I didn't say *yes*.

"So that's it, then?" Keegan asked. "Won't your mother be pissed that we're busting out of the clink? Won't she send her underlings after us?"

"Tonight, they'll be too busy celebrating the return of their princess," Elora said. "Probably, too, there will be a spectacle made of Naeve." We both smiled at that. Maybe the darkness inside of her was the same darkness I recognized in myself. Maybe all the darkness in the world was born of experiencing things no living being should experience, and adjusting accordingly. We made ourselves darker to survive. As long as we never used it to destroy someone innocent, it wasn't such a terrible thing.

My gut didn't respond well to that thought. It clenched as if in warning. *Who decides who's innocent?*

I didn't have time to ponder it. Someone was coming down the steps. Elora waved us closer, whispering, "Don't call me by my name. Don't behave as if I understand Faerie. And," she said, fingers grasping mine for what could be the last time, "when the guards leave again, do not wait for a sign to escape through the tunnels. That is your sign. Run."

We nodded and, sitting in a circle like ragdolls, held each other's hands. We swayed a little bit. We could've started a round of "Kumbaya." Everything we did, we did to make ourselves look more pathetic. And it must've worked, because when Alexia came striding in, wearing Elora's form like she'd been born into nobility, she gave us the saddest look of pity. She was striding fast, keeping the guards several feet behind her, and when she reached the bars, she beckoned to us with a hand.

"Everything is in order, I trust," Elora murmured.

But Alexia shook her head. I realized, then, that the look of pity wasn't forced. The Queen of Deception wasn't putting on an act.

"We have a problem," she whispered. "Naeve's begged an audience with the Dark Lady. He spelled out his words with his own blood on the castle floor. He swears he can prove your disloyalty if she just gives him the chance."

"How?" Elora asked, but Alexia didn't answer. The guards were gathering in, and besides, her eyes said everything her lips couldn't say. Fluttering across the group like a nervous butterfly, they settled on me.

24

ELORA

The door to the cell clanked open, and much to her chagrin, I dove at Alexia, pulling us both into the shadows. Drawing in a cloak of darkness, I pulled away both of our glamours. Alexia glared, and I shrugged as if to say, *Now we're even.*

Truly, it was better this way. If the dark faeries thought I hated Alexia, they wouldn't bother making an example out of her. She was the safest of them all.

Together, we went to see the fairest.

The guards led the humans along. These were the faeries I'd inspired to revolt. The creatures who'd been battered and beaten by the nobles of the Dark Court, who'd been neglected and treated as less-than for centuries.

These creatures were on my side.

Still, if they knew the truth about my affection for the humans, they might abandon the cause. How could they trust me if they learned I'd been fraternizing with *both* of the Unseelie Court's greatest enemies? In bed with a mortal *and* the Bright Lady, albeit figuratively speaking in the latter case. They wouldn't understand, not now. But after the revolution, when the Bright Queen disbanded her court as promised, they'd see that everything I'd done had been for them. For freedom.

I just had to keep them in the dark a little longer. I just had to hope no one discovered my house of straw, and blew.

As we entered the foyer, where the Queen sat rigidly in her obsidian throne, I realized the flaw in my logic. My house of straw had already been discovered, and there, on the Dark Lady's left hand side, was the wolf.

"I should've shut you up when I had the chance," I snarled at Naeve, striding past him with nary a glance. "Surely, Lady, you've come to your senses and realized I couldn't care for vile, pathetic beings."

Not a lie, because I didn't care for vile, pathetic beings. Beings like Naeve, perhaps like Brad. As for Taylor . . .

I kept my gaze from him as I spoke, pretending he didn't exist. Trying to pretend, and failing.

"My darling, you've put me in a difficult position," my mother said. *Darling*, she said, as if there were love between us. But she only meant to taunt me. "You see, I have here an unprecedented occurrence. Two faeries, telling me two *very* different stories. Two faeries, unable to lie . . . and yet one of them must be."

She reached out, as if to touch my cheek. But when her fingers met my flesh, she was so cold, I thought of dead things. I wondered if perhaps she was a dead thing, if all the things that made her alive had bled away from her years ago. Now she lived on hate.

"What am I supposed to do?" She pursed her ruby lips, as if genuinely distressed. "I cannot simply take your word for it. That would be showing favor."

"Oh, certainly. Don't ever be one to show favor."

She grinned, and I scowled, because she showed favor depending on her mood. Some days, she only favored the beasts of the forest. Other days, she favored Naeve, merely to toy with his emotions. Most days, she showed favor to me, but not in loving embraces or encouragement. Simply by punishing my servants for performing some tiny task wrong.

"If one of the faeries of my court has learned to twist the laws of nature, to bend the truth as mortals do"—she sneered in disgust—"I must know of it, and they must be punished."

"Twist the laws of nature," I repeated, circling her throne, and thus Naeve as well. "Like … using iron against their own kind?"

"Using iron is a punishable offense," my mother said. "Punishable by death, punishable by exile. But lying in a mortal's bed is much worse, and requires a punishment that is drawn out over centuries."

Of all the words to stick on, my mind got stuck on "worse." I hadn't shown her my wings yet, hadn't revealed the damage Naeve had done. Still, she'd obviously heard about the sword, and she was excusing him. *If* I'd lain in bed with mortals, she was excusing him.

My confidence faltered and, for a moment, I fought to keep from sinking to the ground.

"Why so glum, proud Elora?" Naeve taunted, sniffing out my weakness and threatening to lunge. "If you're telling the truth, you will have justice for my little indiscretion."

Oh, Naeve. I'd forgotten your proclivity for innuendo. "Indiscretion." That's a good one. That really hits home.

"What are we to do?" I asked, turning back to the Dark Lady, ignoring Naeve entirely. "And what of my celebration?"

"Oh, there will be a celebration," my mother said, "but with a twist of my own. Whether you're guilty or not, I am happy to have my daughter home. So we shall perform a simple test, and if Naeve proves to be the traitor, I will punish him for all to see."

"And if the traitor is Elora?" Naeve's voice burrowed into my brain, though I refused to look at him. I was too busy looking at the Queen.

She wore the most curious smile. And her gaze turned to the mortals when she said, "There will be a different kind of sacrifice."

25

TAYLOR

Here's the thing nobody tells you about being a human sacrifice: there's a lot of preening involved. The servants of the Dark Court dragged us to the forest, forced us to undress, and pushed us into the snow. They didn't want to touch me, so they mostly used sticks with patches of moss to scrub me clean, which would've been comical if it weren't so painful. The icy water made my skin splotchy and raw, and the sticks only deepened the damage. I could feel cuts opening all across my back, and I couldn't help but think of the way Naeve had broken his iron sword into tiny pieces, and slid each shard into Elora's back.

Was this my punishment for causing her to be caught by him? Did I deserve this treatment? Did it make her and I *closer* somehow?

Okay, maybe I was trying to find some explanation for all of this horror. Maybe I was trying to turn my sacrifice into some grand romantic gesture, the way people romanticize the suicide of Romeo and Juliet. But in the end, hurting yourself for another person isn't anything but stupid. And Elora wouldn't have wanted this.

Where is she?

When the "bath" ended, we were ordered to our feet, which was hard enough for the four of us who didn't rely on a wheelchair to get around. For Kylie it was impossible. At least the dark faeries had the decency to let Alexia help her—or maybe they just didn't want to get human filth on their precious skin, and decency wasn't a factor. Either way, I could hardly look at any of my friends, or myself for that matter, because our skin was blotchy and we were all shivering, and I wondered if one of us was going to die before we even made it to the sacrifice.

But something funny happened then. As the faeries picked up thicker branches, not to cleanse us, but to "properly put us in our place," I heard a voice at my back. It said, "My mistress has requested your safe passage."

"I don't suppose you mean *safe passage from these lands*," I muttered, too frozen and, all right, *terrified* to turn around.

"I'm afraid not," the faerie replied, taking a swing with a stick. My whole body tensed, waiting for the blow, but it never came. It stopped just short of my back. Still, my skin was so raw that I felt the wind crashing against me, and I cringed.

"Just do it or don't," I snarled, wrapping my arms around myself. Lot of good that did. "The anticipation is kind of the worst part."

"You say that now," the faerie said, *almost* hitting me a few more times. "But trust me when I say the impact is worse." A single, delicate wrist made its way in front of my face, the pale skin barely visible through all the discoloration. Blue bleeding into purple bleeding into black. A multi-colored tapestry of pain. "And the bruising after."

"It's gotten bad, hasn't it?" I asked, meaning the treatment of the servants by the courtiers.

"It has never been anything but bad," came the reply. "Now turn. They are watching from the windows."

I turned, but there wasn't time to take in the sight of the sickly pale faerie in front of me. Suddenly I was surrounded, hair combed and skin smoothed by faeries who didn't have the social standing to refuse this kind of work. Still, they did their best to keep from making contact with my skin.

Old habits aren't murdered easily, I thought. *But some things are. Me, Kylie, Keegan, and—*

Damn, I was rambling. And even though it was only happening in my head, it scared me that I couldn't focus on my impending doom. I needed to be plotting our escape, but I didn't know where to start. How could I convince the Queen that I hadn't sullied her daughter's virtue? I mean, sure, we hadn't had *all-the-way* sex, but sullying was sullying, in the eyes of the dark faeries, and virtue was...

Wait, were dark faeries even concerned with virtue? Or was there something else I had done to her daughter, something worse in the eyes of the court? Elora had been raised to believe that humans were vile, disgusting creatures, and the minute she stopped believing that was the minute she threw out her mother's teachings. So maybe *that* was the insult, more than any physical indiscretion.

"Ow. Back to beauty school, asshole," I heard Keegan say, and it shattered my train of thought for the moment. Across the way, some faerie was combing his hair. Except it seemed more like "attacking," and the comb was so white, it could've been made of ivory. Or maybe human bones. I didn't want to think about human body parts raking through my hair, so I looked away, into the trees.

That's when I saw her. She was half-hidden by the snow, her frog's body blending with the bark of the tree. Or maybe she was using glamour. Her skin looked darker than it had before.

Yes, I recognized her. She was a friend of Elora's. At least, I thought she was, because I'd seen her at the borderlands when we'd crossed into the Unseelie Court. I didn't know her name, or how close she was with Elora. All I knew was, when Elora had come home, this faerie had cheered with the others, and that was enough.

I smiled at her.

She nodded back. Her lips didn't even twitch.

Ah, so it's like that, is it?

She must've hated humans, just like the rest of the dark faeries. I didn't know what Elora was doing, keeping all these secrets from her servants. Regardless of the revolution's outcome, how did she think they were going to react when they knew she was in bed with the enemy?

In bed-*ish*.

God, if I managed to survive all this, I'd better get some time alone with her. Even if we just lay together in bed and looked into each other's eyes, not saying a *word*, it would be worth it. I could play with her hands, and she could touch my face in that way that drove me crazy, my heart racing and my body rising and my *entire being* feeling like it belonged in the universe for once.

Feeling like it was *home*.

And just like that, I got my second wind. Okay, maybe it

was my fifty-second wind, but still. I would survive this, damn it, and I would get to kiss her again. We'd live an unbelievable life.

Even we wouldn't believe it, sometimes. How good it was.

"So, what do you think my chances are?" I said, not really expecting the faerie with the messed-up wrist to help me. But what could I lose, at this point?

She leaned in close, speaking so only I could hear. Her jet-black hair tickled my shoulder. "There are many among us who would like to see Naeve suffer," she muttered. "But he cannot be appealed to by humans."

"And, what, the Dark Lady can be?"

"Not appealed to, no," she said, running her hand through my hair with a swiftness I couldn't follow with my eyes. Pulling her hand away, she examined it like she expected it to be covered with insects. "But taken off guard, perhaps." Even though her hand was clean, she brushed it against the rags of her dress. She caught me looking and blushed, as if ashamed. "I…"

"Old habits?" I offered through gritted teeth.

She nodded, barely. "Turn, now," she said, apparently incapable of forming the word "please." I did as she asked, and something warm fell over me. Something warm and *dry*. A cloak.

"Thank God," I murmured, though the sentiment would probably sound weird to her. Where she came from, faeries had the powers humans attributed to gods, and they sure as hell weren't in the business of salvation.

I hugged the cloak around me. It really only covered my shoulders and back, but if I bunched it up in my hands, it covered more. A quick look around showed more of the same: my friends pulling their cloaks around themselves. Even Brad had the sense to draw his in like a blanket, which was somewhat counterproductive, considering he was squatting in the snow.

I turned away. I couldn't deal with my conflicting feelings about Brad right now. Couldn't deal with the hatred that still swam inside of me, dulled by pity. Dulled by compassion. Caring for him felt too much like forgiveness, but hating him felt too much like sealing his fate. Leaving him to die. Why had it fallen on me to protect or abandon him?

Like Kylie said, this wasn't about avenging her anymore. Maybe it had never been about avenging her, not entirely. Even back in the human world, when his actions had hurt her directly, *I'd* felt responsible. If I'd stood up to him before the end of my senior year, he might've realized that his actions had consequences.

Then maybe he wouldn't have hurt her in the first place.

Suddenly I felt warm. It wasn't due to some kind of realization or epiphany; the faerie servant was using her power to warm me. It felt so good, I almost fell to my knees. The small bit of sanity I had left kept me standing, and I managed to say: "Why are you helping me?"

The faerie was quiet a minute. "Not helping," she said, and I thought that was what she needed to believe. "But not hurting either. There comes a point when any violence, even the justifiable kind, becomes too much. And how can I long for peace if I am not its greatest proponent?"

"I don't know," I said honestly. "But I think we're a long way from peace, even if..." *The battle goes as planned*, I finished, not knowing how much Elora would want me to say in her servants' presence. She'd left us all in the dark about something. I hoped that didn't come back to bite her in the ass. I hoped she was as smart as she thought she was, because all of this secrecy could lead to some pretty major misunderstandings.

Case in point: we were supposed to be racing down a tunnel right now, preparing to fight. But Naeve had thwarted that, and since the servants didn't know we were good people, they wouldn't risk the wrath of their queen by helping us escape.

Still, they *were* helping us, in their way. Instead of beating the crap out of us with branches, they were covering us with a glamour that made us look beaten. I know, it was pretty messed up. But I'd take a magical shit-kicking over the literal kind any day. My skin looked practically purple, patches of white peeking through. In this weird way, I fit in with the landscape better than before.

"So how do we catch the Queen off guard?" I said, speaking to the faerie at my back. The one in the tree, too.

"The Queen will only ever see humans in one way. Maybe all of us will," my faerie groomer said, and I wasn't sure if she was ashamed or just stating a fact. "But Elora's part in things ... the princess ... if you could convince the Dark Lady that her daughter was innocent of any wrongdoing, that you'd coerced her, or ... "

Acted like Brad, I thought. *Acted like Naeve.*

"No, why should I do that? The Queen will kill me and let Elora go."

Oh. You know that moment when you answer your own dumb question? Reality hit me like a branch to the face. And maybe she was right—maybe the only way out of this was to sacrifice myself for the good of the group. There was honor in that.

Sure, tell that to my shaking ass.

It was true, I was shaking; the uncontrollable kind. The faerie must've realized what I was thinking, because she narrowed her eyes at me. "You *do* care for her. That much is true." Her eyes went wide, and she touched her hand to her lips. I guess the world was turning on its head. But I didn't have time for an episode of *That Moment You Realize You're a Bigot.*

I had to know if there was another way.

"Is that the only possible plan?" I asked as she placed a crown of thorns on my head. When she yelped, pulling back her hand, I realized she'd been pricked. *Poor baby,* I thought with a snarl. *It really sucks when you injure yourself in the name of torture.*

I guess I was starting to feel furious, in spite of the fact that she was man-handling me nicely. This situation was *entirely wrong,* even with all of her gentleness. She was handing me over to be killed in the name of her princess.

After everything Elora had done.

"Wait a minute," I said, trying to catch her eye. She squirmed under my gaze, like I was a spider who was sizing up a fly. *Isn't that ironic?* "Do you believe Elora? Do you believe she went to the human world to steal us for the Queen?"

I could've been a faerie myself, the way I worded that. She *had* gone to the human world to steal Brad for the Queen. Just, you know, not *her* queen.

But the faerie didn't catch my trick, and she seemed to genuinely ponder the question. "I believe the truth lies somewhere in between. The princess must've gone to the wasteland to capture you, otherwise she couldn't have said it. But while she was there, I believe ... "

"I corrupted her with my wicked human wiles?" I asked, thinking of the way Elora had talked about humans her first week in my world. Of course, at the time, I thought she was some sort of runaway who'd escaped a cult and was skeptical of civilized society. Of people who relied on microwaves and running water. People who were wasteful and didn't realize how easy their lives were.

I guess some of that was fair.

The faerie looked at me as if sizing me up. It was uncomfortable, considering the whole *naked* thing. "I cannot speak on what happened there, only the consequence," she said. "Clearly, the princess's ... perception changed. Otherwise this process would be a lot less comfortable for you."

"You try standing naked in the snow. You do that and tell me it's comfortable."

"It can always get worse," she said, and it sounded like a promise. Or maybe she was just speaking from experience.

"So you believe both Naeve and Elora are telling the truth."

"They have to be. Or, at least, they believe they are. What is the other explanation?"

"And you believe he was justified in hurting her? You think she had it coming?" I tried to hide my fury, because I knew it would give too much away. I was in an impossible position: unable to show my love for Elora without putting her in danger. Unable to be indifferent without proving them right about humans.

The faerie stepped closer, her eyes ablaze. "I love my princess," she said fiercely, "And not just now, with freedom hovering on the horizon. I've loved her since her birth. She never once raised a hand to me, or spoke to me cruelly." A small smile, with a hint of a taunt behind it. "She saved her cruelty for those that were cruel first. It's as if she was born with an innate sense of justice."

"*What does that tell you?*" I said, gesturing to my friends.

The faerie froze. The humans froze. The entire damn ensemble froze.

Frozen, to match my feet.

"It tells me she is worth saving," the faerie said after a minute. "And perhaps, so are you. But I cannot be certain, and I will *not* sacrifice her to save you. Do you understand?"

"Yes."

"The Queen requires a sacrifice, and she will have one. The best you can do is divert her attention from the both of you."

"What, to my *friends*?"

The faerie shrugged, like we weren't discussing murder. "Unless you can make Naeve look like a fool."

"He's mighty good at doing that himself."

Her eyes were cold as ice when she said, "Not this time."

26

ELORA

Night fell, but it was an unnatural sort of night. The darkness that covered the lands came from *within*. Within the Dark Court. Within the Dark Queen. In this part of the world, the sun had a penchant for shying away entirely during the winter months, but in the summer, it shone furiously, forcing us underground.

Still, if the occasion called for it, we might be inclined to climb out of the earth with grasping hands, and use our collective power to cover the lands in pleasant darkness for one night. Our strength would be depleted in the morning, with or without the dancing, with or without the drink. But for one glorious night, we would revel in the blackness, in the sky so beautiful a person could disappear into it.

If you are a good little faerie, the sky might open up her arms and swallow you whole.

This is the story I was told, as a child. And now, in spite of the danger, and the word *sacrifice* running constantly through my mind, I felt a single rebellious thrill as the first sliver of darkness curled out of the earth.

I stood at the topmost tower of the Unseelie Castle,

watching the darkness unfold. Down below, at the back of the castle, the mountain jutted out into a near perfect circle, and there, in the center, was my mother.

Perhaps she was drawing on the strength of her courtiers. Perhaps the darkness of the court just *responded* to her. But here, from a distance, it seemed as if all the darkness in the world existed inside her body, and she was letting it out.

Black tendrils leaked out of her, circling and trickling and expanding to cover the world. Soon that darkness skittered over the grounds, covering the dirt and the snow like a low-hanging fog. Soon that wicked sun was blotted out.

I stood, staring down at my mother, my body filled with fear and awe. She was so powerful; how could I defeat her? She was so beautiful; how could I betray her? All the parts of me—dark and light, cruel and kind—converged and surged within me, and I felt, for the first time, that only a part of me would survive. How could I be so …

In love with a human.

My mother's child.

At war with my people.

My father's daughter?

What had Naeve meant, there in the graveyard, about being destined to visit the human lands? Had my father become entangled with humans as well? Is that why my mother abandoned him? Or worse … harmed him?

I couldn't think on it now. Couldn't wonder about her proclivity for death. For a moment, the most curious image entered my mind, of a blue-haired naiad dragging her lover down to the depths. Had my mother done such a thing to my father, but only to see him scream? Naiad may have felt remorse for her murderous mistake, but the Queen of the Dark Faeries would suffer no such regret.

Oh, Lady, I thought as she finished her wicked work and turned to face me. Perhaps she knew I'd been there the whole time. The smile on her face stretched to terrible heights, and suddenly I felt the sensation of falling, of being pulled. If she'd sacrifice the humans, would she sacrifice her daughter for loving them as well?

I would know the answer by the end of this night.

But first, the celebration. My mother lifted a great, gnarled staff and pounded it into the earth. Her signal for the Unseelie beasties to rise.

And rise they did. They crawled, like dead things, out of the earth, dressed in their finest. Torn velvet, with fraying ropes around their necks. Mortal-decadence-meets-sex-and-death. Skirts slit up to the thigh, or the breast. Naked ladies with thorny crowns pressed into their heads. Everything would be blood and darkness, even if the mortals weren't here to witness it. Everything would be unholy, chaotic, madness.

But oh, there was a part of me that responded to it. A part of me that wanted to wrap my hands around the darkness and dance.

I began my descent.

There, at the back of the Unseelie Castle, a stairway wound its way in circles to the ground. I took one step, then another. The servants of the Dark Court burst out of the lower doors, carrying food for the gluttons and wine for the lushes. Five more steps, and I was halfway down. Then the dancing began. The Queen had a weakness for music made from the body, so here a quartet of pixies rubbed wing against wing, quite like a string quartet except for the pain it brought. Dust drifted through the air, but those smiles never left their faces. To frown would be to suffer worse things.

Oftentimes, at the start of a celebration, the Queen required the satyr servants to dance, but tonight, dancing was everyone's revelry. Masked courtiers spun in circles while the servants swayed, saving their strength for the morning.

Then, everything stopped. For a moment, I couldn't understand it. Had a servant tripped over his feet, causing the Queen to rustle her drink? Would some small indiscretion bring the whole thing crashing down?

Then I realized the distraction was *me*. I was the guest of honor. Dressed in an ebony gown, with Kylie's gold-and-black crown atop my head, the Princess of the Dark Court had returned.

The crowd parted around me. And as the band struck up again—something wild and raucous with great, thundering beats—I made my way to the throne to my mother's right. The throne opposite of where Naeve sat.

Naeve.

I felt a sudden thrill at the thought of her sacrificing him in front of an audience.

I felt a thrill, and then the crushing weight of guilt. But did I *need* it? Guilt exists to keep us from doing bad things, and I wouldn't be doing anything bad tonight. Besides, that anger would keep me sharp come morning. Come time for battle. I shivered when I thought of all that was to come. And then I didn't think of anything anymore.

A satyr appeared beside me, his face hidden by a mask, and he bowed low, his hand held high, as if asking me to dance.

For the first time, after seventeen years of attending unnecessary celebrations, each one designed to showcase the difference between the courtiers and the servant class, I accepted the offer to dance.

And dance I did.

I spun and I spun, trading partners as I pleased, and for once, at these galas, I felt I could breathe. And even though I refrained from drinking the wine or letting the fruit slip past my lips, I began to feel drunk from the wildness of it all. I began to feel special, and royal, and appreciated.

I began to feel like I was home.

After an hour, the music climbed into my bones. It burrowed its way into my head. When a phooka stepped up and brushed my cheek with her lips, I actually smiled, a tiny laugh escaping my mouth. And when my mother looked down at me from her place on high, her lips set in a terribly firm line, I nodded, as if to say, *It's all for you, Lady.*

Then she gave me something in return. Across from the thrones, a stage was rising up from the ground. Velvet curtains swung down from above, unfurling like waves. In the center of the stage, five actors appeared, lit up by a single spotlight. Linked together by chains. Each wore a peculiar costume, their skin adorned in bruises.

Too late, I realized a look of horror had taken over my face.

My mother smiled then, a smile of true joy. "Now for the sacrifice," she said.

27

TAYLOR

I was living a nightmare. My arms were bound at the wrist, held over my head by invisible hands. Down below, Elora was bound too, in a way. The faeries of the Dark Court were closing in around her, holding her back. Wasn't that a funny turn of events? If she'd never met me, they'd never have dared to touch her that way. All of this was my fault.

I had to make it right. I just didn't know how. I looked to my left, to Kylie spinning slowly in the air, one slippered foot pointed toward the ground, one bent at the knee by magic or vines. The dark faeries would add insult to injury every chance they got. So Kylie played the prima ballerina she'd never be in real life. Alexia was the clown, her penchant for beauty exaggerated to the point of mockery, and Keegan was the guard, because he hadn't been able to protect himself, let alone his sister.

Brad was the animal, with a furry coat and floppy dog ears, because his mind had been decimated at this point. At least, I had little hope for him bouncing back, and a nagging fear of what would happen if he did.

Would the darkness that already existed inside of him spread? I mean, you don't start out an asshole, get tortured, and turn into a nicer guy. Reality just doesn't work that way. Right?

As for me, well, I wasn't entirely certain who I was supposed to be. My skin was glistening with oil and they'd given me what pretty much amounted to a flap of burlap to cover my unmentionables. Plus the crown of thorns. Maybe they just wanted me to look pretty, so it would hurt Elora more when they killed me. As if she'd betrayed her entire court because she thought I was good looking. As if she was that superficial.

They really didn't know her at all, and I hoped she would use that to her advantage. I hoped we all would. Because now that we'd all been trotted out like ponies, like slaves, the Dark Queen was rising from her throne and creeping closer. Elora, too, was led closer, dragged along by Olorian and the Lady Claremondes. It was hard to look at her, not only because I hated to see her hurt, but also because thin strands of darkness were crawling out of the Dark Lady, twisting in the air like tentacles that would reach out and choke me, and I needed to be on alert.

It was bad enough that my wrists were bleeding. I didn't need my windpipe choked off as well. I was already pretty close to freaking out.

The Dark Lady slid across the grounds, moving easily through the air like smoke. She hovered over us at an angle, something that would be impossible for a mortal, and her dress billowed out around her in jagged wisps, not unlike Elora's wings. Her *original* wings, that is. The ones that had been tattered from the start.

Wait, why had they been tattered from the start? Was it

because light and darkness were battling it out inside of her? When Elora had first come into the Seelie Court, the symbols on her arms had faded. The parts of her that were *dark* had faded, and only returned at night. But here in the Dark Court, she still had her snow-white skin. She still had her fiery hair.

The darkness wasn't washing away her light.

Because it isn't light, I realized. *Her father isn't a bright faerie.* He couldn't have been, since light erased the darkness. The second he'd touched the Dark Lady, she would have faded. Maybe disappeared entirely.

She was a being of pure darkness.

I thought of the Bright Queen's story then, of Naiad and Dryad. They'd loved each other, but they'd never actually touched. Not in the scenes that Maya de Livre had created to illustrate the story. But Naiad had touched her lover with no problem at all.

"The creature of the land," I whispered.

"Excuse me?" The Dark Lady's voice was soft, but there was a rumble beneath it, like an earthquake skittering under the ground.

"I know your secret," I said, my mouth dry and my heart thundering. "The reason Elora was born with tattered wings. The reason she went to the mortal world in the first place—"

"Stop!" The Queen lunged forward, the glamour dropping from her face. Beneath it, I caught a hint of her fury. Her anguish.

"Don't worry, your secret's safe with me," I said quickly. Darkness was creeping toward my mouth, ready to shut me up if I said too much. "In fact, I'm willing to take it to my grave, if you give me one small thing."

"I am not letting you go," she said, sneering.

"I'm not asking for that. I'm not selfish enough to bail on my friends. I just want you to hear me out."

The Queen jerked back, affronted. "Why should I do anything for you?" she demanded. "Why shouldn't I kill you now, with a flick of my wrist—"

"Because you'll never know who's been whispering behind your back. You'll never know who's been sharing your *deepest shame*."

She froze, her cheeks flushing crimson.

"Admit it," I said, glancing out at the crowd, "If you kill me now, you'll be denying yourself the chance to sacrifice the betrayer."

"That would be a pity," she agreed, her hair dancing around her head. It was hard to see in this darkness, but thin strands of scarlet ran through her hair, like blood in the blackest of lakes. "Although, if I torture you slowly, I'll be able to pluck the name of my betrayer from your muddled brain, and then I'll have everything I want."

"You could," I said, shrugging as best I could. It was hard, being captive and all. "Of course, if you do that, I'll *definitely* spill the secret."

Her smile slipped.

"Face it, Lady, I have you trapped. If you torture me slowly, I'll spill your secret to the world, and if you kill me fast, you'll never know who stabbed you in the back. So ... do we have a deal?"

She was silent a minute. Finally, she turned to the crowd. "What do you say? Shall we let the wicked wretch entertain us?"

The faeries shrieked and clapped.

"You have three minutes," she said, turning back to me. "After that, I will revert to Naeve's plan and torture each of you to see if my daughter reacts. *You*, I think, I will suffocate—"

"And if Elora doesn't react, you'll know that she's telling the truth and that Naeve's lying?"

She peered at me coolly. "I suppose. Yes."

"And if Elora's telling the truth, you'll let her go."

"Yes," the Queen said again.

I took a deep breath. "So what if Elora *isn't* telling the truth?"

The dark faeries gasped. It was beautiful, all these self-righteous assholes totally blown away by one little sentence. Elora's eyes were bugging out of her head, but I hadn't *said* she'd lied, now had I? I'd just asked a question.

Faerie-style.

"Well?" I pressed.

The tendrils of the Dark Lady's gown floated forward, tickling my face, brushing against me in a way that made me feel sick. "Then the princess will be properly punished."

"That's not what I mean," I said, trying to keep from shaking. "If Elora told the truth, and she was only intercepting humans the Bright Queen had targeted, then you can feel justified in stealing us for yourself."

The Queen raised her eyebrows, her lips twitching the tiniest bit. With one small movement, she might unhinge her jaw and swallow me whole. The way she was hovering over me reminded me of a cobra.

I swallowed, looking away. "But if Elora's lying, and she entered the mortal world of her own accord, for her own twisted gain—"

"Then she must be taught a lesson—"

"Yes, but *we* shouldn't be. Do you understand?"

She scowled, unhappy with the boy who had the audacity to cut her off, but what did I have to lose at this point?

"You only have claim to us humans if the Bright Queen went after us *first*," I said. "Our torture would be *retribution* for her breaking the sanctions agreed upon by both courts."

"He's right," Elora breathed. "I didn't even think of it, because…" She let the thought dangle, let the faeries believe she hadn't thought of it because she'd been telling the truth. "If I interacted with humanity of my own accord, then *I'm* the one who broke the sanctions, and you're complicit in the treachery by torturing them. The Bright Queen will have recourse to take humans of her own."

"She'll have recourse to wage war," I said, not wanting the faeries to focus on Elora for too long. I wanted to shift the focus from *we must punish the princess!* to *we can't punish the humans.* "Even holding on to us is cause for the Bright Queen to retaliate, if Naeve is telling the truth and Elora broke the sanctions first."

"Oh. *Oh dear.*" The Dark Queen lifted a hand to her mouth, and I knew she was mocking me. I knew, because Elora had used that same gesture to mock Brad back home. A shudder ripped through me, and I couldn't stop shaking.

She really is her mother's daughter, I thought, and shook my head. Naeve had said the exact opposite, in the graveyard.

But which was true?

I studied the Dark Queen's face for answers. "Should we let you go, then?" she asked with that same mock concern.

"What do you think, beasties? Should we give them a running start to the Bright Court?"

The dark faeries laughed. Even some of the servants snickered. I guess old prejudices weren't murdered easily, but still. These were our *lives* we were talking about. A little respect would've been nice.

"So you're just going to ignore the possibility that *you're* the one breaking the rules and let the Bright Queen come after you?" I asked. "I have to say, it's kind of a ballsy move."

"To be *ballsy*, one requires..." Her eyes draped over the burlap that barely covered me, and her lips curved into the most hideous smirk. "Well, you know. What I have is much more powerful. Still, you make a valid point. I'd hate for my daughter's wretchedness to bring trouble right to our door. So let's make this interesting."

A titter laced through the crowd, and I felt like ants were crawling over my skin. When I looked down, creatures *were* crawling over me, creatures the size of ants, and just as hungry. I knew it was the Queen's darkness, or some kind of illusion, but it stung, and I could see my feet disappearing inside of it. All five of us were being swallowed.

"If my daughter is telling the truth, we are entitled to you by law."

"Not human law," I said, "but go on." I wanted her to think she didn't scare me, even though she did. If I'd been wearing pants, I probably would've pissed them, but without anything to cover it up, I did my best to remain continent.

"But if my daughter lies... if *somehow* my daughter has managed to lie, or twist her words enough to fool her own mother, then perhaps an adjustment is in order." She lunged forward, those teeth just inches from my face, stretched into an impossible smile, the kind of thing you only see in dreams. In nightmares.

"So I will be the merciful ruler I have always been, fair and just and protective of my people."

I waited for the faeries to snicker, but they didn't. Even the few servants who had to clap their hands over their mouths to keep from screaming did so with grace. And the Queen leaned closer, so that I could smell her stale, rancid breath, the breath of a dead thing. "I will give four of you directly to the Seelie Queen, and keep only one. She cannot possibly find folly in that."

"And how will you choose?" I asked, fearing I already knew the answer. But I didn't, not the worst of it.

"Oh, I'm not going to choose," she said, spinning around to face her daughter. "She is."

Elora gasped. In the span of one second, that carefully crafted façade slipped away, revealing her true fear. Revealing her love. I wanted to offer myself up to the Queen, just to spare Elora the torment. Whether she ended up choosing me or not, the Queen would find a way to figure out I was the favorite. I was pretty sure she already knew.

"Wait! I'll … I'll … " The words died on my lips. God, I couldn't do it. Here, when Elora needed me *again,* I faltered, unable to protect her.

But maybe that wasn't the entire truth, considering I was the one who was bound. Maybe I needed to get better at trusting other people to help *me* when I needed it. It certainly hadn't been my parents' way, but not everyone was like them.

I turned to Elora. I expected her to look back at me with frightened eyes, but she'd replaced her fear with a look of pure curiosity, as if we were performing an experiment in science class.

"How, exactly, am I supposed to differentiate between *humans?*" she said, tilting her head to the side. All of that red hair spilled over her shoulders and rippled down her back. Red on white. Blood in the snow.

"I'm going to ask you a simple question," the Dark Lady said. "And you're going to answer honestly. If everything is as you say, you won't be able to lie, isn't that right?"

"Yes," Elora said without hesitation. "I am incapable of telling an untruth, just like any faerie."

"Any pureblood faerie," her mother said, and I didn't understand the distinction. Pureblood, like of royal descent? Wasn't that just a made-up title here? Wasn't that just a made-up title everywhere?

But maybe she wasn't talking about royalty at all. Maybe she was confirming what I'd already figured out.

Elora stepped forward, her handlers pulled along behind her, and suddenly it was as if she was running the show. As if they were simply there to do her bidding, should she require it of them. "Ask away," she said, all confidence, and for a second, I thought anything the Queen threw at her, she could handle.

My chest inflated like a balloon.

"Which one of these mortals do you *most* want me to release?"

The breath whooshed from Elora, and from me. I'd been expecting something simple, like "Which of these humans do you love?" or "Which of these mortals has shared your bed?" In the case of the first, Elora could've named any of us, except for Brad. And as for the bed question, well, we'd all lain together on beds of moss in the Seelie Court. In a manner of speaking, she'd "slept" with all of us. Kissed Keegan and Kylie on the cheek at some point. Wrapped her arms around Brad when they'd danced on prom night. If the Queen had asked about something purely physical, or even emotional, Elora could've handled it, but this?

This was a riddle, and one wrong move, and the mortal she *wanted* the Dark Lady to release would be the mortal who was flayed to death on this very stage.

But Elora, even if she was one step behind the Queen, was one step ahead of me. "Release from bondage, or from life?" she asked.

"Ooh, clever girl. Trying to ruin my fun." Her mother pouted, but only for a second. "Let me rephrase the question: which mortal do you most want me to release from these bonds, and hand over to the waiting hands of the Seelie Queen, completely unharmed?"

"Except for the damage you've already done."

"Except for the damage *they've* already done," the Queen said, nodding to her servants, determined not to take responsibility for our wounds. As if she hadn't ordered the dark faeries to bind us, and worse.

"And if I refuse to answer?" Elora asked.

"Then I will sacrifice them all, and take my chances with the Seelie Queen."

Elora was silent for a minute. All of us were silent, all mortals and all faeries. I wondered if they were thinking what I was thinking: if Elora really loved her people, she'd save them from the wrath of the Seelie Queen. She'd choose one of us, and let the Queen pick a sacrifice from the remaining four.

The Dark Lady's smile deepened, and I hated her so much in that moment. Hated the way she treated humans, yes, but hated the way she treated Elora even more. This was her *daughter*. The baby she must've held in her arms, if only for a second. They'd come from the same flesh, yet torturing Elora came so easily to her. And I thought I knew why.

But spilling the Dark Lady's secret would only get me killed faster at this particular moment. And naming Naeve as her betrayer wouldn't change the game she was playing with her daughter. Only a sacrifice would do that.

A personal sacrifice.

Confidence swelled in my chest once more. Confidence, and courage. I could do this. I could take the fall. Elora wouldn't have to choose, or reveal to her followers that she loved a mortal. She wouldn't have to risk her revolution.

I lifted my head, wanting to look at her one last time before the end. I opened my mouth to say: *Don't choose. I'm the one you should sacrifice. I'm the one who made Elora stay in my room, and sleep in my bed, until I was finished with her. I tricked her, trapped her, and forced her to strike a bargain.*

I am everything you expect humans to be, and worse.

I opened my mouth to say the only thing I could to save her, and my friends. But Brad beat me to it. Brad, the boy who'd caused harm wherever he went in the mortal world, and suffered every day for it in Faerie, lifted his head and said, "I know the name."

28

ELORA

For a moment, I felt as if I were underwater. I watched Brad's mouth open, so slowly I could hear the hinges creak, and the words came out, but I couldn't really process them. I was too afraid of what he might say next.

Afraid and something else, something like hunger. A hunger that creeps under your skin and burrows into your bones. A hunger born of starvation, of a life of emptiness, of wanting. Deep down in the darkest part of me, I wanted Brad to offer up himself. I wanted it not because I hated him, and not because I didn't value his life. I wanted it because there was no possible answer that would leave my true love safe. For the riddle was ...

"Impossible," I breathed.

"What was that, darling?" my mother asked, the darkness surrounding her body reaching out and slipping into Brad's mouth. Stifling him. Shutting him up for the moment.

He squirmed, but could not speak.

I spoke in his place. "The riddle is impossible," I said. "Even if you actually free the mortal I name, you will simply pursue him *after* you've handed him over to the Seelie Queen."

"*Him?*" my mother said, her lips parting into a startled O. "Who said anything about it being male?"

I rolled my eyes, as if I were back at Unity High. "Naeve has already told you I care for a male, now hasn't he? Between the one I allegedly stole from the mortal world, and the one I allegedly saved in the graveyard, you're already convinced I've fallen for a boy. Aren't you?"

I grinned, as if to say, *Your move*, but it was a mistake. I may have been able to outsmart my mother this one time, but she would wield the final blow.

"I have my suspicions," she said, and two mortals jerked to the front of the stage. The other three drifted backward, their bodies jangling like skeletons. "Naeve told me who those mortals are as well."

Damn, damn, damn.

Why did I have to take my little swing? Even if I knocked her off her feet, she'd never stay down for more than a few seconds. Not unless someone bigger was throwing the punches. Someone bigger, and older, and much more powerful than me.

I closed my eyes and reminded myself that I simply had to make it until tomorrow. Tomorrow morning, the Seelie Queen would bind my mother, the battle would wage, and without the Dark Lady to protect them, the dark faeries would fall.

Their court would.

I just had to stall. "Thank you," I said, staring up at the two mortals as if my mother had done me a favor. "This will make it much easier to prove my point."

"What point?"

"That the riddle is impossible. Suppose I choose boy number one." I gestured to Taylor. With a flick of the wrist, my mother pulled him forward until he dangled above the front of the stage. "You send boy number one to the Seelie Court, and kill the other. Am I correct so far?"

The Queen smiled but did not nod. She would not show her hand until I was finished.

Still, I said, "I thought as much," as if to fool the faeries who couldn't see her as clearly as I could. "So what happens then, exactly? What sordid scenario have you created in your mind? I run off to the Seelie Court to meet my chosen mortal, and together we live out our days amongst the bright ones?" I curled my lips in disgust, shaking my head. "You'd never let that happen. It would be too much of a slight to your court, and to your pride. You'd hunt us down and flay us in front of your congregation."

"And if I promise to leave him alive?" the Queen asked, her brow raised the tiniest bit. It was clear I'd piqued her interest, but she wouldn't show the strength of her emotion. Not now, and not if I burst into flames this very minute.

"Then someone from your court would do your dirty work for you. Isn't that how it's always been?" I asked.

"Not always," she said with a smile. "But I could easily forbid it."

I actually laughed. That startled the smile from her face. "What good would that do? Every faerie in your congregation knows you've lost control of your court. Naeve snuck away to the mortal world without your blessing. He *tortured your daughter* behind your back. That's why you're so insistent on proving that *I've* done wrong. Because if I'm innocent, that means your greatest devotee betrayed you. He went against his queen, and his people, and did whatever his wicked heart desired. And what would that say about you, then?"

Her face was redder than I'd ever seen it. In all my years in the Unseelie Court, I'd seen her turn opalescent white on the night of the full moon, or impenetrable black on the night of the dark moon. This was something new entirely. "How *dare* you—"

"You've lost your power, Lady. Even if Naeve acted in your best interest, he did it *without your permission.* Attacking the Dark Princess can only be interpreted as an act of aggression against your court. And what do you do in response? You go after *me*, the person who has been slighted in the first place, all to save your precious pride. How dare *you*—"

"ENOUGH." The Dark Queen's fury shook the ground. The mountain beneath us trembled at her rage. But something more terrible happened then. That darkness stopping up Brad's tongue crept farther into his throat, choking him. Beside him, Taylor began to shake. She was suffocating them both, punishing them for my transgressions. If I didn't choose quickly, both mortals would fall.

"Wait," I said, trying to stop my voice from shaking. If she hurt him, I wouldn't be able to keep my feelings a secret. She would know.

They would all know.

"You've given me a choice," I said, but the darkness was flooding out of her. Pouring out of her, with faces and hands and little claws scritch-scratching at the dangling mortals. Opening their skin. Licking the wounds with blackened tongues.

"Then choose!" the Dark Lady shrieked as Taylor's face

began to pale. First white, then blue. Soon purple. I had to think quickly. But I couldn't think. My heart was racing and my mind was filling with darkness.

There is no safe answer. The minute you choose one, you're giving her free license to murder the other. Then she'll go after the first.

"Choose, now!"

"I…I can't—"

"Have it your way." The Queen ripped the darkness away from Brad, her face positively glowing. Brad sputtered, coughing blood onto the ground. "Speak, mortal, and seal your fate. Which boy does my daughter love?"

Brad lifted his head, and there was so much clarity in his eyes. In that moment, he'd finally come awake. As his gaze shifted to Taylor, something inside of me snapped. No, something broken slid back into place. And I realized what I'd been denying for some time. I was not a bright and shining angel, come to save my people with benevolence and light. I was the Princess of the Dark Court, and I'd come to claim my birthright.

"Don't hurt him," I screamed, and dove in front of the mortal. The mortal named Brad.

29

TAYLOR

For five brief seconds, I didn't understand. Then I understood too much. "Don't speak," Elora cried as she leapt in front of Brad. "You don't have to lie to protect me."

The faeries shrieked. The Dark Lady gasped. And part of me died. A lot of me died.

The Unseelie Queen let go of her hold on all of us, and together we fell to the stage. Still bound at the wrists, but no longer forced to hang in the air like some kind of demented puppet troupe. Breathing didn't come easy, at first, and I wished I could touch my hands to my throat. I wished I could touch my hands to my wrists, to soothe the feeling of wire slicing into my skin. Then Brad began to rise, spinning in circles, and I wished I could cut out my eyes.

"No," Elora screamed, blocking his body with her own. "You mustn't harm him!"

"Oh, mustn't I?" her mother said. "It seems you have made your choice."

"All the more reason."

The Dark Queen shook her head. "But you didn't *speak* your answer, my darling. You didn't tell me which boy to free."

"I—"

"The riddle was simple, Elora. But you refused to comply. Now I can kill whichever mortal I choose."

"But—"

"If I were a crueler person, I'd use your shortcomings as an excuse to kill all the mortals."

Elora went so pale then, I knew my suspicions were right. She wasn't protecting Brad because she cared about him.

She was *sacrificing* him.

Cold liquid flooded my veins. In that moment, I thought of all the stupid times I'd been jealous of Brad. Back in the human world, Elora had flirted with him, but only to gain his trust. All that time, I'd been worried about the wrong thing. I shouldn't have worried that she cared about him. I should've worried that she didn't care about him *at all*.

I should've worried that she would sacrifice him to save us.

But she isn't sacrificing him, I insisted as the Dark Lady neared the stage. *Her mother is.*

Still, I couldn't shake the thought. Elora would steal one mortal to save all of Faerie. Elora would sacrifice one mortal to save four. Elora was the Dark Princess.

"But I am a merciful Queen," the Dark Lady continued, snapping her fingers and calling on her guards to seize Elora. They dragged her off the stage, away from her pretend lover, kicking and screaming.

God, how she'd fooled them.

"And I will keep my end of the bargain, though you did not," the Queen said to her daughter, who stood struggling before her. "Let this be a lesson to you of my true greatness, of my true *superiority* to you. I need not be spiteful, darling. If you'd ever truly been on my side, you would know that."

"If you'd ever truly been a mother to me, I'd have *wanted* to be on your side." Elora spat in her mother's face, and I knew she was being honest in that moment. The girl couldn't lie, but she deceived better than anyone I'd ever known. How was that possible?

"So you say," the Dark Lady said, wiping her face with her hand, and she motioned to us, the humans who would be spared by her *mercy*. "Place them in front of the stage, so they can watch properly. After that, I'll gift them to the Bright Queen as an offering. How happy she will be that the sanctions need no longer be in place." She grinned, and I closed my eyes. Behind my lids, all I could see was blood. "And then, thanks to my lovely daughter," she said, forcing my eyes to open again, "we will usher in a new age of sacrifice and bloodshed. Won't that be fun?"

Elora turned to her mother as the servants dragged the four of us from the stage. Her face was impassive as a stone. "Perhaps that was my plan all along."

"Let's put that theory to the test." The Dark Lady clapped her hands, and a strange, eerie light bled down onto Brad. That light was tinged red. "Make certain they can see it," she said to the faeries holding us captive, and suddenly there were fingers poking into my eyelids, holding them open. I struggled furiously to blink. I struggled to look away from Brad. I failed.

Brad's body was still circling, but his head was hanging limp. Could he even breathe with his arms jerked over his head like that?

"Aw, has the baby grown tired of being held upright?" the Queen said, her gaze drifting over the crowd. It settled on the Lady Claremondes. "Won't you be a darling and wake him up?"

No, no, no. Please. I can't watch this.

But I didn't have a choice. Those fingers had slid under my eyelids, holding them against my brow bones. Eyelashes broke away and fell into my eyes. I couldn't get rid of them. It was terrible. But it was about to get so much worse, because the Lady Claremondes was slithering across the ground, her long, ethereal tail sloughing off skin as she went. She didn't have as much of a tongue as she used to, thanks to Naeve. He'd ripped off the poisonous appendage to use against me in the graveyard. Elora had stopped him then, sacrificing her body to save mine.

My heart ached at the thought. Ached with love, and with sorrow. She wouldn't just sacrifice Brad to save me. She'd sacrifice herself, her life, and her wings. It was sick, but I really knew she loved me in that moment. Really accepted it. And, as horrified as I was with what was about to happen, I wished she was the tiniest bit closer to me, so that I could grasp her hand. I could slide my thumb over her palm in the way that I knew soothed her nerves. I could tell her that, no matter what happened, I really did love her. My heart belonged to her.

Forever.

When Kylie's hand slid over mine, tears sprang to my eyes. This was it, even if the Queen was telling the truth. Even if we survived. This was the final moment before our humanity got swallowed by the darkness. No matter the outcome, the dark faeries would win. We would be destroyed.

"Here," I said, so quietly that only Keegan could hear. He felt my hand reaching, and took it. Alexia followed suit. Luckily, our shackles were loose enough that we could find each other. Together we stood, the four of us, mere mortals in a Court of Dark Faeries, and watched a human lose his life.

It started with a snap. The Lady Claremondes was all set to unleash her venom on Brad's neck, when she stopped and reached out to break a single finger instead. *Snap*. So easy, just like that.

Brad shook, but didn't lift his head.

"Just checking," she hissed. The faeries laughed.

My whole body felt cold. I squeezed Kylie's hand, but it didn't help.

"Now then," the Lady Claremondes said, and trailed her stump of a tongue over Brad's neck. I could *hear* the poison sliding over him. I waited for the silence that lulled you into a false sense of security. The silence and then the scream. It's so much louder that way. So much worse. Brad's scream began in his gut and ripped its way through the length of him, almost shattering our eardrums. I actually forgot my hands were bound and scrabbled to cover my ears.

Then pain, so much pain, shooting through my wrists. So much fear, pouring off of Brad's skin. He was shaking, the poison spreading through his bloodstream. Now the Lady Claremondes wrapped one long, sugar-white dreadlock around his neck. Her built-in noose.

She turned to the Unseelie Queen. "Shall I give him a rest?" she asked.

Elora's mother grinned. Whatever magic she'd used to keep Brad in the air slipped away, and he careened to the ground. Just before he hit the stage, the Lady Claremondes caught him with her noose.

Elora screamed. Brad scrambled wildly, clawing at his throat, but he couldn't free himself.

"Stop," Elora sobbed, sinking to her knees. That golden crown went tumbling from her head.

The Lady Claremondes rose higher in the air, using Brad's agony as leverage against the girl who appeared to love him. Elora covered her face with her hands. I honestly didn't know if she was devastated by the torture of Brad, or if she was acting. The thought chilled me to my core. Even my spirit shook with the force of it.

"Stop?" the Lady Claremondes asked Olorian, her partner in crime, who'd reached the base of the stage and was watching hungrily. In just three steps, he joined her up above, his footfalls shaking the earth.

"Should we?" she asked.

Olorian chuckled, his inky black body crackling with excitement. "Let us leave it up to him."

The Lady Claremondes nodded silently, wrapping her arms around a struggling Brad. For a minute, it looked like she was cradling him. She smoothed his hair away from his face, whispering sweetly into his ear.

Then Olorian wrenched his arm from its socket.

Kylie wailed and tried to break free. She didn't, but in the commotion, her captor lost hold of her eyes. When the three of us saw her eyes close, we followed suit, jerking away from those hands. Even one second away from this horror would be better than none.

The Queen said, "*Wake him up*," and I realized Brad must've passed out. Kylie moaned, leaning into me. "One little lick makes baby sick," I whispered, remembering the rhyme the

Lady Claremondes had chanted in the graveyard. "Two on the neck is baby's death. Remember? It could be over soon."

Kylie was quiet a minute, watching the faeries transform Brad into a pile of mortal ruins. One finger snapped after another, but the Lady Claremondes didn't run that tongue over him again. "I don't remember much from that night," Kylie said.

"What about the earlier part?" I asked, as the faeries struggled to hold our eyes open. But now that we'd proven we could shake them off, they were less enthusiastic. Or maybe they actually felt bad and were giving us a break from the horror. "Remember getting ready, and the actual dance?" I said. "Remember when Alexia announced that she loved you in front of the entire school?"

Kylie inhaled, a baby sound. Twisting to the side, I could see the tiniest flash of a smile.

Keegan's voice surprised me. "I about pissed my pants at that."

"Me too," I admitted. Now that all of Brad's fingers were broken, he was coming awake again.

Close your eyes, stupid, I told myself.

"Remember when stuff like that seemed important? School shit?" Keegan asked.

"It was important. That was our life, then," I said. Even if we couldn't block out what was happening, maybe we could put something else in front of it. Something brighter. Less horrifying.

"Then you disappeared from the dance," Keegan said, picking up on my game. For a brief second, I wasn't in the

Unseelie Court. I was on the grounds outside the prom ball-room. Alone with Elora.

"I actually thought I might get some that night," I said.

Alexia snorted, nearly drowning out Brad's strangled cries. The Lady Claremondes was tightening her noose. It was almost time.

"Really?" Kylie asked, her voice rising in pitch. We were all so desperate to escape this.

"No," I admitted, and we laughed. We couldn't help it. It was either laugh or start screaming. "No, I knew it wasn't going to happen. I never thought it was going to happen."

And that was it. That brought us back to the present moment. Because it still hadn't happened. Elora and I had never had our moment. Not the way I'd wanted it. Not just the two of us, tucked away in some normal place, in the mortal world, making love for the first time. Sure, I'd said "get some" to my friends, but it had always been about more than that. Being with Elora made me feel alive, loved, exhilarated.

"Please ... let him go," Elora whispered from her place on the ground. She looked weak, like she couldn't even stand up. And I knew, in that moment, she wasn't faking this agony.

"You said the magic words, *princess*." The Lady Clare-mondes grinned. She had no teeth. Had she ever had teeth?

Why am I focusing on this?

She looked down at Brad. "Should we let you go?"

He stared at her with anguished child's eyes. He tried to speak.

The Lady's smile deepened. "Release you from this cruel creation and the filth of your wicked kind?"

Brad nodded in little jerks, choking on eagerness and bile.

"No," I breathed. Kylie was shaking her head. Elora still knelt, frozen.

The Lady Claremondes tilted her head. "Let your body give way to sweet release?"

"Yes," Brad croaked, crying into her chest. "*Please*."

"As you wish." She twisted his neck until it cracked.

30

ELORA

The Queen was true to her word. After the decimation of Brad was complete, she waved a regal hand, and the servants of the Dark Court carried the remaining humans away. I should've been happy that she'd released them into the hands of my followers. But happiness was a far-off island that I dared not hope to reach. I felt entirely depleted, as if all my blood had seeped out onto the ground.

Of course, it hadn't. Only Brad's insides were feeding the earth at this very moment. As crows swarmed around him, diving into his warm places, I turned away, facing my congregation. My people. Only … they didn't feel like my people anymore. *My* people were the ones scurrying away, to be delivered to the eager hands of the Seelie Queen. Given. As if people could ever be given.

Why had it taken me so long to learn that lesson? Even Brad, who'd caused only destruction in his world, was not mine to remove. Funny I should realize the flaw in my justification the moment I was too late to remedy things. His blood streaked the stage, entrails hanging out like fat, juicy worms. Even though I wasn't looking anymore, I could still see it.

I would always see it.

I stepped farther away, watching the progress of the humans as they slipped into a passage that led into the earth. I tried to focus on this, their freedom. Their escape. And right before he stepped into the shadows, Taylor turned and looked my way. His eyes were alight with fear, or sadness. I shook my head. As much as I wanted to run to him, draw him into my arms and beg forgiveness, for understanding, I knew there was no point in blowing our cover now. The dark faeries had fallen for my ruse, believing Brad to be the one I wanted. Taylor was safe. Even if he never wanted to touch me again, he would live.

That was enough, for now.

Five minutes after the human sacrifice, the Dark Queen clapped her hands and the music commenced. Trolls stomped their feet to create a drumbeat, and the winged section jerked fervently. As tactless as it was to dance in circles before the blood had even dried, the servants of the Dark Court did not dare rebel against the Queen now. It had been a long time since they'd seen a show of her true power and how easily she could kill. How easily she could torture without batting those beautiful eyes. The faeries of the Dark Court may have simply been a manifestation of the earth's darker aspects, but their queen was evil.

And she needed to be taken down.

"Mother," I called out, sounding desperate without even trying. The Dark Lady turned to me, head cocking to the side like a bird listening for the sound of worms under the earth. Again, an image of Brad flashed through my mind, and I shuddered involuntarily.

"You dare speak to me, wretch?"

"Please," I begged, playing at obedience, though it was the last thing I felt. "You granted Naeve an audience. You believed he betrayed you, yet you granted him an audience. Won't you do the same for your own flesh? Your own blood? Please. I can explain."

"I've no cause to believe you," the Queen said. "You've sullied your flesh with human filth. You've stood before me and lied. You are as far from a faerie as I can possibly imagine, and I care not for your twisted words." She rose from her throne and made a simple flicking motion with her wrist. "Away with this aberration. I will deal with her when I have finished celebrating Naeve's exoneration."

In his seat on her left-hand side, Naeve grinned like I'd never seen him grin. I actually wondered if the Queen would take him to her bed tonight. As far as I could tell, she hadn't taken a lover since the day I was born, but I was as good as dead to her now.

Naeve gave me the tiniest nod of the head, as if to say, *enjoy your exile.*

A shiver went down my spine. Exile would be my best-case-scenario punishment. "Lady, please, I can explain myself. It isn't what you think."

"No," she agreed. "You aren't."

"You *must* give me a chance." I was growing angry. "You gave him a chance, and he isn't … "

"My flesh and blood, yes. You've said that. But that can be amended."

Naeve perked up at that, like a puppy long-starved of attention. It was pathetic. Sad. And I was just as desperate. When the Queen lifted her arm, I expected her to pat him on the head. But she did something stranger. She lifted her wrist to his lips. "Drink," she told him. "Become 'my blood.'" Her eyes turned to me. "By the time I'm done bleeding out the princess, you'll be the only child left with royal blood."

Oh, Darkness. What have I done?

Naeve's teeth sank into her royal flesh.

Without me to defend them, and with Naeve as the Unseelie heir, the faeries of the Dark Court would be cast into a future of bloodshed and war. They would crawl over the human world, covering it like a blight of Darkness, sucking the life out of everything. The earth would live on, but at what cost? The very ocean would be choked with blood.

I had to find a way to turn the tides.

"Please, Lady," I said, gesturing to Brad. My stomach churned like a blood-spattered sea. "You've taken the boy. Naeve's taken my wings. Have I not been punished for my alleged transgressions? Will you at least grant me an audience, *one minute* of your time? What is one minute out of eternity?"

The Queen's head was bent back, her eyes closed. Naeve seemed to be sucking her dry. For a moment I thought it might work to my advantage, this weakening of her strength. Then I felt sicker than ever, always relying on the dark faeries' ability to weaken and manipulate. To trick. Always looking for the way to gain the upper hand by stepping on another's head.

I really was my mother's daughter. How ironic that she'd never know.

After a minute of frenzied slurping, Naeve lifted his head. His teeth were stained red, and he was shaking a little, as if dizzy. One drink, and he was already addicted.

Junkie.

The Queen's eyes fluttered open. I had no doubt Naeve was waiting for her final blow, but he didn't know her as well as I did. We were so alike after all, she and I. And if she could bolster my spirits, only to drop me from a much greater height, she'd do it.

It's what I would've done.

"Very well," she said quietly, so that only those closest could hear. "If you perform one simple task, I will grant you an audience."

"Yes, Lady?"

She looked at Brad, at what remained of him, and smiled. "Go have a tea party with your darling."

No...

I inhaled shakily, remembering the stories of my mother's "tea parties" in the Middle Ages. Less tea and cake, and more blood dripping from little cups. Chairs made out of mortal bones. "I...don't think I can."

"If you are my daughter, you can." It was as if she was reading my thoughts and wanted to test me on them. To snuff out the last of my compassion and make me give in to my wickedness. If I could sit in a puddle of my beloved's blood and drink of his body, I would become like her, unfeeling as a stone. Or I would break, and be useless to my people. Either way, she'd win.

"Please, Lady."

"This is your choice. One cup for one minute of my time. Or I can punish you now..."

I shook my head. The minute she bled me out, the revolution would be lost. The servants were already shaken from witnessing her true wrath and my affection for a mortal. To expect them to stand against her tomorrow, without me to stand with them, and without the Bright Queen's binding...

I did not want to imagine the slaughter that would ensue.

I did not want to imagine it, and yet my feet were moving forward, toward a slaughter of a different kind. On shaky legs, I climbed the steps of the stage. My dress for the party was black, so Brad's blood seeped into it like water. Creeping over the edges. Staining me before I'd begun.

"There's a good princess," my mother said as I sat among the wreckage, and now I was the dog, the pup waiting to be rewarded.

Punished, then rewarded.

I struggled to keep the contents of my stomach from rising, and I hadn't even taken a sip yet. My mother procured a cup out of *nothing.* "Darlings?" she said to a pair of midnight blue pixies hovering at her back. Dark horns curled out of their heads, and their wings buzzed so quickly, I could hardly see them. Within seconds, they'd delivered the cup to my hands. The porcelain was white, a strange color for my mother to choose, but then, it would help me see the blood.

I cannot do this.

Of all the laws of Faerie that had been broken, this was the worst.

"Lady, there is iron in mortal blood. This will poison me."
Again.

She nodded, and her lips did not twitch toward a smile. Her eyes did not soften to reveal remorse. She was as unfeeling as a stone. "Hence the *little* cup," she said. "Wasn't that nice of me?"

I bit my lip and tasted blood. That was a mistake.

"Besides, you've felt the sting of iron before and survived," she reminded me, and it sounded like a taunt. A challenge. "What faerie can say that?"

What was she suggesting? Already the world was spinning before my eyes as I lowered the little cup to Brad's body. His blood was pooling in places where his wounds were the worst. My vision swam with red as I tilted the cup.

Blood poured in, a little whirlpool churning and churning.

My world was churning. I fought to stay conscious as I lifted the cup to my lips. My hand shook so terribly, blood was sloshing over my fingers. In the background, my mother's voice drifted in from another galaxy. She whispered, "Only you, darling."

Then my world turned to black.

31

TAYLOR

I didn't think I was going to make it. My legs were so heavy. I kept trying to think of something that weighed more than lead, but I couldn't think straight enough to do it. I couldn't *think* at all, but all the while, images kept flashing before me.

Here, I saw the packed-in dirt of the tunnel up ahead. A dead end, I thought. No, I didn't think it. I *saw* it. My eyes transmitted messages to my brain, but before they could be analyzed, they slipped away like rain. Like blood from a lifeless corpse.

Brad.

And just like that, I saw him in front of me. I could barely process the fact that I was walking *through* the dead end— *another glamour among millions*, I thought, and then that, too, slipped away from me. I was slipping in Brad's blood, drowning in the depths of it, trying to carry the both of us to safety, and sinking in the process.

A body smacked the ground. His body?

No. Mine.

"Get up," a faerie said, yanking me to my feet. *Another faerie among millions.* I knew the creatures that led us to safety—*Ha! Safety?*—were not the ones who'd attacked Elora on prom night. Were these faeries on our side, eager to get us to the Seelie Court so their rebellion could begin?

Or were they only acting on the order of their precious Queen? A woman I could go my entire life without seeing again. God, it was a wonder Elora hadn't turned out completely wicked, with a mother like that. It was a wonder she could love anything, let alone a forbidden human. Now I could see her face in front of me, as we turned to the left and headed down. As we moved through another tunnel that looked like a dead end.

She beckoned me forward, eyes glistening with tears of love. But her dress was torn and muddy, and blood stained her hands. Blood stained her lips. Had she been drinking it? Would she drink mine?

My guts twisted, and I shook my head. I couldn't stop shaking. And Elora kept beckoning to me, a vision with blood-covered hands, and I kept walking to her, no matter what it meant. No matter the danger.

Was I so desperate to feel her one more time that I'd let those crimson hands run through my hair, staining me? Would I taste the blood on her lips, and smile?

Was there anything I wouldn't do for her?

Is there anything she hasn't done for you? a voice whispered, and I swear, it came from outside of me.

"Just a little longer," the vision of Elora promised. And I listened. God help me, I followed her. She led me from the darkness into the light.

It started with a flash, like the first spark of a raging fire. It happened so quickly, I worried I'd imagined it. Then I realized there were branches up ahead, shifting and twirling and revealing the world in little patches. I thought, *Here we'll come upon the entrance to the Seelie Court, and hands will reach out to guide us over the border. Hands that are brown and strong like the earth, like nature, not like evil and darkness and death. Hands that stroke rather than choke, in a court that was created to protect us.*

Then an image of Brad tied up in the Seelie Court flashed through my mind, and I realized I'd never be safe again. Realized safety didn't exist.

I stopped in my tracks. Two faeries ran into my back, and Kylie mumbled, "What are you doing?"

I turned and found her clutched in Alexia's arms. "I have to go back."

"We are going back," she said, pointing to the light. That's when I realized what I should've noticed from the start: we weren't moving toward the light. *It* was moving toward us, bobbing and weaving between the trees. A single orb of light, illuminating the dark forest.

Shit.

"I don't want to see her," I said, backing into the darkness. The faeries were staring at me like I'd lost my mind, and maybe I had. But I couldn't go back to the Seelie Court just to get trapped there. Not with the Seelie Queen, who knew my full name. Not with Maya de Lyre, who was no longer a prisoner now that Brad had died.

"Please, I can't go back there," I said, but the faeries weren't looking at me anymore. Now the light was spilling through the forest, and they shrieked, covering their eyes.

A faerie with shimmering cobalt skin stepped forward, braving the light. "You are not welcome here," he snarled as the orb of light broke free from the shadows. It spilled over the darkness, obliterating it.

The dark faeries screamed and raced away from us, seeking sanctuary in the forest behind us.

Both Kylie and Alexia slumped to the ground, unable to move any farther. Keegan fell against a tree, and I followed suit. "I have to go back," I told them.

"I understand," Keegan said. "I'll try to hold her off."

I almost laughed because the idea was so ridiculous. But still, it was ridiculously nice of him to offer, to put my safety before his. I squeezed his hand. "I'll come back for you," I said, and it was a promise.

"She has no claim to us," he replied.

I nodded, backing away into the darkness. "Don't let them trick you," I said. "Don't split up."

"Promise."

I nodded again, throat tight at the thought of leaving them. But I had to help Elora, and I had to trust them to take care of themselves.

That was the problem with loving somebody, I guess. You wanted to do everything in your power to protect them, but if you did that, you might keep them trapped in a clearing somewhere, safe from harm. Safe, and caged.

I let my friends go. They let me go, and I raced into the darkness. I leapt over logs, like I had that first day in the Seelie Court. But now, with the Bright Queen's light *behind* me, I couldn't see very well, and I tripped over a root.

I tripped and went flying.

My head scraped a rock as I went down.

No, no, no, I begged as light danced behind my eyes.

Behind them. In front of them. God, I couldn't get away from that damn light.

But slowly, painfully, I opened my eyes. The fall hadn't knocked me out. I could do this. I tried to push myself to my knees.

But I couldn't. My body had used up the last of its energy bolting away from the Queen. The Dark Queen. The Bright Queen. Here, now, it was rebelling. My arms shook and refused to hold me. My legs stopped working entirely. As light spilled over me, I thought of Elora's face. I promised her that this wasn't the end, that I'd come back for her, somehow.

Then I didn't promise anything anymore, because darkness came for me. It was beautiful, and it came from within. I saw wings, and an endless obsidian sky. I saw the universe, galaxy upon galaxy. Eternity unfolded.

And then I saw nothing.

32

ELORA

I awoke in a bed. *My own bed.* For a moment, I sprawled out, tangled up in velvet and satin, in red and black. Those colors I couldn't escape. Those colors that *were* a part of me, but not the only part. Each one of us is a spectrum filled with darkness and light. Filled with violet twilights and golden dawns, crimson sunsets and emerald leaves. Emerald eyes.

Taylor.

I sat up in bed. My mother sat beside me, upon the actual bed, rather than in the ever-present throne that she'd built into every room of the castle as a symbol of her omnipotence.

What did this closeness mean? Was she coming to me as an equal? The idea seemed ridiculous, but so did the thought that she'd kill me here, so far from her congregation.

Why not make it a show?

I licked my lips and came away with the foulest taste.

"Here," my mother said, holding out a goblet of silver. I lifted the liquid to my nose.

"It's *water*," she said, and I almost laughed, it was so unexpected. "To flush out the iron."

"Why?" I asked, drinking all the same. She was right. It was water. It tasted amazing.

Beside me, my mother kneaded the blankets silently. No matter, I had more pressing questions to ask.

"How long have I been asleep?"

"Hours," she said simply, studying my face. Was there something wrong with me? Was I covered in blood?

Oh, Darkness.

The night was coming back to me slowly. But if I closed my eyes, I could almost push it away.

My mother caught me before I fell back onto the bed. What was *happening*?

"Is it morning?" I managed, dread creeping over my gut. I had to open my eyes to see she was shaking her head.

"Several hours until dawn."

"And the congregation?"

"Some continue to dance. Others are sleeping wherever they might fall."

Yes, perfect. Perfect, perfect. I can still finish what I started.

"And you?" I asked, giving her doe eyes. Trying, but my body wanted to sleep so badly, possibly forever. I didn't remember drinking Brad's blood, but I could taste iron on my lips. "Have you come to grant me my minute?"

"More fairly, your *second*," she said, confirming my suspicions. "You were unable to complete my simple request for a tea party, but you did manage to fall into a puddle."

I swallowed thickly.

"You ingested but a little blood," she said. "There, where it splashed on your lips."

I turned to the side of the bed and retched.

"Probably more effective than the water," she said, ever calm and unperturbed. Then again, she wouldn't be the one to clean up after me.

"I'll use my second wisely, then," I said, wiping my lips. She handed me the water again. I didn't even remember her taking it.

How am I going to fight?

"Whenever you're ready," my mother said, glancing at an invisible watch. Good Darkness, was she making a joke? Who was this creature? Had the Bright Lady somehow taken her place?

It didn't seem possible, and I wasn't taking any chances. I spoke quickly. "When I arrived at the Unseelie Palace, I traded places with the mortal girl in the burgundy gown, using glamour, and *she* is the one who lied to you about my feelings for the mortals. I remain a humble servant to Faerie, unable to tell an untruth."

My mother stared into me, her eyes widening to illustrate her surprise. "That was more than a second, but well used." She inhaled slowly. "I must admit, it frightened me to learn you could lie so easily. To see Naeve spell it out in his own blood. That was the moment I knew that I'd lost you."

"You never *had* me," I said, and tears sprang to my eyes. "Never held me. Never spoke to me of love." How could she claim to have lost me?

She lowered her head, but she did not cry. My mother could never, would never show such emotion. Still, the idea that she might actually *feel* it, and keep it hidden, did more than surprise me. It called my entire life into question.

I lay back in the bed, promising to only close my eyes for a moment. Promising myself. Promising my people. I only had a few hours left to accomplish my task.

My mother's voice brought me back. "Suppose I believe you," she said, and even in my exhaustion, I murmured, "You *do* believe me."

"I want to. But suppose it is true, what you say. What then? You've put me in an impossible position, Elora. Whatever your intentions, you *cared* for a *human*. And thus, the laws of Faerie *have* been broken."

"Those aren't the laws of Faerie," I exclaimed, and I was startled by my own outburst. "Those are *your* laws."

She shook her head. "The earth has guided everything I have done."

"But all of us believe that. You, me, the entire Seelie Court. How can it be the earth's will for us to destroy each other, and all humans? What purpose would that serve?"

My mother shrugged. "Clean slate," she said simply. I realized, then, how deeply her hatred of humanity ran. She would destroy all of Faerie if it meant the death of humanity. "The earth will survive. That is the bottom line."

"There's more to life than a bottom line. Why focus on a perfect world instead of improving this one? Certainly, an earth devoid of all beings would have the *purity* you crave, but we would cease to exist."

"As long as the earth survives, there will be faeries."

"But not these ones. Not *us*."

"I would sacrifice myself for that cause."

"Easy to say, Mother, but you haven't. I'm the only one making sacrifices. I've been making them all night. Why did you do that to me? If you truly believed I loved him, it was evil. And if you didn't—"

"I *didn't*," she shouted, and the ceiling shook. "How could I believe that? Good Darkness. Elora, my precious daughter, sullied by—"

"You put on a good show." I shook my head. "But so do I, so I've learned to recognize it. And you knew there was a possibility that I cared for one of them. Even a little."

"Must you make me say it? Yes, I knew there was a possibility. But in my heart of hearts, I never thought you would react so pathetically."

"Is that what I did?" I asked, thinking: *That was the show.* Of course, I had felt awful for Brad, but that original cry, and throwing my body in front of him, had been intentional. *Answering* the riddle would've revealed my true feelings. But *showing* feelings for Brad, well … that was the only way to save Taylor.

"Yes, you made quite a scene. I wasn't expecting it."

"What did you expect?"

"I expected you to be smart enough to control yourself, to behave like a princess. Don't you see? If you had simply allowed me to kill one of the *other* mortals, and refused to react, I could've freed you of the charges! You would be sitting beside me on your throne, with Naeve as your footstool, instead of lying in bed half-alive with blood on your lips."

I am not the only one with blood on my lips, I thought, an image of Naeve flashing through my mind. But I did not say that. I was too filled with sorrow, too filled with regret. The idea that my mother had being trying to *help* me with her riddle seemed impossible. And yet …

"Lady—Mother," I amended, and pushed myself onto my elbows. "I want to tell you everything. I want you to understand that what I did was not an abomination of nature. I went to the human world to help our people. I *promise* you."

She couldn't argue with that. Not if she believed I couldn't tell a lie. And I *couldn't*, in spite of the fact that mortal blood was now swimming in my veins. It was only a taste, and besides, I'd meant what I said: I remained a humble servant of Faerie.

Whatever the price.

"Now that we've spoken our truths … " I lowered my head, feigning shyness. "Could we go somewhere, away from all this? Away from the foolish dancing, and Naeve, with newly royal blood in his veins. Somewhere we won't be bothered?" *Or found.* "I want you to know everything, but I don't want them to overhear and use it against me. It will not make as much sense to … simpletons."

I smiled wickedly, and she smiled to match me. I wanted her to think we were cut from the same cloth, the only faeries good enough, *royal* enough, to understand what others could not. That false sense of superiority would be her downfall.

But for now, it was the key to separating her from the rest.

"Perhaps the forest at the base of the mountain?" I suggested. There, we would be close enough to the borderlands for the Bright Queen to come to my aid, but not too far from the castle to return by morning.

"Ah, and perhaps you'll catch a glimpse of the humans on their travels?" the Dark Lady said suspiciously.

I rolled my eyes. "Trust me, Mother. The last thing I want is to cross paths with them tonight."

And that, too, was the truth. The farther away they were from this place, and from *me*, the safer they would be.

But my mother, poor darling, did not catch my meaning, and she smiled down at me. "Very well," she said, lifting my golden crown from the ground. It must've fallen off during the sacrifice. "I do grow tired of the same old thing. Let us venture from this place, and if you can prove your intentions were favorable to the dark faeries, I may find a way to spare you yet." She placed the crown atop my head.

I smiled, as if joy was flooding my heart. Really, I was drowning in a sea of darkness. By the end of this night, the Dark Lady's foolishness might well spare my freedom.

Pity I couldn't say the same of hers.

33

TAYLOR

I was having the strangest dream. I knew it was a dream, in spite of the fact that it felt *so real*, because Elora was in it. She was sitting right in front of me.

"You're here," I whispered, pulling her into my arms. I was in the Dark Court, just like I'd been when I passed out. Elora felt unusually hot. Like, lit up from the inside. Like a burning ball of light come to set me ablaze.

I guess I was a little delirious.

"God, is it really you?" I asked, touching her cheeks, her lips, her hair. "I thought I wasn't going to see you..."

Until tomorrow? Ever?

"I know," she said, her voice strangely garbled. It must've been the dream. You know how you try so hard to remember something correctly, and it just gets more distorted?

"I missed you so much. I love you." I pulled her back into my arms, and she hugged me back, kind of. "I'm going to stand with you tomorrow. I'm going to fight."

"It's too dangerous," she said. "You've only just escaped—"

"But that's the point. Now that I know what they're capable of, I can't abandon you there."

I started to feel hot, like intuition was reminding me of something. But that's the thing about dreams: you don't have to focus on anything you don't want to. So Elora's mother had sacrificed Brad. That was a problem for Real-Life-Taylor. Dream-Taylor was only going to focus on the girl in front of him. The girl he needed to be close to before morning came.

Who am I kidding? It's already here.

I tried to chart the sun's progress across the horizon, but it was difficult. The darkness hovered over everything, blotting out the light. Wait, why was the dream world exactly like the real world, except for Elora's presence?

She couldn't *really* be here.

"Listen close, for we do not have much time," she instructed, and I nodded, forgetting my thoughts so I could focus on her. She looked blurred around the edges, like she'd thrown on a glamour while racing through the forest. "I refuse to forbid you," she said. "But I need to preserve you—"

"Like a jam," I muttered, but what I thought was: *Like a non-corpse.* God, my mind was jumbled.

I needed to gather my thoughts. They fluttered like insects in my brain. They wiggled like worms. I tried to hook one. "But I owe it to you to fight," I said, drawing the thought out of the muck of my mind. "I owe it to you, and us, and the world. I have to do what's right."

"I thought you might say that." Elora's lips curved down on the ends. I don't think I'd ever seen her frown so completely. Then her body flickered with light, like a lightbulb turning on under her skin. "I have something for you."

"What is it?" I perked up, thinking she'd give me something romantic. A lock of her hair, or a drop of blood—no, not blood; I'd seen enough of that to last a lifetime. But something else. Maybe a life-affirming kiss.

When she stood and walked toward the shadows, I didn't understand. Then she came back holding something tangled and dark, and my stomach dropped so hard I thought I might fall over. "You still have your old wings," I breathed, hardly able to talk. "But I thought…"

"Oh these? These are not for me."

I narrowed my eyes. In the dim light, I watched her pull a needle and thread out of her pocket.

"Think on it, Taylor. Think on what we have learned about faeries and mortals. If I give you these, perhaps you can—"

"What… fly?"

"Why not?"

"Uh, because I never had wings in the first place. Because I don't have anything to attach them to. What's going on with you?"

There was something strange about this entire operation—I mean, besides the obvious lack of logic. She was plotting something. Something she wasn't saying.

"You worry too much," she said, brushing the hair away from my neck. "Now, won't you be a good boy and turn around?"

How could she talk to me this way? So casually, like there was nothing between us.

"Let's talk about this," I said, turning my back to her. Wait, why had I done that?

"The time for talking has passed," Elora said in my ear, and it gave me all kinds of shivers. But not the good kind.

The kind that warned of something terrible to come. "I truly believe you'll be happy when this is all over."

"When this is all over? What does that even mean? We're going to battle in a few hours. We're … " Then it hit me. This whole sordid encounter was a means to an end. And all those stories about trusting and respecting me? Total bullshit.

I squirmed away from her hands. But damn, she was strong. Was she always this strong? "You can't do this," I said, trying to catch her eyes. They looked greener than usual, which was strange, considering it was still dark under the trees. "You think this will keep me from going into battle, but it won't."

"Why would I want to keep you away from the battle?"

"Because you don't think I'll survive." I shook my head, talking more to myself than to her. "You said it yourself, that night on the hill. Trying to reattach your wings would have put you out of commission for weeks. Your body would have been too weak to fight. But it'll be different with me, because my body will reject them. This could kill me."

"I would not be doing this if I thought that were a remote possibility."

"How can you know that?"

Finally she looked at me. But the look she gave didn't calm me. It scared me. She had absolutely no emotion on her face. "You're going to make this difficult, aren't you?" she said, putting her hands on my shoulders.

I felt like two rocks were pressing down on me. "What are you doing?" I demanded, struggling to breathe.

She sighed, not even straining to hold me in place. "I had hoped that your love for the princess would allow me to perform the ritual with ease."

"*What ritual?* And why are you talking like that? Is this the royal *we?*"

"The ritual you promised me."

"I didn't promise—"

"You promised forgiveness, too."

"I—"

"Taylor Christopher Alder."

"What?"

"Sit still."

I couldn't argue. I couldn't move. It was like she had complete control over me. But it wasn't until the needle pierced my skin that I realized two things:

This wasn't a dream. And she wasn't Elora.

34

ELORA

My mother and I walked until the commotion was a dull roar, and then we walked some more. Down the twisting ledge that had threatened to pitch the humans to the rocks below. Through the Unseelie Forest. The bright faeries might've had lush, leafy trees, but we had hundreds of beastly things: thorns that bit and brambles that tore. Tall pines reaching into forever, glistening with icicles and glittering beneath the stars. A cluster of rocks here, jagged and beckoning.

One might sit and rest a while. One might be crushed. You never knew. That was the danger of the Dark Court, and the thrill. All of us were chasing death because we didn't know what to do with our long lives. Long, and unfulfilled.

Until now.

"Perhaps we could rest here," I said, gesturing to a cluster of moss-covered rocks. We'd reached a point in the forest where the ground dropped off swiftly, leading almost straight down. If I looked far enough into the distance, I could see the place where the drop-off led directly to the border between the courts, there below.

But a faerie of the Seelie Court wouldn't have to wait for

us at the borderlands today. Today, all sentries of the Dark Court were attending the celebration, leaving the border unguarded.

That was my mother's first mistake.

"Let us seek shelter beneath these pines," I said, and sat beneath the second-to-largest tree. My mother would surely choose the largest, and this served my purposes as well.

"The wicked sun is less bright in the shade," my mother agreed. The darkness that blanketed the Unseelie Palace was more like a film here, a thin, insubstantial veil through which one could see the light. It hung low on the horizon, indicating early morning. The higher it rose, the weaker she would become.

She sat upon a low-hanging branch, just as I'd suspected she would, facing away from the drop-off.

That was her second mistake.

I almost smiled. Down below, I could see a ball of light moving through the forest like a second sun, bold and bright and just as powerful. Gold among green. Beautiful in its own way.

"How much time will you give me?" I asked.

My mother shrugged. It seemed too careless a gesture for her. It occurred to me, in this moment, that she'd *never* wandered through the court with me. Never went on a long, leisurely walk. Never took her daughter on an adventure.

Here, with the court's fall imminent on the horizon, like those two shining lights coming from the east, my mother was giving me the things I'd always wanted. Her time. Her attention. Herself, removed from the court and her title as queen.

Surely, that couldn't be a sign?

"My faeries will sleep through the morning," she said.

"Only when the fog lifts, and the sun rises high into the sky, will they scurry back into the earth like worms."

"So…"

"So, you have until then."

"That is more than gracious."

"I told you." She looked at me with pity, with condescension. "I am a most merciful Queen."

"I suppose you could always be worse," I allowed.

She laughed at that. "Indeed I could. I could've slaughtered all the mortals, and my daughter, in a matter of minutes. I could've fed you to the wolves."

"The wolves like me," I said, a petulant child. Still, how many times had I curled up in my mother's bed, amongst her wolves, while she was off ruling her kingdom with an iron fist? The *wolves* had been there for me.

"They may well love you," she said, licking her lips as if the word tasted unfamiliar. As if it tasted funny. For a minute, I thought she might spit. Instead, she smiled. "But not as much as they love to eat."

I scowled, looking away from her. Down below, that moving light had disappeared, which meant the Seelie Queen had reached the bottom of the drop-off and was just outside my line of vision. My heart began to race.

"Let us not waste time with things that might've been," I said. "Or what might still be. Let me explain my interaction with the humans."

My mother swallowed, and then she did spit. Her saliva was laced with red. Had she been suckling on Naeve's wrist, like he'd been tasting her? Or was she ill?

I shook myself, refusing to dwell on the possibilities. The

former was meaningless, in terms of what was going to happen next, and the latter would only help me overcome her.

So why did my chest feel so tight?

"Trust me, Elora. If we could gloss over this part, I'd be a much happier queen."

Enjoy being queen while it lasts, I thought.

But I said, "That makes one of us." She perked up at that. "What I mean is, I *want* to explain myself. I want you to understand."

She looked at me then, looked right into my eyes, and I thought I could see the beginning of time. The first wash of darkness, the first spark of light. I thought I could see, too, how they'd once lived in harmony.

What had happened between them?

"I have little hope of understanding," the Dark Lady said. "But try me."

"I went to the human world because of the Seelie Queen," I admitted. "Because she wanted a human."

My mother inhaled sharply, and I could tell she believed me. So far, she believed me. "But why?" she asked.

"Why did I go, or why did she want a human?"

"Either. Both," she said, as light rose up from below. Even if my mother turned around at this point, she would only think it was the sun. Both lights were coming from the east, one lined up with the other, as if the Seelie Queen had charted her course accordingly. How easily she could sneak up on my mother. How talented she was at trickery.

My heart skipped a beat as I said, "One answer is easy: I do not know. To this day, I do not know the Seelie Queen's reasons for wanting a human. I can only assume she grew tired of the sanctions and wanted a toy. Something to pet, maybe more."

My mother shuddered, the way Illya had shuddered when I'd told her I was sleeping in the mortal world. The way I had shuddered when Taylor had first invited me into his home. If I could learn the truth about humans, maybe my mother . . .

A wicked sliver of light pierced through the trees, forcing me to blink. My eyes closed. Behind closed lids, I saw the lifeless body of Brad sprawled out across the stage. I saw my mother ordering me to drink his blood like tea.

She is too far gone.

I bit my lip. "As for your other question, let me first explain what happened in the mortal world, before I explain why I chose to go there."

She nodded, agreeing to my terms.

That was her third mistake.

If all went as planned, the Seelie Queen would arrive before such an explanation was necessary. My mother wouldn't know I meant to take down her court until it was too late. And as for what had happened in the mortal world, well . . .

I was actually looking forward to telling that part.

"I followed the ocean until I exited the Unseelie Court. From there, I headed farther south, until I reached a forest. The forest was greater than I would've expected for the human world."

"Give them a decade. It will be gone."

"Perhaps," I agreed. I didn't want to argue with her, and besides, she wasn't entirely wrong. Regardless of Taylor's sweetness, or Kylie's, or anyone's, it didn't negate humanity's penchant for tearing down forests and putting up "plants." Ironic,

I know, that they should fill the world with dead things and name them after the living.

I still didn't understand it.

"After a time, I came upon civilization. First the farms, then the little towns. Then something a bit larger. I knew the Seelie Queen wanted a boy…"

My mother's scowl deepened. But Darkness, she didn't know the half of it.

Not yet. "A boy old enough to lead, yet youthful enough to be considered 'young.' Color me conceited, but that made me think of my own age."

My mother smiled, and I thought she was proud of my affinity for leadership. Then she said, "Who would follow you but leaves and worms?"

"Someone would," I whispered. She looked up, and for a moment I feared she was going to turn around. That light was creeping up the base of the hill, crawling toward us like vines. The Queen must be close.

The Seelie Queen, that is. Not my queen.

I don't have a queen, I reminded myself.

"A mortal would follow me," I said, drawing my mother's attention back to me. "But I'm getting to that. You see, once I realized she wanted someone my age, I lingered on the edges of a mortal school, in search of a leader. What I found was a loner."

She tilted her head, as if listening for the part where I drew the mortal's blood, or led him into the sea. *Something* to prove I was the daughter of the Dark Lady and not a total disappointment.

But I did not need her approval anymore. "I watched him

for the better part of a week. Watched the way he was pushed around by other students, or brushed aside entirely. Watched the way he slipped away to the park behind the school whenever he could manage it. There was something about this mortal boy, something that drew me to him."

"Oh, Darkness." She paled, though I didn't think it possible for her to get any lighter. In the brighter months, she would fade to almost nothing if she didn't stay underground.

"The mortal boy had a secret," I explained. "That was all right. I had a secret too. I thought, who better to protect my privacy than someone who was trying so hard to hide his own demons? That is something I learned from you, dear mother: seek out a person with commonality, and use it to your advantage."

She smiled, but it was short-lived.

"When he offered to take me home, I accepted," I said, and that smile slipped from her face like a stain that had been wiped away. "He lived above his parents' garage, which afforded us a certain level of … freedom."

She closed her eyes, to block out the horror of my words. To block out the glowing light. I realized, then, that the Seelie Queen must've been holding back some of her light. If she'd come at us with the full force of her brightness, we'd never have mistaken her for the distant sun.

The element of surprise would be ruined.

Now she was rising beyond the halfway point of the hill. I had minutes—minutes!—until she reached the summit. I'd have to forgo the creative version of my story and go for the final blow. Well, three blows, in succession.

First: "I'd been there a day when I allowed him to hold my hand."

My mother's eyes snapped open, and rage flashed across her face. "You lie."

"Oh, my darling mother," I said, rising so that she would stand as well. "By the time I am finished with my story, you will wish I had the ability to lie."

She stood, not disappointing me, as the Bright Queen's light spilled over the base of the hill. I could see the top of her head, all those leaves and flowers, a crown befitting a nature queen. My mother wore thorns and animal bones in her hair, amongst blossoms of poppies.

"By the second week, we were lying in bed together, and when he trailed his fingers across my skin, I didn't push him away." I flashed a wicked smile, startling her with the strength of my conviction. "I *welcomed* it."

"No," she whispered, eyes filled with horror. "No, they've done something to you. It's happened before, when faeries lingered in the wasteland..."

"God, mother, you're *rambling*. If only you could hear yourself—"

"God? *God?* Do *you* hear *yourself?*" She reached for me then, and whether she wanted to cradle me to her chest or snap my neck, I did not know. "Oh, love, they've corrupted you."

"No." I shook my head, pushing away the word *love*. She didn't mean it. Couldn't mean it. "I wanted him to corrupt me. Do you know what I mean? *Corrupt?*" I stepped forward, forcing her back to the edge of the drop-off.

That was *my* mistake. Any sane person would've turned around to see how close she was to the edge. But my mother was not sane.

She looked at me with anguished eyes. "No, she cannot do this to me. She cannot take you, as she took—"

"*Mother.* You're ruining my story," I snapped, barely able to follow her line of thinking. Who was "she"? The Seelie Queen?

Just as I thought it, I saw her face. She rose like the wicked sun—*no, like the natural sun,* I reminded myself, *a sun that is necessary*—behind my mother, the night. For a moment, darkness eclipsed the light. And my mother was buried deep in the depths of her despair, unable to witness her own undoing. Unable to witness anything but the daughter who'd betrayed her.

I wielded my final blow. "By my third week in the mortal world, we'd become entangled, body and spirit, and I was wrapping myself around him, wondering how it would feel to—"

"*Stop,*" she commanded, and the forest trembled at her fury. Icicles fell around her, shattering on the ground. "Please, I cannot suffer it. Not again. I'm trying to save you. But I can't, unless…" She reached out, clutching at my arms. Practically clawing me in her desperation. "Tell me he trapped you, please. Tell me he tied you down."

"You see, Mother, that is the problem with people like you. You'd rather I be tortured than love him willingly. Rather I be raped than lie with him of my own free will. Do you know how *sick* that is? Do you know what that does to a girl who is growing up in this world, desperately trying to love her own body? And her *heart?* Her desires. My life could've been a wonderful thing…"

She looked at me, uncomprehending.

I stepped closer, my own darkness swirling to meet my mother's. But those strands didn't intertwine this time. They were strangers, like we were strangers. We'd never understand each other again. "And I feel *sorry* for you," I said, subtly slicing a nail across my wrist. Skin parted, and three drops of blood fell to the earth. "Everything I went through taught me to trust my warm, bleeding heart over your hateful one. Everything I cast aside made me surer of my love. So thank you, mother, for forbidding me to love a mortal boy. Don't you know teenage girls always rebel against their mommies?"

My mother gasped and stumbled against the trunk of the pine tree. The Seelie Queen rose up behind her then, a phoenix rising from the Dark Court's ashes. My heart was thundering, my mouth dry from all this confessing, all this fear, and I could barely breathe as she chanted the binding spell under her breath, calling on the branches to do her bidding.

"Thank you, Elora," the Bright Queen said as the branches reached out for my mother.

The Dark Lady shrieked, turning in horror, but it was too late. Those branches gripped hold of her like hands. The tree itself opened up, the trunk parting to draw her into its darkness.

A proper binding for a Dark Queen.

"You've weakened her quite nicely," the Bright Queen said as my mother screamed. It was hard to watch, this great Unseelie creature taken down by blood and branches. I had to remind myself of the spectacle she'd made of Brad. Had to remind myself it could've been Taylor.

My resolve strengthened.

The branches clawed at her, but my mother clawed back. I feared she'd break free. The Bright Queen draped an arm around me, a taunting gesture that my mother didn't miss. "Why don't you finish the job?" she asked me.

For a moment, I was confused. Was there a new part of the binding I was supposed to perform? The blood had been spilled, the spell had been chanted. Then I realized my part was what it had always been.

Weaken her, the Bright Queen had whispered when we'd first planned our coup. *Make her feel the crushing weight of betrayal.*

Well, I could do that. "Oh, mother dear," I cooed, stepping close enough that she could *almost* grab me. "You'll find this quite interesting. Lyndiria?"

"Yes, sweet?" the Seelie Queen said.

"How does my true love fare? The boy I fell for in the mortal world?"

"A little worse for wear, but healing quickly."

"Good." I smiled, and warmth rushed through my chest. "You see, Mother, the boy you killed was not my lover. That was a trick. I fooled you."

My mother struggled against her bonds, snapping one of the branches. Roots leapt up from the earth and wrapped around her.

"I'm going to see him soon," I said.

"No. *No,*" she begged as roots wove into her hair, yanking her into the darkness.

"I'll give him a kiss for you, okay? But everything after that … " I flashed her my wickedest smile as the trunk began to close. "That'll be for me."

My mother's face caved in. It looked as if a great, ominous mountain was collapsing under its own weight. A moon crumbling to dust. She howled, and tears sprang to her eyes.

Tears! On the Unseelie Queen!

I didn't understand it. But it didn't matter, because the pine swallowed her whole. It cut off her howl and left us in silence. It closed around her, trapping her inside.

"Now only blood will free her," the Seelie Queen said.

"The blood of someone who loves her," I murmured.

"Enough to cover the ground at her feet. But after the battle is won..."

No such faerie will exist, I thought. But I didn't say it. I couldn't say it.

"Let us go, then," I said softly, tearing my eyes away from the tree. My mother's cage. My mother's grave? "The revolution is about to begin."

"Yes." The Bright Queen turned to me and smiled. "It is." Her lips were so dark, she could've been suckling on blood herself. And she knelt beside the tree, scooping a handful of dirt from the ground. Dirt speckled with my mother's blood.

"What are you doing?" I asked.

"Finishing what I started," she said. And she trickled that dirt over my feet, chanting under her breath.

I turned to run, but I wasn't fast enough. The branches of the smaller pine were already reaching for me. "You tricked me!" I cried, as sharp claws curled into my hair and wrenched my head back.

"There's a lot of that going around." The Seelie Queen grinned. She had a madness in her eyes, as if goblins were feasting on her mind. "Sweet dreams, princess," she said, yanking the crown from my head.

Then the forest swallowed me alive.

35

TAYLOR

I expected to wake up in a cage. I expected, at least, to wake up in the Seelie Court under the Queen's watchful gaze, but I didn't. I woke up several yards from where I'd fallen asleep, with my friends right beside me.

Well, two of my friends. Keegan was missing.

I tried to stand. I tried to sit up and shake off the most psycho of all psycho dreams, and that's when it hit me.

The pain, I mean. The realization came more slowly.

First, the agony. It started at my spine, and went shooting through my back like spindly webs. I pushed myself to my elbows, heaving with the weight of it, and fell back onto my stomach. It was all I could do not to throw up.

"Oh, God," Kylie said.

My eyes fluttered open for about two seconds before they closed again. They were heavy. Everything was heavy, and I was sinking into the ground.

"Here, drink this," said Alexia's voice. Of course, knowing the faeries and the way they used glamour, it could've been anybody. Kylie might not've been Kylie. I might not've been me.

Oh, crap. This was not the time to be having an existential crisis. But still. Who could I trust, under the circumstances?

"What is it?" I managed, as Alexia held what looked like an acorn cap to my lips. I shook my head, spilling some of the liquid. "No. Did *she* give it to you? I don't want it."

"She didn't," Alexia said, and this time I was able to glimpse her eyes. Barely, but they looked like hers. That was the thing about glamour, the thing I'd realized too late. There was something about the look in a person's eyes that was hard to replicate. Maybe because of that whole window-to-the-soul-thing. Or maybe because a person's eyes showed flashes of their personality. Either way, this was Alexia.

I was sure of it. But I still wasn't drinking the Kool-Aid. "No way," I said, turning my head. "I'm not drinking anything the Bright Queen—"

"I told you, *she* didn't give it to us. They did."

I lifted my head, and, for the first time, I noticed the figures lingering in the darkness. The dark faeries. I started to crawl away. But I couldn't move very fast because of the weight pressing down on me.

The wings.

Oh, God. I have wings. The Bright Queen gave me wings. She held me down, shoved a needle into my skin, and ...

"Stop," Alexia said, which was a relief. I was barely moving anyway, and every movement was agony. Better to just lie here and play possum. "They helped us."

"What do you mean?" I asked.

"The Bright Queen wanted to take us, but they flooded the clearing, refusing to let us go. Drink."

I eyed the acorn cap suspiciously. "What is it?"

"Your medicine."

I gave her a look.

A faerie ducked out of the shadows, his body as black as the darkness itself. All I could see were his horns and his red, glowing eyes. "It isn't as potent as the Bright Lady's light, but it will dull the pain for a few hours."

That's all I need, I thought, taking the cup. The cap. The cap-cup.

Get a grip.

"Will it make me sluggish?" I asked.

The faerie shook his head. "The effects are purely physical. Your mind will be fully intact."

"Good." I tipped back my head, swallowing the juice. It was sweet, and it burned my esophagus. It was a miracle it didn't come right back up.

"Let's go then." I tried to push myself to my feet. I tried, and failed, just like before. "Third time's a charm, right?"

This time, when I pushed, I felt like parasites were crawling out of my back. Like alien creatures had laid eggs in my body, and now they were hatching and breaking free. Really, it was just the wings hanging down on each side.

Still, I made it to my knees.

"Success," I joked, and almost threw up.

"It takes a few minutes to kick in," the faerie said, eying me with suspicion.

Whatever, I thought. *They all look at me like that. And I've got places to be.*

One. Two. *Three.* I pushed into a crouch and just sat there, shuddering. "You know, just for the record, this is really uncool," I said, speaking to no one in particular. Maybe to the universe. "And really unfair."

"Why did she do that to you?" Kylie asked. At any other time, the thought of a human gaining wings might've made her smile, but here, she looked horrified. That's the thing about reality. It's so much uglier than fantasy.

Most of the time.

I reached for a branch above my head, and pulled myself to my feet. "Mother f—"

"Taylor?" Kylie pressed. She was looking at my back like she might be sick. Well, that made two of us.

"She didn't want me to fight in the revolution," I said. "But she wouldn't flat-out forbid it, because then she'd be like the dark faeries. No offense," I added, glancing up at the faeries who lingered in the shadows. Unlike their royal masters, they seemed uninterested in controlling us.

Of course, that's what I'd thought about Maya de Lyre, and look where that had gotten me. Look where it had gotten Brad.

I swallowed, leaning against a tree for support. "She sewed the wings into my back because she thought it would keep me from fighting. Like it would've kept Elora from fighting if she'd tried to get her wings back."

"Was that actually a possibility?" Kylie asked.

I nodded, breathing heavily. I felt like a dog on a hot summer day, except, you know, a dog that's been kicked around a lot. Maybe run over by a car. "Elora wanted to fight. But if she had her wings sewn into her, she would've had to rest."

"Like you need to rest," Alexia said. Kylie was just staring at me with those big brown eyes.

"Where's Keegan?" I asked.

"He went with the Queen. To safety," Kylie added. "She promised not to trap him."

"And you didn't go?"

"We wanted to stay with you."

"We wanted to fight," Alexia said. "I mean, we told you we would. That's what the past few weeks have been building toward."

"And Keegan didn't want to?"

"I guess he got scared," Kylie said. But she didn't look convinced, and a chill went through me.

"We've got to get up there." I gestured toward the mountain and looked to the faerie with horns. "Will you help us?"

The faerie stepped closer, making tiny steps. He was a great beast of a thing, but he was scared of me. "Yesterday, I would have laughed at such a request. But in the past few hours, I have seen things I never thought I would see."

"Yeah?"

He nodded, dipping his horned head. "I saw mortals offer themselves up to the Dark Lady so that the princess could return home. A false offering, yes, but clever, very clever." He chuckled. "And watching you outsmart the Dark Lady as she sought to humiliate you ... such a sight."

"I didn't outsmart her, though. She forced Elora to choose one of us, and Brad got killed because of it."

"Yes, him and not you. Him and not the princess. You protected her. You all did." He paused, looking conflicted. "I did not believe the stories about what happened in the graveyard. Did not believe you defended her out of goodness—"

"You thought we wanted something from her?" I said, and

I was sick with anger. Sick with pain. Just sick. "A prize? A pot of gold? Is that what you thought?"

"That is what we know of humans. Not only from the Dark Lady's stories, but from what we have seen. Many of us have lived very long ..." He trailed off, looking into the darkness. "We have seen the worst of this world."

"And last night? When you watched the Dark Lady string us up and tear one of us to pieces? Does that rank in the top ten?"

He frowned, and I thought he was going to shake his head. "I have seen mortals do that a thousand times over," he said. "Seen it done to children. Seen women torn apart in ways ..." Again, he trailed off, and this time, I didn't push him. Instead, I pushed myself. I took one step, then two. I could walk.

It was a start.

"Will you help us?" I asked.

"You watched your friend get torn apart, and still, you would face them?"

"Yes."

"For love of the princess?"

"Yes. And because I want to do what's right. I know you don't understand that, coming from a human, but I don't care. We don't have to understand each other. We both want the same thing, and that's enough."

"Then we will help you," he said. "But you're in no condition—"

"I'll be the judge of that."

"Fine. We can provide you with the proper attire. But it would be best if you were stationed in the trees surrounding the battle. Acting as—"

"Defense, fine." So Elora would get her wish after all. What a fair fucking compromise. "Do you still have our armor?"

The faerie wrinkled his nose. "Ah, yes. It is safe in the dungeon."

"You won't be able to wear it," Alexia said to me. "Not with your..."

Wings. I shuddered. "But you guys will."

"We'll need horses," Kylie broke in, and the faerie bristled. "I know we don't *own* them, and I know you can't own an animal, but we need their help to get back to the castle in time."

"Horses are scarce here," the faerie said as others crept out of the forest. I caught glimpses of horns, of feathers, but mostly I saw shadow. "And yet, we may be able to help you."

Kylie nodded, a show of respect, and a centaur stepped out into the light. The sky was dim—that moment when the moon is already asleep but the sun is taking its sweet time— but still, there was no mistaking that half-man/half-horse form. Soon others joined him in the clearing, not to be shown up in front of a bunch of humans. There were ladies with feathers for skin and talons for feet.

"Sirens," Kylie whispered to me.

There were men with bulls' heads and human-like bodies.

"Minotaurs," Kylie said.

Those guys, at least, could've used a pair of pants. But I didn't say that because, you know, we were negotiating. And it was all fascinating, in spite of the occasional flash of man-junk.

"Thank you for your help," Alexia said, averting her eyes from the nakedest of the faeries. "We appreciate your sacrifice."

I cringed at that word. But she was right. Touching "dirty"

humans would be a sacrifice for these faeries. Carrying us was a big deal.

I tried to look appreciative. "Three more things," I said, as Kylie whispered, "Pegasuses! Pegusi?"

"What things?" the horned faerie asked me.

"I need you to glamour my back," I said. "Hide the wounds, so it looks like these wings are mine." I didn't want to go charging into battle looking like I was already half dead.

"Fine." The faerie nodded, and I thought, *that was easy.* "And?" he asked.

"I want a sword."

He glanced at my back. "It will be nearly impossible for you to duel in your condition. Arrows would be best, and even then, it would be wise to—"

"Keep one trained on Naeve at all times, to protect the princess. I know. I still want a sword."

"That can be arranged. But why?"

"Because the time may come when arrows aren't enough and I need to get closer. To fight *with* her. And if that time comes—"

"Is this your third request?"

I nodded. "Stay out of my way."

36

ELORA

In spite of the Bright Queen's binding, I could still hear everything. I could even see, just barely, through a hole in the tree that held me. Could see a splash of the forest. Could see the light receding as the Seelie Queen returned to court.

But hers or mine?

What had I been thinking, inviting her into this place on the one night the sentries were away? Why had I helped her bind my mother? Now the Bright Queen could enter the Unseelie Palace, glamoured to look like the Dark Lady, and do whatever she pleased. Would she lay waste to the Unseelie servants before I could return and defend them?

Would she take over the court?

From there, it was a small step to controlling all of Faerie. All this time, I'd truly believed she wanted to be free. Free of her court, free of the bloodshed that followed nobility at every turn. Free of that damned Sword of Damocles hanging over her head.

Now I feared she wanted to wield that sword with absolute power. Kept at bay by no one, she could cut across our entire world, making the dark faeries her subordinates and sending her shining courtiers into the mortal lands to do as they pleased.

For seventeen years, I'd hated the power struggle between the High Faerie Courts. Only now did I wonder if each had kept the other from taking over the world. The dark faeries would've laid waste to as much of humanity as they could, but the bright faeries? They would take prisoners.

They had prisoners already.

I had to stop her. But how? The laws of blood binding were not exactly open to interpretation. Though I struggled, throwing the weight of my body against the inside of the tree, I only managed to scratch my already delicate skin. Though I screamed, it was like screaming into an abyss. No one could hear me. I couldn't even hear myself, not really, because the blood rushed so loudly in my ears, I wasn't certain if I was screaming audibly or merely making noise in my own head. The darkness poured over me completely, and for the first time in my life, I longed for light. A spark of gold in eyes so green, they broke your heart with their beauty.

Their openness.

When I heard a slight skittering across the forest floor, I thought it might be him. I hoped it wasn't, because I didn't want him to spill any more blood for me. I wanted him out of this place, and out of my life, because it was the only thing that would protect him. I loved him so much, I needed to set him free. Butterflies, and letting go, and all that nonsense.

But he wouldn't come back to me. I wouldn't let him.

When the voice came, my heart leapt into my throat. The voice wasn't Taylor's, but something much smaller and just as familiar.

Illya!

"Lady," she said in response, though she couldn't have heard me. "I heard you speaking."

What is happening?

"To the Bright Lady," she added, stepping closer. "I heard everything. I will free you."

Yes. Yes, thank you! I shrieked, but only to myself. My lips weren't so good at making noise. *Go and get help, and you can free me.*

But Illya was not leaving. I could hear her coming closer, as leaves and twigs rustled beneath her amphibian frame. I wanted to hug her, to clasp her gently in my hands and hold her to my chest, but beneath the excitement was a trickle of dread. The binding could only be broken with blood. *Enough blood to cover the ground.* Surely, if Illya knew this, she'd know to find someone not quite so small, someone whose offering would not mean risking her life. I could not bear another sacrifice after last night.

I held my breath, waiting for Illya to detail her plan, as we always did with one another. I waited for the rush of information and the promise to return. But Illya was not promising anything, and those steps were coming closer still. My heart, red and raw from the previous events, started to harden, as if someone were turning it to stone. Heavy it hung in my chest. Weighted it pressed against me.

Still, I could feel everything. *Illya,* I called, with every fiber of my being. *Go get someone else. Now.*

Illya did not hear me. Instead, I heard her come to rest at the base of the tree. Now my heart grew the wings of a dragon, and beat against the cave of my chest. I struggled against the branches, trying to peer out the little hole in the tree. Trying to reach my friend.

At first, I could see nothing. Nothing of her skin, brown and green and blending with the leaves. Nothing of her eyes, cerulean blue around a golden iris. Part sun and part sky. If ever there was a case for faeries being both dark and light, Illya was it.

But she wouldn't hear me if I said that. She wouldn't hear me if I said *anything*, and now, as I fought to break from my bonds, I was able to press my eye against the opening and look down. What I saw there almost broke me.

Down below, my oldest friend stood looking up at me. Her wings were curled up, burned like paper, and she wore no glamour to hide it. Unlike me, she'd always wanted to be herself, nothing more. Nothing less.

Just perfect, brave Illya. Alone in the woods with a knife.

"My Lady," Illya breathed, looking up as if she could see me. Smiling because she loved me. "I hope you will take this as a token of my gratitude." Her eyelids fluttered closed, and I thought I saw a tear trickle down her cheek. But she shook herself, ever hiding her emotions in front of me. Her fear. "It has been an honor serving you."

No!

Still, my lips made no sound. Still, my voice had no power, but soon I would have all of it. My voice, my freedom. I would be able to speak the moment she could no longer breathe.

No, Illya, please.

She paused, tilting her head in that familiar way of hers. Eyes crinkling at the sides, as if she could see inside my soul.

And I thought, for one perfect moment, that she would wait for me, wait until I could speak somehow. Wait for my direction.

But I had taught Illya that she deserved to be free, and it was a lesson she would not easily forget. I may have been her princess until the end, but she'd never be my servant again.

Illya looked down at the blade, speaking softly. "I want you to know that you were right about the mortals. Maybe not all of them," she added quickly, as if unable to let go of her teachings entirely, "but about the boy. The one you've chosen. You were right, and I … I hope you will forgive me for doubting you."

Of course I will, I said without speaking. *We made mistakes, each one of us. But now that we know the truth—*

"And I hope you will remember me." She lifted the dagger. I saw blood before she'd pierced her skin. I was screaming and clawing and my vision swam with dark, dark blood.

"Goodbye, Lady." She shoved the dagger into her belly, and blood climbed up from my throat. I could taste it as it blossomed on her lips. I could feel it, spreading over my belly as it covered hers. Staining skin, covering hands.

Drowning me.

When Illya shuddered, I felt the first crack in the tree. The sound was so loud, it deafened me. But the crack was thin, and it was difficult to see through it. Then she dropped to the ground, so easily, like a child falling into pleasant sleep. There was nothing loud or final about it. One moment, she was alive. The next, nothing.

The crack widened, and I pushed my hand through it. Skin caught on bark and parts of me came away bloody, but what did it matter at this point? Illya's blood soaked the forest floor at my feet. She'd loved me, and she'd sacrificed herself for me. Now I was free.

I pushed out of my prison only to sink to my knees. "Why did it have to be you?" I whispered, gathering her up in my hands. Why couldn't it have been someone who would've survived this?

Of course, I knew the answer to that. Only Illya had followed me to the places she wasn't supposed to go. Only Illya had risked life and limb to defend me, and only Illya would have risked following me down here.

Only Illya was that devoted to me.

Used to be, I thought, and then felt horrible the moment the words entered into my head. My gaze flickered to the red dotting the forest floor, but already it was fading, sinking into the dirt. As quickly as the offering had been made, the earth was swallowing it up, ravenous after a long, painful drought.

"Oh, sweetness." I lifted Illya to my chest. Her eyes were open, the bright, cerulean orbs now cold as glass. No gold. I couldn't look at them anymore, couldn't remember her this way, without that spark, so I cradled her against my chest, holding her delicately.

"I love you," I whispered, finally offering the words I'd kept so close to me. The words I'd guarded lest they be used against me. Lest they be used against the people I adored.

Little good that's done me.

"I have always loved you. From the moment I met you, as a child. You have always been my greatest friend."

I choked back a sob, and in doing so, lifted my gaze. In spite of the dark, ethereal haze that still covered the Unseelie

Palace, the sun was rising higher in the sky. Morning had come, and with it, my revolution.

Our revolution.

As gently as I could, I carried Illya out of the clearing, laying her to rest several yards from my mother's tree. Waving my fingers in the brisk morning air, I covered her in a protective glamour. Tomorrow I would return to bury her, here in the land that she'd loved in spite of the Dark Court's tyranny. In spite of her bondage.

I stood, glancing down at my glamour. The shape was rough, but if one knew where to look, one would see a little stone resembling a heart. It wasn't much, but it would suffice until I could return and give Illya a proper remembrance. For now, I could only offer one thing.

"Today, as I stand against our enemies, I do it in your name. And for generations after, when people speak of this revolution, they will speak of you, brave Illya. Your sacrifice will be the catalyst that frees the faeries from bondage."

With that, I pressed a hand to my lips and touched it to the glamoured stone. And I rose, walking in the direction of the Unseelie Palace, the dawn at my back like a fiery wave that would wash over the faerie lands, burning away its wickedness and leaving only possibility in its wake.

37

TAYLOR

My arms ached as I climbed from a winged horse into the trees. My entire body ached, and I wondered if this was a fraction of what Elora had felt after she'd lost her wings. For a minute, I allowed myself to feel close to her, even though I only had a vague idea of where she was, or at least, where she was supposed to be.

Everything will be an illusion.

That warning taunted me as my friends settled in around me, Alexia up above and Kylie below. It made me feel like the ground could fall out beneath me, the tree could turn into a dragon, and that dragon could burst into flames, taking me into oblivion.

I mean, if I really thought about it, *everything* couldn't be an illusion. I was real. Kylie and Alexia were real, even though Keegan was absent. Was *that* an illusion? Fear tugged at my confidence, weighing me down.

I'd always depended on my brain to outwit the faeries, rather than any illusion of strength. I mean, I could've been some big hulking mammoth, and they still would've stopped me. Magic trumps muscle. Just ask Brad.

My back shuddered at the thought, and I almost fell out of the tree. I knew I'd insisted on coming here today, but *damn*, these wings hurt. It felt like they were killing me, slowly sucking my life away. What the hell was the Seelie Queen thinking, torturing me like this?

Oh, I won't infringe on your free will, but I will operate on you in freaky-deaky ways.

Sure, that made sense. Fucking faeries and their lack of logic. Or bendable logic. Un-understandable logic. Could I even outsmart them?

Elora can. The voice came to me from a distance, like the Dark Princess herself was reaching out to hold my hand. *She* understood them. *She'd* grown up with them, was one of them. She knew their strengths and their weaknesses.

Me, I was still learning. So I watched carefully as the Unseelie servants slipped away from the palace grounds. They had to be careful not to step on the sleeping courtiers, who were sprawled out haphazardly like teenagers after a rager. And this had been quite a rager.

Drinking and dancing and human sacrifice, oh my!

I guess I kept joking about it because I couldn't really handle it. Sure, the servants had taken pity on us and allowed us to finally close our eyes, but by then we'd already seen enough brutality to last a lifetime. Even now, my gaze strayed to the stage where they'd put on their elaborate show, and I searched for signs of blood, for signs of *Brad*, but there was nothing.

They'd cleaned everything away. Or maybe they'd just glamoured him. Before I could get a decent look at the stage, the entire scene was glamoured over, slowly, like light slipping over a forest to reveal everything the darkness had hidden. My heart caught in my throat. Then, just as thoroughly, *that* was glamoured over too, and I understood what Elora had meant about double illusions. I understood everything, and it was a good thing, because the Unseelie servants were circling the sleeping courtiers in a spiral, wave after wave of voluntary soldiers, wrapping around the courtyard and down the mountain.

I held my breath.

"This is it." Kylie's voice filtered up from below. She was sitting in that faerie-made saddle, on the back of a chocolate-colored horse. To my left, Alexia was perched in the branches, crouching like some sort of warrior.

I'm glad one of us is confident.

Then again, she was the better shot. As it was, I'd be lucky if I could lift my bow. My arms were shaky as hell and I kind of felt like throwing up. I told myself I was just scared, but really, my body was trying to heal itself. And failing. I swore that, if I managed to survive this battle, I'd find a way to break the Seelie Queen's hold on me. And if my body gave out before that, it'd be because I'd summoned my strength and shot the arrow that saved Elora's life.

"I promise," I whispered, so quiet that only the trees could hear me. It was enough.

"I guess the time for hand-holding is over," Alexia said. Kylie looked up, and I suspected she was thinking of Keegan. Whatever his reasons for staying behind, it was probably a good thing.

No, definitely. The dark courtiers were waking up.

It happened slowly, bless their drunken hearts. I guess it was pretty honorable that Elora hadn't just drugged them with sleeping potions and cut them down while they slept. She wanted to stand against them, but she didn't want to become them.

Also, where the hell was she?

I didn't see her anywhere, and it was getting a little late to make a fashionable entrance. Meanwhile, the nobles of the Unseelie Court stumbled to their feet, the bright morning sun beating down on their already throbbing heads, and they looked to their queen—that is, her empty throne—and squinted, as if to see more clearly. They couldn't. The sun was too bright, they had partied too hard, and besides, they had bigger things to worry about. From my perch in the distance, I could see the place where the dark servants' army trailed halfway down the mountain; there were that many of them.

Wait, there were *that* many of them? How had the Dark Court controlled them for so long? I guess I didn't have time to get into the nature of oppressive regimes. My eyes were getting frantic, scanning the crowd for Elora. Instead, they fell on Naeve.

He seemed to be recovering quicker than most. Rising to one knee, and then to his feet, he strode across the grounds, which now appeared to be covered in grass. Elora's followers had glamoured the space to look like a forest I'd never seen. Even the trees surrounding us had changed. No longer the tall and rigid pines, straight as the back of the Unseelie Queen, they curved out into flowered branches, sprouting pink blossoms on the ends. Not exactly the perfect site for a battle. But maybe the servants wanted some beauty in the impending bloodshed.

Impending. Encroaching. Inevitable. Yet, nothing happened right away. Even Naeve, who was scouring the grounds like a vampire desperate for a vein, hadn't drawn a weapon yet.

"Where is she?" he snarled, climbing the stage that now looked like a grassy knoll. The kind of knoll you'd expect to find faeries in, the cute, tiny kind who danced to tinkling music. Nothing like this nightmare. Nothing like reality. Naeve's golden eyes darted this way and that, searching the forest and the sky. His shiny black hair was matted on one side. The asshole probably spent time every morning getting those curls just right. I wanted to hold up a mirror. But this wasn't a fairy tale, and Naeve wouldn't dissolve into a pile of dust at the sight of his reflection.

Running a hand through his hair, he turned in a circle, showcasing those golden wings. The ones that cast shadows over the land. "Is this your army?" he called. From his position, he could only see the first wave of faeries. "My poor princess, it's nearly as crippled as you are." He let the comment hang as Elora's silhouette appeared in the sky.

She rode on the back of a winged horse, in a long black dress with a high, regal collar. Kylie's golden crown sat atop her fiery head.

A thrill went through me.

She's going to trick him. It's going to work. Yes.

Fifty feet above the camp, Elora came to a stop, her body framed by the light of the sun. Her hair flowed around her face as she stared at the faeries with compassion, like she loved each one of them, even those she aimed to destroy.

Her voice filtered down. "Those of you who wish to join us and live in a world without nobility, do so now, and you will be spared." She waved a hand toward her troops. "Those of you who wish to fight ... prepare to fall."

The courtiers murmured, but none of them budged. *Big surprise.* They'd live in a world of hatred, or not at all.

Elora descended. She was so stunning, both vulnerable and powerful, as she lowered herself to the stage, that my heart squeezed, halting my breath. I wanted to cry, or kill; I wasn't sure which. I decided, right then and there, that I would do anything to protect her, even if it meant my own horrific death. Cautiously, I inched toward the trunk of my tree, preparing to climb down. It would hurt, but not as bad as losing her would.

A hand landed on my shoulder, stopping me in my tracks. "Don't be stupid, little boy."

I spun around, to face Alexia. "Don't talk like you're one of them," I warned. "You aren't one of them."

"I know what I am, and what I'm not," she said. "But I'm starting to understand how they think."

"That's a mistake too."

"Don't lecture me on mistakes," she hissed, leaning close to my ear, "when you're about to ruin everything by trying to do something heroic. You can't save her. She's smarter than all of us."

"I think I've known that from the start," I confessed as Elora dismounted. "I always wanted to protect her, and I always worried that when the time came, I couldn't." I scowled. "I can barely lift a weapon."

"Your mind is a weapon, if you use it right." Alexia smoothed the dark brown tunic the faeries had given me, adjusting the opening in the back.

I winced. "It makes me crazy that I can't help her."

"You are helping her." She slunk back into the shadows, behind me. "This is what she wants."

I exhaled, my body shaking from exhaustion and relief. And I wondered: even if we did survive this, would Elora's love be able to heal me? Or did that only work for faeries?

Down below, she walked toward Naeve with smooth, unflinching steps. I had the most terrible sense of déjà vu. Naeve waited, tapping his fingers against his leg in mock-impatience, his black cloak falling around him. The red powder of dried leaves decorated his ebony curls, and his eyes flashed, feral and bright.

"Clever girl," he drawled as Elora stopped in front of him. "You've come to kill me with your repugnant stench. I can smell mortal filth all over you." He lifted a hand toward her face. "Let me give you a bath. No slave of mine will wear the gown of human grime."

Elora slapped him away. "No slave of yours hides here, little prince."

Naeve chuckled as a bubble of rushing liquid encircled him. It was oily, and I thought of oil spills, of baby seals slick and drowning. "Save your tricks," he warned, his voice resonating within the bubble. "My defenses can't be penetrated by your pathetic spells."

Elora laughed wildly, clutching her stomach as she bent over. "Save your challenges. I've no desire to *penetrate* anything of yours." She paused, licking her lips. "So you learned one defensive spell." She turned to the faeries below. "Who taught this dog a new trick?"

Laughter rippled throughout the crowd. Even the courtiers grinned.

Naeve didn't like that. Circling Elora, he smirked at her back. "How darling, Elora, you've glamoured yourself some hideous wings to replace the ones you lost in battle."

"The 'battle' where you used an iron sword against me?" she asked. "You and I define the word very differently."

"Still, your costume pleases me." He reached for the wings, but she jerked away. "You miss them, don't you? How does it feel to be locked to the land, unable to fly of your own accord? Does it pain you?"

"After our last meeting, Naeve, little pains me."

I narrowed my eyes. That sounded like a lie. Naeve noticed it too, because he said, "Liar."

"Maybe I am."

The Dark Prince shook his head. "You've always found ways around the truth. Look at you, sporting wings you no longer have. Look around you." His arm swept through the air, all melodramatic. I wanted to punch him. "This landscape reeks of deceit. Are you afraid to show me where you've really taken me? Are we sitting in some hovel you now call home?"

Elora shrugged, and I felt a thrill of excitement. She was setting him up, twisting her words to manipulate him. "See for yourself. I'm sure you can remove the glamour if you *really* try."

"Effortlessly," Naeve replied. Still, he stood a minute in quiet concentration before lifting his arms to the sky. He didn't know it, but the servants of the Unseelie Court must've been concentrating too. I realized there was a reason Elora hadn't ordered them to attack.

She needed them for this.

When Naeve pulled down his arms, the glamour ripped away, revealing a strange world beneath. His laughter died in his throat. The bubble of protection crashed to the floor, and he gawked at the landscape with terrified eyes.

A city stared back at him, cement and iron and glass flashing in the sun. A squat, brick building rested under his feet; a skyscraper loomed at his back. Where a forest floor had been, thick strips of asphalt stretched out as far as the eye could see. Buildings shot up in the distance, and farther off, a great suspension bridge stretched over a murky, stagnant river. Cars sat parked on the outskirts of the courtyard, colorful and gleaming.

"Holy mother of mortals," Alexia breathed at my back. I almost laughed. I felt the strangest sense of pride. Staring out at the city, and the park at the edge of the battlefield, I marveled at how life-like it all looked, and how familiar. But it was no wonder I recognized this landscape.

I'd drawn it.

A single, high-pitched tone rang out across the open space, informing the first wave to attack. Far below, another ringtone wailed in the distance, signaling the second and third waves to approach.

The moment was perfect. The courtiers were disoriented, slack-jawed and uncoordinated as they took in the sights all around them. They may have anticipated many things, but none of them expected this. Then, just as they'd started to gather their wits and shake off their hangover, that strange ringing attacked their ears, and for a few seconds they were frozen with confusion. Frozen with fear. And in those seconds, the revolutionaries attacked.

In the center of the grounds, the first wave of faerie servants poured over their captors like insects covering a corpse. Still, the courtiers pushed back. I saw Olorian shove a nymph against a signpost that was really a tree. The nymph's lips opened slightly as she asked the tree to come to her aid. A second later the post bent down, encircling Olorian in its grip.

On the other side of the space, the Lady Claremondes fought furiously with three ogres, cackling as she slithered between their feet. The first fell, unbalanced and confused, and the others looked as if they were going to go hurtling to the ground as well. The Lady shrieked, thinking she'd won, when a dozen minuscule arrows whizzed across the battlefield, piercing her neck. A group of brownies shouted in triumph.

They're winning, I thought, my hand subconsciously threading an arrow through my bow. It hurt like hell, but it was better than being useless.

We're winning.

Then, just as suddenly, a terrible feeling bloomed in the pit of my stomach as I watched Elora stare down Naeve.

I crept to the edge of my branch.

"Taylor," Alexia said.

I shook my head. It made me dizzy, but what didn't, at this point? "This whole thing is a sham."

"What?" Kylie hissed, looking up.

"Our place in the trees. Playing 'defense.' It doesn't mean anything." I gestured to the stage. "If he grabs her, none of us is a good-enough shot to take him out, without risking…"

Alexia opened her mouth, but she didn't say anything.

That told me everything I needed to know. "We're just pawns. Even she's a pawn in her own game. She'll do whatever it takes to distract him, to keep him busy until…" I slid my arrow into its quiver. "I'm not playing anymore."

"Taylor," Alexia said softly. "Every part of this has been planned—"

"You can't plan for everything! That's the point." And then I was gone, slipping down the trunk of the tree. Kylie watched me as I hit the ground, but she didn't try to stop me.

Up on the stage, Naeve was drawing a sword from his cloak. "After an impressive, surprising day, you choose such a pathetically uninspired end?"

Elora said nothing. She made no move to defend herself.

I started to run.

Naeve took a step forward. "So typical of you to sacrifice yourself for the good of your kind. Elora the valiant. Elora the fool."

"Bravery always did elude you," she said, absently adjusting her crown as I pushed between two trolls.

"Such an insolent tongue," Naeve snapped, his gaze drifting to her head, where her hand had lingered. "Yet I still believe, with the proper training, you will make a suitable servant to the Unseelie Prince."

"Ha." Elora scoffed and spat in his face.

Naeve twirled his sword. "All I need is one little sign of subservience." His golden eyes flashed. "Give me your crown."

Elora frowned, like she'd forgotten she'd put on the crown in the first place. "No."

"What?" Naeve asked, pleased by her somber reaction. "A faerie who willfully relinquishes nobility is undeserving of such ornamentation."

"No," Elora murmured again, touching the crown with her fingers. "It was a gift."

Naeve's face flushed, instantly angry. "Then you will

watch the blood drain from everyone you love." He slashed the blade across her face.

Elora gasped, cupping her cheek. Down below, I'd reached the bottom of the stage. For a second, our eyes met, and something in Elora's eyes changed.

"All right," she said, taking the crown from her head. Blood dripped through her fingers onto the jewels. "You can have it. Just don't hurt my friends."

Naeve grinned. "All I ever wanted," he said as Elora stepped toward him with the crown, "was to see you kneeling at my feet. You'd be much more appealing from that angle."

"You have no idea," Elora said in a sultry voice, lifting the crown to his head. "Too bad you never will."

She shoved the iron spikes into his flesh.

Naeve stumbled forward, his eyes rolling dizzily. The sword clattered from his hand. I watched him from below, my arms screaming as I tried to pull myself onto the stage. When he drew something out of his boot, I cried out in vain.

Elora lifted a shimmering sword from the folds of her dress as Naeve rose to his knees. She swung the sword in a way that was so familiar, it made my chest hurt. She lifted her blade. He lifted something too.

Isn't it funny, the difference a second makes?

Just as she brought the blade down, Naeve flung his dagger into her throat. Red blossomed over the white.

"You lose," Naeve said.

A scream ripped from my lips. Then Elora was falling, sliding into a puddle on the ground. I tried to catch her eye, to tell her I loved her one last time. Kiss her cheek. Stroke her hair. But a funny thing happened then. Elora looked out at the grounds, and *grinned*. As I followed her gaze across the battlefield, I saw faeries slumped in the dirt, both servant and courtier. But of those standing, there were hardly any courtiers left.

"*I* win," Elora said. I thought she did, but something about the voice made me loosen my grip. The voice wasn't Elora's.

The building slipped from my hands.

Everything will be an illusion.

The voice was Keegan's.

38

ELORA

I arrived to find the battle in full swing. So perhaps my people did not need me after all. Or perhaps everything had been plotted so perfectly, my presence was less important than all the arrangements I'd made. I'd gathered the servants of the Unseelie Court. I'd made certain my mother was absent, so more faeries would survive.

I did that, I told myself as I reached the top of the mountain.

I set this up, I thought as the body hit the ground. *My* body, or so it seemed, but looking down at my hands, I knew what was mine and what wasn't.

Still, I had one quiet moment of denial where I forgot everything that had led to this eventuality. I told myself it couldn't be my fault. I told myself I couldn't have prevented it. Then reality hit me like a knife to the gut.

A knife to the throat.

"*No!*" A voice screamed, as the glamour bled away from Keegan's body. Looking to my left, I saw a figure on horseback traveling along the outskirts of the grounds, trying to reach the place where Keegan had fallen.

Where her brother had fallen.

"Oh, Darkness," I breathed, wishing for wings that could lift me into the sky. Wishing for someone to carry me. Wishing for magic that wouldn't come. Then, as beings often do in times of trauma, I remembered the parts of me that did work. The parts that were magic, whether anyone realized it or not.

I picked up my feet. I curled my fingers into fists.

And I ran.

Into the fray I went, past centaurs trampling nymphs with their hooves. Past nymphs choking pixies with vines. Blood streaked my arms, and I hadn't even done anything yet. Brambles nipped at my ankles, taking away my skin in little bites.

When I reached the center of the battle, I sought out the key players. I already knew where Naeve was, but where were his favored courtiers? And where were Taylor and Alexia? As an arrow buzzed past me, landing at Naeve's feet, I found one question answered.

But what of the others?

My heart began to race. Really, it was an amazing muscle, withstanding torture, witnessing sacrifice, and still managing to be surprised by such a scene. Brother fighting brother. Sister fighting sister. All of us, so righteous in our indignation. And oh, we'd have our equality!

Death makes equals of us all.

I stumbled over the bodies of fallen faeries. I searched for green eyes and golden hair. I was flinging my darkness haphazardly, inky webs shooting out of my fingers, binding but not suffocating. I needed to find him, to make sure he was all right.

It was foolish, and I focused on it anyway. Love can kill us or save our lives, depending on the minute.

That minute, I chose love over self-preservation, and ran smack-dab into my third greatest enemy. The Lady Claremondes, in all her hideous glory. Even more hideous since Naeve had wrenched her tongue out in the graveyard and used it against me. First I'd been poisoned with her venom, then with iron. Another kind of girl might've been irritated at the injustice. But all's fair in love and war, and I was about to rain *fairness* all over this wretch.

"Ooh, hoo, hoo!" the Lady crowed, that stump of a tongue making me feel sick. I took a step back, a wave of nausea washing over me. "If it isn't the broken princess."

"You aren't exactly the belle of the ball."

"You're speaking like them," the Lady Claremondes said, twirling her sugar-white dreadlocks. Her skin was so pale, she might as well have been a ghost. And she would be when all was said and done. A doomed spirit, haunting this land. Unable to grab. Unable to poison.

Yes.

Come closer, I thought, and beckoned with my hand.

She grinned. "You think you can best me? You cannot even fly."

"Then I guess I will have to kick your face in."

"Have at it," she said, slithering backward. It was easy for her, as her bottom half trailed behind her like a snake, more vapor than substance.

Fair enough, I thought. *I'll just pin her top half against something.* But with what?

Glancing around, I saw the ground was littered with knives. *Kylie*, I thought, my eyes drifting to the outskirts again. I couldn't see her, but it didn't matter. A quick look around the battlefield showed what she'd been doing. Rather than aiming her knives at people's hearts or temples, she'd been wounding them, so that they'd stumble and be overcome by dark servants.

Clever trick. Clever and merciful, for she wasn't taking their lives. She was only incapacitating them. Still, as I watched Naeve yank the crown from his head, swaying dizzily, I knew Kylie would not be merciful with him. If she reached him before I could reach him, things would get uglier than they already were.

Better make this quick.

I swooped down, plucking three knives from the ground. In quick succession, I hurled them at the Lady Claremondes' chest. The first pushed her back, into a tree that looked like a signpost. The second lodged in her chest, stealing her breath. But with the third blade, I gave a little extra oomph, and it slid through her body like she was made of butter.

It pinned her to the tree.

I should've walked away then. Should've sought the stage and taken down Naeve. Should've used the vantage point to locate Taylor and come to his aid. But I didn't. I didn't even think about what I was doing. I just walked toward her with a grin. "Funny how a flightless faerie can still take you down, isn't it?" I said, grabbing a strand of her hair. The long, circular dreadlock she used as a noose.

"You speak like them. You fight like them. You'll fall like them."

"I've already fallen, and come back." I wrapped the hair around her neck. Not like a noose, but over and over again, the way a python wraps around its victim.

A punishment befitting a snake.

Still, it wasn't enough. I couldn't just let her die quietly, allowing her world to fade to black. I didn't have such mercy in me. I wanted her to bleed. To shake. To scream. I wanted to poison her the way she'd poisoned me. And, as I looked to the trees, locating a thin, delicate web, I knew how to do it.

"Come lovelies," I whispered, and started to chant under my breath. I felt it in my fingers first, prickling like sweat, as the spiders in the forest lifted their heads to listen to me. And slowly, like sap seeping from a tree, their venom leaked out of their fangs and crawled through the air, dancing toward me.

Oh, the dance! I hadn't even realized how much I'd missed fighting until this moment. But Naeve had made my childhood hell, and I'd risen to the occasion. Drown me, and I'll suffocate you. Toss me off a cliff, and I'll bring back the waves to crash over your head.

Poison me and, well, wait and see . . .

I grinned as the venom settled under my fingernails, making a home there. The Lady's face was turning blue from the choking, and I lowered my lips to her ear. "This is for me. This is for him. This is for the life I could've lived."

I dug my nails into her neck. And that wicked, poisonous creature, oh, how she screamed. Shaking, her face a pleasant purple, she shrieked with a vengeance, her body suffering spasms.

"Oh, beautiful," I said. But I didn't feel joy. Not like I used to feel when I'd bested Naeve. Quiet guilt settled over me, and I thought of Kylie. I thought of how she'd shaken when the Lady Claremondes had licked her neck.

Here, she was vindicated, but it didn't matter. Her brother

was still dead. I saw a flash of her between two buildings. She was closing in on Naeve.

This game of torture had to end. Yanking the knives from the Lady Claremondes' chest, I tossed her to the ground, calling to the pixies that fluttered around me.

"Hungry, my darlings?" I asked.

They flashed sharp teeth. Of all the beings in the Unseelie Court, the Lady had tortured the pixies the worst. She loved the way their bodies crunched when she bit into them. Loved to snap their necks. She loved to whip them and break them and laugh.

Now they hovered about, gossamer wings flapping furiously, so tiny and beautiful except for those fangs. The least I could do was feed them. The least I could do was step aside and let them have their vengeance.

"Dinner is served," I announced, pushing away into the crowd.

I heard them surround her, buzzing in a swarm. I heard tiny teeth sinking in. I heard screams, then, nothing. Or rather, everything else, as the battle reached a fever pitch. I pushed forward, tuning the noises out, until a horse brayed.

I spun around, my heart racing. Across the battlefield, Kylie's horse reared up on its hind legs, nearly tossing her to the ground. She'd almost made it to Naeve. Now she hung in midair, trying desperately to keep from falling as dark courtiers circled below.

I changed direction, racing toward her. I ran as fast as my legs would carry me. And I knew, with crushing clarity, that if she dropped to the ground, I wouldn't reach her in time.

39

TAYLOR

As I watched Kylie dangle in midair, I wanted to race over to her. Wanted to swing my sword like a madman, cutting down anyone in my path. But I couldn't. Something was holding me back.

Literally. A hand around my neck.

I turned, twisting out of his grip, feeling the bruises forming. Damn, this guy was big. But I guess you'd have to be, to play bodyguard to the Dark Prince.

"Guess the nymph didn't kill you?" I snarled, circling him.

Olorian waved a hand. His skin was as black as the Unseelie Forest, as black as the polished spires of the castle. I followed his gesture to the twisted body of a nymph on the ground.

No, no, no.

I felt my muscles clenching, to protect me from the nausea. I felt my brain whispering stories: *she might not be dead.* I felt my reflexes bending over backward as waves of shock washed over me, making it impossible to process such destruction. Death. Game over. The end.

Who could process that?

Even now, as that great, hulking mass stumbled toward me, his footfalls shaking the ground, his hands large enough to crush me like a soda can, my body just acted, leaping out of his grip. Doing what was necessary to survive.

A miraculous thing, really.

Sure, think of miracles. Think of beauty, as bodies lie twisted all around. That's appropriate.

But I couldn't stop it. Couldn't stop searching for signs of life, of beauty, amongst all the blood and broken bones. I needed that balance. I needed that hope.

Especially now, as Olorian approached, grinning. "Well, well, well," he said, his mouth a gaping abyss. "If it isn't the boy who sullied the princess."

"Maybe after I kick your ass, I can sully her some more."

Whoa. Did I just say that? It seemed like the guy I was in my mind and the guy I was in real life were merging into the same person. The one who stared into the face of danger and laughed. The one who didn't let insecurity keep him from doing what he wanted.

Well, this I could work with.

I reached into my belt, drawing out my sword. "Maybe after all is said and done, I can sully her brains out." I grinned, swinging the sword with expert precision. (At least, this is what I told myself.) "And she can sully mine."

Olorian swiped at me, his nails catching my shoulder as I jumped away.

"See, that's the problem with big guys," I taunted, swinging the sword again. My back didn't even hurt anymore, not like it had. That's what happens when you mix faerie drugs with adrenaline.

A dangerous cocktail, my friend, I thought and laughed.

"You think you're so tough, but you move too slow, and this happens." I sliced the sword once, then twice, slashing a long, red X across Olorian's stomach. "That's why, in a bet, I'd take a scrapper over a big guy anytime." I lashed out again.

This time, his hand went *around the blade* and pulled forward.

Shit. I'd forgotten how easily faeries could heal. If I was going to do damage, it needed to be of the mortal variety. And it needed to be fast.

Kylie was shrieking from her corner of the battlefield as faeries clawed the air, waiting to welcome her into their circle. When an arrow hit one of them in the back, I knew Alexia was closing in.

Time to join her, I thought, and tightened my grip on the sword's hilt. I yanked the blade out of his hand.

Olorian yelped like a dog that's been stepped on, and I stumbled backward. I mean, I pretended to stumble. Then I pretended to fall, angling my head so it landed on a rock. In reality, I was using my arm to cushion the fall, but Olorian was distracted, staring at his mangled hand.

When he looked at me, the sword resting loosely in my palm, my eyes closed, he thought I'd been knocked out.

He started to laugh. Then he strode over to me. Those footfalls were heavy, and I had to close my fingers, just a little, to keep the sword from clattering to the ground.

Olorian stood over me, chortling loudly. "That's it? That's all you've got?"

He kicked my gut, and I tried not to wince.

Just a little closer, I thought.

And yes, he leaned in. "That's the problem with you mortals," he said. I closed my hand around the hilt. "You think you're so incredibly special, but you're *nothing*. You've no power and no magic, you weak, pathetic parasite."

Come on, I thought. *Threaten Elora. Threaten my reason for living, so I can slice you into pieces.*

It was an odd thought to have, but probably not uncommon. How many of us would defend our loved ones before we'd defend ourselves? Like Kylie had said, she might not kill to save her own life, but she'd kill for Alexia.

Wait, what did that say about us? We would kill for others, but not for ourselves? No, I couldn't be that person. I needed to live for myself. Needed to believe I was worthy of life. After that, Elora and I could fight alongside each other.

But first, I needed to live for *me*.

"Sweet dreams, foolish mortal," Olorian said, preparing to smash me into oblivion. When he lifted his arm, I lifted mine.

Mine had a sword in it.

He lunged, and I lunged too. Together, we found each other, but his fist didn't meet my flesh. My blade met skin, then muscle, then bone. It slipped into him like a hand slips into water. And it just kept slipping, as red, gushing liquid rushed out of him. (It helped to think of it as "liquid" and not something else.) It didn't stop slipping until the hilt slammed into his ribs. The sound was ... unfortunate. Sharp and grating, but also wet. Like grinding a stone in a swamp. I almost lost my lunch then. Almost lost everything I'd ever eaten.

And then I did.

It happened as he fell forward, crushing me beneath him. Across the way, I heard a horse bolting for the trees. Heard

Kylie falling to the ground. Calling for Alexia, who had to be close, but was she close enough?

I tried to free myself. But it was hard. This fucker was big. And now I could feel everything, every place where the Bright Queen's needle had pierced my back. The wings dug into me as I turned, pushing, pulling.

It can't end like this. Please. God. Mother Earth. Anyone.

I heard a voice responding in my ear. Asking for a sacrifice. And I almost said no, because I was so sick of sacrifices.

But I needed to survive this.

The scream tore out of me as I pulled my body in an unnatural direction. It was the only way, the only opening between him and the air. His body. Olorian. Yeah, he was dead, and now my leg was broken.

I heard it crunch as I pulled away.

Come on, shock, I thought as I pushed myself to my feet, then fell again. *Come on, adrenaline. I need you.*

Nope. Nothing.

Well, how do you like them apples? Olorian was lying on my sword, and there was no way I was getting it back. Shooting a final glance in his direction, I started to crawl across the courtyard.

One foot in front of the other, I reminded myself. Then, *No, one hand in front of the other.* Either way, I would make it. I'd throw Kylie a knife, and together, we'd save ourselves. Yes.

Fairy tales are nice when you're nearing the end.

When I caught a flash of red hair, all the way across the battlefield, I almost cried from relief. Then I looked up and saw Naeve watching her too.

No, no, no.

First he took Keegan. Next he'd take Elora. The dark faeries would take Kylie. Then they'd come for me.

Together, we'd fall.

"Not this time," I told Naeve, though he couldn't hear me. "You can't have them," I told the earth, which was soaking up the blood so quickly. Lapping it up like sustenance, like we were just nutrients, not bodies and hearts.

Now Kylie was screaming. Alexia was moving through the trees, but she could only move so fast.

Just a little longer. Please.

At the edge of the battlefield, close to where Kylie had fallen, there was movement, and I saw something golden behind the buildings. *Bright faeries,* I thought, but it didn't soothe me. More faeries meant more soldiers. More soldiers meant more bodies. More blood. More broken bones.

But I was wrong, I realized, as deer flooded the courtyard. Within seconds, they'd surrounded the circle of faeries. Surrounded Kylie. A great, spotted buck with skin as gold as it was brown slipped into the center and knelt down. I couldn't see him. I thought he was using his body to cover Kylie. Across the grounds, Elora was curling her fingers in the air, calling on the vines that lived in the forest. They slithered toward the circle, toward the dark faeries.

I closed my eyes, waiting for the screams to start up again.

But here in the faerie realm, where things don't do what you expect, the buck surprised me. Kylie surprised me.

The deer shot up, bounding out of the circle, and on his back was the girl with the warmest eyes I'd ever seen. Dark hair disheveled. Arms wrapped around the deer's neck. Vines snaked around her lower half, lashing her to the animal. I'd never seen anyone look so fierce.

Together, they soared over the crowd and landed on the stage beside Naeve. Beside Keegan, who was the only one in our group who couldn't fight anymore.

Didn't have to.

Couldn't.

I held my breath. As the deer reared up, hooves curling in the air, Naeve dove for the dagger that had stolen Keegan's breath. In an instant, he could fling that blade into Kylie's chest. In an instant, the deer could trample him.

I heard a voice at my back. "Shall we finish what we've started? Together?"

"It's going to have to be," I said, gesturing to my leg. The Princess of the Dark Faeries wrapped her arm around my waist, and together, we made our way to Kylie.

To Naeve.

To the end.

40

ELORA

On the morning of the seventeenth, I held a meeting with mercy and asked her how to live with what had transpired. And unlike death, who took but never gave, she offered to play a game. A game of numbers.

How many? she asked. *How many will live? How many will die?*

I pulled Taylor onto the stage. I could hear bone grinding against bone, but I would not tell him to rest this time. That choice was not mine. So instead, I lifted him onto the final battlefield just as Alexia climbed up the back of the stage, rising behind Naeve.

Four humans, I counted, my heart thundering wildly. *Three living, one dead. Two faeries. One dagger. Two swords.*

Naeve spun around, nearly catching Alexia in the chin. But she was ready for him, and she ducked, causing him to spin. Just when his back was turned to her, she kicked, sending him flying. Unfortunately, he sailed past Keegan's body, landing next to one of the swords.

I knelt down, lifting the other. "Alexia," I called, holding it out to her. But Alexia had other plans. Crouching down, she scooped Naeve's fallen crown from the stage. Then she dove, scraping the iron spikes across his chest.

"Yes. Get him!" Kylie yelled as Naeve howled, hitting the ground. Reaching over his body, Alexia grabbed his sword and jumped to her feet. She lifted her sword and I lifted mine.

No, no, no, mercy said. *You are now in the service of death.*

I froze, ready to cut off Naeve's head. Alexia looked ready to cut out his heart. But as Taylor inhaled beside me, I wondered if I could murder a person in front of him. I wondered how Kylie would feel when her fury bled into sadness.

I pushed the sword into Taylor's hand. "This is your moment," I whispered. "Use it wisely."

"Alexia," Kylie called from up above. "Toss me the sword."

Alexia turned, staring at her. Naeve was clambering to his feet. Blood dripped from his chest, but he was healing quickly. Alexia's blow would not be the thing to kill him. As for Kylie's...

"Trust me." Kylie reached out her hand.

"I do," Alexia mouthed, and let go of the sword. No, she tossed it, perfectly, into Kylie's hand. All of her strength and grace were visible in that arc. All of her calculations that, in the end, she relinquished.

We both did.

"It's all you, baby," she said, as Naeve pulled back his hand. The dagger glinted in the mid-morning light.

Taylor leapt in front of me, lifting his sword.

41

I dove across the stage, bringing down my sword. Kylie brought down hers. Naeve howled and fell to his knees. But he couldn't cover his face with his hands, not anymore. Kylie had taken them.

And I'd taken his wings.

The hands fell quickly, tumbling to the ground like I did, but the wings, well, they wanted to put on a show. Fluttering quietly, they fell to the stage like leaves. Like feathers.

I thought they would never hit the ground.

But *Kylie* did. Slicing the vines that held her in place, she slid from the deer onto the floor, next to Naeve's severed hands. But where was the dagger?

Oh, there, between my ribs. As soon as I saw it, I *felt* it, and my whole body swayed. Elora dropped down beside me. "Taylor? No, no, no. *Please…*"

My vision started to blur. I blinked, but all I could see was the blood spattering my skin.

"Is it deep? Taylor? Is it—"

"Tell me it isn't," I managed. "Faeries can't lie."

Elora smiled softly, her hands wrapping around the dagger's

hilt. "It can't be," she whispered, and pulled. My body jerked forward, then snapped back like a taut rubber band. But I could breathe. I could breathe, and I wasn't bleeding too badly. Elora tore strips from her dress and wrapped them around me.

Now the dagger lay on the ground. Naeve would never grab one again. Never cut off someone's wings. Never hold someone hostage. Never fly.

Poetic justice, I thought as Alexia stepped up to him. He was moaning and writhing as she lifted her boot. She brought it down on his head. He slumped to the ground, no longer conscious.

"See, I can be helpful too," she said, flashing a grin.

Kylie looked up, smiling the tiniest bit. Then her face crumpled and she dissolved into sobs. Together, we crowded around the body that used to be a boy. A beloved companion. A twin.

Kylie brushed the chestnut hair from Keegan's eyes. He'd looked a little wild, at the end. We all had, probably.

We all grew wild to survive.

"It should've been me," she whispered, studying his face for signs of life. Like at any moment, he'd jump up with a mischievous grin and announce he'd been kidding. She waited. We waited.

Still, nothing.

"Let us take him away from this," Elora said when I thought all of the blood had poured out of him. "Somewhere you can be alone together."

"And Naeve?" Alexia asked after a minute. Her hand was on Kylie's back. But I didn't think Kylie could feel it, didn't think she'd feel anything for a very long time. I wanted to comfort her, but I knew how pointless it would've been.

"Naeve..." Elora said softly, scanning our faces.

"It's your decision," I said. Just as Brad's fate should've been left to us, Naeve's fate was up to Elora. She'd judge her people. We'd judge ours. Until the time came when we could live together, in peace.

If that time ever came.

"I have an idea," she said, her teal eyes glittering. Those flames were lighting up, giving way to something wicked. "The faerie world gained five humans. Shouldn't the mortal world gain something?"

Alexia looked up, smiling softly. I nodded. Kylie didn't even glance in our direction.

"We'll have to bind him with iron, to weaken his magic. Glamour him to look mortal." Elora stared off into the battlefield. The clangs and screams were dying down. Scanning the space, I couldn't see any courtiers left standing. But many servants stood tall, cheering and hugging and declaring their victory.

We've won, I thought, warmth surging in my chest. Then my gaze trailed back to the place where he rested. To Keegan.

We've lost.

42

ELORA

That night, we buried our dead and laid crimson petals over their graves. That night, Keegan was laid in an enchanted casket, which would keep his body preserved until Kylie was ready to say goodbye. And that night, as we settled into our chamber in the Unseelie Palace, where we would rest until we were healed, Taylor turned to me and said the last thing I expected.

"I don't think I can do this." He turned to the window. Outside, the sun hovered low on the horizon, all bloody and red. Too much blood. Too much darkness.

Still, I pretended not to know what he was saying. "What do you mean?"

He gestured to the bed. His skin was pale. Once golden, now dulled by lack of light. He looked like he'd aged a hundred years.

Did you Rip van Winkle us? Kylie had asked.

No, I have done something worse. I have aged your heart. I have aged your soul.

I placed my hand over his chest. When he looked down, it was as if he didn't even know me. Or perhaps he knew me too well.

"I can't stay here tonight," he said. "I can't stay with you. I'm sorry."

I climbed off the bed. Like I'd done in our hotel room after prom, so many weeks ago. So many centuries ago, it seemed. I knelt before him. "Talk to me."

His hands went to my hair. It seemed like a reflex now, like something he couldn't help.

Yes, run with that, I thought, dying to feel his lips on mine. *Give in to it. Don't think. Just feel.*

These thoughts were dangerous. But what could I recognize, if not danger?

"I keep trying," he said, staring into my eyes. "If you'd asked me yesterday, or a week ago, or a month, where I wanted to be forever, it was here." Again he gestured to the blankets, all tangled up beneath him. "With you. In bed." He laughed, the tiniest bit.

It sounded brittle, like twigs snapping. Like bones breaking. Bitter, like blood on your lips.

"I could never have imagined a scenario where I wouldn't want this," he said.

"And now?" I asked, my heart falling into darkness.

"Now, I keep thinking about sleeping here with you tonight, and I just can't *get* there. It doesn't feel right. I keep trying to force it, when I know that's wrong. I thought we'd be celebrating, but how can we, after what's happened? I thought we'd be so much in love, and showing each other that, but how can I, if—"

"You don't love me anymore?"

His face crumpled the way Kylie's had. "I love you more

347

than anything in this world. I love you enough to kill or die. That's what scares me."

"But you didn't kill. Not when it wasn't required."

"No. But you..." He looked away. "You let Brad die."

My gaze fell to the bed. My bed, all dressed up in black and red. Blood and darkness.

Oh. So he's right about me.

"Yes. I let Brad die," I said, touching the blankets. Changing their hue with the slightest bit of effort. "Threw him to the wolves, even." But we did not say "threw him to the wolves" in the Dark Court. We said "threw him to the humans."

The Dark Court has fallen, I reminded myself, but then, it had only just happened. And old habits weren't murdered easily.

I shuddered, taking hold of his hands. "I had to protect *you*," I said.

He nodded. "I keep thinking about it. Wondering if there was another way out. But there wasn't, was there? She was going to kill one of us. If it wasn't him, it was going to be me."

"Yes." With shaking fingers, I lifted my hand to his cheek. He was pale, but he was still warm. Pale and warm, like the dark faeries.

Is he right to protect himself from me?

"I know why you did it, I understand your reasoning. But I still can't get past it," he said. "Can't get past that it happened. *Seeing* it..."

"Maybe in time—"

"I know about Keegan, too," he said. "I know what he offered to do. I heard you talking in the forest."

My breath caught in my throat. "I wouldn't let him do it."

Taylor nodded, but his gaze was so far away. Trapped somewhere in the past where I couldn't reach him. "So you did everything you could to stop him?"

"I told him it was forbidden. Told him I'd never sacrifice him to protect myself."

"Never," he said softly, and his meaning was obvious. *Never* couldn't be that long if Keegan was dead.

"You think it's my fault?" I realized, my hand jerking to my side defensively.

"I think it's Naeve's fault. And Keegan's. And the Bright Lady's."

"And mine."

He was quiet a minute, but his silence spoke volumes. "I don't think it's your fault."

The breath rushed into me. The life rushed into me. And then he knocked it out again. "But I think you could've stopped it. I think you could've tried harder, and forbidden the Queen."

"I…" The words died on my lips. "I didn't think to forbid her," I confessed. "I didn't think I had that power."

"But you would've tried, if it were me. If I'd offered myself, you would've tried anything to stop it."

"How can you punish me for loving you?"

"I'm not. I'm not even mad." He took his head in his hands. I wanted those hands to be mine. But they weren't, just like he wasn't. "I'm just heartbroken and furious with myself and I can't *look* at you."

Those words were like shards in my back. And I should know. I'd actually felt them. But as for a dagger in the throat, well…

Keegan had suffered that for me. Was Taylor right, then? Would I have fought harder to protect *him*?

Of course I would have. I would have done anything. I would have thrown my body in front of the knife.

"I did everything I could think to do, logically. I promise you—"

"But you would've done more to protect me?"

"Yes," I said. His eyes closed at the sound of it. "Because I am not logical with you. You are not logical with me. This love, this thing between us ... it makes us do stupid, reckless things. But I cannot be punished for being logical with others. That isn't fair." I reached for him, and he pulled out of my grasp. It made me feel desperate. I would kill just to touch him. But that was the problem, wasn't it?

"If I had it to do over, I would try harder," I told him. "But you said it yourself, I can't control what any of you do. It isn't my decision."

When he looked up, his eyes were red. He looked as if he was on the brink of despair. Well, good. We could meet each other there. "*Why* were you late to the battle? *Why* was he in your place to begin with? It should've been—"

"Me."

"No. Not you." He shook his head, hair falling around his face. I wanted to grab it, wrap my fingers around it, and ...

Stop.

"Who else could it have been?" I asked. "It was him or it was me. There was no other choice."

"It could've been me."

"And you could've been dead. And then, Taylor my love, you would not want to have seen your wicked princess. You

350

would not want to have seen the darkness I would've unleashed on them. All of them. I wouldn't have cared who—"

I stopped. The look on his face stopped me. He was crawling backward, away from me.

"The Bright Lady tricked me," I explained, but it was too late. The damage had been done, and he knew who I was now. A monster. The Dark Princess. "She bound me, alongside my mother. She used my own trick against me! I only broke free because..." But I couldn't say the rest. Couldn't speak of another sacrifice among many. My beloved Illya. Even as tears filled my eyes, I realized the uselessness of trying to bring him back to me. Illya had died and Keegan had died and Brad had died.

Because of me.

"You're right," I said. "I should have been up there. I shouldn't have trusted the Seelie Queen. I should have done everything I could to protect all of you, and I didn't. And I'm *sorry.*" I lowered my head to my hands. All of it was washing over me, the sadness, the grief. "I'm so sorry. I understand why you don't want me."

"I want you," he said, and my head snapped up. My tears stopped. "I want you, and I would have you, with blood still on my hands. That's the problem. My love for you does something *bad* to me."

"No."

"Your love for me does something *bad* to you."

I have always been bad, I thought, but I did not say it. It would just drive him away from me.

He's already leaving.

"Please, just a little more time," I begged, asking for the

thing he had always asked of me. "Please have the mercy to grant what I could not grant to you."

He shook his head. "You were right. All along, you knew this was impossible."

"Just *one night*. One small thing." I could see us, showering together in the falls. Washing the blood off each other's skin. Washing the tears. Hands so delicate. Kisses so sweet.

I did something I am not proud of then. I crawled onto the bed and pressed my lips to his. I appealed to the body, when I should have appealed to the heart. The soul. But such things are not as separated as humans believe. My heart responded to him as we kissed. My soul wrapped around him as my body did.

"Please," I whispered, kissing him fiercely. *Please, you don't know how hard it was for me to trust you. To trust anyone. Please don't prove I was right all along*, I thought. But all I said was, "Please."

His hands curled into my hair.

"I love you," I whispered, fingers trailing past the bandage on his chest. If I could just heal him, maybe things would be different.

"Your love is dangerous," he said as I passed his navel and fumbled with the buttons of his pants.

"Yes, but not only," I promised.

"Your love could kill me."

"But it won't." My hand slid down, and for a moment, time stilled. For a moment, we were cradled in the center of the universe, and no one could reach us and pull us back. "We have seen the darkest parts of love," I told him as he pressed into me, kissing me so fiercely, it almost hurt. "Now, let us see the brightest. Love can kill, but love can also save your life. You saved mine."

"I didn't," he breathed, leaning into me.

I had almost reached him. "You have no idea."

Everything stopped. Our breathing stopped. Our kisses stopped. I knew I had him, but only physically.

I took my hand back.

"Where are you going?" he asked.

I took my body back, though my heart stayed with him.

"I'm sorry," I said.

"Why?" he asked, breathing heavily.

Because I wanted you so badly, I would've used your body to get to you. And I couldn't, because love doesn't do that. Love doesn't hurt to get what it wants. It doesn't use, or trick, or manipulate. The very idea goes *against* love.

"Why are you sorry?" he pressed.

I lowered my head, feeling the distance between us. "Because I don't know how I'm going to live without you."

He was quiet a minute. Finally, he said, "I just need some time. A couple of days. I need to figure things out."

I nodded, waiting silently. I knew he had more to say. I knew him so well. My hands were closing in on themselves.

"It's just… ever since I met you, everything I've done has been for you."

"Yes, but Taylor, I didn't ask for that—"

"You didn't have to," he said. "I wanted to be in your service. You were my queen from the minute we met. I would've bowed at your feet. I would've tied myself up and cut my wrists with the vines." He swallowed, closing his eyes. "I would've sat like a dog waiting patiently if it meant I could have you. Because that's what I thought it would take."

"But you have me."

"And what did it cost me? I've been shackled for you. I've killed for you. I almost died for you. I gave up my freedom for you. My family—"

"We've been reckless," I said.

"No." He shook his head. "I wasn't reckless. I was *deliberate*. I knew what I was doing."

"You were merciful in the end. You didn't kill Naeve."

"Right. Killing is—"

"What I would've done."

"Yes. And you wouldn't have felt bad."

"Not as much as you would have."

"Because we're different," he said.

"No."

He nodded, taking my face in his hands. For a moment, I thought he was going to kiss me, but he didn't. He couldn't.

We're different.

We're different.

We're different.

All my life, I'd felt different. *Why are you playing with us?* the servants had asked, scurrying away from me. *Why are your wings so tattered and ugly?* the courtiers had teased. Naeve couldn't stand me. My mother couldn't look at me.

"You're the only one who made me feel like I belonged." I searched Taylor's eyes. "You are my home. The home I've been searching for."

My true love said nothing.

That's all right. I know what to do now, I thought. There

was one piece of unfinished business, one last battle to fight, and though I was not as strong as she was, if I caught her by surprise, I could still take her down. Together, we'd risen to power. Together, we'd fall to dust.

Only, always, together.

"I will give you what you want," I said, rising from the bed.

"It isn't what I want." There were tears in his eyes. There were tears in my eyes. "It's what I need. I want you," he added softly.

"You had me," I told him.

But not now.

I leaned in and kissed my sweetest salvation. My reason for living. The only joy I'd ever had. "I love you," I whispered. "Always, I have loved you. From the moment my spirit came into being. Before it even made sense."

"I love you," he said, but I couldn't hear him. He'd only mouthed the words. I waited for him to pull me back to him. To show me his love.

But he didn't.

And I didn't pull him back either. Backing away from the bed, my arms still stained with the blood of my enemies, the blood of my friends, I went to meet my mother.

I went to seal my fate.

43

TAYLOR

That night, I expected to dream of bloodshed and violence. Of shackles and faeries who torture you while they grin. But I didn't. I dreamt of my house in the human world. My bed.

I looked down at the blankets, thinking, *This is the real world, and that was just a dream. Keegan isn't dead.*

I sat up with a smile on my face. The sun was filtering through the windows, softly, like you'd never see in the faerie courts, and I stretched my arms above my head lazily. I couldn't wait to face the day.

Everything is perfect, I told myself. *Everything is as it should be. I'm safe. My family is safe. My friends are safe.*

The calendar was hanging over my desk, and I walked up to it. May hadn't even happened yet. It was still April.

It was the day I'd met ... somebody. But it didn't matter, because everything was as it should be.

And so it went. I brushed my teeth and showered. Went rummaging through the house for breakfast. I wanted to hug my parents, even though they'd driven me crazy before. I wanted to, but I couldn't find them.

That was okay. My mom was probably at the store, and

my dad was … well, wherever my dad always went. Absent, even when he was here.

That was okay. I walked back to my room, past the pine tree in our yard. Something about it bothered me, but I couldn't remember what.

Clouds passed overhead.

The school day went by quickly. I was anxious to get to the soccer game, to play against Brad. No, alongside Brad. We were on the same team; he just wasn't a team player. That was okay. Everything was okay. The stupid little things that had bothered me before didn't bother me anymore. I strode onto the field with confidence. I offered Brad a high-five, so relieved to see him standing there, but he didn't offer one back. Whatever.

Worse things could've happened.

The game started on time. And everything went how I remembered it: our team was behind. Brad was trying to cheat. The coach was ogling the cheerleaders. It all felt so unnecessary. So pointless. Like, this was their life? This was my life? Kicking around a ball on a field? Kicking at a net?

I told myself to calm down. Everything was okay. *Look to the stands, wave to your parents.* I tried, but they weren't there. They were never there. Not a single time.

Okay. Okay. Okay.

I missed an easy kick, and Brad pushed me aside. God, he was a dick. No, he was an okay guy. No, he was a jerk, but he wasn't a dead jerk, so I should be relieved.

I mean, I was relieved.

Still, he kept bumping into me and I just didn't have the patience for it. The game wasn't important to me. The people in the stands weren't important to me. We were kicking a ball into a net. In my dreams, I'd been a hero on a battlefield. I'd saved a princess. And now...

Race, dodge, kick. Race, dodge, kick.

This is your life?

I walked off the field at halftime. On my way out, I stopped by the other team and told them to watch out for Brad, and then I just bailed. I thought about calling Kylie, but I didn't have her number. We weren't even friends.

That was okay. We would be friends.

But I couldn't remember how or why. We didn't run in the same circles. We'd only talked a couple of times. And honestly, when I thought about going to school and sitting through Math and English and stuff, I just... couldn't muster up the enthusiasm.

I mean, quadratic equations? Sonnets? There were people being blown up. There were people being murdered and raped. But hey, let's talk about Socrates! Let's sit at lunch tables and trade stories about almost getting laid. Let's tell lies and wear masks.

I walked right past the parking lot into the trees. It was cooler back here. Nice and dark, with these tiny shafts of light. I walked over to the swing set and sat down. I was waiting for something.

But what?

The game let out. The moon rose higher. Ten o'clock. Eleven o'clock. Midnight. Soon, morning.

No one came. I was alone. My parents hadn't even called my phone.

I started to feel heavy again, started to feel sweaty and panicked. I was alone? *What about Alexia?* I thought.

Wait, I didn't even like her, I remembered. We hated each other. At least, we looked at each other with the appropriate amount of disdain. Popular vs. unpopular.

Wait, this is your life? This is your life?

I stood from the swings, thinking I could change it all. I could connect with Kylie before it was too late. Help her bring her girlfriend to the prom. Talk to my parents. Make friends. Make peace.

Yes.

I hurried to my car and drove home in a daze. But when I got there, my parents' cars were gone. The windows were open, and no blinds were covering them up. Looking in, I saw empty rooms.

I raced to the garage. There I climbed the stairs with heavy legs. I struggled to pull my keys from my pocket, thinking it would take three tries to get my key into the lock. My hands were so shaky. But it turns out it wasn't a problem.

Because there was no door.

I walked through the open entryway and found what had been missing. The unhinged door was lying on the floor. And in the center of the room sat a single box holding the remainder of my belongings. A ball. A sketchpad. Three books: *Peter Pan, Othello,* and a history textbook. My heart squeezed when I picked up *Othello.* It reminded me of something, but I didn't know what.

Then I saw it. A single sleeve, streaked red. Pulling it out, I found it was attached to a shirt. And then I just slid to the ground, clutching the shirt to my chest, the last remnant of my home.

Because this place wasn't my home. My family was gone,

or they would be soon. My friends would go off to college, get jobs, maybe follow me on Twitter or whatever networking site would exist when we were adults.

And here I'd be, alone, rocking in the same damn place I'd always been. Wanting to be a hero, but paralyzed by fear.

No, *immobilized* by fear, by loneliness.

Maybe I'd get married. Maybe I'd have kids. Pass down the same harmful bullshit my folks passed onto me. Or hell, maybe I'd be a great dad, but what would I be doing for the world? What would I be giving back? Forests would fall to build my home. My furniture. Books. Papers. Napkins. We'd eat animals raised in factories.

Blood would follow us everywhere we went. The blood of the forest. The blood of the earth. I might live, and I might love, but all I would do was destroy this place.

Lead it closer to the end.

Outside my window, I heard a great cracking sound, and I looked out to see the tree had split open. There, at the base, darkness was creeping out, like it was searching for me. But I didn't run from it, not this time.

I ran toward it. Into it.

I ran home.

44

E̲L̲O̲R̲A

I did not go to meet my maker dressed in blood. Oh, no. I stopped beside the falls and cleansed the crimson from my arms. I even tinged the water a pleasant blue before I left. Little known fact about glamour: it was easier for me to put one on than tear one away. Another thing Taylor didn't know about me.

One of many.

My legs grew heavy as I walked. Probably I was suffering from exhaustion. Probably I was in some kind of shock. One thing was for certain: I was not in a state to be making important decisions. But when everything you love has been lost, you cease to care about such things. When you've gained everything you've worked for and still come away feeling empty inside, you'll do anything to fill that chasm. Even fight. Even die. Rage slips in so easily, when love has bled away.

And I had lost a lot of love that night.

I stopped outside the space where my mother had been bound and gave my oldest friend a proper burial. I dropped petals of white upon Illya's grave. So tired of red and black, I knelt and pressed my forehead to the earth, and said, "It was not in vain."

As I lifted my head, a petal stuck to my forehead, and I laughed softly, saying, "Yes. I will keep a piece of you with me always. I will—"

I stopped, my gaze trailing through the forest toward my mother's tree. There, in the center of the clearing, was a body.

A nymph, her skin pale. Her blood coating the ground.

"No," I whispered, pushing to my feet. I hurried over to check the creature's pulse. Her skin was cold, as if she'd been dead for hours. She must've stumbled here during the battle, and used her blood to free the Queen.

Yes, I thought as my gaze traveled to the great, cracked pine. The empty pine.

My mother was gone.

For a moment, a sense of vertigo washed over me as I tried to put the pieces together. How had the nymph come so far? I'd seen her in battle, fighting a satyr. Trying to choke him. I'd turned away just as he'd rammed his horns into her belly.

So much blood, and yet she had made it here. So many trees, and yet, she had known where to look. How?

One glance at the ground showed a single green leaf, the kind of leaf another queen might drop. Of course, she had been here earlier, so it made sense that there would be leaves. Except this leaf was curled up in the nymph's hand, like the morbid calling card of a murderous queen.

A glittering queen.

I shook my head, unable to make sense of it. The Bright Lady was the last person who'd want to unleash my mother on the world. Wasn't she? The first thing the Dark Lady would do is destroy her. At least she'd try. And then, she'd come for …

"No." My gaze trailed to the castle, to the place where the humans slept. The place where he slept.

Oh, Darkness.

I realized it didn't matter how my mother had broken free. All that mattered was what she did with that freedom.

I picked up my skirt and raced to the castle.

45

TAYLOR

When I woke up, the first thing I noticed were the blankets. Elora must've glamoured them blue, but I'd been too mired in my own self-loathing to notice. All the little things she did for me, I managed to miss.

Instead, I'd focused on the bad things, the murderous things.

But all along the way, she'd been sweet to me. Telling me stories to help me sleep. Sitting through the most awkward dinner of my life while my parents rejected me, and then telling them off. Holding me when I felt guilty over my brother's death. Kissing me when I was too afraid to ask for what I wanted.

Kissing, and other things.

I bolted from the bed. I needed to see her, needed to tell her I'd been wrong, and the battle had messed me up. That battle would mess anyone up, and watching Keegan die... no human could bear witness to that, and be okay.

No person could.

But we could heal together now, and I wouldn't push her

away again. I'd just needed some time to work through what I'd witnessed. To work through what I'd done. What we'd done.

Yes.

I raced from the room. But rather than tearing through the castle and out into the trees, I stopped at the room down the hall, knocking softly.

Alexia answered the door, hair plastered to her face. Eyes red. But it didn't exactly look like she'd been crying. It looked more like she hadn't slept or eaten in twenty-four hours and maybe she needed a little help.

"Is Elora in here?" I asked.

She shook her head. "She came by earlier and hugged me and Kylie, but she didn't stay."

I nodded, anxious to go find her. But Kylie was my family too now, all three of them were, and Alexia looked like she was going to pass out.

"How's it going?" I asked softly.

"Intense." She ran a hand through her hair and it got stuck. "She hasn't gotten up. She just lies in the bed and cries and doesn't go anywhere. Not even to see him in his ... "

Casket, I thought, and an image of Snow White flashed through my mind. Keegan's casket was made of glass too, and it was supposed to be magic. But nobody would wake him with a kiss.

Not his true love, whoever that might've been. He never got to find out. I swallowed, grabbing the doorframe for support.

"I should come in," I said, and it was halfway between a question and a statement.

Alexia nodded, and stepped out of my way.

Inside the room, the air felt heavy. Humid, like all of Kylie's tears were hovering in the air. And since this was Faerie, I guess it was possible. Maybe tears turned into clouds, and rained back on us when we needed a reminder of what we'd lost.

As if we could ever forget.

And there she was, lying on a bed with burgundy blankets, which Elora had probably glamoured to suit Alexia's tastes. Or maybe it was just a coincidence. It didn't really matter, but sometimes stupid thoughts like these kept me from breaking down when things got too heavy.

Not heavy. Heartbreaking. Our friend is dead.

Don't you love it when your brain reminds you of things? I started to break down before I even made it to the bed. Kylie saw me, and I guess I was speaking her language, because she didn't wave me off.

She opened her arms.

I crawled onto the bed and wrapped her up in my arms, and together we lay there crying and not saying anything. The words would come later, the stories of what had made Keegan amazing. I could see us sitting up every night for the rest of our lives, telling stories around the campfire. Eventually, the stories would repeat, because he hadn't been that old, and—

Oh, God.

I closed my eyes against the pain, and she clung to me. And I just started saying "I'm sorry," as if that could do anything. I was sorry for her. Sorry for him. Sorry for me.

So sorry, so sorry, so sorry . . .

Eventually, she pulled back. Her face was puffy, like she'd been hit. And she had, over and over again, in the gut. In the soul.

The heart.

"What am I supposed to do?" she asked.

I shook my head. "I don't know."

"I mean, me. My future. My life. Where am I supposed to go now?"

You could go home, I thought. But home was a complicated place for Kylie, and for me.

Home is where the heart is, I thought, and then, *Home is in the casket.*

"I have no family," she said. "I mean, I could go home to Auntie Jane, and what? Bring back his body? Explain his death to a bunch of humans? They wouldn't understand. They'd put me into therapy or, or … " She stopped, running a hand through her hair. "Lock me in a psych ward. How could I explain any of this?"

"You couldn't," I said, brushing a tear from her cheek. I felt weird doing it, but I couldn't be afraid of these things anymore. I'd looked death in the face. Hell, I'd caused it. I couldn't let insecurity keep me from helping my friends.

My family.

"None of us could explain it," I said. "I mean, we could make up a story. Say we were kidnapped, you know? We *were*, in a way … "

"Yeah, then my life would become about that. Inventing a kidnapper. Doing the talk-show circuit. *Woohoo*." Her face crumpled, and that calm bled away. No, it fell away. "I won't let them make a spectacle out of me."

"No," I said, stroking her hair awkwardly. Even if I wanted to be supportive, I'd still have to learn how to be affectionate with people. I'd still have to learn how to touch people without it feeling *wrong*, like I didn't know what I was doing. "I don't think any of us belongs there anymore. Or maybe we never did. But now it just feels—"

"So far away," she said, looking up at me. Her eyes were still warm, in spite of the redness. In spite of the tragedy.

"In a different space and time," I said.

"But we don't belong here. We don't belong there. We don't belong anywhere. Should we lie down and die?"

"We belong together," I said. I didn't even have to think about it. It felt natural to say. "You, me, and Alexia. Elora too. We're a family."

"You don't mean that." She wiped at her nose.

"I do. What, like we're just going to bail? Go off on adventures without you? What if we need help from a *deer*?"

She started to laugh. It was gone in an instant, but still, it had happened. I'd made her laugh. "God, that was ... "

"Incredible. You were incredible."

She smiled, and Alexia, lingering by the door, swaying a little, came to kneel next to the bed. "We can do this," Alexia said, taking Kylie's hand. "It'll be hell for a while, a part of it will always be hell, but we can do this. Together."

"I guess there was never any question about you staying here, huh?" I said, shifting my gaze to Alexia. "You hate humans," I explained.

She laughed.

"She hates everybody," Kylie said. "Except me, and ... " Just like that, she dissolved into tears again. She probably would for a while. Every mention of him must've felt like a knife in the heart. Worse than bones cracking.

I stretched my leg. I hadn't taken any more faerie drugs,

but my body didn't hurt so badly. *Maybe I'm still in shock*, I thought as Alexia leaned over the bed. "I hate everyone, but I loved him," she said softly.

"He won you over, in the end. It was the sex jokes, right?" I asked. I was trying to get her to smile, to get a laugh from Kylie. Anything but tears and sadness.

But Alexia bit her lip, and tears flooded her eyes.

Well, shit.

"Yeah," she said, laughing through the tears. "It was. He made me feel so normal. I've never felt normal before. Everybody treated me like I was different."

"You were the queen of the school," I said.

"Yeah, and I worked my ass off to get there. I dedicated my life to it." She shook her head. Her eyes were dark, and her light brown cheeks were flushed with red. "Even then, I knew it was a precarious arrangement. If I wasn't perfect every second, they'd turn their backs on me."

"You *are* perfect," Kylie said, sniffing quietly. Holding our hands.

"No," Alexia said. "But I am loved. That's what matters. I'm loved, and I can kick some faerie ass. So I'll get by."

"We all will," I said, my eyes drifting toward the window. Darkness was rising there, warning us of an arrival.

No, not warning. Just telling, I thought, but my heart felt heavy in my chest. I couldn't explain it.

"She's here," I said. "I'll bring her up, and we can make plans. For dinner tonight," I added when Kylie's eyes went wide. Probably it was too soon to be making other plans. Plans meant moving on, and Kylie needed to stay in this moment for a while. That was all right. We'd stay here with her.

"I'll be right back," I said. Out of the room I went, down the twisting stairs, into the entryway.

She was here. She was *here*. I couldn't wait to pull her into my arms. I'd tell her I was sorry until she forgave me, kiss her until she was dizzy with love.

I pulled open the doors. And there she was, the Lady of Darkness, inky black swirls circling her arms like jewelry. Beautiful and terrible and wild.

But it wasn't Elora who reached out for me with porcelain skin. Black dress flowing around her. Wings shooting out of her back.

"I've been waiting a long time for this," the Dark Lady said.

"How is that possible?" I asked, staggering backward. "We only just met..."

To my surprise, she grinned. Her teeth slipped past her lips, sharp as a vampire's and stained on the ends. "And yet you remind me of someone I knew long ago."

How long ago? I thought. *Seventeen years? Eighteen?* But I didn't say it. I kept one bullet in the chamber of my mind. It was the only bullet I had left. Even now, I was afraid it wouldn't wound her enough. With no witnesses, how much power did a secret hold? I could tell her, and she could bury me.

The end.

"It isn't fair to punish me for what someone else did," I said finally, taking another step toward the stairs. Like I stood a chance against her. Like I could just run.

Already she was smiling down at me, so smug with herself. "I am not punishing you for what others have done. I am punishing you for what *you* have done."

"And what, exactly, is that?"

For a second, her smile slipped. I knew what she was thinking, even if she wouldn't *say* it. And I couldn't convince her that she was wrong. Couldn't convince her I hadn't *sullied* the princess.

"Fine, don't say it," I spat. "But if I'm going to be punished, I should at least get to stand trial. Plead my case. Call witnesses."

It was the wrong thing to say. Her teeth cut into her lips as she said, "There will be no witnesses. Now, come."

She tugged on me, the way a toddler tugs on a puppy's leash. She wasn't even touching me—oh, she wouldn't *deign* to do that. Still, she pulled, her darkness wrapping around my neck, yanking me through the doors, along the path to the Unseelie cliffs. No forest led gradually down the mountain here; instead, there was a steep drop-off, with an ocean spreading out far below.

Even the water was black.

"What are you going to do?" I asked as we neared the edge. Down below, that water was not smooth and inviting. Sharp rocks jutted up to impale me. To grind my bones to dust.

"A little experiment." The Dark Lady grinned. Her lips were ruby red, matching the strands that laced through her ebony hair. "I want to know if a mortal with faerie wings can fly."

"It's glamour," I lied.

"Once upon a time, I would've believed that," she said, forcing me closer to the edge. "I would have seen what I wanted to see. But now—"

"Oh, sure. You're not punishing me for past transgressions at all. Keep telling yourself that. Keep lying."

"Faeries do not lie."

"Maybe not to me. But to themselves..."

"One flick of the wrist, boy, and I could end your life." She slid toward me, like ink sliding through water. Like a knife sliding into a body. "And even then, I would be granting you a mercy." Her black eyes shifted to the cliffs. "Much more delicious would be to tear you limb from limb—"

"Blah, blah, blah, and have a tea party with my blood. Dance on my bones. To be honest, I'm over it."

She scoffed. "You're over it? He's over it!" she announced to the sky, to the darkness that was so much a part of her. "And why is that?"

"Because you haven't killed me yet, which means you want something."

Her body tensed. Behind her, I saw a glimpse of movement. A flash of red coming up the hill. My heart leapt. Then it crashed. I couldn't expect Elora to risk her life for me this time.

I would go down swinging, and Elora would survive.

"You want to know what I know," I told the Queen, or the *fallen* Queen, as Elora approached. On soft feet she ran, skirt clutched in her fists. Her mother didn't hear her. I didn't hear her.

But I caught her eyes, and tried to say *I'm sorry* without words. *I'm sorry I rejected you. I'm sorry I didn't handle things better. I'm sorry it had to end this way, before I got to tell you the truth: That one second with you was better than seventeen years alone, and I've lived, really lived, through knowing you. Through loving you.*

I stepped up to the Dark Lady, and she stepped back in surprise. It was beautiful. "You want to know who told me your secret, and who I told. But you're too late."

"No."

"You didn't stop me from telling Elora."

The Queen shook her head, her eyes wide in desperation. Her hair was writhing like a nest of snakes. "No, *please*. It cannot be true."

Elora had reached the summit. Her eyes were so bright, and I knew she would do anything to save me. She'd go up against the one faerie she knew she couldn't beat. Hadn't she enlisted the help of the Seelie Queen to avoid this? Now, here, she would die for me.

Unless I stopped it.

When the Dark Lady said, "When did you tell her?" I actually smiled.

"Now," I said, and turned to the love of my life. "Your father was a human."

Elora gasped.

The Dark Lady shrieked, lashing out, and then I was flying. In spite of the agony, I tried to flap my wings. But wings don't simply work because you want them to, and this wasn't a fairy tale.

Pain shot through my back, knocking the breath from me. I reached out, but Elora was too far away.

I fell, and no one caught me.

46

ELORA

I didn't think. I didn't breathe. I dove, and together we fell. Soon, we'd be splayed across the rocks. The gulls would feast on our entrails. The rocks would feast on our blood, and that blood would slip into the sea, feeding it.

No.

In spite of logic, I dove. In spite of danger, I opened my wings. I knew they were much too new, much too fragile, to carry us back to the cliffs. I'd be lucky to even reach him before the end.

But I did. Halfway down the cliffs, I wrapped my arms around his waist and tried to lift him with my newly budding wings. He was too heavy. *We* were too heavy, together, and if I hoped to survive, I would have to let him slip through my hands. But survival without love seemed too heavy a cost, and besides, what was the point of being a faerie if I couldn't believe in magic?

I believe, I thought, and felt more foolish than I'd ever felt in my life. *I believe in magic. I believe in love.*

But I do not believe I have the power to carry us up to the cliffs, I admitted, and that's when the answer came for me.

I did not have to carry us *up*. I only had to slow us down enough to keep from crashing against the rocks.

I flapped my wings. The pain came sharp and fast. But even screaming, even enduring this agony, I fought to survive.

I fought to save the mortal's life.

His arms wrapped around me, and he buried his face in my hair. He whispered, "Let go. It's okay."

Or, I thought he did. But the wind was rushing fast, and I could not hear him very well. Still, I could feel him, and it was enough.

I held fast.

My body shrieked, and yet, I held on to him. My lungs ached, and I thought of darkness. Of peace. Still, I flapped my wings, slowing our descent. When we came upon the rocks, we crashed against them, skin tearing and blood spilling, but no bones broke. The ocean claimed us, pulling us into the depths, and together we sank.

Together we rose.

I broke the surface first, pulling him up as best I could, and his arm went around my waist. He started to swim. He must've known I was tired, near exhaustion. Maybe near death. He must've known the sacrifice I had made for him, and here, he was paying me back.

So I'd saved him from dying on the rocks. He saved me from drowning in the sea. Together, we crawled from the foam onto the sand. And we lay there, breath heaving, in each other's arms, too tired to assess the damage, as my mother approached.

"No more," Taylor murmured, and I laughed, kissing him while I still could.

"I have always, will always love you," I said.

He nodded, his eyes fluttering open. "I know."

And then she was upon us, darkness slithering toward us like a whip. When Taylor lifted his head, I thought he would bargain, but instead, he laughed. "Fancy meeting you here," he said.

I held him close, protecting him from her. I held him close because it was what I wanted. This faerie loved a human, and I was not ashamed of it. But as for my mother...

"Is it true?" I asked, pushing myself to my elbows and then falling back. My left arm was turning black, bruises darkening with every breath. "Was my father a human?"

"Yes, it's true." She knelt before us. She did not look angry anymore. There were tears in her eyes. "But I did not know it at the time. Lyndiria tricked me. She—"

"Oh! She glamoured him to look like a faerie," I finished, realizing the truth.

"Yes." She glared at Taylor. "So you did tell her before now."

"No," I broke in. "The Bright Lady did. That is, she told me the truth disguised as a fable."

"Clever trick," Taylor said, taking my hand. If I didn't get him out of here soon, he'd bleed out in the ocean. We both would.

"She told you a fable?" the Dark Lady asked. *My mother* asked. "And you understood it?"

"No." I shook my head, laughing a little. "It didn't even occur to me that she was speaking of you. But I suppose we see what we want..."

She looked off, to the horizon. Light was gathering there.

"Yes, we do," she confessed. "I saw what I wanted to see in him."

"And you … loved him?" I asked, hardly daring to hope.

But she said, "Yes." Without even hesitating, she said yes. My mother. The Dark Queen.

It should have made me happy, to hear she was capable of love. But it didn't. It *broke* me. "You loved him," I said, swallowing back tears. "You loved him, and not me."

Taylor squeezed my hand. He was pushing himself to his knees, though it must've been agony. Slashes adorned his limbs. Bruises were blossoming.

"You *are* him," my mother said. "You speak like him. You *think* like him. To be around you was … "

"Too painful, of course. What a simple, easy explanation." I turned away, but not before she shook her head.

"It was not simple. It was anything but simple. Look at me, Elora."

I did, and a tear dropped from her eye. But it could've been glamour, and either way, I would not be swayed by it.

It was far, far too late.

"When you were born, and I saw that you … embodied him, it was everything I wanted, in a way. But I would not love again only to lose, so I pushed you away."

"Well, that's pretty stupid," Taylor said, and I loved him more than ever in that moment. Even now, he was fighting for me. "You didn't want to lose her, so you made sure you did. Well played, Queen of Darkness."

Shadows flickered across my mother's face, but she did not lash out. She looked exhausted. "I was born with the dawn of the earth. I have seen civilizations rise and fall. There are thousands of ways to break a person, to betray, to wound, and I have witnessed them all. After a time, I closed myself off to love. Eventually, I could not even feel its heat ... " She trailed off, looking to the light again. "Until him."

"And when I was born—"

"I did not want to feel it, if it meant being destroyed again. And so I kept away from you, until ... "

"Until I decided to overthrow your court, and then, suddenly, my existence mattered to you."

She smiled. My mother, that old, wretched creature, smiled out of joy rather than wickedness. "Oh no, my darling. That was the moment I realized you were like me. That was the moment I realized you were *mine*. And that was the moment *she* tried to take you away from me. Oh, it wasn't enough to take him—"

"But she didn't take him," Taylor said. "You killed him, accidentally."

"But didn't she know there was a risk? And did she try to stop it?" My mother's eyes were wide, and her hair was dancing around her face like fire. Like black tendrils that could wrap around your neck and pull.

"You blame her," he said softly. "That's why you hate her. Before it was just a rivalry, but after that—"

"I wanted to destroy her. I wanted to make her suffer, the way she'd made me. But then she came for my only child, and she poisoned her against me. Sent her to the one place where history would repeat."

"But it didn't," I said, as the light grew brighter. Something was approaching from the east. But was it the sun, or something closer?

Something wilder?

"When Taylor fell, he didn't die. That's what happened to my father, isn't it? He fell?"

"The Bright Queen said they were swimming," Taylor said.

"But it was a fable, and she was speaking of Naiad." I turned to my mother. "But you wouldn't have been swimming. You would have been soaring through the sky. All of this, the location, the fall ... " I looked to the cliff. "You were recreating what happened. You wanted to break me as you'd been broken. And then we really would be the same."

I thought of my words, then, from earlier that night: *You could've been dead. And then, Taylor my love, you would not want to have seen your wicked princess. You would not want to have seen the darkness I would've unleashed on them.*

Perhaps I really was my mother's daughter.

No, my father's daughter.

No, *both*.

"I want to know what he was like," I said. "My father. I want to know before you kill me."

"I am not going to kill you." My mother reached for my hand, yanking me to my feet. Pain shot through me, but what did it matter? I was alive. I would survive.

We all would.

"But *why*?" I asked, leaning against her for support. I did not want to, but it was difficult to stand on my own.

"Because you dove after him." She gestured to Taylor. "You did what I would not do."

"You let him *fall*?" I closed my eyes. "My ... "

"I let him crash upon the rocks." For a moment, she was

silent. "It was not my intention," she explained, shaking her head. Now that she had calmed, her hair fell around her like a cape, no longer reaching for us like ravenous flames. "We'd been playing in the trees, there." She pointed up, past the cliffs, to the forest beyond. "I thought, it'd be so easy to slip into the air. To be *together* in the place where sea meets earth meets sky. But he was hesitant, and I did not understand it." Her lips curled, the tiniest bit. "Faeries aren't exactly known for our propriety. But as I pulled him from the safety of the trees, he struggled so badly, I had no choice but to let him go. To free him from whatever was terrifying him."

Her gaze dropped, the way he must've dropped, from the cliffs to the sea. "For a moment, his hands were scrabbling in the air, as if reaching for something. He was not even trying to flap his wings. And as I realized why, a cold clarity settled over me. I hesitated, just an instant, and it was enough. He fell against the jagged mouth of the sea. There." She pointed to a rock off to the left. I half expected his blood to have stained it.

But it hadn't.

"I hesitated for an instant, in fury, and he died because of me. Because of himself. Because of *her*." Her eyes trailed to the light approaching.

That is not the sun, I thought, and steeled myself for a confrontation between the two queens.

But my mother surprised me a second time. She stepped back, as if retreating. "You risked your life for him. You did not hesitate. You are not like me."

"I am," I said, stepping forward. "I have your fierceness. Your wicked humor. I have your protective streak."

"I never protected you," she said.

"No, you were concerned with bigger things. You were trying to protect the earth."

"Trying, and failing."

"It is not over yet." I met her gaze. She met mine. Together, we held each other in the only way we knew how. For once.

"So you will not murder me, or him? Do I have your word on that?"

She nodded. "I did not believe you would dive after him, not without your wings. I ... " She paused, glancing at my back. She could not make sense of it.

I did not know how to explain it to her. So I simply said, "Love healed me."

His love. My love for him. But really, hadn't it been the connection between us? The mutual trust, and understanding? Our spirits dancing?

"Someday, I hope you know how that feels," I said.

"I won't," she replied. "There is only one person left who understands me, and if we were to touch ... "

What happens when the light touches darkness?

A shiver ripped through me. Now, the light was pouring in. My mother retreated farther.

"Wait," I called. "You really aren't going to hurt us?"

She was silent a moment. Finally, she said, "I have caused enough harm to those I've loved."

My breath caught in my throat. A part of me wanted to ask for more. But this was the closest she was ever going to come to saying she loved me, and it was enough. It would be enough.

"And what of your throne?" I asked.

I expected her to laugh, to tell me she was already rebuilding her court. Instead, she lunged forward, bringing with her the darkness. "Let me tell you a secret," she whispered as tremors shot down my back. "The clever reign of chaos lends its subjects the illusion of free will. But the strength of the dictator is born of the disorder of revolution. You think yourself full of ideas that are new, belonging to you alone, but the cycle of rule and rebellion is as old as the earth, and sovereignty will rise again, when it is time. Until then ... " She lowered her lips to my cheek, and kissed. "Keep my throne warm for me."

Summoning a wave of darkness, the Queen of the Dark Faeries rose into the sky and disappeared.

Taylor pushed himself to his feet. "Holy mother of ... "

"Unholy," I said with a smile. The light was pouring over us. "Let us get you somewhere safe. I can tend to your wounds, and—"

"Not so fast, young princess," a voice said, and I spun around to face the sun. To face the Bright Queen. She was carrying a crown made of flowers and leaves, a crown befitting the ruler of the Bright Court.

She walked right up to Taylor and placed it on his head. "Your Highness," she said with a bow.

47

TAYLOR

The branches of the crown dug into my skin. The leaves tickled my ears. Any way you sliced it, I didn't like it, but when I went to remove it, the Queen stopped me.

"Wait," she said, lifting a hand. "Think on it a moment."

Elora stepped up, ready to fight for me. My unstoppable princess.

No, not a princess anymore, I thought. *Just a faerie I love desperately.*

"Can we just ... *relax* a minute?" I said, swaying a little. Everything hurt, but it could always get worse. "I think I've seen enough fighting for—"

"Ever," Elora finished for me.

"Yeah. That."

"I came not to fight," the Bright Queen said. "I came to fulfill my part of the bargain."

Elora shook her head, placing herself between me and the Queen. Protecting me again. "You promised to disband your court. You said if I took down the Dark Court, you would—"

"Did I?"

I felt like hands were tickling my spine. Now, after a night of surprises, I didn't think I could handle any more.

But that was too bad, because the Queen had three tricks up her sleeve, and she revealed them one after the other. "I did not say I would disband my court," she corrected Elora. "I said I would relinquish my throne."

"What is the difference?" Elora demanded.

The Queen nodded to me. That is, she nodded to my crown.

Oh my God.

"I relinquish it to him," she said with a grin. "Whether or not he disbands the Seelie Court is up to him."

Surprise, I thought.

"So you are taking over our world," Elora snarled, advancing on shaky legs. "He will simply be the puppet who does your bidding—"

"You misunderstand me," the Queen said, plucking an object from the ground. Dusting the sand away, she handed it to Elora.

For a second, they just stared at it. We all did. The circular frame curved up into spires. The poppies were bright against the bone. Red on white.

"My mother lost her crown," Elora mused.

"And now it is yours." The Bright Queen bowed a second time.

Elora frowned. "How . . . no it isn't," she said.

"You destroyed her court. Her people are waiting for your orders. All you have to do is put on that crown and you will rule our world. Together, with our new king, you'll both rule."

"That's why you asked for a leader," Elora said. "In your riddle. *A young leader of men…*"

Surprise.

Elora touched her lips. "You wanted a king for the Seelie Court, a mortal your people could follow. And you wanted me to love him, so that we could join both courts."

The Queen nodded.

She isn't the queen anymore. She isn't the ruler.

I am.

Elora stared at me. "That doesn't make sense. The faeries of the Bright Court might welcome a human king, but my people won't. They'll *never* bow to him."

"Why not? They bow to you, and you have mortal blood in your veins." The Bright Queen smiled.

"They do not know—"

"They will. And they'll still follow you, won't they, darling? You freed them from bondage."

"But if I *rule* them, how am I any better than—"

"You freed them from a corrupt queen, and from Naeve. They're no longer servants."

Elora was silent a minute. Finally, she said, "So what if that's true? Having a mortal father is not the same as being a full-blooded human. They will not follow him. Their prejudice is strong. It will take time, and—"

"Blood," the Queen said softly. I mean, the *former* Queen, but I couldn't remember her name.

"Enough blood has been spilled," Elora said.

"I am not speaking of blood *spilled*. I am speaking of blood *sewn*."

"Blood… what? I don't understand."

But I did. Because now the Queen was looking at me. "Turn around, my young leader of men."

"I ... don't want to," I said, swallowing. "And if I'm the king—"

"Taylor Christopher—"

"*Unfair,*" I said, turning on my own. I might as well do it if she was going to make me. I might as well act on my terms.

"I don't see ... " Elora began, but the Queen cut her off.

"I have not shown you yet." Then she did. There was an odd tingling in my back, and a rush of air, and then I was on the ground. The glamour had been torn away.

"Oh, Darkness." Elora stepped up close. I felt more exposed than I'd ever been. "What have you done to him? Why did you—"

"To give him your blood, of course. Don't you see?"

And she did see. She must've, because she knelt down beside me. Touching the redness with soft hands, she whispered in my ear, "Does it hurt, love?"

"Actually, the fall was worse."

Elora laughed. It made my heart hurt to hear it. It made me want to hold her.

"If I had known—" she began.

"You could not have known," the Queen said, coming to face me. Coming to face us.

Together, we stood against her.

She took a step back. "You could not have known that you would connect with humanity, but I did," she said to Elora. "I have known it since you were born. Why do you think your wings grew in so tattered when you were a child? All your life, a part of you was missing."

"The human part."

"Yes."

"And when I came to you with my plan, you sent me to go find it." Elora swayed, and I linked my arm through hers to keep her from falling. She looked to me and smiled. "But how did you know I would fall in love?" she asked the Bright Queen.

"I didn't. But I knew you would connect with them more than expected, and it would be enough to make you question your mother's teachings about humanity. I knew you would find one among them who was strong, and sweet, and by the time you brought him back to me, perhaps your feelings would have—"

"Why did it have to be a *he*?"

The Queen looked amused. "It did not *have* to be. But if we are to survive as a species, and continue to create life—"

"Oh. Oh my God." I turned to Elora. "You survived because you're half human."

"Survived what? The iron in the graveyard?"

"Yes, but not only. Your human side is the reason you were born."

Elora looked at me, eyes narrowing. God, they were bright. "What are you saying?" she asked.

I thought of the faerie story she'd told me, back in the human world. "I'm saying that iron is poisonous to faeries, right? And the more humans produce it, the less often faeries are born. But *centuries* after the last faerie baby was born, you arrived. Why?"

Elora sucked in a breath. "Because of my human side."

"Because you are *both*," the Queen said. "Because you are

better. Stronger than any of us, in a way. Able to withstand iron *and* use magic. But it wasn't until you engaged both sides of yourself that you came into your power. It wasn't until you walked in both worlds, and—"

"This is all conjecture," Elora broke in. "The Bright Court's way of thinking. Where I came from, my tattered wings made me inferior."

"Yes, because your mother believed you were inferior, that it was an act against nature to lie with a human. She thought your wings were a punishment for that."

I expected Elora to look hurt. Expected tears to spring into her eyes. But this time, she surprised me. She laughed. "I suppose it was quite a shock to see me flying then."

The Bright Queen started to laugh. Then I was laughing. We all were laughing.

"The Dark Lady does not know everything," the Queen said after a minute.

"No," Elora agreed.

"None of us does," I said.

"So you sent me to find a human, believing I would connect with a human," Elora said. "My human side would. And then, once I brought him back, he would take over your court, and I would take over mine."

"Only if you wish."

"But I still don't understand. You gave him my wings—"

"To give him your blood, dear princess. To make you one and the same. You have mortal blood in your veins, and now he has faerie blood in his. Whoever follows you will follow him."

Surprise.

"I could really be a king?" I touched the crown. It still dug into my head, but it was bothering me less and less.

"Together, you two can connect both courts, and eventually connect with humanity. And your child would be a symbol of that union."

I said, "Child?" as Elora said, "Symbol?"

She turned to me. "What do you think, young leader of men? Do you think I am a superior being, come to usher in a new age of human and faerie entanglement?" She said it in a joking way, but I knew there was seriousness behind it. I knew this was important.

"I think you're the most beautiful, wonderful, powerful being I've ever met."

"But?"

Oh, she knew me so well. I knew her. Maybe that was the point. "But I think placing one person, or one group of people, above others is what got us into this mess, both humans and faeries. I think it's what keeps getting us into this mess."

"So I will not be better, or worse." Elora looked to the ground. "I will only be *different*."

"And yet … " I laced my fingers through hers. "We'll be the same."

"You know what you have to do, then?" the Seelie Queen said. The former Seelie Queen. A person, just like us.

I looked at Elora.

She looked at me.

Together, we dropped our crowns in the sand.

48

ELORA

For a minute, our crowns mingled with the sand. His, of earth and leaves. Mine, of poppies and bone. Then slowly, quietly, they sank into the earth.

I turned to face the Queen. "I have seen too much bloodshed under the guise of *ruling*."

"And I've seen too much control disguised as protection," Taylor agreed.

The Queen stared at us a long moment. Finally, her face broke into a grin. "Well done," she said, clapping her hands. Then, more softly, "Better than I have done."

I stared at her. "We'll see."

Taylor was standing beside me, his fingers still laced through mine. *Please, don't ever let go,* I thought. Now, with my blood in his veins, he would live longer, though not for eternity. But here, in this moment, it was enough.

"I will leave you now, if all your questions have been answered," Lyndiria said.

I nodded, letting the light recede. But when she had almost disappeared into the darkened forest, I called, "Why did you bind me?"

She turned, a curious smile upon her lips. "I underestimated you," she said simply.

"What does that mean?" Taylor asked.

The light was lapping at our feet. "I wanted a boy who was able to lead, but one who would not risk his life in battle," Lyndiria said. "I wanted the same from you."

"That does not make sense," I argued.

"Doesn't it? How long did your mother and I languish on our thrones? How many centuries did we send others to fight, while pretending to be brave ourselves?"

"Too many to count," I said.

"And so, I loved that you were willing to fight, loved the bravery of it, but did not think you would actually survive the battle."

"Harsh," Taylor muttered.

"Ye of so little faith," I agreed.

The Queen smiled, looking down at us. Even now, I expected her to turn on us, to reveal herself to be an enemy.

"So you bound me to protect me. And you *sacrificed* a person—"

"I did not intend for Keegan to fall. I only intended to give him what he desired most, and protect you in the process."

I frowned, shaking my head. "And what of Taylor, then? What did you do to 'protect' him?"

"She sewed the wings into my back," Taylor explained. "She did it right before the battle, thinking it would incapacitate me."

"But it didn't?"

"It came close."

"And you still fought for me? In such agony?"

"Worth it."

I closed my eyes. We needed to be alone. "Lady..."

"I am sorry for causing you pain," Lyndiria said, shocking me. Faeries rarely apologized, and queens?

Never.

But she is not a queen, a voice reminded me. *Neither is your mother. Neither are you. There are no queens or kings anymore.*

"I had a good reason for everything I did," Lyndiria said, bowing her head. "But I am sorry for your suffering, and your losses."

"Thank you," I replied. Then, "What are you going to do about it?"

She looked up, surprised. "Excuse me?"

"I was only thinking, since you have moved us around as pawns, perhaps you could do us a favor?"

Her lips twisted up, amused by my boldness. "I suppose I could try."

I pulled Taylor closer to me. "Make certain no one bothers us tonight. Tomorrow, we will begin to rebuild our world. But tonight..." I brushed my lips across his cheek. "Tonight is his and mine."

"It would be my pleasure," said the fallen Seelie Queen. But as she slipped away, I called her back a second time.

"Let me rephrase that," I said. "Do not *force* people to stay away from us. Use your words, and use them nicely."

"Yes, Princess."

"Elora," I said. "Only Elora."

"Whatever you say, my little beacon of light." And then she was gone, leaving trickles of gold in an otherwise sapphire sky.

"Finally," Taylor said, turning to me. Wrapping his arms around me gently. "What's wrong?" he asked after a minute.

He must've noticed the look on my face. The way I kept staring in the direction of the Queen. "She called me a beacon of light."

"Yeah?"

"That's what my name means. *The light in the darkness.*"

"Wait, what?"

"Elora va Darchali," I whispered, so no one else could hear me. "*Darchali* is an old fey word for the darkness. And Elora is—"

"Greek," he said, surprising me. "For light."

"Yes, how did you—"

"Alexia."

"Ah, of course. Our cunning little linguist." I shook my head. "I haven't even thanked her for everything she's done for me. I haven't even thanked *you*." I brushed the hair from his eyes, leaning in for a kiss.

But just as I reached his lips, he said, "Maybe your father named you."

I pulled back, blinking at him.

"Maybe *she* named me, through him," I said, glancing in the Queen's direction. *Lyndiria's* direction. "Just to stick it to my mother."

"Maybe … " Taylor said, following my gaze. "You don't think she knew—"

"No." I bit my lip. "You?"

"No, it's impossible. She couldn't have planned this entire thing. Couldn't have known you were going to be born. Couldn't have known you'd bring the courts to their knees."

"I did, didn't I?" I said, grinning. "*We* did."

"And now we're going to rebuild the world."

"But not tonight."

He froze, staring at me with a wild look in his eyes. His hair was messy, the way I liked it. "So you meant it?" he said. "I have the whole night with you? *For once?* No one can bother us?"

I wove my fingers into his hair, pulling him closer. "You and me. All night."

"I could use some healing," he confessed.

"As could I." I kissed his lips once, then twice. He tasted so sweet. "You forgive me, then?" I asked softly.

"For what?"

"For everything I've done." I was clinging to him. He was clinging to me. "Everything you said to me, back at the castle."

"I was being an idiot."

"No. You were coming out of shock. You had blood on your hands."

"I still have blood on my hands."

I looked down. Always, I was hurting him. Putting him in danger. But perhaps we could change that now. Perhaps the bloodshed was ending, sliding back into the earth like the tides.

"I am not evil," I said, looking up into his eyes. Those emerald spheres were shining like the light. But darkness is as necessary as the light, and I would draw strength from both. "I would simply do *anything* to protect you."

"I know." He brushed the hair from my face. "I understand that now. I think I understood it then. That's what scared me."

"Because you would do anything to protect me?"

"Yes. Kill. Die. But I would rather live."

"We can do that together." I lowered my forehead to his.

The waves were crashing against our feet, and I imagined pulling him down to the shore.

I kissed him.

He kissed me.

It would be so easy to fall right into the sand. To fall right into his arms. To *heal* each other, right here, right now...

Taylor must've realized what I was thinking, because he said, "You know you have a room here, right?"

"It is not my room anymore."

"Wow, you've slipped out of that princess role quickly."

I laughed, touching his cheek. "This feels natural. That was the abomination." I paused, grinning slyly. "Of course, time spent in my room was always restless. It would be a shame to leave that place behind without giving myself *one good memory...*"

He leaned into me, lips tickling my ear. "If that's what you want."

I smiled. "You are what I want."

"Yeah, I'm going to need to hear that about a million more times before I believe it."

"Doable."

"And I'd like that to be my nickname."

"Oh my Darkness."

"I don't like that one so much."

I placed my hand over his mouth, playfully, and he nipped at me. "Come on," I said, leading him along. Once, he had led me to his bedroom. Now, I would lead him to mine. But no walls could contain us anymore. No rules could tear us apart.

Together, we ascended the mountain, climbing a staircase

made of jagged rocks. Together, we ascended the rules our people had made.

The rules our families had made.

We would not spend our lives plotting new and extreme ways to kill each other, as had been my mother's dream. Nor would we join together simply to create life, to please the Seelie Queen. We would not be mere instruments of creation or destruction.

We would be more.

"Come on," I said, but I did not see a bedroom laid out in front of us. I did not see a single night. I saw eternity. I saw a sky filled with endless stars. And we would meet that mystery, that world of possibility, together.

Only.

Always.

Together.

Acknowledgments

Thank you to Sandy Lu for her enthusiasm, insight, and belief in this project, and to Brian Farrey-Latz for his continuing editing excellence. Thank you to everyone at Flux, including Mallory Hayes, Sandy Sullivan, and Kevin Brown, for making this book shine, and for being all-around fantastic.

Thank you to Marwane Pallas for being a magical genius, and for saving the day.

Thank you to my irreplaceable, unstoppable betas, Adri-Anne Strickland, Kayla Whaley, and Justina Ireland, for being the fabulous people that they are, and for helping me in all kinds of wonderful ways.

Thank you to The Lucky 13s and the folks at #WeNeed DiverseBooks, for awesomeness-related reasons.

And thank you to Chris Hauth, for always inspiring and encouraging me.

© www.cameronbrowne.com

About the Author

Chelsea Pitcher is a karaoke-singing, ocean-worshipping Oregonian with a penchant for wicked faerie tales. She began gobbling up stories as soon as she could read, and especially enjoys delving into the darker places to see if she can draw out some light. She is also the author of *The Last Changeling* and *The S-Word*. You can visit her at chelseapitcher.com and follow her on Twitter at @Chelsea_Pitcher.